Laurie Fletcher

Andrea Levy was born in England to Jamaican parents. She is the author of five novels, including her most recent title, *The Long Song*. *Small Island* won both the Whitbread Book of the Year Award and the Orange Prize for Fiction: Best of the Best. She lives in London.

Also by Andrea Levy

Every Light in the House Burnin'
Never Far from Nowhere
Fruit of the Lemon
The Long Song

Praise for *Small Island*

"Honest, skillful, thoughtful, and important. This is Andrea Levy's big book."
—*The Guardian*

"Levy writes with remarkable insight into . . . lives circumscribed by race, class, and circumstance. There is passion and anger, but also warmth and humor in her acute observation of their workings. . . . Panic and emptiness, the failure to connect lurk beneath the surface. This is a largely neglected period. Levy, in this novel, does it justice."
—Rt. Hon. Paul Boateng, MP, cited on
Small Island's receipt of the Orange Prize

"In this lively, crisp, raw voice, young black Londoners may have found their Roddy Doyle."
—*The Independent*

"An engrossing read—slyly funny, passionately angry, and wholly involving."
—*Daily Mail*

"Here is the book I have been waiting for . . . an ample, sprawling story mirroring an expansive inner and outer landscape, spanning two islands and three continents, and incorporating a hybrid cast of humanly idiosyncratic characters; and above all, a book in which the author, Andrea Levy, never once forgets she is telling a story, delighting us, improbably, in this nasty tale of race, with the effervescent style of Dickens."
—*The Globe and Mail* (Toronto)

"Powerful . . . rigorous . . . bittersweet . . . touching. What makes Levy's writing so appealing is her evenhandedness. All her characters can be weak, hopeless, brave, good, bad—whatever their color. The writing is rigorous and the bittersweet ending, with its unexpected twist, touching. . . . People can retain great dignity, however small their island."

—*The Independent on Sunday*

"Levy's skill and cunning leave the reader shaken."   —*The Voice*

"A brilliantly deft and humane account of two ordinary couples in postwar London . . . *Small Island* is never less than finely written, delicately and often comically observed, and impressively rich in detail and little nuggets of stories."   —*Evening Standard*

"A cracking good read . . . I think what appealed to me most was that the passion and anger in the writing were always leavened with a particularly wry sort of humor—the sort that, though you find yourself smiling, you at the same time realize you almost shouldn't be."

—Margaret Forster

SMALL
ISLAND

ANDREA LEVY

Picador
New York

For Bill

SMALL ISLAND. Copyright © 2004 by Andrea Levy. All rights reserved. Printed in the United States of America. For information, address Picador, 175 Fifth Avenue, New York, N.Y. 10010.

www.picadorusa.com

Picador® is a U.S. registered trademark and is used by St. Martin's Press under license from Pan Books Limited.

For information on Picador Reading Group Guides, please contact Picador.
E-mail: readinggroupguides@picadorusa.com

ISBN 978-0-312-42952-2

Originally published in Great Britain by Headline Book Publishing, a division of Hodder Headline

Second Picador Edition: May 2010

20 19 18 17 16 15 14 13

Prologue

Queenie

I thought I'd been to Africa. Told all my class I had. Early Bird, our teacher, stood me in front of the British flag – she would let no one call it the common Union Jack: 'It's the flag of Empire not a musical turn.' And I stood there as bold as brass and said, 'I went to Africa when it came to Wembley.' It was then that Early Bird informed me that Africa was a country. 'You're not usually a silly girl, Queenie Buxton,' she went on, 'but you did not go to Africa, you merely went to the British Empire Exhibition, as thousands of others did.'

It was a Butchers' Association trip. Every year there was an outing organised for the butchers, the butchers' wives and children and even the butchers' favourite workers. A day out. Mother liked to go. 'It's like a holiday,' she would say to Father.

'Bloody waste of time,' he'd grumble. But he went all the same.

Some years nearly everyone from our farm went. The inside girls who helped Mother with the pies. The outside girls who fed the pigs and poultry. Even the stupid boys, who helped Father in the shed, changed out of their splattered aprons and into their ill-fitting, fraying best suits for the trip. We always got dressed in our best to paddle in the sea at Blackpool or ride a red bus round Piccadilly Circus or laugh at the monkeys in the zoo. Then it was time to go home again. The men would be dozing from too much beer and the children would be snivelling after being whacked for dirtying their clothes or getting a piece of rock stuck in their hair. As often as not one of the farm girls would go missing with one of the farm boys only to turn up later, looking sheepish and dishevelled.

The year we went to the Empire Exhibition, the Great War was not long over but nearly forgotten. Even Father agreed that the Empire Exhibition sounded like it was worth a look. The King had described it as 'the whole Empire in little'. Mother thought that meant it was a miniature, like a toy railway or model village. Until someone told her that they'd seen the real lifesize Stephenson's Rocket on display. 'It must be as big as the whole world,' I said, which made everybody laugh.

We had to leave my brothers Billy, Harry and Jim behind. They were too small and everyone agreed with Father when he told the grizzling boys that they would get swallowed up by the crowd. 'I'm not scared of being eaten,' Billy whimpered. They sobbed and clung to Mother's coat. So she had to promise to bring each of them back something nice – a model engine or soldiers. She left them with the inside girl Molly, who stood at the window sulking, giving us all a look that could curdle milk.

I was dressed in a white organza frock with blue ribbons that trailed loose down the front and my hair was set in pigtails adorned with big white bows. All the way there on the train Mother and Father chatted with other butchers and butchers' wives about, of all things, the bother of humane killing over the poleaxe. Which left me sitting between two of our farm helpers, Emily and Graham, who spent the time giggling and flirting over my head.

Emily had been our outside girl for two months. She had a kindly foster-mother, who lived in Kent and made pictures from spring flowers, and a father and two uncles in London, who drank so much that they had not been awake long enough to take part in the war. Graham helped Father in the shed. He looked after the fire under the copper of pig swill, took the pork pies to the bakehouse when needed and generally ran round doing everything Father asked, only not quite quick enough. Father called Graham Jim. On Graham's first day he had said his name to Father who looked him up and down and said, 'I can't be bothered with a fancy name like that – I'll call you Jim.' Consequently some people called him Jim and others Graham – he'd learned to answer to both. But Graham's only ambition, as far as I could tell, was to get a feel of Emily's bust.

Hundreds and hundreds of people were tramping in through the gates of the exhibition, past the gardens and the lakes. Or milling about, chatting. Little kids being dragged to walk faster. Women pointing, old men wanting a seat. 'Over here! No, over here . . . Over here's better.' The Empire in little. The palace of engineering, the palace of industry, and building after building that housed every country we British owned. Some of them were grand like castles, some had funny pointed roofs and one, I was sure, had half an onion on the top. Practically the whole world there to be looked at.

'Makes you proud,' Graham said to Father.

At which Father looked his butcher's boy up and down for a minute and said, 'Will you listen to him?'

There was a lot of discussion about what we should see – the whole world and only one day to see it. Mother was not interested in the different woods of Burma or the big-game trophies of Malaya. She said, 'Maybe later,' to the coffee of Jamaica. 'Ooh, no,' to the sugar of Barbados. 'What for?' to the chocolate of Grenada. And 'Where in heaven's name is that?' to Sarawak. In Canada there was a lifesize model of the Prince of Wales made in yellow butter. I had to struggle to the front to get a good look. I pressed my face close to the glass and Mother came and dragged me back. 'You hold Emily's hand,' she told me. 'I don't want you getting lost.' Then she moaned at Emily in front of the crowd, who strained to look past my mother and her blushing outside girl, everyone muttering, 'Butter really? Butter? Never.' Mother told Emily that she had only been brought along to look after me and that if she lost me then she would be in trouble – very big trouble indeed. So Emily attached herself to me like soot to a miner. And where Emily went Graham followed.

Australia smelt of apples. Ripe, green, crisp apples. A smell so sharp and sweet it made my teeth tingle. 'We'll have some of them,' Father said, as he joined the queue to buy a small brown bag of the fruit. Mother saved hers until later, but I ate mine and gave the core to Emily. Graham then told us all that he was going to live in Australia. 'Australia – you? You daft beggar,' Father laughed.

I was promised that I would see a sheep being sheared in New Zealand but we only arrived in time to see the skinny shorn animal trotting round a pen with the fleece at the side. Hong Kong smelt of drains, and India was full of women brightly dressed in strange long colourful fabrics. And all these women had red dots in the middle of their forehead. No one could tell me what the dots were for. 'Go and ask one of them,' Emily said to me. But Mother said I shouldn't in case the dots meant they were ill – in case they were contagious.

The smell of tea in Ceylon had Mother swallowing hard and saying, 'I'm dying for a cuppa and a sit-down. My feet!' At which Father began grumbling that he hadn't seen the biscuit-making or cigarette-packing machines yet. I cried because I wanted to see more countries. Emily called me a little madam and Mother told her to watch her mouth. So Father gave instructions to Graham – which he had to repeat twice to make sure he was understood – to meet him and Mother later in the rest lounge of the gas exhibit. Mother and Father then went off to find modern machinery and refrigeration, while me, Emily and, of course, the soppy Graham carried on travelling the world alone.

That's when we got lost in Africa. We wandered in, following the syrupy-brown smell of chocolate. Emily trailed behind Graham only looking at me every so often to shout, 'Come on – hurry up.' I wanted one of the cups of cocoa that everyone was sipping but instead Emily pulled me by one of my pigtails and told me to keep up. Then we found ourselves in an African village with Graham looking around himself, scratching his head and telling Emily he was wanting the toilet.

We were in the jungle. Huts made out of mud with pointy stick roofs all around us. And in a hut sitting on a dirt floor was a woman with skin as black as the ink that filled the inkwell in my school desk. A shadow come to life. Sitting cross-legged, her hands weaving bright patterned cloth on a loom. 'We've got machines that do all that now,' Graham said, as Emily

4

nudged him to be quiet. 'She can't understand what I'm saying,' Graham explained. 'They're not civilised. They only understand drums.' The woman just carried on like she'd heard no one speak – pushing her stick through the tangle of threads.

'Have you seen the toilet?' Graham asked her, but she didn't understand that either.

'I want to go,' I said, because there was nothing interesting to look at. But then suddenly there was a man. An African man. A black man who looked to be carved from melting chocolate. I clung to Emily but she shooed me off. He was right next to me, close enough so I could see him breathing. A monkey man sweating a smell of mothballs. Blacker than when you smudge your face with a sooty cork. The droplets of sweat on his forehead glistened and shone like jewels. His lips were brown, not pink like they should be, and they bulged with air like bicycle tyres. His hair was woolly as a black shorn sheep. His nose, squashed flat, had two nostrils big as train tunnels. And he was looking down at me.

'Would you like to kiss him?' Graham said. He nudged me, teasing, and pushed me forward – closer to this black man.

And Emily giggled. 'Go on Queenie, kiss him, kiss him.'

This man was still looking down at me. I could feel the blood rising in my face, turning me crimson, as he smiled a perfect set of pure blinding white teeth. The inside of his mouth was pink and his face was coming closer and closer to mine. He could have swallowed me up, this big nigger man. But instead he said, in clear English, 'Perhaps we could shake hands instead?'

Graham's smile fell off his face. And I shook an African man's hand. It was warm and slightly sweaty like anyone else's. I shook his hand up and down for several seconds. And he bowed his head to me and said, 'It's nice to meet you.' Then he let my hand go and stepped out of our way so we could pass. Emily was still giggling, looking at Graham and rolling her eyes. She grabbed my arm and pulled me away while Graham mumbled again that he needed the toilet. And the African man must have understood because he pointed and said, 'Over there by the tree is a rest room where I think you will find what you need.'

5

But Graham never found the toilet. He had to wee behind some bins while me and Emily kept a look-out.

Father said later that this African man I was made to shake hands with would have been a chief or a prince in Africa. Evidently, when they speak English you know that they have learned to be civilised – taught English by the white man, missionaries probably. So Father told me not to worry about having shaken his hand because the African man was most likely a potentate.

To take my mind off the encounter Father promised me a trip on the scenic railway. 'Come on, we'll be able to see for miles up there,' he persuaded Mother. She was reluctant, worried I might be sick over everyone on the ground. Father called her a daft 'aporth, then promised her the most wonderful view she'd ever see. I waved to Emily and Graham as our little carriage slowly nudged further and further up. They'd stayed behind – Emily chewing toffee and Graham smoking a cigarette. But then they disappeared. 'They'll turn up later,' Mother sighed.

We went up and up into the heavens until people were just dots below us. As we hung right at the top – the twinkling electric lights below mingling with the stars – Father said something I will never forget. He said, 'See here, Queenie. Look around. You've got the whole world at your feet, lass.'

1948

One

Hortense

It brought it all back to me. Celia Langley. Celia Langley standing in front of me, her hands on her hips and her head in a cloud. And she is saying: 'Oh, Hortense, when I am older . . .' all her dreaming began with 'when I am older' '. . . when I am older, Hortense, I will be leaving Jamaica and I will be going to live in England.' This is when her voice became high-class and her nose point into the air – well, as far as her round flat nose could – and she swayed as she brought the picture to her mind's eye. 'Hortense, in England I will have a big house with a bell at the front door and I will ring the bell.' And she made the sound, ding-a-ling, ding-a-ling. 'I will ring the bell in this house when I am in England. That is what will happen to me when I am older.'

I said nothing at the time. I just nodded and said, 'You surely will, Celia Langley, you surely will.' I did not dare to dream that it would one day be I who would go to England. It would one day be I who would sail on a ship as big as a world and feel the sun's heat on my face gradually change from roasting to caressing. But there was I! Standing at the door of a house in London and ringing the bell. Pushing my finger to hear the ding-a-ling, ding-a-ling. Oh, Celia Langley, where were you then with your big ideas and your nose in the air? Could you see me? Could you see me there in London? Hortense Roberts married with a gold ring and a wedding dress in a trunk.

9

Mrs Joseph. Mrs Gilbert Joseph. What you think of that, Celia Langley? There was I in England ringing the doorbell on one of the tallest houses I had ever seen.

But when I pressed this doorbell I did not hear a ring. No ding-a-ling, ding-a-ling. I pressed once more in case the bell was not operational. The house, I could see, was shabby. Mark you, shabby in a grand sort of a way. I was sure this house could once have been home to a doctor or a lawyer or perhaps a friend of a friend of the King. Only the house of someone high-class would have pillars at the doorway. Ornate pillars that twisted with elaborate design. The glass stained with coloured pictures as a church would have. It was true that some were missing, replaced by cardboard and strips of white tape. But who knows what devilish deeds Mr Hitler's bombs had carried out during the war? I pushed the doorbell again when it was obvious no one was answering my call. I held my thumb against it and pressed my ear to the window. A light came on now and a woman's voice started calling, 'All right, all right, I'm coming! Give us a minute.'

I stepped back down two steps avoiding a small lump of dog's business that rested in some litter and leaves. I straightened my coat, pulling it closed where I had unfortunately lost a button. I adjusted my hat in case it had sagged in the damp air and left me looking comical. I pulled my back up straight.

The door was answered by an Englishwoman. A blonde-haired, pink-cheeked Englishwoman with eyes so blue they were the brightest thing in the street. She looked on my face, parted her slender lips and said, 'Yes?'

'Is this the household of Mr Gilbert Joseph?'

'I beg your pardon?'

'Gilbert Joseph?' I said, a little slower.

'Oh, Gilbert. Who are you?' She pronounced Gilbert so strangely that for a moment I was anxious that I would be delivered to the wrong man.

'Mr Gilbert Joseph is my husband – I am his wife.'

The woman's face looked puzzled and pleased all at one time. She looked back into the house, lifting her head as she did. Then she turned to me and said, 'Didn't he come to meet you?'

'I have not seen Gilbert,' I told her, then went on to ask, 'but this is perchance where he is aboding?'

At which this Englishwoman said, 'What?' She frowned and looked over my shoulder at the trunk, which was resting by the kerbside where it had been placed by the driver of the taxi vehicle. 'Is that yours?' she enquired.

'It is.'

'It's the size of the Isle of Wight. How did you get it here?' She laughed a little. A gentle giggle that played round her eyes and mouth.

I laughed too, so as not to give her the notion that I did not know what she was talking about as regards this 'white island'. I said, 'I came in a taxicab and the driver assured me that this was the right address. Is this the house of Gilbert Joseph?'

The woman stood for a little while before answering by saying, 'Hang on here. I'll see if he's in his room.' She then shut the door in my face.

And I wondered how could a person only five feet six inches tall (five feet seven if I was wearing my wedding-shoe heels), how could such a person get to the top of this tall house? Ropes and pulleys was all I could conceive. Ropes and pulleys to hoist me up. We had stairs in Jamaica. Even in our single-storey houses we had stairs that lifted visitors on to the veranda and another that took them into the kitchen. There were stairs at my college, up to the dormitories that housed the pupils on two separate floors. I was very familiar with stairs. But all my mind could conjure as I looked up at this tall, tall house was ropes and pulleys. It was obvious that I had been on a ship for too long.

In Gilbert Joseph's last letter he had made me a promise that he would be there to meet me when my ship arrived at the dockside in England. He had composed two pages of instructions telling me how he would greet me. 'I will be there,' he wrote. 'You will see me waving my hand with joy at my young bride coming at last to England. I will be jumping up and down and calling out your name with longing in my tone.' It did occur to me that, as I had not seen Gilbert for six months, he might have forgotten my face. The only way he would be sure of recognising his bride was by looking out for a frowning woman who stared embarrassed at the jumping, waving buffoon she had married.

II

But it did not matter – he was not there. There was no one who would have fitted his description. The only jumping and waving that was done was by the Jamaicans arriving and leaving the ship. Women who shivered in their church best clothes – their cotton dresses with floppy bows and lace; their hats and white gloves looking gaudy against the grey of the night. Men in suits and bow-ties and smart hats. They jumped and waved. Jumped and waved at the people come to meet them. Black men in dark, scruffy coats with hand-knitted scarves. Hunched over in the cold. Squinting and straining to see a bag or hair or shoes or a voice or a face that they knew. Who looked feared – their eyes opening a little too wide – as they perused the luggage that had been brought across the ocean and now had to be carried through the streets of London. Greeting excited relatives with the same words: 'You bring some guava, some rum – you have a little yam in that bag?'

As my feet had set down on the soil of England an Englishwoman approached me. She was breathless. Panting and flushed. She swung me round with a force that sent one of my coat buttons speeding into the crowd with the velocity of a bullet. 'Are you Sugar?' she asked me. I was still trying to follow my poor button with the hope of retrieving it later as that coat had cost me a great deal of money. But this Englishwoman leaned close in to my face and demanded to know, 'Are you Sugar?'

I straightened myself and told her, 'No, I am Hortense.'

She tutted as if this information was in some way annoying to her. She took a long breath and said, 'Have you seen Sugar? She's one of you. She's coming to be my nanny and I am a little later than I thought. You must know her. Sugar. Sugar?'

I thought I must try saying sugar with those vowels that make the word go on for ever. Very English. Sugaaaar. And told this woman politely, 'No I am sorry I am not acquainted with . . .'

But she shook her head and said, 'Ohh,' before I had a chance to open any of my vowels. This Englishwoman then dashed into a crowd where she turned another woman round so fast that this newly arrived Jamaican, finding herself an inch away from a white woman shouting, 'Sugaaar, Sugaaar,' into her face, suddenly let out a loud scream.

12

It was two hours I waited for Gilbert. Two hours watching people hugging up lost relations and friends. Laughing, wiping handkerchiefs over tearful eyes. Arguing over who will go where. Men lifting cases, puffing and sweating, on to their shoulders. Women fussing with hats and pulling on gloves. All walking off into this cold black night through an archway that looked like an open mouth. I looked for my button on the ground as the crowds thinned. But it would not have been possible to find anything that small in the fading light.

There was a white man working, pushing a trolley – sometimes empty, sometimes full. He whistled, as he passed, a tune that made his head nod. I thought, This working white man may have some notion as to how I could get to my destination. I attracted his attention by raising my hand. 'Excuse me, sir, I am needing to get to Nevern Street. Would you perchance know where it is?'

This white man scratched his head and picked his left nostril before saying, 'I can't take you all the way on me trolley, love.' It occurred to me that I had not made myself understood or else this working white man could not have thought me so stupid as to expect him, with only his two-wheeled cart, to take me through the streets of London. What – would I cling to his back with my legs round his waist? 'You should get a taxi,' he told me, when he had finished laughing at his joke.

I stared into his face and said, 'Thank you, and could you be so kind as to point out for me the place where I might find one of these vehicles?'

The white man looked perplexed. 'You what, love?' he said, as if I had been speaking in tongues.

It took me several attempts at saying the address to the driver of the taxi vehicle before his face lit with recognition. 'I need to be taken to number twenty-one Nevern Street in SW five. Twenty-one Nevern Street. N-e-v-e-r-n S-t-r-e-e-t.' I put on my best accent. An accent that had taken me to the top of the class in Miss Stuart's English pronunciation competition. My recitation of 'Ode to a Nightingale' had earned me a merit star and the honour of ringing the school bell for one week.

But still this taxi driver did not understand me. 'No, sorry, dear. Have you got it written down or something? On a piece of paper? Have you got it on

13

a piece of paper?' I showed him the letter from my husband, which was clearly marked with the address. 'Oh, Nevern Street — twenty-one. I've got you now.'

There was a moon. Sometimes there, sometimes covered by cloud. But there was a moon that night — its light distorting and dissolving as my breath steamed upon the vehicle window. 'This is the place you want, dear. Twenty-one Nevern Street,' the taxi driver said. 'Just go and ring the bell. You know about bells and knockers? You got them where you come from? Just go and ring the bell and someone'll come.' He left my trunk by the side of the road. 'I'm sure someone inside will help you with this, dear. Just ring the bell.' He mouthed the last words with the slow exaggeration I generally reserved for the teaching of small children. It occurred to me then that perhaps white men who worked were made to work because they were fools.

I did not see what now came through the door, it came through so fast. It could have been a large dog the way it leaped and bounded towards me. It was only when I heard, 'Hortense,' uttered from its mouth that I realised it was my husband. 'Hortense. You here! You here at last, Hortense!'

I folded my arms, sat on my trunk and averted my eye. He stopped in front of me. His arms still open wide ready for me to run into. 'Don't Hortense me, Gilbert Joseph.'

His arms slowly rested to his sides as he said, 'You no pleased to see me, Hortense?'

I quoted precisely from the letter. ' "I will be at the dockside to meet you. You will see me there jumping and waving and calling your name with longing in my tone." '

'How you find this place, Hortense?' was all the man said.

'Without your help, Gilbert Joseph, that's how I find this place. With no help from you. Where were you? Why you no come to meet me? Why you no waving and calling my name with longing in your tone?'

He was breathless as he began, 'Hortense, let me tell you. I came to the dock but there was no ship. So they tell me to come back later when the ship will arrive. So I go home and take the opportunity of fixing the place up nice for when you come . . .'

14

His shirt was not buttoned properly. The collar turned up at one side and down at the other. There were two stray buttons that had no holes to fit in. The shirt was only tucked into his trousers around the front, at the back it hung out like a mischievous schoolboy's. One of his shoelaces was undone. He looked ragged. Where was the man I remembered? He was smart: his suit double-breasted, his hair parted and shiny with grease, his shoes clean, his fingernails short, his moustache neat and his nose slender. The man who stood jabbering in front of me looked dark and rough. But he was Gilbert, I could tell. I could tell by the way the fool hopped about as he pronounced his excuses.

'So I was just going to go to the dock again. But then here you are. You turn up at the door. Oh, man, what a surprise for me! Hortense! You here at last!'

It was then I noticed that the Englishwoman who had answered the door was looking at us from the top of the steps. She called from on high, 'Gilbert, can I shut the door now, please? It's letting in a terrible draught.'

And he called to her in a casual tone, 'Soon come.'

So I whispered to him, 'Come, you want everyone in England to know our business?'

The Englishwoman was still looking at me when I entered the hallway. Perusing me in a fashion as if I was not there to see her stares. I nodded to her and said, 'Thank you for all your help with finding my husband. I hope it did not inconvenience you too much.' I was hoping that in addressing her directly she would avert her eye from me and go about her business. But she did not. She merely shrugged and continued as before. I could hear Gilbert dragging at my trunk. We both stood listening to him huffing and puffing like a broken steam train.

Then he ran through the door, saying, 'Hortense, what you have in that trunk – your mother?'

As the Englishwoman was still looking at us I smiled instead of cussing and said, 'I have everything I will need in that trunk, thank you, Gilbert.'

'So you bring your mother, then,' Gilbert said. He broke into his laugh, which I remembered. A strange snorting sound from the back of his nose, which caused his gold tooth to wink. I was still smiling when he started to rub his hands and say, 'Well, I hope you have guava and mango and rum and—'

'I hope you're not bringing anything into the house that will smell?' the Englishwoman interrupted.

This question erased the smile from my face. Turning to her I said, 'I have only brought what I—'

But Gilbert caught my elbow. 'Come, Hortense,' he said, as if the woman had not uttered a word. 'Come, let me show you around.'

I followed him up the first stairs and heard the woman call, 'What about the trunk, Gilbert? You can't leave it where it is.'

Gilbert looked over my shoulder to answer her, smiling: 'Don't worry, Queenie. Soon come, nah, man.'

I had to grab the banister to pull myself up stair after stair. There was hardly any light. Just one bulb so dull it was hard to tell whether it was giving out light or sucking it in. At every turn on the stairs there was another set of steep steps, looking like an empty bookshelf in front of me. I longed for those ropes and pulleys of my earlier mind. I was groping like a blind man at times with nothing to light the way in front of me except the sound of Gilbert still climbing ahead. 'Hortense, nearly there,' he called out, like Moses from on top of the mountain. I was palpitating by the time I reached the door where Gilbert stood grinning, saying: 'Here we are.'

'What a lot of stairs. Could you not find a place with fewer stairs?'

We went into the room. Gilbert rushed to pull a blanket over the unmade bed. Still warm I was sure. It was obvious to me he had just got out of it. I could smell gas. Gilbert waved his arms around as if showing me a lovely view. 'This is the room,' he said.

All I saw were dark brown walls. A broken chair that rested one uneven leg on the Holy Bible. A window with a torn curtain and Gilbert's suit – the double-breasted one – hanging from a rail on the wall.

'Well,' I said, 'show me the rest, then, Gilbert.' The man just stared. 'Show me the rest, nah. I am tired from the long journey.' He scratched his head.

16

'The other rooms, Gilbert. The ones you busy making so nice for me you forget to come to the dock.'

Gilbert spoke so softly I could hardly hear. He said, 'But this is it.'

'I am sorry?' I said.

'This is it, Hortense. This is the room I am living.'

Three steps would take me to one side of this room. Four steps could take me to another. There was a sink in the corner, a rusty tap stuck out from the wall above it. There was a table with two chairs — one with its back broken — pushed up against the bed. The armchair held a shopping bag, a pyjama top, and a teapot. In the fireplace the gas hissed with a blue flame.

'Just this?' I had to sit on the bed. My legs gave way. There was no bounce underneath me as I fell. 'Just this? This is where you are living? Just this?'

'Yes, this is it.' He swung his arms around again, like it was a room in a palace.

'Just this? Just this? You bring me all this way for just this?'

The man sucked his teeth and flashed angry eyes in my face. 'What you expect, woman? Yes, just this! What you expect? Everyone live like this. There has been a war. Houses bombed. I know plenty people live worse than this. What you want? You should stay with your mamma if you want it nice. There been a war here. Everyone live like this.'

He looked down at me, his badly buttoned chest heaving. The carpet was threadbare in a patch in the middle and there was a piece of bread lying on it. He sucked his teeth again and walked out the room. I heard him banging down the stairs. He left me alone.

He left me alone to stare on just this.

Two

Gilbert

'Is this the way the English live?' How many times she ask me that question? I lose count. 'This the way the English live?' That question became a mournful lament, sighed on each and every thing she see. 'Is this the way the English live?'

'Yes,' I tell her, 'this is the way the English live . . . there has been a war . . . many English live worse than this.'

She drift to the window, look quizzical upon the scene, rub her gloved hand on the pane of glass, examine it before saying once more, 'This the way the English live?'

Soon the honourable man inside me was shaking my ribs and thumping my breast, wanting to know, 'Gilbert, what in God's name have you done? You no realise, man? Cha, you married to this woman!'

Queenie was still standing by the open door when I dared fetch the trunk that Hortense had sailed across an ocean. 'Everything all right, Gilbert?'

'Yes, thank you,' I tell her.

'What did you say her name was?'

'Hortense.'

'Funny name.'

'What, funnier than Queenie?'

She gave a little laugh although I had not made a joke. 'You'll have to move that trunk. I need to shut the door. Someone will be away with it if you're not careful.'

'If they can lift it, it's theirs,' I muttered, before adding, 'I moving it now, Queenie.'

My idea was to sort of slide the trunk up the stairs. Now, I could do this for one stair perhaps – two stairs if I could rest up me feet for an hour after. But this trunk lifted like the coffin of a fat man turned to stone. I would have to get one of the boys to help me. So I knock on Winston's room.

Now, the man that answer the door was not Winston. True, him look like Winston, him talk like Winston and him dress like Winston. But Winston was half of a twin. Identical as two lemons on a tree. This was his brother Kenneth. To tell them apart, try to borrow a shilling. Winston will help you out but pester you all over London till him get it back. Kenneth, on the other hand, will persuade you to give *him* a shilling, assuring you that he could turn it into a pound before the week's end. Kenneth's home was in Notting Dale with an Irish woman named Noreen. I knew this was not my friend Winston when, after I asked him to help me with my wife's trunk, the man before me said, 'So you tell me she jus' come from home? You know what she have in that trunk?'

'No, man.'

'Come, let us open it. Mango fetching a good price. You think she have rum? I know one of the boys give me half his wage to place him tongue in a guava.'

'Is my wife's belongings in that trunk.'

'Me caan believe what me ear is hearing. You a man. She just come off the boat – you mus' show who boss. And straight way so no bad habit start. A wife must do as her husband say. You ask a judge. You ask a policeman. They will tell you. Everyt'ing in that trunk belong to you. What is hers is yours and if she no like it a little licking will make her obey.'

And I asked this smooth-tongue man, 'How come you in Winston's room? Noreen throw you out again?'

Silly as two pantomime clowns we struggled with this trunk – but at a steady pace. That is, until the trunk fell back down one whole flight when Kenneth, letting go, insisted that a cigarette – which I had to supply – was the only thing that would help him catch his breath. How long did it take us to reach the room? I do not know. A fine young man when we start, I was a wheezing old crone when we eventually get to the top. And there is Hortense still sitting delicate on the bed, now pointing a white-gloved finger saying, 'You may place it under the window and please be careful.'

Kenneth and I, silently agreeing with each other, dropped the wretched trunk where we stood, just inside the door.

It is not only Jamaicans that like to interrogate a stranger with so many questions they grow dizzy. But the Jamaican is the undisputed master and most talented at the art. And so Kenneth began. The hands on a clock would have barely moved but he had asked Hortense which part of the island she came from, how many members in her family, her daddy's occupation, where she went to school, what ship she sailed on, did she meet a man on the ship from Buff Bay named Clinton and, of course, what did she have in the trunk? Now, him never wait long enough for any answer and Hortense, although listening polite at first, gradually come to look on Kenneth like she just find him stuck to her shoe.

'Thank you for your help, Kenneth,' I say.

'Oh, you have curtain up here,' Kenneth say.

'Goodbye,' I tell him.

'You goin', man?' him say.

So I have to give him the sign. All we Jamaican boys know the sign. When a man need to be alone with a woman, for reasons only imagination should know, the head is cocked just a little to one side while the eye first open wide then swivel fast to the nearest exit. Even the most fool-fool Jamaican boy can read this sign and would never ignore it in case it should be they that needed it next time.

'Oh!' Kenneth say. 'I must be gone. And don't forget what I tell you, Gilbert. Winston know where to find me.'

As he left the room Hortense turned to me to sneer, 'He your friend?'

I shut the door. Now, to get back into the room, I have to step over the damn trunk.

'What you doing?' she say.

'The thing in me way.'

'That is a valuable trunk.'

'What – you wan' me sleep in the hallway? You no see I caan step round it. Your mummy never tell you what caan be step round must be step over?'

She rub the case like I bruise it.

'Cha, it come across an ocean. You tell me this one skinny Jamaican man gon' mash it up. What you have in there anyway?'

She sat her slender backside down on the trunk averting her eye from mine, lifting her chin as if something in the cracked ceiling was interesting to her. Stony and silent as a statue from Trafalgar Square. I began to crave the noise of her 'English live like this?' questions again.

'You wan' take off your coat?' I say, while she look on me like she had forgotten I was there. 'You don't need on that big coat – the fire is on.'

Cha! Would you believe the gas choose that moment to run out? I know I have a shilling somewhere, but where? Searching my pocket I say, 'Oh, I just have to find the money for the gas meter.' It then I notice my shirt was not buttoned properly. I had not done up a garment so feeble since I was a small boy – me shirt hanging out like a vagabond's. And now she is watching me, her wide brown eyes alert as a cobra's. If I change the button on the shirt I will look like I am undressing. And this, experience tell me, would alarm her. So I just tuck the shirt in me pants like this mishap is a new London fashion.

Let me tell the truth, I had been asleep before she come. But I had gone to the dock. You see, she tell me she coming at seven and I know she is sailing with bananas, because she coming on the Producers boat, to Jamaica dock. Everything work out fine – I am on the late shift at the sorting office, and when I finish around six in the morning I go to the dock. The sun is rising pretty as an artist's picture, with ships sailing through a morning mist slow up the river. Romantic, my mind is conjuring her waving majestic to me, my shoulders, manly silhouetting against the morning sun, poised to receive her comely curves as she runs into my arms. Only they tell me, no. She and her bananas are coming seven at night. Am I to wait there all day? I get a little something to eat, I go home and I even tidy up a little. Then I lie on the bed intending to doze – just doze. But I have been working twelve hours, I have been to the dock – man, I have even tidy! Is it a sin that I fall asleep?

The shilling must have drop out the pocket of me pants into the bed. So now, she is watching me having to look under the bedclothes for the money. 'You keep your money in the bed?'

Cha, I knew she would say that. I just knew it! 'No, it's just when I was sleeping . . .'

'Oh, you were sleeping, then.'

'I just lie for a minute and I must have—'

'So, that why you no there to meet me?'

'No, I come but—'

'I know, you tell me, you tidying the place.' And she look around her and say, 'See how tidy it is?'

I was not foolish enough to say, 'Shut up, woman,' but I was vex enough to think it. But instead I show her the shilling and tell her, 'I will put this in the meter.' She is looking on me, sort of straining her neck to see where I was moving, so I say, 'Come, let me show you how to put the money in the meter.' And you know what she say?

'You think I don't know how to put money in a meter?' and she turn back to that fascinating crack in the ceiling, patting at the tight black curls of her hair in case any should dare to be out of place.

But this is a tricky meter. Sometime it smooth as a piggy-bank and sometime it jam. Today it jam. I have to stand back to give it a kick so the coin will drop. But, oh, no, one kick did not do it. I hear her demurely sucking on her teeth at my second blow. How everything I do look so rough?

When I light the gas fire again I say, 'Take off your coat, nah?' And victory so sweet, she finally do something I say. Mark you, she leave on her little hat and the blessed white gloves. I had no hanger for the coat. 'You wan' a cup of tea?' I say. I had been meaning to get another hanger – the only one I have has my suit on it. 'I'll just fill the kettle,' I say. I go to throw the coat on the bed but, I am no fool, just in time I hang it over me suit instead.

Now she is walking about the room. Looking on the meter. Perusing the table, wobbling the back of the chair. As I am filling the kettle she is running her hand along the mantelpiece. She then look at her hand. And, man, even I get a shock: her white glove is black.

'Everything filthy,' she tell me.

'Then stop touching up everything with white glove.'

'You ever clean this place?'

'Yes – I clean it.'

'Then why everything so dirty?'

'Is your white glove. You touch an angel with white glove it come up black.'

Everywhere she feel now – the wall, the door-handle, the window-sill, the curtain. I tell her, 'Now you are just putting dirt on everything – those gloves are too mucky.' A smile dared on to my face but she stern chased it away again. 'Come,' I say patting the armchair, moving it nearer the fire, 'sit down, I make you a nice English cup of tea.'

Oh, why the little bit of milk I have gone bad, the cups both dirty and the kettle take so long to boil on the ring? I am wondering what I can say next by way of chit-chat, but then she say, 'Who is that woman downstairs?' Let me tell you I was relieve for the conversation.

'Oh, Queenie – she own the house.'

'You know her?'

'Of course, she own the house. She is the landlady.'

'She married?'

'Her husband lost in the war.'

'She on her own?'

'Yes.'

'You friendly with her?'

Wow! Friendly. Every Jamaican man know that word breathed by a Jamaican woman is a trap that can snap around you. Tread careful, boy, or she will think this woman hiding three children for you.

'I knew her during the war,' I say. 'She was kind to me and now she me landlady. And lucky I know her – places hard to come by, especially for coloured boys.'

'She seem to know all your business.'

'No,' I say.

Now, why Queenie choose that time to knock on the door calling out, 'Everything all right in there, Gilbert?' Of course I trip over the damn trunk getting to the door. I open it just a crack. 'I can smell gas,' Queenie say.

'It just go out, but I see to it. You want something?'

'Just checking everything was all right.'

'Yes, thank you,' I say, and shut the door.

When I turn back the rising steam from the kettle has Hortense fading away. A lady in the mist, she just sitting there swallowed up in vapour. I trip over the damn trunk again.

'You no see the kettle boiling?'

'So, she no wan' know your business?'

I so vex I forget to use a cloth to pick the wretched kettle off the ring. 'Ras,' I drop it quick it scald me so. 'The thing hot,' I tell her.

'Then why you no use a cloth?' she say.

Reason tells me if I am not to kill this woman I must take a deep breath. 'Please forgive my language,' I say, while she is looking on me like I am the devil's favoured friend. 'Come,' I tell her, 'I will show you how to use this gas-ring.'

'Why?'

'You will need to know so you can cook on it.'

'I will cook in the kitchen.'

'This is the kitchen.'

'Where?'

'You see this ring and that sink, that is the kitchen. The dining room is over there where you see the table and two chairs.'

'You tell me you cook on just this?'

'Yes, that is what I am telling you.'

'Just this one little ring?'

'Yes, so let me show you how it work.'

And she is back looking round the room, her mouth gaping like a simpleton's.

'You watching me? See when you come to cook you have to turn it . . .' I stop. She looked so quizzical I wonder if I am talking in foreign tones. 'You can cook, can't you?' I asked.

'I was taught to cook in domestic science at college,' she tell me.

'It not science we need, it food. Man, you telling me you caan cook . . .'

She stood up. 'Where is the lavatory? I presume there is a lavatory?'

'Downstairs,' I tell her, and she is stepping over the trunk to leave the room so quick she is a blur before my eye.

I am making the tea in the little pot when I hear, 'A dump it may be, ducky, but you ain't weeing in here. What's the matter with you lot? Does this look like a ruddy toilet?'

I am chasing down the stairs now. Jean, the woman in the room underneath, does not like to be disturbed at this time of night before she is about to go out for work. She is standing in her doorway wearing only a pink slip and underwear. Half her head has hair rollers, the other half, in the process of being combed, has the brush stuck in it like a hatchet.

Hortense is asking, in slow deliberate English usually reserved for the deaf, 'Would you be so kind as to tell me where I might find the toilet?'

Jean, frowning, says, 'What? What? This is not the toilet.' Then seeing me, 'Thank bloody God! Gilbert, can you help me? This one thinks I'm a bloody toilet.' Then suddenly Jean laughs, a cackle like pebbles falling down a washing-board. Placing her hand on Hortense's shoulder she leans in close to her, all the while sniffing like she is smelling something. 'Bloody hell – she's so fresh off the boat, I can smell the sea.' Hortense still smiling wide-eyed polite then feels Jean's door shut in her face.

It was with a frantic whisper that Hortense shouted at me: 'You tell me the toilet is downstairs. This is downstairs.' The frown that pinched her eyebrows was from a little girl confused.

I touched her arm. She pulled away. 'Okay – I am a disease not to be caught,' I say, stepping away from her. 'Just follow me.' I take her to the toilet, which is at the bottom of the house opposite the front door. 'You can find your way back?' I ask.

'Of course,' she tell me. 'I make a simple mistake but I am not a fool.'

Puffing noisy as a pipe organ I hear her returning from way down the stairs. She was breathless but still she find air enough to chide me. 'You mean to tell me that every time I must go to the lavatory I must walk first down then up all those stairs?'

Now, I know plenty boys would have told her to stick her skinny backside out the window if she no like it, but I tell her, 'No, you can use this.' And I stoop down to feel under the bed for the potty. Cha, nah, man, I was so pleased to have a solution that I pick up the pot without any thought. Only after I place it under her nose did I ask myself, Gilbert, why the hell you no empty it before Hortense come? The contents is slopping over the side and spilling on to her dainty-foot shoes.

She jump like a flea. 'Disgusting – you are disgusting,' she cry. 'This place is disgusting. How you bring me here?'

Now I am having to calm her, to raise a finger to my lip to shush her. 'I caan believe you bring me to a place like this. You tell me you have somewhere to live. You wan' me live like this?' She is waving her arms so her white gloves could bring a plane safely into land. And I am still holding this pot saying, 'Listen, Hortense. Hush now. I sorry.' But the thing spilling more as I am trying to compose her.

'Get away from me,' she say. 'I caan believe you bring me here. You live like an animal . . .'

There is no room to put the pot back down and I am making it worse following her round slopping this stuff everywhere. So I throw the contents down the sink. Oh, why the two cups still in the basin – surely I had already washed them for our nice cup of English tea? For one blessed moment she was silent. You know, I heard a clock strike and a woman giggle in the street before she began, almost tranquil: 'Wait. You tell me you wash your cup in the same place you throw your doings.'

'No, no, I don't,' I say, 'I take it down to the toilet but—'

She is not listening. She rage at me, 'You wash in filth! This place is disgusting. I caan believe you bring me all this way to live like this. You make me come here to live like an animal?'

Man, this woman is a barb under my skin – she irritate me so I lose me temper. I tell her, 'Yes, and you know what else, little Miss Stick-up-your-nose-in-the-air, you will have to wash your plate, your vegetable and your backside in that basin too. This room is where you will sleep, eat, cook, dress and write your mummy to tell her how the Mother Country is so fine. And, little Miss High-class, one thing about England you don't know yet because you just come off a boat. You are lucky.'

Before

Three

Hortense

The sound of my father's name could still hush a room long after he had left Savannah-La-Mar. Every generation in our district knew of my father and his work overseas as a government man. His picture was pinned to parish walls — cut from the newspapers of America, Canada and England. My father was a man of class. A man of character. A man of intelligence. Noble in a way that made him a legend. 'Lovell Roberts,' they whispered. 'Have you heard about Lovell Roberts?'

When you are the child of someone such as he, there are things that are expected that may not be expected of someone of a more lowly persuasion. And so it was with I.

I was born to a woman called Alberta. It was she who suckled me until I was strong enough to drink from the cow. I recall a warm smell of boiling milk. Being rocked in the sun with a gentle song and 'me sprigadee' whispered until my eyes could do nothing but close. I remember a skirt flapping in the breeze and bare black feet skipping over stones. I do not recall the colour of her eyes, the shape of her lips or the feel of her skin. Alberta was a country girl who could neither read nor write nor perform even the rudiments of her times tables. I was born to her out of wedlock — it would be wrong to say otherwise. But it was she who gave birth to me in a wooden hut. And it was

31

she who bought me shoes for the journey I was to take holding the hand of her mother, Miss Jewel.

I grew to look as my father did. My complexion was as light as his; the colour of warm honey. It was not the bitter chocolate hue of Alberta and her mother. With such a countenance there was a chance of a golden life for I. What, after all, could Alberta give? Bare black feet skipping over stones. If I was given to my father's cousins for upbringing, I could learn to read and write and perform all my times tables. And more. I could become a lady worthy of my father, wherever he might be.

Mr Philip Roberts was almost as important a man as my father. Short with a round belly plump from plantain and his beloved dumplings. He had a house that sat in its own green acres of land, which was befitting of his status as the wholesaler for the grocers of the district. All produce came through his hands. So trusted was he that low-class people from all around would call at his door to settle any fuss in the neighbourhood. He was not the law but he was authority, and his face drooped two fleshy jowls with the weight of that responsibility.

Martha Roberts was known throughout the district for her pale grey eyes, a rarity on a face that everyone agreed should not have been so dark. Two inches taller than Mr Philip, her frame, over the years, had obligingly hunched shorter so as to spare her husband that indignity. She had given birth to three children: two girls and a boy. Her hair turned overnight from black to startling white when her dearest daughters died – together, only days apart – from measles. Mr Philip and Miss Ma, as I was allowed to call my father's cousins, were then left with only one child to nurture. Their precious son, Michael.

Miss Jewel, Alberta's mother, wore her good hat and her best blouse to lead me to the house of my father's cousins. I, a tiny girl, tripping along beside her in sham-patta shoes. My only words were Mamma and na-na (which I believe meant banana). I remember staring at white shoes tied neat with laces, two bloody knees and a grinning boy, who held a gecko on his palm for me to see.

With a nod and the assurance of money from my father, it was all agreed. Alberta was to leave Jamaica and take up work in Cuba and Miss Jewel would stay as a servant of my father's cousins. She would watch me grow. In those years she washed, dressed and fed Michael and me. Calling him Massa Michael and me Miss Hortense. (Miss Hortense when there was someone to hear and 'me sprigadee' when there was not.)

I sat a quiet vigil in the henhouse. Waiting. Watching the hen pushing out her egg – seeing it plop soft and silent on to the straw.

'Hortense, where are you?' Michael padded around outside in his rubber-soled shoes. His shadow playing on the wooden slats in the wall. His one eye, with lashes that curled like a girl's, looked through a hole in the wood. 'Come out, Hortense.' He slapped his palms on the walls, which shook this tiny world and startled the hen into deserting her egg. Michael liked to see chickens flapping their wings, scattering in fright, screeching until he could do nothing but laugh and cover his ears against the sound.

I pushed him aside as I carried the newly laid egg into the house, him leaping around me saying, 'Let me see, Hortense, let me see.'

'No,' I said, 'you have no patience, Michael Roberts, to sit and watch the egg coming out. So you have no reason to look upon the egg.'

Miss Ma thanked Michael for the egg I brought into the house. Her hands enclosed mine, the warmth of her touch gradually pulling the egg from my hand. Devotion lit her pale eyes as she gazed on Michael's face. He puffed out his chest like a cock and said, 'Shall I bring you more, Mamma?'

She only looked on me to say, 'Hortense, I don't want you in the henhouse. Leave the chickens alone. You hear me, nah?'

'You are a nuisance to me, Michael Roberts,' I told him. A boy one year older than me and one foot smaller who led me into mischief. For one, I was not supposed to climb trees. Mr Philip told me that it was not godly for girls to lift themselves into branches as a monkey would. Or come home wet from the stream, our bellies full of star apples, raspberries and mangoes, my skirt clinging to my legs with Michael running behind me dangling a wriggling fish from his hand. I was not supposed to hunt for scorpions, tipping them from their hiding-place, tormenting them with a stick. Or dress the goat in a bonnet and attempt to ride her like a horse.

'Leave me alone, Michael. You can play all day but I have work that must be done,' I told that wicked boy daily. I had washing to do in the outhouse sink, cleaning of the shades on the kerosene lamps. I was responsible for keeping the area under the tamarind tree free from dirt and a pleasure to sit in. But he was always, 'Come, Hortense, come, Hortense. Let us see the woodpecker's nest.' Him impatient, wriggling underneath me as I stood on his back trying to see into the hole in the tree that the bird flew from. 'You see anything yet? Come, Hortense, it's my turn now.' Tipping me on to the ground just as I was to look on the nest.

'Why you do that, Michael? I just about to see.'

'It's my turn, Hortense. Bend over.' This boy, older than me, climbing on my back, complaining all the time. 'Stand still, you make me fall, nah.' And saying, 'I think I see. Stay still. I think I see,' as the woodpecker flew from the hole and pecked him on his head. Oh, how that boy screamed from the little cut the woodpecker made.

If Mr Philip knew of the devilment I had been tricked into he would have sent me away. Little girls did not climb trees! 'Principle,' he bellowed at every meal. 'We must all have principle. Each one of us will stand accountable — puny and small in front of the magnificent throne of the Almighty.' After he had blessed the food with a grace that sometimes went on long enough for my neck to get stiff with the prayer, Mr Philip started his sermon: 'Life is preparation for the day when we finally look upon the face of the Lord, our Maker.' He rose from his seat clutching his Bible like a weapon. 'I am the way, the truth, and the life.' Sometimes he banged the table — Miss Ma looking nervous, seizing a vibrating bowl or wobbling water jug. 'It is only through the Lord thy God that we will reach the kingdom of heaven.' Larger than a mountain, Mr Philip stood looking down between Michael and I. Michael did not attempt to catch my eye for fear it would start us giggling. No words came from our mouths. Not one word. Spittle often hit my cheek but I did not dare brush it away. Or look on Mr Philip's face, scared I would be entranced by the lines that came and went as his forehead danced with the wonder of the scriptures. Miss Ma placed food on to Mr Philip's plate, nodding her approval, then held out her hand to serve Michael and I. We kept our heads bowed to eat as Miss Ma instructed us on appropriate table manners. 'Take your elbows off the table while you are eating. Hortense, please sit straight. Michael, do not put so much food into your mouth. Only a horse chews with its mouth gaping.'

I pinched myself at the table on the night before Michael was to leave to attend boarding-school. Squeezing my nails into my hand until blood pricked on my skin. I did not want to cry. I did not want to paw at the table and beg them let me go with him. I had been told, when there is too much pain, tears nah come.

'Remember now thy creator in thy days of youth,' Mr Philip began. 'But it is time to surrender the deeds of thy younger years. And walk in the way of God as a man.'

I gave Michael my bottle of perfumed water with which to clean his slate at his new school. I did not want his slate to give off the stinking vapours that the boys' slates at my government school did.

He took it, saying, 'I will learn about the whole world, Hortense. And you will be staying at the penny-a-week school, skipping silly rhymes and counting frogs at the base of the tree.'

I pushed my fingers into my ears and sang, ' "What are little boys made of? Moss and snails and puppy dogs' tails . . ." ' He poked out his tongue and handed me back the bottle. It fell and I finally cried when the earth claimed the sweet-smelling liquid.

Tiddlers swam in the rivers without worry. Woodpeckers went about their business. The goat looked as a goat should. Scorpions stayed in their hiding-place. Even Mr Philip cut short his nightly Bible readings, asking for his glass of water to be poured long before Miss Ma had given me any table manners. And, without Michael, I sat in the henhouse undisturbed.

Miss Jewel called me every day after school, 'Miss Hortense, di boy gone, come help me nuh.' Her colossal leather-worn hands squeezed waterfalls from washing. Her breasts wobbled: two fallen fruit trapped by the waistband of her skirt. Her legs bowed.

'Miss Jewel,' I asked, 'why your legs stick out so?'

She solemn, sucked her teeth and said, 'Me nuh know, Miss Hortense. When me mudda did pregnant dem seh smaddy obeah'er. A likkle spell yah no.' And she sang as she washed. ' "Mr Roberts wash him sock at night. And sidung pon de ground." '

'No, Miss Jewel,' I told her, 'you are singing the wrong words. It is "While shepherds watched their flock by night".'

'Weh you mean shepherd, Miss Hortense?'

'A shepherd is a man who looks after sheep.'

'Sheep? Dem nuh have none ah dat in Jamaica?'

'No, it is England where the shepherd is, Miss Jewel.'

'Oh, Hengland. Ah deh so de Lawd born ah Hengland?'

'Of course. And in England sheep live everywhere. They wear wool to keep out the winter cold.'

She looked to me for all her knowledge of England.

'Miss Jewel,' I told her, 'you should learn to speak properly as the King of England does. Not in this rough country way.'

'Teach me nuh, Miss Hortense?'

I taught her the poem by Mr William Wordsworth that I had learned to recite at school.

> I wander'd lonely as a cloud
> That floats on high o'er vales and hills,
> When all at once I saw a crowd,
> A host of golden daffodils.

Even though she asked, 'Weh yoh seh it name – daffodil?' and did not stop fussing until I had drawn the flower in the dirt, she learned every word. Watching my lips like a child enthralled, moving her own to form the same shapes. Recounting every perfect word with her chin high and her arms folded under her breasts. But soon she was rehearsing her own version as she went about her day. ' "Ah walk under a cloud and den me float over de ill. An' me see Miss Hortense a look pon de daffodil dem".'

* * *

My government upper school had to lose its star pupil when I reached the age of fifteen. Upon leaving I was pressed by Miss Ma and others to continue improving myself by assisting with the education of young children (from good families) at a private school. I marked their dictation, underlining any wrongly spelt word and supervising as they rewrote the offending item six times. I listened to the reciting of times tables, correcting the bright pupils and encouraging the backward ones to speak up during the repetition of their mistakes. My favourite task was to hand out the books at the beginning of term. Those children all had new books, whose turning pages wafted a fragrance of sun on sweet wood; a scent of knowledge. They did not have the musty stench of decay that emitted from the dog-eared Nestfields grammar books at my government school.

This private school was run by Mr and Mrs Ryder, a married couple who had sold everything they had in America to set up the school.

'It is for the poor people that we have been sent to do this,' Mr Ryder told me, on our first meeting.

Mrs Ryder, in her movie-star accent, remarked, 'Someone must help these poor negro children. Education is all they have.'

Many people wondered if Mr and Mrs Ryder were aware that their school took only the wealthiest, fairest and highest-class children from the district. Or whether these polite, clean and well-spoken pupils nevertheless still looked poor to them.

The Ryders were evangelists and Mr Philip had no time for evangelists. He did not like the way that people moved by the spirit of the Lord threw themselves to the ground shaking and frothing at the mouth like beasts. He could not understand that, as the service came to a close, those same people could be seen politely shaking the preacher's hand as they left the church. He said, 'The spirit of the Lord cannot come and go in people so quickly.' I asked him to make an exception of Mr and Mrs Ryder as the spirit only ever moved them to raise their eyes to heaven and sway.

Mrs Ryder was, without any doubt, the whitest woman I had ever seen. Her short blonde hair sat stiff as a halo around her head. Her delicate skin was so thin that in places it revealed a fine blue tracery of veins. But her mouth looked unfinished – a gash in her face with no lips to ornament the opening. Mr Ryder had so very little hair that a naughty boy from the school claimed to have counted the strands that were left. Sixty-five was the number that escaped from the schoolyard out into the town. His poor shiny hairless head was red as a berry ripe to burst, and when the sun caught his face a fever of brown freckles was produced.

They had a car, which was the envy of every black man who ever walked from the fields in slip-slop shoes. Even Mrs Ryder drove this car, sitting low at the wheel in a hat adorned with a long brown bird's feather. The car drew head-turning stares from anyone it passed. So it was to no one's surprise that gossip about the Ryders followed close behind: in shops, under the shade of trees, on street corners, at food tables, busybodies discussed when they last saw Mr Ryder where Mr Ryder should not have been. When a pretty young woman produced a fair-skinned baby with a completely bald head, the men who sat at their dominoes sucked their teeth and whispered that Mr Ryder was spreading more than just his love of learning. Some looked in pity on Mrs Ryder as she sauntered through the district unescorted. Although plenty of young men would leave their game of dominoes undecided to rush to her assistance.

For Michael's homecoming, I wore a pink floral dress that was given to me by Mrs Ryder. She had no more need of it so I asked if I might take it to have something pretty to wear for Michael. I sat into the night in the feeble flicker of a candle, adjusting the bust for a tighter fit, attaching ribbons of lace and sucking my pricked finger to avoid staining the garment red.

On the morning of Michael's homecoming we assembled ourselves on the veranda. Mr Philip and Miss Ma fidgeted nervously as the *Daily Gleaner* van could be heard crunching along the stones of the path.

Michael had been home for holidays many times before. Once he even appeared when Mr Philip had a fever. He read the Bible to his father, talked close into his mother's ear until she was consoled and left only when Mr Philip demanded his dumplings. But each time he visited something of him had altered.

'Michael Roberts, what is wrong with your voice?' I had teased him. We were sitting in the tamarind tree swinging our legs.

'You can see Cuba from here,' he said. But his voice cracked like an instrument with a loose string.

'You sound funny – like this.' I sang high like a girl, low like a man and something like a goat in between. 'What is wrong with you?'

He jumped silent from the tree and did not speak until it was time for him to leave. I did not recognise the deep bass noise that came from his mouth the next time I saw him.

'Come, Hortense,' this growl from within him said. 'Stand on my shoulders and see the woodpecker's nest.' He was firm and solid under me. 'Can you see?'

'I can,' I said, looking on the empty hole. When I got down I gazed up at his face, him realising at the same moment as I that there was no chance he could stand on my back to look. He would snap me in two.

Was it the suit, the crisp white shirt, the brown-and-green-striped tie held in place by a pin? Was it the hat tipped at an angle on his head? His thin moustache, perhaps, or the crooked smile that lit his face? His eyes, it may have been his black eyes where a mischievous boy could be glimpsed laughing within. Or perhaps it was Miss Ma's breathless exclamation, 'Look at you, son. I send a boy to boarding-school and see what they send me back – a man!'

He stepped down from the van in his shiny city shoes. He shook Mr Philip by the hand and bowed his head politely, like a man of class, a man of character, a man of intelligence. Noble in a way that made me want to shout, 'Michael Roberts! Have you seen Michael Roberts?' Or perhaps it was the way he looked at me then. Over my curves, across my breasts, up and around my lips as he said, 'But, Hortense, you are all grown-up.' Whatever it was, I knew – from the moment my eyes first beheld this handsome, dapper, newly made man – I knew that I loved him.

Michael was gazing on me as we all sat down that night at our usual places for dinner. His eyes willing me to look up into his. I did once – briefly. He smiled so sweetly I nearly pass out at the honeyed taste of it on my lips. Miss Jewel arrived in the room carrying a plate of fried chicken. Michael's eyes closed as he inhaled a waft of fragrant air. 'Oh, boy, Miss Jewel,' he said, 'how I miss you' spice-up chicken.' Mr Philip looked up as startled as if a bird had flown through the window. A voice at the table – a child of his had dared speak at the table. But Michael simply patted his stomach as if unaware of this transgression.

After we had eaten, Mr Philip lifted his Bible as he had at every meal I could remember. Miss Ma slapped gently at my hand to stop me playing with my hair as Mr Philip began. 'And God said, "Let there be light," and there was light. And God saw that the light was good; and God separated the light from the darkness. God called the light Day and the darkness he called Night.'

Mr Philip then paused for the briefest second – just enough time to clear his throat. His lips were poised to open again and complete his sermon when Michael's voice said, 'I have been taught that the earth moves around the sun and that it is this movement—'

Miss Ma, agitated, quickly interrupted with, 'It is rude to speak at the table, Michael.'

'Oh, Mamma, I am a grown man now – not a boy.' It was only shock that kept Mr Philip mute in this situation. While Michael carried on with, 'It is this movement of the sun which causes night and day.'

'Boy or man, there will be no back-chat at this table. We will have hush,' Miss Ma said.

Mr Philip glanced from the Bible to his son with the fierceness of all Ten Commandments, then continued. It was mid-reading when Michael interrupted Mr Philip for a second time. God was making man in his own likeness, as he had done on many occasions before. But this time the Lord's endeavours were cut short when Michael said, 'Tell me, Papa, what do you think to the notion that men are descended from monkeys?'

Miss Ma was on her feet shouting, 'Michael, that is enough.'

Mr Philip's voice broke like overhead thunder: 'Are you questioning the Lord thy God? Are you presuming to question the teachings of the Almighty, the King of Kings, the Lord of Lords, thy Maker?'

'No, Papa,' Michael said, with a calm that is usually placed before a storm. 'I am asking you about a subject on which my teachers saw fit to enlighten me. It is, I believe, a popular scientific opinion that man is descended—'

I jumped a full foot in my chair when Mr Philip cried, 'Enough!' His chair fell behind him – a terrifying clatter. 'I will not have blasphemy in this house. I will not have blasphemy at my table.' Mr Philip prepared to strike Michael, his hand rising in the air ready to fall and crack around Michael's head, when a loud laugh came from me – not with mirth but the strangeness of the circumstance. Michael stood out of the blow's way as I felt the full force of Miss Ma's hand strike against my own ear. Her pleading, 'Please behave, both of you.' But Michael, standing tall above his father, looked to all the world as if he was about to lash him. Mr Philip at his table was no longer a mountain only a man, stunted and fat and incapable of instilling fear. Was it the ringing in my ear that made my head throb so? Or the exhilaration of Michael staring on his father's face, saying, 'I would like for us to discuss this, Papa.' And Mr Philip – silent – taking up his Holy Bible and leading Miss Ma from the room.

With love it is small signs you have to look to. When Romeo scaled a wall I have no doubt that Juliet swooned with the certainty of what she then knew. Even Miss Jewel had a suitor who wooed her by sleeping overnight at the base of a tree so as to be near her early the next morning. (Although she misunderstood – thinking him just drunk and incapable of movement.) Declarations of love are for American films or books that are not read by educated people. Michael refused to accompany me to the Shirley Temple film. As I praised the sweetness of her voice and the bounce of her curls, he looked on me deep and steady. 'Shirley Temple is a little girl and I prefer women, Hortense.' All the world knows teasing is a sign. And he liked to tease me with his learning, urging me to test him on all the capital cities of the world. Australia, New Zealand, Canada. He knew them all. 'Ask me something harder. Surely you can ask me something harder than that?'

'For what is the city of Sheffield famous?'

'No. Test me on my understanding of geography, not this childishness. Ask me of ox-bow lakes and sedimentary plains or the fishing-grounds of the continental shelf. Come, test me on my knowledge. Ask me of the League of Nations or beg me explain the Irish question.'

41

He knew I knew nothing of these, but boasting to impress had been used since Adam first looked upon Eve. There was a time when I would have punched him for his conceit and told him little boys are made of moss and snails and puppy dogs' tails. But when he patted my head all sensible thought was gone. I feared he could hear my heart beating when he came close; on days when I walked by his side in the shade, leaping to take the same length steps as he; or the moment when, looking into clear water, our faces rippled together as one.

But I could not play the game of love all day. Miss Ma insisted I return to my work. 'But,' I asked, 'what will Michael do?'

'Michael can get along without you,' she said. 'You are not children – he is a man not a boy. He will help his father.' Mr Philip's face had set like a stone since his son's return. Carved into an expression of 'too much to bear'. I had not heard him utter one word that was not the Lord's since he had yelled, 'Enough', at the food table. He looked so pained that I dreamed of taking his hands and making him dance.

'Could I not assist here at the house, Miss Ma?' I asked.

'What, you think you are a white woman now – a lady of leisure?' she said. There was no choice for me.

But would the morning sun rise if I could not look on Michael's face? Could it set if I had not heard him call my name? I need not have fretted, for as I stepped on to the veranda that first dark, silent morning Michael was standing at the foot of the stairs; dressed in his finest ready to escort me to the schoolhouse. 'Michael Roberts,' I said, 'I hope you are not neglecting your duties for my sake.'

Despite the absence for his education Michael was as well loved and respected in the town as his father. He knew everyone. Hello, good day, good morning accompanied every step we took. He was even acquainted with Mrs Ryder.

'Was it not at church that we met, Michael?' Mrs Ryder said, when I asked of their first encounter.

Michael put both hands in the air and shook his head. I knew he would not remember. So I said, 'No, you must be mistaken as Michael does not attend the same church as you and Mr Ryder.'

'Oh, in a grocery store, then,' Mrs Ryder said hastily. She was embarrassed – her white cheeks flushing.

And that mischievous Michael made it worse by laughing at my employer saying, 'Was it in a grocery store?' which made her glow like a lantern.

Mr Ryder shook his head when I enquired if he knew Michael. 'I don't believe I have met Mr Roberts's son since his return. Although I have heard people speak of him.' But then, without a word, he turned back to stamping books when I remarked that Mrs Ryder thought she had met Michael at church.

'Oh, Hortense! What does it matter where I first met the woman?' Michael was vexed when we walked home. 'It is no concern of yours. Just hush now.'

Michael frequently chaperoned me along the dirt road from town. He always made some feeble excuse to be there with me – on a little business or an errand. Sometimes he held out his gentleman's elbow for me to slip my arm through and we would catch the stares of people who thought we looked a fine young couple. At other times I would find him hiding – pretending he had not come to see me at all. He would feign surprise when I tapped his shoulder or waved at him from a distance. And I played along by giggling gracefully at the joke.

A hurricane can make cows fly. It can tear trees from the ground, toss them in the air and snap them like twigs. A house can be picked up, its four walls parted, its roof twisted, and everything scattered in a divine game of hide-and-seek. This savage wind could make even the 'rock of ages' take to the air and float off as light as a bird's wing.

But a hurricane does not come without warning. News of the gathering storm would sweep the island as swiftly as any breeze, scattering rumours of its speed, the position of its eye, the measure of its breath. I was too far from home to return safely on the day of the hurricane and Mrs Ryder needed my assistance. Luckily no children had yet arrived for the school term but the building had to be prepared for the onslaught to come. And her husband was nowhere to be found. 'He'll be somewhere safe – I know it,' Mrs Ryder told me, without concern. 'This will be my first hurricane and I don't mind telling you,

Hortense, I find it quite exciting.' She skipped like a giddy girl, bolting the shutters with a delighted laugh. She hummed a song as we stowed chairs and desks and locked cupboards. She looked in the mirror, combing her hair, before we secured the doors. And turning to me she said, 'Wouldn't it be something to stand in a hurricane, to feel the full force of God's power in all its might?' But I was saying a prayer that the schoolhouse roof would stand firm and did not bother to answer such a ridiculous notion.

It was no surprise to me when Michael knocked at the door of the schoolhouse. For how could he stay at home during a hurricane? After leading the agitated goats and chickens, flapping and straining, into the safety of the barn; after securing the shutters, shaking them as ferociously as a man could, then checking them again – twice, three times; after leading Miss Jewel and Miss Ma to gather up lamps, chocolate and water, he would have to sit confined in the windowless room at the centre of the house with Mr Philip. And the rage inside would have blown as fierce as the tempest outside. So Michael ran two miles to be with me on the day of the hurricane. Two miles through an eerie birdless silence that scared as much as the wind that followed.

Was his shirt wet from the rain or the exertion of running? It cleaved to the muscles of his body, transparent in patches, revealing his smooth brown skin underneath. His chest was rising and bulging with every lungful of panted breath. Sweat dripped from his forehead, down his cheek and over his full lips. 'Michael Roberts,' I told him at the door, 'I am capable of looking after myself. You do not have to come all the time to protect me.' Looking in my eye without a word he pulled the clinging shirt from his body, flapping at it gently. He wiped his hand across his neck, over his forehead and let his chest fall.

But then, catching sight of Mrs Ryder over my shoulder, he looked suddenly alarmed. And pushing me, not gently, to one side he went straight to her. He flew so fast towards her I feared he was going to embrace her. He called her Stella – a familiar name that even Mr Ryder would not use in my company. 'Stella,' he said, 'I saw your husband in his car and I thought you might be . . .' he hesitated, looking over to me before saying '. . . alone.'

The three of us sat tender as bugs caught in the grasp of a small boy as rain pelted the walls. Fear gradually began to appear in the eyes of Mrs Ryder. Her girlish enthusiasm for the hurricane evaporated every time the roof bounced like a flimsy skin. At times the wind would just knock at the door, no more frightening than an impatient caller. At other times it would shriek like a dreadful choir of the tortured. And the bumping, the thumping, the crashing, the banging, no matter how distant, all made Mrs Ryder wail, 'Oh, Michael, thank God you are here.'

And all the time I wondered, How did Michael know her given name was Stella?

A shutter flew open. A gust exhaled into the room. Suddenly everything — books, papers, chairs, clothes — took on life and danced in the unseen torrent. And a shoe soared in through the opening, hurtling to a stop against the blackboard. Michael struggled to secure the shutter while Mrs Ryder looked on the dead cloth shoe and screamed. Michael forced the shutter closed until the room breathed a sort of calm. But Mrs Ryder was sobbing. Her blonde hair a little ruffled but her cheeks still white, her skin still delicate with a fine blue tracery of veins and her voice, when she said, 'Oh, Michael, I'm scared,' still sounded like a movie star's. He had no hesitation when he went to her to place his arm round her shoulders.

'Hortense, light another lamp,' was all he could say to me. The lights threw our shadows on to the wall. On what hour of what day did this married woman tell Michael to call her Stella? Stella, he spoke softly to her. Stella, he calmed her with. Stella, he caressed. In what grocery store did Mrs Ryder give Michael the freedom to speak as familiar as her husband?

'Mrs Ryder,' I said softly, 'are you thinking where your husband might be?' She looked tearful eyes on me but made no reply. Michael put his hand over Mrs Ryder's, slipping his fingers delicately through hers. She cast her bewitching blue eyes at him and squeezed his fingers tight.

With a hurricane, when you think you can take no more it grows stronger. It should have been I that was in need of a chaperone — a single young woman caught in a darkened room alone with a handsome man for who knows how long. It should have been I who feared for the talk that would fall from the mouths of busybodies. A married woman like Mrs Ryder should have looked out for my good name. But every sound made them hug up closer. Every gesture drew them together. Until the shadow of their heads took the shape of a heart on the wall. At that moment I wanted to burst from the room, to blow through the windows, to blast through the walls, and escape into the embrace of the dependable hurricane.

No living person should ever see the underside of a tree. The roots – that gnarled, tangled mess of prongs that plummet unruly into the earth in search of sustenance. As I fled from the schoolhouse after the hurricane had passed, the world was upside-down. The fields to my left, to my right, undulated with this black and wretched chaos. Trees ripped from land that had held them fast for years. Branches that should have been seeking light snuffled now in the dirt – their fruit splattered about like gunshot. Tin roofs were on the ground while the squeaking wheels of carts rotated high in the air, disordered and topsy-turvy. I stumbled through this estranged landscape alarmed as a blind man who can now see.

At first I only saw four people huddled around an upright tree, pointing and shaking their heads. Then others came – five, six, seven. Some running from across the field. Some shouting at others to come. All stopping to stare when they reached the old tree. Then, round the legs of a tall man, over the heads of two small children and past the white handkerchief of a woman who dabbed at tears in her eyes, I saw the body of Mr Ryder.

He was dead. Wrapped around the base of the tree like a piece of cloth. His spine twisted and broken in so many places it bent him backwards. He was naked, his clothes torn from him by the storm with only one ragged shirt sleeve still in place. His mouth was open wide – was it a smile or a scream? And around him his butchered insides leaked like a posy of crimson flowers into a daylight they should never have seen.

I believe I might have screamed. I think I screamed, 'He is a jealous God.' I might have held my head and yelled, 'Thou shalt not commit adultery. Thou shalt not covet thy neighbour's wife.' For the small crowd looked on me for a brief moment, frowning, before they resumed their yapping: 'Where is Mrs Ryder? . . . Mrs Ryder should be informed . . . Someone must bring Mrs

Ryder.' I cannot be sure whether the howling that I heard was only in my head. But I am sure of what I said next. I am certain of what I said, out loud for all to hear. I can clearly recall what I said, in my strong and steady voice – for I said it until all were staring on me.

'Mrs Ryder is alone in the schoolhouse with Michael Roberts.'

There was confusion when I finally reached home. Was it the same crowd of people who had been looking on the broken body of Mr Ryder who were now crowding the veranda of our house? Was it the same woman dabbing at her eyes with a white handkerchief? Was it the same tall man? Or were they different people who now jostled around a grave and sombre Mr Philip, waiting to hear what he could do about the fuss in the neighbourhood? And was Miss Jewel sobbing at the death of Mr Ryder? Or did her tears flow because the crowd was whispering, 'Michael Roberts – have you heard about Michael Roberts?'

Miss Ma grabbed my wrist to pull me past the crowd and into the house. As she closed the door on an empty room she slapped my face so hard I fell to the floor. 'Did you know what my son was doing with that woman? Did you know my son was committing a mortal sin with Mrs Ryder – a married woman?' I tried to run from the room but she held me back with the strength of fury.

'Why are you treating me like this?' I asked.

'My son with that woman.' She had lost her senses. She hit me again, this time her hand rounded as a fist. 'My son was found in an ungodly embrace with that woman,' she screamed.

Suddenly her strength left her. She collapsed, falling on to a chair as her body returned to that of a frail old woman. I looked on her and gently placed my hand on her shoulder. As fast as a snake she puffed herself up again. Her eyes fixed on mine, her hand raising to strike me. But I escaped from the room. I ran to the henhouse and squeezed my adult body in with the bewildered hens. There I sat a quiet vigil, looking out on the turmoil through the hole in the wood that was once used to spy on me.

❉　❉　❉

I went to the town to stay awhile in the now empty schoolhouse. I had to make sure the school was safely closed up. And to turn back the children who might arrive for their school term. I pinned a notice to the door concerning the tragic accident. Mr Ryder was not yet in the ground. Mrs Ryder was abiding with the preacher from the evangelical church, waiting on the day when her sister would arrive to carry her far away from this island. But all around the town rumours flew on the breeze. How had Mr Ryder died? Was he trying to feel the power of the hurricane? Was he caught where he should not have been? Some said that Mr Ryder's death was not an accident. Gossip appeared in the newspaper – a picture of Mrs Ryder's grieving face with Michael caught in the flashlight's glare. And everywhere I walked the whispered name of Michael Roberts became as familiar as birdsong.

It was three days before I finally returned home from the schoolhouse. The man who came and sat at the dinner table was Mr Philip. Still short, still with a round belly plump from plantain and his beloved dumplings. But he had no Bible. His empty hands shook as they hung above his knife and fork. His water glass wobbled and spilt its contents, the liquid dribbling down his chin, which remained unwiped. Miss Ma sat down and placed her napkin neatly in her lap. But there was no grace spoken even though we looked on Mr Philip to start the prayer. There was no thanking of the Lord. And there was no Michael. No Michael staring on me from across the table. No Michael attempting to catch my eye.

As usual Miss Jewel came in the room with a bowl steaming with rice. But after she had placed it on the table she laid her two hands on my shoulders and held them there for all to see before returning to her work. I could still feel the warmth of her touch long after Miss Ma had stopped staring her open-mouthed surprise at the two of us. It was then that, for the first time in my living days, I dared speak at that table. 'Where is Michael?' I asked. Mr Philip raised two weary eyes to look on me before lifting himself from his chair. Leaving his plate of food untouched he withdrew from the room.

Miss Ma did not look in my eye when she said, 'Michael has gone.'

'Gone?' I said.

'Yes, Michael has gone.'

'Gone?' I shouted.

'Hush, child, this is still the table.'

'Gone? Gone where?' I had no reason to talk calmly.

'England,' Miss Ma said, casually lifting an empty fork to her mouth.

'England!' I rose from the table. 'England?' I screamed.

'Child, hush yourself or you will feel my hand. Sit. Sit and eat.'

I sat down again to ask quietly, 'England?'

'Of course England,' she said, as if he had not travelled an ocean but just walked into town. 'Michael has been planning to go to England from a long time ago.'

'When did he go to England?'

'This morning – if it is any business of yours.'

'He did not tell me.'

'You think he tells you everything? It should be obvious that my son does not tell you all his business. He is a man.' She went on: 'He has gone to England with the purpose of joining the Royal Air Force.' I could do nothing but watch her lips as they formed words that made no sense to me. 'They need men like my son. Men of courage and good breeding. There is to be a war over there. The Mother Country is calling men like my son to be heroes whose families will be proud of them.'

'But for how long has he gone?'

Again, she lifted the empty fork to her mouth, then realising I could see she was eating no food she laid the fork down and dabbed at her cheeks with a napkin. But she gave me no answer.

I heard the gentle drip, drip, on to my plate before I felt the tears on my cheeks. Was my last view of Michael Roberts to have been that shadow on a wall? Or the snatched flashlight picture in the newspaper? Michael was gone? No matter how hard I dug my fingernails into my hand this time I could not stop myself from weeping.

Four

Hortense

I never knew that electric light could be used so extravagantly. At home just one bulb came and went with the whim of the weather. One single bulb that attracted every buzzing, flying, irritating insect from the district to flutter mesmerised in its timid glow (and also Eugene, a feeble-minded man who would trek miles from the fields in his bare feet to stand gaping in our yard until the light was turned on). The two-storey college building was illuminated by lamps that could have made a blind man cover his eyes. Cars attracted by the brightness arrived at the gates bringing pretty-dressed girls who also buzzed around in the light, giggling and chattering and hugging up old friends.

I was tired and hungry from my journey in the *Daily Gleaner* van. I had sat on what looked to me to be an upturned bucket. Eustace White, the driver, had somehow attached this implement to the floor for his passengers to sit on. All feeling was lost from both my buttock cheeks before the wretched van had even left Savannah-La-Mar. When I complained of the paralysis in my hind region, Eustace White informed me bluntly that he was not meant to take passengers in the newspaper's van and only did so to supplement his income so he might have money to pay for the treatment of his mother's eye complaint. Going on to explain the past, present and future of this eye condition in unnecessary detail for the rest of the long journey. By the time we arrived in Kingston my eternity had been lived listening to this man – I was convinced I had had no other life than that which took place on the upturned bucket in the *Daily Gleaner* van. The winding path from the road to the college grounds bumped and jiggled me for an infinity before leading us out into that floodlit fairyland that glowed before my eyes like salvation.

Mr Philip and Miss Ma had taken no more notice of my leaving the homestead than if I were a piece of their livestock whose time had come to be sent for slaughter. Had they forgotten that my father was Lovell Roberts? A man whose picture had been pinned to parish walls. Their cousin who, somewhere, was still a man of honour, still noble in a way that made him a legend. Those diligent years of my upbringing – feeding me with the food from their plates, dressing me in frocks made of cotton and lace, teaching me English manners and Christian discipline – were they to mean no more than the fattening of a chicken on best coconut, which, after they had feasted on its carcass, stripping it of all goodness, they threw out as waste? And their son, Michael, could have been anywhere on God's earth: flying across the English Channel, sipping coffee in a Paris café, taking tea in London. The only place I could be sure he was not was at that joyless home, where the tamarind tree, the henhouse and the dusty walk from town were the only things that ever spoke softly to me of missing him.

It was Miss Jewel alone who waved me off when I departed for the teacher-training college in Kingston, standing in her best blouse, her legs bowed so that the hem of her skirt nearly touched the floor. As the van collected me, crunching along the stones of the path as always, she handed me a tiny parcel.

'A likkle spell?' I asked.

The parcel contained one well folded pound note and two shiny shillings tied in a white handkerchief that had been stitched, unevenly, with my initials in blue and red. 'You nah need a likkle spell, me sprigadee. De Lawd haffe tek care a yuh,' was all she said.

Like butterflies, we new girls dazzled in our white gloves, our pastel frocks, our pretty hats. Girls from good homes from all across the island.

Girls who possessed the required knowledge of long division, quadratic equations. Girls who could parse a sentence, subject, object, nominative, and name five verbs of manner. Girls who could recite the capital cities of the world and all the books of the Bible in the perfect English diction spoken by the King. We new girls were to be cultivated into teachers and only after three years of residential study would we be ready for release into the schools of Jamaica.

The hall in which we waited on that first evening was loud with the silence of fear. Fidgeting was kept to a minimum, only necessary when someone needed to straighten the hem of their garment to prevent it creasing or wipe away a tear of sweat that had developed with the heat. Only one girl coughed.

Outside this room there was great commotion – the older pupils going about their business as raucous and shrill as parrots on a branch. Until, in one instant, it stopped as if, suddenly, all the parrots had expired or taken flight. The principal was making her entrance, parting girls to her left, to her right, like Moses through the Red Sea. She was tall and broad with a top lip that carried such a profusion of dark hair that the impression she gave was of a man in an all-too-inadequate disguise. She walked with dainty yet lumbering steps – full of feminine grace that nevertheless shook the floor beneath us. And following on behind in the gap that her ample gait created were five teachers. In the shadow of this colossal woman those attendants looked as flimsy and puny as leaves blown in by the wind. The teachers mounted the stage and faced we new girls. They were all white women but their complexions ranged – as white people's tend to do – through varying shades of pink depending on how long they had been on the island. The principal carried a seasoned ruddy glow on her cheeks while others bore the blotchy roaring-red of newcomers.

A smile should light up a face so that a person might seem friendly and kindly disposed to those they are smiling at. Unfortunately the principal, Miss Morgan, had a smile that was so unfamiliar to her face that it had an opposite effect – rather like the leer of a church gargoyle, it made her look sinister. She first smiled after the words, 'Welcome, girls, to our teacher-training school. You have a hard yet stimulating three years of study ahead. If each of you attends to your work with diligence and courage I am sure you will get on well with us here.' Her voice rang with a soft, gentle lilt as if soon to break into song, yet her smile made me recoil. But it was during her second grin, after the register of names had been taken by her bashful deputy, that I made the contrary vow never to do anything that would cause her to smile on me directly.

Miss Morgan was not an Englishwoman as the other teachers were, her country of origin was Wales — a corner in Britain famous for its coal, its capital city Cardiff, and for being where clouds tip excess rain before moving on to the pastures of England. While the five teachers seated themselves delicately upon the chairs provided on the stage, the principal paced stately to the piano and lowered her substantial backside on to the shaky stool. For a brief moment she paused as if in prayer — her hands splayed chord-shaped over the keys — before we new girls were ordered, by some imperceptible yet demanding movement of her eyebrow, to stand. She began to play, thumping out the chords to the hymn 'Immortal, Invisible, God Only Wise'. While thrashing and beating the instrument into a tune, her hair, which had sat as neat as if cast in resin, gradually began to give up one lock. The rogue hair shook looser with every note until the passion of her playing let it fall free over her forehead. 'Most blessed, most glorious, the ancient of days'. With one mighty voice we new girls sang along, fired by the emotion of her performance and the vigorous quivering of the fallen lock. 'Almighty, victorious, thy great name we praise'.

Michael was holding his closed hand out to me. This fully grown man with stubble hair piercing the skin of his chin was grinning on me as a schoolboy would. Opening his hand he revealed, resting in his palm, an ink-black scorpion, its tail erect and curled. I wanted to warn him of the danger of its murderous sting, but no words would come. I moved to strike the insect from his palm but my arm was being pulled away. Someone had my wrist clasped in their hand as tight as vine round a tree.

I had never had such a rude awakening. The cover on my bed was pulled back. I could not for a moment remember where I had laid my head to sleep.

I was revealed half naked on the mattress – my nightdress rolled and twisted at my waist with the movement of my dreams. I was being pulled so hard I could do nothing but follow. My feet fumbled for solid floor as I tugged at my nightdress to hide my shame. And before I was entirely convinced I was no longer dreaming I found myself running for my life. My captor was before me still squeezing on to my wrist, she turning to look on me only to say, 'Hurry nah.' Other girls were running alongside us. The doors they hurtled through slammed behind them like gunshot. The slapping of our bare feet echoed on the stone floor of every long corridor we ran down, before we were funnelled to one single door where I was pushed and jostled through the hole by other girls, whose manner insisted they should get there before me. The room was so bright with sunlight that at first I could not see. But then I observed overhead shower pipes and felt wetness under my feet. My captor released my wrist now and in one deft movement pulled her nightdress over her head and stood before me as naked as Eve. She gestured for me to copy her but became exasperated, sighing and tutting as she watched me untying the buttons and bows that modesty had stitched at the neck of my nightclothes.

'Come, hurry,' the girl said, slapping my useless hands out of the way and fumbling at my buttons. She began to lift my nightdress but I held it tight, not wanting to be naked in front of so many strangers. She hit at my hands again. So I hit hers and for a second she stopped, startled, before hitting mine so hard I gave up the fight. And I stood, with all the other girls, exposed – clutching my elbows to me, trying to hide my breasts, between my legs, my backside, my unattractive knees. Then the water came on, pouring down on us in a rain of icy water. Every girl screamed. One deafening sound that drowned all others. Mouths open so wide I could see deep into pink throats, as girls with tendons that stood out on their necks like rope yelled with the force of beasts. And as I looked on my captor – naked, shivering, screaming, a glistening waterfall running down her black skin, past nipples that stood as erect as bullets – I detected a gleam of pure abandon on her face. So I closed my eyes, opened my mouth and let my lungs give forth the most savage ferocious cry my body had ever produced. The blessed relief of this noise cleansed like a silent prayer. I screamed until I became aware that the water was no longer flowing, the room was calm and I was gently being shaken by my captor, who was saying softly, 'You can stop now.'

It was Celia Langley who pulled me from my bed that first morning. She believed it was the duty of a third-year pupil such as she to teach an untrained new girl (such as I) about the necessity of arriving early for the morning shower. The first out of the shower, dressed and smelling of sweet-scented soap would, on arriving for breakfast in the dining room, get a cup of chocolate that was still hot and drinkable. If you were second, third, or a deliberately dawdling fourth, then the chocolate would not only be cold but have a skin on it so thick it could be stitched into a hat. When Celia Langley took hold of my wrist that first morning – I the new girl in a bed next to hers – she placed me not only in the shower but firmly under her wing.

Celia came to my bed every evening after assembly, roll-call and prayers. Smelling of jasmine, she sat close beside me in the hour before the electric lights were extinguished. With everything Celia said, even if only telling me the time of day or commenting on the heat, she leaned with her lips close to my ear to whisper as if disclosing a hush-hush truth. These breathy tête-à-têtes were always accompanied by the gentle clatter of her knitting needles as she fashioned socks for men who, like Michael, were travelling to England to fight in the war. In those dusky evenings Celia, being a year older than I, coached me in what to expect from my lectures.

'Geography will be taught by Miss Wilkinson,' she told me. 'She will try to tell you of glaciation or something of this nature. But if you are to mention, even if only in passing, the Pennine Hills – and only the Pennines will do this – her eyes will focus somewhere only she can see and instead of the geography lesson she will tell tales of her childhood in Yorkshire. While these tales are not particularly interesting they do allow you to look out the window on the trees.'

Celia whispered that Oliver Cromwell had a large ugly wart on his face when she found me struggling with a composition on this man's accomplishments. Placing a delicate hand on my shoulder she informed me that Miss Newman who taught history held a theory that Mr Cromwell's wart was a conspicuous sign that he had been sent by the devil to destroy the English monarchy. Mention this wart, Celia hushed, and Miss Newman, who believed coloured girls had a better understanding of these sorts of things, being less civilised and closer to nature, would write in my margins that I was astute. And all girls classified as astute were given the honour of entertaining everyone at evening assembly with a recitation.

I could not choose between Henry V's speech before the battle of Agincourt or Alfred, Lord Tennyson's 'The Charge of the Light Brigade'. Both allowed for rousing dramatic interpretation. The daffodils, however, Celia thought too simple – no girl at the college would be unable to recite that.

'Once more unto the breach, dear friends, once more.' It was Celia who instructed me to physically intimate the expressions referred to in the text – to stiffen the sinew and summon up the blood by raising my shoulders while holding my head aloft, so my chin could rise with the dignity of the oration, and to end with a genteel cry, but not too loud, for Harry, England and St George.

I was the talk of the college for several weeks. And when I thought my spirits could go no higher, my fairy cakes – with their yellow cream and spongy wings – were declared by the domestic-science teacher, Miss Plumtree, to be the best outside the tea-shops of southern England.

There were sixty pupils in the first class I had to teach. Sixty children fidgeting like vermin behind rows of wooden desks. Sixty nappy-headed, runny-nosed, foul-smelling ragamuffins. Sixty black faces. Some staring on me, gaping as idiots do. Some looking out of the window. Some talking as freely as if resting under a lemon tree.

I was used to children from good homes. In Mr and Mrs Ryder's school wealthy, fair-skinned and high-class children sat ruly waiting for my instruction before lowering their heads to complete the task satisfactorily. In that school no child ever wiped their running nose across their sleeve before raising their hand high into the air and waving it around like semaphore. No child would chant, 'Miss Roberts, Miss Roberts', over and over until I could not recognise my own name. And no child ever subtracted five from ten and made the answer fifty-one.

Job himself would have wept genuine tears trying to get this rabble to face the board at once and Solomon would have scratched his head trying to understand what the wretched boy Percival Brown did with all the pencils. This light-skinned, green-eyed boy had looked the most trustworthy pupil for the task of handing one pencil to each member of the class. Half-way round the room he came to me saying the pencils had run out.

'How they run out? I gave you sixty pencils,' I queried him. 'Did anyone get more than one pencil?' I enquired of the class. Every one of those senseless children was suddenly attentive enough to shake their heads. 'What you do with the pencils?' I asked Percival Brown again. And this thieving boy just looked on me with a rascal's eye and shrugged. I searched in his pockets, I went through his desk, while this class of seven-year-old ruffians peered at me and silently laughed.

And all through this mockery I was closely observed by Miss Cleghorn, who sat at the back of the class, her glasses on the tip of her nose, writing a report marked: 'Progress and suitability of trainee teachers'. As every one of my classes ended – the herd of children stampeding to their play – she would approach me. Cocking her head to one side and looking to her notebook as if reading she would say, 'Miss Roberts, you must try to maintain better discipline among your pupils.' Or: 'You are, I am afraid, Miss Roberts, letting these children get the better of you.' Or: 'You cannot expect a child to respect and obey a teacher who cannot maintain order within the classroom.' While I, nodding impotently, mumbled that I would undertake to improve my performance.

I hungered to make those children regard me with as high an opinion as I had for the principal and tutors at my college. Those white women whose superiority encircled them like an aureole, could quieten any raucous gathering by just placing a finger to a lip. Their formal elocution, their eminent intelligence, their imperial demeanour demanded and received obedience from all who beheld them. As I prepared my lessons ready for the next day I resolved to summon every tissue of purpose within me to command that class to look on me with respect.

But in the morning their grubby little faces would file past me. Percival Brown grinning and picking at a scab on his elbow before handing me a browning star apple as a gift. Those sixty black children started the day by looking on me eagerly as we put our hands together ready to pray. But then as we lifted our heads after the devotion their fickle minds would start wandering again, roaming the classroom, drifting round the yard, their gazes fixed upon anywhere but me and the lesson I was about to give.

Celia waited to greet me after teaching practice one afternoon. Standing pretty by the gate of the school in a pale blue and yellow dress, her feet pressed together elegantly, she looked like a flower growing out of the dirt. I was so delighted to look on a familiar face at that school for scoundrels I had grown to despise that I refused to notice the trail of a tear, which ran through the dust on her cheek and collected in the cup of her Cupid's bow. And she smiled brightly. I had no reason to think she was anything but cheerful as she said eagerly, 'The men of the RAF are parading in the town. They will be leaving for England soon – we must wave them goodbye.'

It was on a weekend stroll, after I had been at the college for only a few weeks, that Celia and I had come across a place where, if we climbed to the first branches of a citrus tree, we could see over the barracks on the men who were being trained to go to war. At first all we heard were the bellowed commands that soared so loud into the air they were almost visible – by the left . . . quick march . . . attention . . . stand at ease. It was Celia's notion to lift our skirts and scale the tree. She was hoping to discover, if only by a glimpse, how these instructions were enacted. Our view was from further away than the yelled commands had implied, yet we could clearly see a pattern of parading men manoeuvring as balletic as birds. And even at that distance it was apparent to us that those brave fighting men carried wooden broomsticks over their shoulders instead of guns.

After that, I decided to join in Celia's war effort by starting to knit the only thing my talent would allow – long plain strips (which were always useful) – while Celia, tiring of socks, added hats to her repertoire. We tipped as much money as we safely could into the collecting tins that sat at the door to the dining hall. A picture, cut from the *Daily Gleaner*, of the fighter planes our money had helped to buy was pinned to the noticeboard. And every time Celia and I passed we pointed to the part – sometimes a wheel, sometimes a window – we decided our coins had purchased.

Marching in disciplined rows through the streets that afternoon, these men, dressed entirely in thick blue cloth, looked as uniform and steely as machinery. On their heads every one of them wore a strange triangular hat that was tipped at an impossible angle. I followed Celia as she nudged and poked her way through people come to stare. Women mostly, who pushed and jostled us back. Wives, mothers, sisters, aunts lining the street. Some were there just to see the spectacle, while others strained anxiously for a glimpse of a man they loved. But close to this fighting machine was merely composed of line after line of familiar strangers. Fresh young boys who had only just stopped larking in trees. Men with skin as coarse as tanned leather, whose hands were accustomed to breaking soil. Big-bellied men who would miss their plantain and bammy. Straight-backed men whose shoes would shine even through battle. It seemed all the dashing, daring and some of the daft of the island walked there before me.

So many men.

'Why must so many go?'

I thought I had spoken these words only in my head but Celia, facing me sombrely, replied, 'You must understand, if this Hitler man wins this war he will bring back slavery. We will all be in chains again. We will work for no pay.'

'Celia, I work for no pay now,' I said, thinking of my worthless class.

Perhaps she did not understand my joke, for she did not laugh or even smile. A look of distaste passed carefully across her features. I made no attempt to placate her. I could understand why it was of the greatest importance to her that slavery should not return. Her skin was so dark. But mine was not of that hue – it was the colour of warm honey. No one would think to enchain someone such as I. All the world knows what that rousing anthem declares: 'Britons never, never, never shall be slaves.'

A woman heavy with child, recognising a man she knew on the march, howled, 'Franklin, where you goin'?' And weeping loud she held her arms up to him like a child waiting to be carried along. Her companion wrapped two hands tight round her big belly to keep her from running to him. Franklin, turning his eye to her as he passed, broke his step, tripping forward as if he had been struck, before regaining his soldier's composure and moving on.

And Celia, looking distressed by the trouble this woman was creating, turned away, asking me, 'I wonder who has on my socks?'

Pleased at her change of mood I replied, 'Celia, it is possible that every one of those men and most of the crowd are wearing them.'

She smiled at this joke and, locking her arm through mine, she leaned in close to whisper, 'Hortense, let me give you a secret. When I am older, I will be leaving Jamaica and I will be going to live in England. I will have a big house with a bell at the front door and I will ring the bell, ding-a-ling, ding-a-ling.' Her black hair caught by the sun shimmered golden strands in the light. 'I will ring the bell in this house when I am in England. That is what will happen to me when I am older.'

It was another commotion that brought Celia's dreaming to a halt. A woman's voice rising louder than the marching feet, more clamorous than the chattering crowd. One and all turned to follow the approaching cry – even airmen's eyes swivelled to where the noise was emanating from. It became clear to me that this woman's voice was shouting the name 'Celia'. Everyone who was not called Celia strained to look at the caller. The only motionless person was Celia herself who stood lifeless as a cadaver.

Walking towards Celia was a tall, dark-black-skinned yet elegant woman. Her back straight, her head high, she carried the imperious air of a proud white lady. As she came closer the crowd parted, some almost jumping out of her way, some looking on her with pity, because it was obvious that this graceful woman was wearing two dresses. One dress had black skirts flowing along the ground and sleeves buttoned to the wrist. With just this dress she would have received only the comment that she was a little old-fashioned. But over the top she wore what looked from a distance to be a pretty blouse, but was revealed as a lacy pink frock made for a small girl. The short puffed sleeves were pulled up achingly taut over the sleeves of the other dress, while the tiny bodice stretched and gaped across her adult frame. She raised her hand, waving a white handkerchief, and shouting, 'Celia,' so vociferously it sounded to be coming from a deity not from the mouth of a mortal such as she. I looked to Celia for an explanation as to why this strange woman was trying to attract her attention.

But Celia's eyes were tight shut, her lips mumbling, 'Oh, no,' and a fresh tear was running down her face to her Cupid's bow.

This woman was now upon Celia, chattering noisily as if she had been at her side all afternoon. 'Celia, you will see . . . he will be along soon. You must just wait, me dear, and I will show you him. You will see . . . you will see.'

She waved her handkerchief in front of her nose. 'Oh, this heat . . . this heat, I will never get used to this heat.' Her perfume was so sickly pungent that I coughed with the taste of it in my throat. Her hair, which at first impression looked a distinguished grey, transpired to be a brown wig soiled with dust. Slipping slightly to one side this wig revealed a patch of the matted black hair it was trying to conceal. Oblivious to the spectacle she created she stood fanning herself as haughty as nobility. Yet there was no spirit in her eyes: they remained as expressionless and unengaged as the simulated gaze of a doll.

Celia gently took this woman's arm and leaning close to her ear she said, 'Mamma, hush.'

Even though this woman was chattering loudly, 'Now where is that man? . . . Where has he gone? . . . He is always missing,' she stopped as suddenly as if a control had been turned to off.

I did not need to ask if this curious woman was Celia's mother, it was there to see. Dark skin on a once-pretty face and lips that carried the same pronounced Cupid's bow. Celia avoided my eyes as she spoke closely and carefully to her mother: 'Mamma, you should not have followed me here. We must go home now. I will take you back. They will be worried for you.'

Her mother, heeding Celia as if in a trance, let her gently guide her by her elbow away from the crowd. Until without warning she came to life once more. 'He is here, Celia. He is here! Look.'

The crowd responded readily to her cry – some watching her antics while others, more curious, looked to where she was indicating. Celia's soft hand on her mother's arm became a grim-faced knuckle-clenched grasp, which her mother wrestled violently away from. Unfortunately the procession of airmen momentarily stopped and Celia's mother ran to one airman and, pointing him out like a dress in the window of a shop, called, 'Celia, this is your daddy. I told you he would come.' The airman had obviously never seen this woman before. This young boy – younger even than Celia – glanced around confused while his compatriots jeered.

'Winston.' Celia's mother examined his face. 'Don't you know me?' The airman would have shaken his head, would have said, 'Oh, no, madam, no,' but, before he could reply, Celia's mother threw her arms round his chest constricting him with a hug that could have taken the breath from a bear. He looked to be choking and unsure whether to hit this madwoman or surrender to her clasp.

Celia approached and her mother fearing she would lose her prize held tighter to the poor man. 'Mamma,' Celia said, leaning close to her mother, 'leave him.' But her plea fell on to an ear that was deaf to it. Raising her voice sharply to a level I had never heard, Celia said, 'Mamma,' once more. Some in the crowd began to see this as a comical situation – an airman off to fight for the Mother Country terrorised by a lunatic woman attached to his chest. But Celia was shamed. Humiliation flowed through every grimace and frown as she started to pull her mother from the man, her mother kicking and batting her away, all the time saying, 'Winston, don't you know me? Is Evelyn.'

Another airman broke rank to help with this struggle. Then another and another. Three uniformed men were trying to remove this wriggling woman, while restricting their hands to touch her only on those parts that would not offend her modesty. The little pink dress she wore ripped this way and that as she strained to keep her grip. Her wig slipped over her eyes then fell to the ground. I retrieved it from under a large boot, while Celia, in what looked to be a well-practised manner, began peeling her mother's arm from around this beleaguered man.

All the time his fellow airmen taunted him, 'What you do to her, man? You look too young. You one for the ladies?' And a sergeant paced up to see the commotion, which was holding up the march. Finally, in a composed desperation, this young man said quietly to the top of Celia's mother's head, 'My name is not Winston, ma'am. I am Douglas.' As quickly as she grabbed him she had let him go. And scattering the crowd as she ran, this vagabond, fluttering pink and black, disappeared.

It was in contravention of most of the college rules for a pupil to be seen in town dragging an hysterical woman (who was wearing two dresses) from around the chest of a marching airman. In public, no eating, no running, no singing, no spitting and no loud chatter was allowed. As teachers in training our behaviour outside the walls of the college was expected to be as exemplary as if we were still under the watchful gaze of the principal. It was true that I had eaten no food and that Celia and I did not sing during this ordeal. But we had run after her mother. We had shouted for her to wait, to come back, to stop. We had held up traffic as we struggled to pull her from a bus and I had spat on to the road when the dusty wig I was holding was accidentally pushed into my mouth in a scuffle. This list of in-town rules – no eating, no running, no singing, no spitting and no loud chatter – was recited like an incantation by the principal every day at assembly. So when I was summoned to Miss Morgan's study I feared that news of this fracas had reached her ears. For Ivy May had heard the tale – her smiling on me as she passed saying, 'Hortense, I see you meet Celia's mother, then,' before going on her way, giggling. So I had my excuse. It was Celia! It was she who met me from the school. It was she who led me to the parade. It was she who, having spent a morning with her crazy mother, left the door open that allowed her to follow. And it was she who insisted we get her mother back to the house of her aunt before returning to the college. All these misdeeds were the fault of Celia Langley. It was she who, like a devil at my shoulder, had led me from the path of righteousness.

For fifteen minutes I paced outside the principal's study assuming Celia would soon arrive to walk up and down with me. But she was not by my side when 'Enter' was called. I took comfort in her absence – she would not be present to hear me cite her name as reason for every rule I had transgressed. She could not gawp on me like I was committing some betrayal or contradict me by saying she had not asked me follow and that I did so because I was inquisitive about her deranged mother.

The desk at which the principal sat was not big enough for her. Like an adult at a school desk made for a child I was afraid when she lifted herself from it that it would be stuck to her front like an apron. What desk could accommodate the majesty of this Welshwoman?

'Hortense Roberts?' the principal asked.

'Present, Miss Morgan,' I said stupidly, as if answering the roll-call. It was as she looked up at me that I noticed both her eyes were not, as I had always believed, blue. One and a half eyes were blue. The left eye was half blue and half light brown. It was my sharp intake of breath that made her enquire if I was quite well. 'Yes, thank you, Miss Morgan, quite well,' I replied, keeping my gaze away from the peculiar eye.

'Hortense Roberts,' she repeated, in a manner that made me ready my excuse. It was Celia, Celia, Celia, I was about to plead. But instead of the anticipated chastisement the principal showed me a letter. 'This is for you. I am afraid it has been opened as it was actually addressed to the principal. But it's certainly meant more for you than for myself. Please – read the letter.'

It was from Miss Ma. The letter began with an elaborate five-line apology for taking up the time of such a busy and distinguished person as the principal. 'However,' it went on, 'I and my husband, Mr Philip Roberts, would be in your debt if at your own convenience and in a manner you deem fitting, you could perchance relay a message to Miss Hortense Roberts, whom I believe is a trainee teacher still in the first year at your establishment.' I recognised the careful script with its flourish that looped at the top of the *h* and curved at the base of the *g*. 'The message concerns a Mr Michael Roberts, who is our eldest and only son and with whom the aforementioned Miss Hortense Roberts is acquainted.' Precious news of Michael! My legs nearly buckled under me at reading his name. I had heard nothing of him since his departure for England. And here on these small, folded pieces of white paper his life was lifting before me anew. He had been sent at first to Canada to train for the RAF. And, typical of Michael, was awarded the highest marks and sent to England without delay to join a squadron as an air-gunner.

'Sit down if you feel the need,' the principal told me. And I did. It was a rare privilege to sit on this padded seat designed for dignitaries. This chair, having been sent all the way from England on a ship, seemed a befitting throne to read news about Michael.

The letter carried on:

Our son, Michael Roberts, was dispatched with his squadron on an operation the consequence of which was to find him perambulating in the skies above the country of France with the enemy residing below. Mr Roberts and I have recently been in receipt of a missive from the War Office in London, England. This authority has informed us that while our son, Michael Roberts, was performing his duty for the Mother Country, the aeroplane on which he was travelling was unaccountably lost.

The meticulous script began to deteriorate, its poise transforming into a childlike scribble with the words: 'Mr Roberts and I have been informed by the War Office in the said London, England, that we should at this stage in the proceedings consider our son, Michael Roberts, to be officially missing in action.'

The strange eyes of the principal were on me when I looked up from the letter. 'Thank you, Miss Morgan,' I said.

'You were acquainted with this young man?'

'Oh, yes,' I said. 'We grew up together.'

She nodded in the sage way I had come to know well. 'I am pleased to see you are taking this news in a befitting manner. It does not do to get too emotional on these occasions. True grief is silent.'

'Oh, Miss Morgan,' I said, 'any news of Michael Roberts is a joy to my ear.'

Coughing genteelly into her hand she shuffled a sheet of paper from one side of the desk to the other. 'I don't think that you have altogether understood the significance of this letter. The young man . . .' she said, shuffling the paper back to the other side.

'Michael Roberts,' I said.

'Michael Roberts, yes. This young man has been officially reported as missing.' She spoke slowly, emphasising each word with a small jab of her index finger pressed against her thumb.

'Oh, he will soon turn up,' I assured her. 'I know Michael. He is always off doing some mischief.'

Closing her eyes, she leaned her head forward on to her two hands, which were clasped together as if in prayer. 'Miss Roberts, there is a war on. When the family of a serviceman is told that their relative is missing in action, the intention is to prepare them for the news that the young man may be dead.'

'The letter says nothing of him being dead,' I said, but foreboding was trembling my hands.

'God willing he is not dead. But prepare yourself and take comfort in the fact that many people, of whom I am one, believe that no matter what their colour, no matter what their creed, men who are fighting to protect the people of Great Britain from the threat of invasion by Germans are gallant heroes – be they alive or dead.'

She held out her hand for me to return the letter to her. But before it had passed from my grasp into hers she did the thing I had a dread of – she smiled on me directly. And all at once this woman appeared devilish to me. So devilish I stood stupefied and gaping as my slackened mouth, like a terrified infant's, quivered with the effort of trying not to weep.

Five

Hortense

The moment I saw him the pawpaw I carried slipped from my grasp, its orange-pink flesh smashing open against my foot, splattering my leg with the pebble-black seeds. He rode a bicycle. The frame, too small to take his long legs, forced his knees to bend like a frog's. Unfamiliar with the machine, he wobbled dangerously, ringing the bell to warn people of his hazardous approach. I ran so I would not lose him – borne on a euphoria that flew me through the street while the sticky pulp from the pawpaw seeped into my shoe. And I called, 'Michael, wait.' Many heads looked but not his. Raising himself from the bicycle seat, he stood to pedal faster.

I turned a corner, and the bicycle – wheels still spinning – lay abandoned in the road, sprawling disorderly as if dismounted at great speed. He was moving through a crowd: a raggle-taggle throng of men pressing together all the way down the street, men stretching their necks, craning for a better view, demanding hush, sucking on their teeth, spitting on the ground, gently jostling each other in this cramped place. He nudged people with his shoulder as he tried to make a steady path through this ragged assembly. And, like a thread pulling between us, I followed in his feet. Soon I was behind him, my hand, with stretched fingers, just an inch from his shoulder when I saw a chair – a part of a chair, the seat and two legs – tumbling through the air towards me. And suddenly I was looking at the dirt floor, a crushing weight on my back and a pain at my knee. Someone was covering me, the pressure of a hand pushing on my head, the vile odour of perspiration filling my mouth. Yelling came in vibrations through a protective chest while an arm slipped round my waist and lifted me from the ground.

The street erupted in commotion. The black men who had been a moment earlier an orderly crowd were now shouting, cussing, jumping and straining to send stones and rocks and wood arching high into the air. Then ducking and skipping to avoid the reply of smashing bottles and sharp projectiles that came back in volleys. A man, his head gashed, oblivious to the pumping blood that ran down his ripped shirt, bent to pick up a jagged stump of a bottle, lobbing it as casual as a ball game. And above this riot a megaphone boomed with words so sonorous and distorted they could not be understood.

I was carried through this chaos. My feet tried desperately to search for a footing so I might run along the ground. But I was enclosed as firm as a knot. Then, rounding a corner, all at once everything was peaceful. People went about their business unaware of the mayhem that could be glimpsed along the next street. In this harmonious place it was a peculiar sight for a man scruffy with dust to be carrying a grown woman whose knee was trickling with scarlet blood. So he placed me gently down and I saw his face. It was him. It was the man I thought was Michael. But it was not Michael. It was a stranger.

'What you doing at this meeting? It's not safe,' he said.

'Get off me,' I replied. His skin was darker than Michael's. His nose was broader than Michael's. His lips were thicker than Michael's. His eyes were rounder than Michael's. His moustache was bushier and his smile was not crooked.

'You hurt?' he said, noticing my bleeding knee.

His open mouth revealed a gold tooth that shone from within. I could have screamed. I shooed his hand away as he reached out to touch my leg. To think that I mistook this uncouth man for Michael Roberts. 'What is all that commotion?' I found I was shaking. The words did not come out with the force I required of them – they rang with tremulousness.

'Busta speaking.' I had no idea what this man was talking about. 'I just come to see what him have to say. But every time we meet there is this rough stuff.'

I was not interested in his explanation.

'Your foot,' he shouted, his face grimacing. 'Your foot is mash-up.'

Calmly I told him, 'That is pawpaw.'

For an instant he gazed on me as if I had mislaid my senses. 'Pawpaw?' he asked.

'Yes,' I replied, offering this man no explanation.

His gold tooth glared as he smiled. 'Your mother never tell you pawpaw is to go in your mouth and not on your foot?' And his smile then became a chuckle at his own joke.

A young man running to the battle line – his arms laden with two big stones and several branches of a tree – tripped in front of us, spilling his load. From his mouth a stream of cusses poured, turning the air rancid. The man who was not Michael grabbed this cussing man by the throat. Their noses only one inch apart, he said, 'You no see there's a lady here? Hush your mouth.' I feared a brawl would begin in front of me. The man who was not Michael released the cussing man's throat, pushed him, and for a second these two stood snarling like savages until the terrified cussing man backed away and ran.

Taking a composing breath, the man who was not Michael looked on me and said, 'Sorry, Miss, for you to hear such language,' before his attention was drawn once again to the uproar that was happening in the next street.

'Go,' I said. 'I am fine.'

'You sure? I can leave you here? You no gonna come back throwing bottles and roughing up the men?' Again he laughed at his own joke as he walked away. And as his back rounded the corner I had to shake myself from the belief that I was once more seeing Michael.

I had sat a quiet vigil for Michael long after the war had ended. The festive balloons deflated, the ribbons lost their sheen. People stopped talking of the shortage of rice and, oh, those miserable days when the condensed milk ran out. Up on the hillside the boats docked below. Even from that distance, if he had been there among the crowd that alighted from the vessels, I would have seen him like a pinpoint of light on a cave wall. Those men who left for the war with spirited cheer returned looking around them as bemused as convicts. In their ill-fitting suits or uniforms that would soon no longer be theirs, they studied the surround as if this were a foreign place – a momentary reluctance trembling in their feet as they stepped on to the dock. Mothers hugged these sons to them while abashed wives looked guilty on the eyes of their returning men. And still he was not there.

What would Michael look like on an aeroplane? I had no picture to conjure with. Was he inquisitive – straining to make out the curve of a coast far below? Or did he gaze skyward, shielding his eyes against the sun as he counted the clouds that slipped past his view? In England the houses are placed so close together, I had been told, that it is possible to look on your neighbour in the adjacent and opposite dwelling. Was someone staring through a window to see Michael sipping at a cup filled with hot tea? Was the window open, a breeze caressing his cheek, or was the closed glass almost opaque with rain? What did Michael do when he was cold? Did he shiver, shaking himself like a dog fresh from a stream, or did he stand erect, wrapped warm in a thick coat? In the eye of my mind Michael Roberts – with his thin moustache and crooked smile – could belong in no other place than on this Caribbean island.

Six

Hortense

My dream was and always had been that I should find employment teaching at the Church of England school in Kingston, for it was there that light-skinned girls in pristine uniforms gathered to drink from the fountain of an English curriculum. But my interview for a position saw the headmaster of that school frowning, concerned not with my acquired qualifications but only with the facts of my upbringing. I evoked my father's cousins and told him of Lovell Roberts, my father, a man of character, a man of intelligence, noble in a way that made him a legend. The headmaster unwittingly shook his head as he asked me of my mother, my grandmother. His conclusion – although no word on the matter passed between us – was that my breeding was not legitimate enough for him to consider me worthy of standing in their elegant classrooms before their high-class girls. It was my old college friend Celia Langley who eventually found me employment teaching in the scruffy classrooms of Half Way Tree Parish School.

Through those first weeks, my hand was clasped by Celia as tightly as it had been on our first encounter in the washroom of our teacher-training college. So popular at the school was she that small boys lined up to place gifts before her every morning. Little girls jostled and pushed so they might find themselves closer to her at the front of the class. Other teachers whispered to me how lucky I was to have Celia's expert guidance. And even the headmaster implored me to watch and learn from everything Celia did. But it was not my first, second or third choice to be returned to that school for scoundrels. The spectre of Percival Brown and those wretched black faces grinning before me for the rest of my days made me feel quite sick. All at once my lofty dreams had soured to pitiful torment.

' "The Lord moves in mysterious ways — his wonders to perform." ' Celia tried to comfort me.

'He surely does, Celia, he surely does,' I said.

For none was so mysterious to me than how, in God's name, a woman such as I found herself residing in the household of people like the Andersons. It was the wife of the headmaster at the school — a woman who not only had received her education at a boarding-school in Scotland but who was well known for having once been invited to take tea with a member of a royal household — who informed me of a room available in the home of a respectable family. I was convinced that such a recommendation would find me lodging with gracious people. Instead I was soon engulfed by the uncouth antics of this boorish family. So shocked was I by their ill-bred behaviour that I invited Celia to their dinner table so she might witness the manners of these vulgar people for herself.

The old woman, Rosa Anderson, began eating her chicken. Taking the cooked bird in her gnarled hands she stripped off the flesh with the few teeth she still had left in her head, gnawing on it with a vulturine concentration until it was just grey bones. Then sucking, sucking, sucking, as loud as water down a faulty drain, while the rest of the family and Celia behaved as if they were not hearing this revolting noise.

Displaying the food she had just put in her mouth Mrs Anderson, Rosa's daughter-in-law, told Celia, with embarrassing detail, about the birth of her twin sons. Shot out and deftly caught by the nurse, these two boys, Leonard and Clinton, looked so alike I puzzled on the need for both of them to exist. Fussing over her little sons, Mrs Anderson cut up their food, stealing pieces from their plates, pinching their cheeks. And then, without warning, she rose from her seat, grabbed these boys, smothered them in loud, greasy kisses while tickling them saying, 'You good enough to eat — just give me a kiss of that neck.'

Mr Anderson pushed back the table at the end of the meal and shook his shoulders, clicking the fingers of one hand while carefully putting on his record with the other. Jazz.

'You like jazz, Celia?' he asked.

Mr Anderson was a public-works officer — a government man, he told Celia with pride, but who, as far as I could tell, spent every day of the week staring and scratching his head over holes in the road. Celia tapped her foot to the noise that came from the gramophone but sensibly declined the offer to dance. She made no conversation at the table, only smiling or nodding or passing or chewing as was politely required. When we were alone she leaned in close to me to say, 'But I like this family very well.' And this family liked Celia so well that Mrs Anderson, who badgered me beyond torment to call her Myrtle, invited her to dine with us on many more occasions.

'Hortense, perhaps you should take the time to know the Andersons,' Celia advised me. But it was not her that had to live in the midst of their cackle.

'So,' Mrs Anderson asked Celia, 'you a pretty girl, you have a young man, Celia? Someone to walk out with?'

Celia blushed and wisely let forth a little lie: 'Oh, no, Myrtle,' she said.

For it was to me, and only to me, that Celia Langley ever talked of the RAF man she had become friendly with. He had been in the thick of the war in England. He knew not only of guns, air-raids and bully beef but of the wintry winds that blew across the English moors, freezing his moustache hair so stiff that he could snap off the brittle strands. She could talk of nothing else. 'Have I told you, Hortense?' she would commence, in that whispering tone of hers, before the descriptions of his eyes, his mouth, his hands, his hair were breathed from her lips in elaborate prose. His voice, she said, lilted with the soft melody of a baritone. Whenever she spoke of him her eyes wandered dreamy, her arms hugged tight round her body holding her together as she rocked from side to side. She had met him in a shop when he asked her, 'Excuse me, don't I know your sister?' And she, forgetting that she had no sister, told him her name. Celia said his face smiled with a hundred happy lines. His eyes sparkled like polished glass, he was charming as a prince. He was a Leo while she was an Aries. This, she assured me, made them very compatible. 'A Leo man will always want to go far. And Aries women are of a similar nature.' But what aroused her more than anything else about this man was the thrill of knowing that he wanted to make a life for himself in England. She could see herself finally ringing the bell on that tall house. 'He wants to return to England soon.' She would sail far away from this island, safe in the arms of her handsome RAF man, to a place where he had told her everyone walked on a blanket of gold.

'Well, Celia,' I told her, 'you must let me meet this man who would take you far away from here.'

Standing, leaning against a wall, casually rifling the pages of a newspaper yet perusing the contents with a concentration that made him oblivious to our approach, was Celia's airforce man. Her voice cracked with elation as, momentarily holding me back, she whispered, 'There he is.' The man lifted his hand and pushed a finger into his ear. His face contorted so with the effort of digging round this cavity that he looked to be killing a buzzing fly in there. It was when he removed his finger, carefully inspected the tip then wiped it down his trouser that I recognised him.

'Well, hello again,' this man said — not to Celia but to me.

Celia, confused, almost squeaked, 'You have met before?'

I heard a plain voice — no lilting baritone — when the man said, 'This is the woman who likes to put pawpaw on her foot.'

I protested, 'I do not. I accidentally step in the fruit,' while Celia's eyes were fixed on me for an explanation.

But this man just kept on jabbering. 'You step in it? Let me tell you, Celia, about this woman. But wait, this woman is not the friend you tell me of?'

Celia, nodding, tried to say, 'We teach at the same—' before this man was off again.

'Celia has told me of her good friend and it is you. Cha, man!' He sucked his teeth, shaking his head. 'You. So you remember me?'

I made no reply, which did not discourage him.

'Celia, let me tell you how I meet this woman. It was the day Busta speaking – by the corporation office. You know Busta? Bustemante? Everybody know Busta. So Busta speaking. Suddenly one quarrel break out. Everything that could be pick up is flying through the air. Boy, the confusion, everyone running this way and that. And there in the middle of the mighty battle is this young woman looking like she strolling to church in her best hat. So I rescue her.'

'He rescued you?' Celia asked.

'You did what to me?' I shouted to this man. 'I did not need rescuing.'

'Oh. As I recall the situation something was about to bounce off your pretty head and knock you flat.'

'He rescued you?' Celia said once more.

'Yes, I rescue her. But the look on her face made me worry she gone turn round and bite me.'

'And what about the pawpaw?' Celia wanted to know.

'Celia, I am glad you ask about the pawpaw – because I am sure your friend here does not tell you she likes to wear it on her foot.'

We waited quietly for this man to stop laughing at his joke. Celia had told me much about him but what she could not say was that sometimes when he laughed – lifting his chin and parting his lips, when he slapped his hand on to his leg and shook his head – he looked so like Michael.

'I have been told you were in the RAF?' I asked him.

'This is true, but whisper what else Miss Celia has been telling you about me.'

Celia looked so abashed I thought she would dissolve.

'You were in England?'

'I am nervous now. You have a question for me, Miss Mucky Foot?'

'Are you acquainted with a Michael Roberts?'

'Who?'

'Michael Roberts. He was also in the RAF. An air-gunner.'

'Your sweetheart?'

If he had not grinned like a cheeky boy when he asked this question I might have answered. But he did, so I did not. Then, searching my face as if a story rested there, he became suddenly solemn. 'There were many Jamaicans in the Royal Air Force but I did not know a Michael Roberts. Can you tell me more about him? Where was he stationed? You say he was an air-gunner, you know his squadron?'

I softly said no, then looked to my feet fearing that if he asked me another unanswerable question I might weep. The embarrassing silence that followed was soon filled with more of his chatter.

'Well, Celia, now you know all about your crazy friend and her very strange ways you must introduce us.'

'This is Hortense Roberts,' Celia said quietly.

'Oh, so this Michael is your brother?' And still looking in my face he asked, 'Celia, you can say something nice about me for your friend?'

She smiled, relaxed once more, saying, 'Hortense, may I present the man who may or may not have rescued you from something? This is Gilbert Joseph.'

I accompanied Celia on several other occasions as she preened herself ready to meet this man. Oh, how my ears got tired of her repetition.

'Hortense, one day I will be going to live in England.'

'I know, Celia Langley, you tell me already!'

She will live there. She will do that. England, England, England was all she ever talked of. She wore me out with it. But I knew that when the day came she would think nothing of leaving her friend alone at that wretched parish school as she sailed the ocean in the arms of her big-talk man. And Gilbert Joseph took pleasure at my presence for no other reason than his big ideas received a larger audience than when it was just Celia alone.

On this day he walked between us through the park looking like a man who had recently purchased the moon and the stars. 'You see how every man envy me. Them saying there is one fortunate man. Two pretty women. Him must have plenty something I have not got.' He laughed, of course, then opened his elbows for us to slip our arms through. Celia held him this way but I did not.

76

'Go on, Hortense,' he urged. 'You want them think I lose me touch already?'

And he talked. He talked tirelessly, beginning sometimes with a question to Celia and myself as if a discussion might take place. 'Let me ask you this one question,' he would say. But he required no reply from either of us. No encouragement was necessary – he simply answered the enquiry himself and carried on. I was breathless just listening to this man. And all his talk, all his chatter was on just that one subject.

'Let me ask you this one question – you ever see a picture of the House of Parliament in London? It is a sight, let me tell you. When you stand there before it, it looks to all the world like a fairytale castle. You think dragons will breathe fire on you soon. You must see this place.'

Celia had to drop her hand from his crooked elbow when the passion of his story required him to wave his arms for effect. 'And Nelson's Column. You heard of Nelson's Column? One man so renowned they stick him so high-high in the air, your neck get stiff looking for him. You can hardly see him. Sometimes when the fog come, him vanish completely – only the pigeons can know him still there.'

As we walked through the dappled shade of a tree he bent to pick a discarded leaf from the ground. Holding it in the flat of his palm he became quiet. As he looked thoughtful at it in his hand his voice – unexpectedly gentle, almost melodious – described how in England the trees lose their leaves before the winter months. Every leaf on every tree turns first red and then golden. With the wind or the passing of time these dazzling leaves fall from the trees covering the parks, the gardens, the pavements with a blanket of gold. 'And you can walk through these autumn leaves. Everywhere. Children kick them up into the air, or pick up handfuls and throw them into the wind. Everybody does it. Everyone delighting in the leaves that float around them like golden rain.' He lifted his palm, which held the browning leaf, closer to Celia, saying, 'Imagine this everywhere.'

'Oh, I would like to see that,' Celia said.

At which Gilbert, throwing his leaf to the breeze, stretched his arms open to her saying, 'Then come now with me to England, Celia.'

Celia's eyes widened like a playful puppy's. 'Shall I go, Hortense?' She giggled.

He took her hands in his. 'We leave on the next boat.'

'And what about my class?'

'Your friend here can teach your class for you,' Gilbert joked. 'Hortense will take care of everything – won't you, Hortense? She will write to us of the hurricanes and the earthquakes and the shortages of rice on this small island, while we sip tea and search for Nelson on his column. Will you come, Celia?'

Celia's eyes were dazzled by that blanket of gold. 'I shall go,' she said.

And Gilbert said, 'Good.'

All seemed to be decided between them so I felt it important for me to ask, 'But what about your mother, Celia? Am I to look after her too?'

The playful light in her eyes was suddenly extinguished. She stood as still as stone.

'Bring your mother. We will row with her on the Thames.' Gilbert laughed before he noticed Celia's eyes steadily gazing on my face. 'Or leave her,' he said slowly, looking first at Celia and then at me. 'What is wrong with your mother?' he asked.

'Celia's mother is not at all well,' I told him. He looked a quizzical eye on me. And I looked to Celia so she might explain to this man the nature of her mother's ailment. But she did not. Instead she dropped her head to gaze on her feet. So it was left for I to tell this man about her mother and the incident with the airmen on parade. Some parts of the story became a little confused in my mind. When was it that her wig dropped off? How many airmen did it take to hold her back? How far did we chase her before she tripped on one of her dresses? I appealed to Celia to help me with clarification but she refused to look in my face. It was kindly that I concluded the tale by telling Gilbert that the reason Celia's mother could not accompany them to England was because she was unfortunately quite mad. I looked between them in the silence that followed the tale.

'I'm sorry to hear that about your mother,' Gilbert said.

Celia lifted her head to him with a tiny smile for the briefest moment only. And I said, 'Yes, I am also sorry for her.'

But she did not smile that thank-you look to me.

The ensuing silence had Gilbert scratching his head in an embarrassed manner when suddenly he said, 'Shall I see if I can get some ice-cream?' The man had disappeared before I could tell him that I was not fond of that icy cold stuff.

I was just about to say something nice to Celia, I forget what but something condoling, when she lifted her face to me. There was menace in her eye. Her ample lips were pulled taut into the line of a vicious glower. I did not see it coming – her fist. It came up from behind her and whacked me full in the head. So hard was the blow I nearly fell off my feet as I stumbled dizzy back. When my eyes could once again focus it was to discern my friend Celia walking haughty away from me at great speed.

'Celia,' I tried to call after her, but that wretched girl had smacked all voice from me.

Seven

Hortense

An intended marriage requires three weeks for the banns to be published. We had just enough time. Three weeks with only one day to spare before the ship sailed for England. The minister sitting us on a pew in the small parish church proceeded to remind us, with an expression as solemn as a Sunday sermon, that marriage was a sanctity. Witnessed by God, it was not to be entered into idly or ill-advisedly.

Gilbert nodded like a half-wit as the minister went on. He threw his head back, looking to the church roof, when asked the question, 'How long have you and your wife-to-be known each other?' Tapping the side of his face with his fingers, mumbling, 'Now let me see . . .' he lingered so long with this deliberation that the minister resumed his sermon without receiving an answer. As the minister talked of the joy of seeing two young people embarking on a cherished life together after a period of unprecedented upheaval, Gilbert, satisfied with his trickery, looked furtively to me and winked.

'Married!' Mrs Anderson yelled. 'But how long have you two known each other?'

'Oh, now, let me see . . . Five days,' Gilbert said.

'It will be three weeks and five days by the time we are married,' I explained.

'And three weeks and six days will have passed when I sail to England to see the place is nice for the arrival of my new wife,' Gilbert added.

There was complete silence at the table – even the old woman ceased sucking her chicken bone to stare on us. Suddenly Mrs Anderson pushed back her chair, leaped from her seat and wrapped her arms round me before moving on to Gilbert whom she hugged so tight his head almost disappeared into the crease of her bust.

'So you like jazz, Gilbert?' was all Mr Anderson wanted to know.

Returning to England was more than an ambition for Gilbert Joseph. It was a mission, a calling, even a duty. This man was so restless he could not stay still. Always in motion he was agitated, impatient – like a petulant boy waiting his turn at cricket. He told me opportunity ripened in England as abundant as fruit on Jamaican trees. And he was going to be the man to pluck it.

'Your brother still there?' he asked.

'My brother?'

'This Michael you ask me of – your brother – he still in England?'

'Perhaps he is,' I told him.

'Well, you must let me know his address and I can look him up for you.'

But this big-ideas man had no money. He had spent all his money, he confided to me, on bees.

'On bees?' I asked.

He had some crazy notion about honey producing money. His cousin in St Mary convinced him that keeping bees was foolproof. All he had to do was give this cousin the money to buy hives, jars and printed labels and soon the money from the honey would send Gilbert winging to England.

'But,' he told me, 'this cousin of mine lost the bees.'

'How you lose bees?' I asked.

His reply? 'It is not easy, but it can be done.'

This small setback had left him undeterred. He had another money-making idea. Postcards. Tourists, he told me, who were now flocking to this island for sun and rum need postcards – pictures, scenes of the many wonders of Jamaica to send back to their family at home. He would swiftly be posted to England on the money he made. He sold two. Both to Jamaicans who tearfully remembered the places in the pictures from their youth. The money he made clinked in his pocket. But he was not downcast. He had another plan, he said.

It was while he was placing an advertisement in the *Daily Gleaner* for his services – as a storeman or a driver or a clerk or a watchman or a dairyman or a messenger – under the ex-servicemen's section headed, 'Help Those Who Helped', that he saw the notice about a ship that was leaving for England. The *Empire Windrush*, sailing on 28 May. The cost of the passage on this retired troop-ship was only twenty-eight pounds and ten shillings.

'Of course, this is twenty-eight pounds and ten shillings I have not got,' he said.

And at that moment – as Gilbert became demoralised for the first time in the face of his impossible endeavour – I had cause to thank Mr Philip and Miss Ma for a lesson they had long taught me. Prudence. A small amount of my wage every week I placed into the building society for a rainy day. And the days before Gilbert left were the rainiest the island had ever seen. 'I can lend you the money,' I told him.

Dumbstruck, he gaped like an idiot before a smile turned one corner of his mouth. 'Your mother never tell you, neither a lender nor a borrower be?'

'You can pay me back.'

'Oh, I know that, Miss Mucky Foot. But what I don't know is why you lend me the money.'

'So you can go to England.' Again he was silent, so I carried on: 'I will lend you the money, we will be married and you can send for me to come to England when you have a place for me to live.'

'Oh, woe!' he shouted. 'Just say that again because I think me ears playing a trick on me there.'

'You can send for me when you are settled.'

'Not that bit. I know that bit. I hear that bit. It was the bit about a marriage.'

'How else will I come? A single woman cannot travel on her own – it would not look good. But a married woman might go anywhere she pleased.'

It took Gilbert only two hours to decide to ask me if I would marry him. And he shook my hand when I said yes, like a business deal had been struck between us.

In the breath it took to exhale that one little word, England became my destiny. A dining-table in a dining room set with four chairs. A starched tablecloth embroidered with bows. Armchairs in the sitting room placed around a small wood fire. The house is modest – nothing fancy, no show – the kitchen small but with everything I need to prepare meals. We eat rice and peas on Sunday with chicken and corn, but in my English kitchen roast meat with two vegetables and even fish and chips bubble on the stove. My husband fixes the window that sticks and the creaky board on the veranda. I sip hot tea by an open window and look on my neighbours in the adjacent and opposite dwelling. I walk to the shop where I am greeted with manners, 'Good day', politeness, 'A fine day today', and refinement, 'I trust you are well?' A red bus, a cold morning and daffodils blooming with all the colours of the rainbow.

Gilbert cut a surprisingly smart figure at the wedding. We were both astonished to see the other looking so elegant. He in a grey double-breasted suit, his trousers wide, his cuffs clean, his shirt white, his tie secured with a dainty knot, his hair nicely oiled and waving. I, in a white dress with a frill at the hem, white shoes with heels and a hat trimmed with netting sitting at a fashionable angle on my head. Gilbert, taking my hand in front of the altar, whispered softly, 'You look nice.'

Gilbert's side of the congregation was made up of his cousin Elwood, who was his best man, and Elwood's ageing mother. Elwood was the cousin who lost the bees, a tall lolloping man who spent the service swatting away flies from his face with such regularity I thought him waving to me. His mother, an old woman with a face as sour as tamarind, sat poking her son, asking, 'Who is he marrying?' through most of the ceremony.

Mr and Mrs Anderson and their two sons made up my wedding guests. But after the service was completed all they wanted to say to me was 'Where's

Celia?' No word of congratulations or comment on my attire, just what a shame Celia could not come – she being such a good friend to me. They liked Celia, they told me. They had been looking forward to seeing Celia. And could I tell them again why Celia had not come to my wedding? I did not utter a word, for what business was it of theirs that my erstwhile friend now chose to ignore me? When they had exhausted me with these questions they started on Gilbert, who told them, 'I have not seen Celia for a long time. Hortense tells me her mother is ill. It is a pity she could not come, I would have liked to see Celia one more time before I left.'

On returning to the Andersons' house the family insisted on making Gilbert and I a party, no matter how I protested. Mr Anderson perused his records asking, 'Gilbert, you like Count Basie?'

'Basie is the best.'

Mrs Anderson brought a mound of chicken from the kitchen and placed it before Rosa, who asked, before devouring, 'Where is Celia? Such a lovely girl. Where is Celia, Myrtle?'

'You must ask Hortense. She is her friend.'

Luckily the old woman was not interested in asking anything of me – she was more concerned to begin her nibbling and gnawing. But for once I paid this intolerable situation no mind, realising that I would soon be living in England and able to rise far above these people, higher than any disdain could ever take me. It was of no significance to me that the wedding present from Elwood and his unpleasant mother was a not-quite-full jar of honey. I thanked them, told them it was a pleasure to meet them and wished them good day as they left.

What did it matter to me that the tuneless music was so loud my head throbbed? Or that the man I had married was prancing around the room screeching while the two little Anderson boys stood one on each of his feet, clinging to his legs, calling out for everyone to watch them? I did not care that on eight occasions I had to find an excuse for why I would not dance as everyone else was. Or that Mrs Anderson painfully landed her abundant backside on me after a complicated step and spin from her husband.

'You like Ellington, Gilbert?'

'Ellington is the best.'

I only smiled when Mr Anderson, leaning on Gilbert, both of them drunk on rum and giggling like schoolgirls, finally said, 'Gilbert, you know nothing about jazz, do you?'

'Well you have me there. No.' Then, as they toasted each other, Gilbert, now leaning on Mr Anderson, said, 'And let me tell you one more thing – I caan dance. But, hush, do not tell Hortense. You see how this woman likes a party? She will regret marrying a man who has two left feet.'

So when I said, 'Gilbert, don't you have to get ready for your trip tomorrow?' and everyone looked at me, I was not as embarrassed as I might have been.

Even when Mr Anderson winked at Gilbert, slapped his back and said to me, 'Of course, Hortense, you want to get your husband on his own on your wedding night.' And Mrs Anderson clapping her hands squealed with amusement.

Gilbert came to the room with two boys still clinging to his legs. 'You must go, boys. I have to play with my wife now.'

He tried to peel them off but they clung tighter, rattling with childish laughing. Mrs Anderson had to be called. She came into the room, grabbed the boys and tucked one under each of her arms. 'Come, we must leave,' she told them. Looking to me she smiled, saying, 'Hortense has something she must show Gilbert.' Then, with both boys howling, she took them from the room.

'So we are alone,' Gilbert said.

He had just one small bag. One small bag for someone travelling so far to start a new life in England. 'Is this all you have?'

He looked to his meagre luggage, then said, 'And I have you, of course, Hortense.'

I took a breath before asking, 'You will call for me? You won't get to England forgetting all about me and leave me here?'

He came closer to me from across the room. He put his hands on my shoulders. 'Of course not – we have a deal. You are my wife.'

'There may be women who will turn your head in England.'

85

'Hortense,' he said, holding me firmer, 'we have a deal. I give you my word I will send for you.'

Then, for the first time, he kissed me gently on my mouth. His breath smelt of rum but his lips were warm and soft against mine. I closed my eyes. When I opened them again he kissed me once more but this time the man poked his wet slippery tongue into my mouth. I choked finding myself sucking on this wriggling organ. I could not breathe. I backed away from him, panting with the effort of catching my breath.

Turning away, I took off my hat to place it delicately in the cupboard. I could have been no more than five seconds but when I turned back Gilbert stood before me as naked as Adam. And between his legs a thing grew. Rising up like a snake charmed – with no aid, with no help – it enlarged before my eyes, rigid as a tree trunk and swelling into the air. I could do nothing but stare.

'Come to me, Hortense,' this man said, holding out his arms for me.

I was going nowhere near that thing. 'What is that?'

'What this?' he said, modelling it for me like it was something to be proud of. 'This is my manhood.'

'Keep that thing away from me!' I said.

'But, Hortense, I am your husband.' He laughed, before realising I was making no joke. The fleshy sacks that dangled down between his legs, like rotting ackees, wobbled. If a body in its beauty is the work of God, then this hideous predicament between his legs was without doubt the work of the devil.

'Do not come near me with that thing,' I screamed.

Gilbert crossed the room in two steps to place his hand over my mouth. 'Ssh, you want everyone to hear?'

I bit his hand and while he leaped back yelping I, trembling, ran for the door.

'Hortense, Hortense. Wait, wait, nah.' He sprang at the door, closing it with a slam. And as he stood panting before me I, terrified, could feel that thing tapping on me as a finger would.

But Gilbert's hands surrendered into the air and that wretched ugly extremity began deflating, sagging, drooping, until it dangled, flip-flopping like a dead bird in a tree. He held his palms up, 'Okay, okay, I will not touch you, see,' then, glancing down, cupped his hands over his disgustingness. 'It's gone, it's gone,' he said.

He struggled into his trousers hopping round the room like a jackass while saying, 'Listen, listen to me.' Buttoning his trousers, he tried to look into my face. 'Look at me, Hortense, look at me, nah.' When I finally looked on him he let out a long breath. Calming himself he began, 'Good, now listen. You listening to me?' As I turned my face away, he tenderly took my chin and moved it back to him. 'You sleep in the bed and I will sleep here on the floor. I will not touch you. I promise. Look – I will give you my RAF salute.' He stepped back saluting his hand to his forehead, smiling, showing me his gold tooth. 'There, that is a promise from a gentleman. I will sleep on the floor. And tomorrow I will rise early, go to the ship and sail to the Mother Country for us both. Because, oh, boy, Miss Mucky Foot,' he shook his head slowly back and forth, 'England will need to be prepared for your arrival.'

Eight

Hortense

'Tell me, Mrs Joseph, how long you say your husband been in England without you?'

Normally I would not have answered a question so direct and presumptuous as that. Especially from a woman such as she. A woman whose living was obtained from the letting of rooms. But I was leaving Jamaica. Getting on a ship the very next day. And I thought I could afford to be charitable. This woman was, after all, very old and probably lonely for company.

I had had to stay in her lodgings the evening before I left in order that I might catch my early-morning sailing in good time. She had been kind. She had prepared me a meal of rice and peas, fried chicken and green banana. 'The last supper,' she joked, as she laid it in front of me. She talked all through my meal, telling me elaborate tales of every member of her family — a saintly dead husband, a thoughtless sister, a feckless son — until chewing felt like an improper response to her tales of woe.

After the meal she had helped me pack. Then, warning me of rationing and the cold in England, she disappeared and returned carrying a blanket she had knitted during the war. She explained, 'You see, Mrs Joseph, I had no time to get it to a cold soldier. I start knitting this blanket from when the King first announce to the Empire that we were at war. And I finish the thing as they all dancing in the street in joy of the conflict over. I am not a fast knitter but this was not taken into account.' She pressed her war blanket into my hand. Squares of brightly coloured uneven knitting sewn together to make a blanket big enough to shelter a platoon. I had room in my trunk so I took it graciously.

So when she asked her question of me instead of evading her prying I answered, 'My husband has been without me in England for six months.' Gilbert was true to his word. He had written to me regularly, sometimes our letters crossing – him asking something I had only just informed him of. But he kept me abreast of his plans. And they came along with a pace that sent excitement and trepidation racing around my veins. Soon everything was set. Everything was go.

But now the old woman's jaw dropped to her chest. Her breath ceased for so long I feared for her health. Then she recovered enough to tell me, 'You must go to England straight away. Those Englishwomen will be up to funny business with him. A young man alone in England. You know these white women like to make sure they brown all over. And these young men have urges. I know, I have a son who would never let an urge pass by him.'

I only smiled at her rudeness and told her, 'Please do not fret on my account. I will take my chances.'

But she carried on with curious anxiety, 'You must go straight away, Mrs Joseph, before him forget him marriage vows and all the Lord's Command-ments too.'

1948

Nine

Queenie

For the teeth and glasses.

That was the reason so many coloured people were coming to this country, according to my next-door neighbour Mr Todd. 'That National Health Service – it's pulling them in, Mrs Bligh. Giving things away at our expense will keep them coming,' he said. He might have had a point except, according to him, they were all cross-eyed and goofy before they got here.

'I don't think so,' I said.

'Oh, yes,' he assured me. 'But now, of course, they've got spectacles and perfect grins.'

I knew he'd be round, as soon as that woman, Gilbert's wife, left her trunk in the road for all to see. A woman. You don't see many coloured women. I'd seen old ones with backsides as big as buses but never a young one with a trim waist. His head popped out of his door then darted back in again. Probably went to get his shoes.

I was right. Not five minutes after Gilbert had taken the trunk inside he was on the doorstep. 'Mr Todd,' I said, 'what can I do for you?'

Another darkie, that's what the look on his face said. The motley mixture of outrage, shock, fear, even – nostrils flaring, mouth trying to smile but only managing a sneer. 'Yes. I just wanted a quick word with you, Mrs Bligh, about your paying guests.'

I bet he did. He'd have told that horrible sister of his that more coloureds had just turned up. How many is it now? they'd have said to each other. Fifty? Sixty? 'You'll have to speak to her, Cyril,' she'd have told him, before bemoaning how respectable this street was before they came. They'd have got all those words out – decent, proper – polished them up and made them shine, before blaming Mrs Queenie Bligh for singlehandedly ruining the country. They were the same during the war, although even they couldn't blame me for that. Too many Poles. Overrun by Czechs. Couldn't move for Belgians. And as for Jews. They moaned about Jews even after we knew what the poor beggars had been through. They were all right in their own country, Mr Todd reasoned, but he wanted none of them down our street. He'd never forgiven me for taking in Jean. Bombed out. Her family dead. Sweetheart blown to no-one-there in North Africa. Why not? She was company even when she started going out all night and coming in with the milk. He asked, bold as anything, what she did for a living. I told him she was a nurse – you know, on night duty. Choked on his cup of tea before enquiring if I was very sure of that.

Three times in one day he once asked me if there was any news of my husband Bernard. Tried to make out it was because they were such good chums. But I knew why he asked. He wanted my errant husband home to put an end to me taking in all the flotsam and jetsam off the streets. Concern for me, he'd say – a woman on her own in this great big house. A nearly-not-quite-widow. No man to protect me, guide me, show me the error of my ways. He looked out for me as neighbours should, Mr Todd said. Our own kind sticking together, just like during the war. Only that's not quite how I remember it, even then.

But I was grateful to him (and, I suppose, his nasty sister). He boarded up the hole in the roof. Got rid of the pigeons. Plastered the ceiling. Replaced the windowpanes. Helped me clear the rubble out of the garden. I knew where to go when a fuse blew – he had the little bits of wire on a card all ready, torch handy. I suppose I was indebted. He even offered to decorate the place, if I could get hold of the paint. 'Stop it deteriorating any further, Mrs Bligh.'

Gilbert moving in had put an end to all that. Darkies! I'd taken in darkies next door to him. But not just me. There were others living around the square. A few more up the road a bit. His concern, he said, was that they would turn the area into a jungle. But I was pleased to see Gilbert. I'd often wondered what happened to Airman Gilbert Joseph. You do with a war – I know that now. Everyone scattered like dandelion seeds. Some people you never think you'll see again – especially on your doorstep. And I hadn't seen Gilbert since the incident. After it I didn't want to see anyone. He wrote to me, more than once, but I didn't reply. It's not that I blamed him. How could I blame him? I bet he thought I did but I didn't. It was the war I wanted rid of, but it was people I was losing. Mother and Father suggested I move back to the farm until the war was over. How many times was I meant to escape from that blinking place? I'd already done it twice. No, I told them, I have to get back to Earls Court – make the place warm for when Bernard eventually gets home.

I did write to Bernard in India – told him all about it. But the next letter I got from him made no mention of his father. Or the one after that. He was not one for talking about things, I knew that, but blinking heck! It was like it never happened. If that's how he wants it, I'll wait until he's returned. Better to look him in the eye and explain it to him, anyhow. But I missed my father-in-law Arthur. And not only for his potatoes and onions. Certainly not for those runner beans. An hour I'd boil them and would still be chewing them from dinner when I was brushing my teeth for bed. 'Send them to Churchill,' I'd told him – secret weapon. 'Give them to Hitler's troops – they'd be too busy chomping to fight a war.' Arthur had laughed at that in his quiet way.

I didn't celebrate VE Day – my husband and thousands more were still fighting out east. I told them that when they wanted me to string up bunting for the celebrations. I stuck out my flags for VJ Day when most of the street didn't bother. With the war over I did my patriotic duty – got myself looking as good as I could. Begged some stockings from Bloom's. Scrubbed the house on my hands and knees, poking into corners that hadn't seen a human face since it all began. Another neighbour Mrs Smith, or Blanche as she liked me to call her then, was waiting too. Her husband was on his way back from somewhere called Rangoon. We were friends at that time. She'd hug me excitedly, 'It won't be long now, Queenie. His ship's arrived.' Gave me the last of an old pot of rouge she had. Not quite my colour but I took it. 'All the girls can talk about is their daddy coming home,' she'd tell me, popping round on some errand or other. And she'd ask me, 'Have you heard anything of Bernard yet?' After the umpteenth time I took to saying no before she'd even opened her mouth. I watched her husband Morris turn up. She ran into his arms like they were in some soppy film. And they kissed in that same way right there on the street, him bending her back like Gable and Leigh. Crikey, I thought, I hope Bernard won't want kissing like that.

Blanche's two little daughters stood watching their mum and dad. Little mites looked scared to death when this strange man held out his arms to them and said, 'Come and give Daddy a kiss.' Both ran into the house screaming.

'It won't be long now, Queenie, you'll see. Then you can get on with the rest of your life. Put this beastly war behind you,' Blanche assured me.

But two years went by and no Bernard or any word from him. All the men had come home. They were back walking round the streets, chatting in pubs, courting on park benches, riding on buses, taking all the blinking seats on the tube. The War Office swore blind they'd returned Bernard. I made an appointment to see them and a self-important little man stared at me with pity in his eyes. He's left you, missus, he's left you, his look said. But they didn't know Bernard Bligh. He wouldn't do anything half so interesting.

Blanche wondered if maybe he'd got a bang on the head – forgotten who and what he was. Perhaps he was wandering forlornly around the country looking for a home. A man up the road said he was sure he'd spotted Bernard driving a bus in Glasgow. I'd prepared to go up to Scotland – travel as many omnibuses as I could. But then my brother Harry said not to bother because a friend of his had spotted Bernard sipping beer in a bar in Berlin. And Mr Todd turned up a grainy photograph of a group of harriers walking the Derbyshire peaks. He pointed to a man in the background saying, 'That's

Bernard, Mrs Bligh or my name's not Cyril.' Frankly, the photograph was so bad it could have been anyone – even Cyril Todd himself. Then a fellow arrived – rode up to the house on a filthy motorbike that backfired twice nearly killing several fainthearts. Said he knew Bernard from Blackpool where they'd trained together, but he hadn't seen him since his posting. Became all flustered when I said I knew nothing about Bernard Bligh's whereabouts. But he still managed to drink three cups of tea and eat the same amount of currant buns before he rose from his seat saying, 'I'd better be off now, Dotty,' and left, puffing foul black smoke from his disgusting machine.

It was Harry who suggested I start proceedings to have Bernard officially declared dead. 'What if he's not?' I asked him.

'Then it'll flush him out of his hiding-place,' he'd said.

I was still young and I had a life to get on with. But I wasn't ready for that. So when Gilbert turned up at my door I thought, I've got the room and I need the money. I took him in because I knew Bernard would never have let me. And if Bernard had something to say about it he'd have to come back to say it to my face.

'How can you think of being a woman alone in a house with coloureds?' Blanche said. She warned me that they had different ways from us and knew nothing of manners. They washed in oil and smelt foul of it. Sent her husband round to reason with me because he knew all about blacks. Morris blushed scarlet telling me of their animal desires. 'And that's both the men and the women, Mrs Bligh.' I was to watch out, keep my door locked. 'You'll never understand, let alone believe, a word that any of those worthless people say to you,' he cautioned.

Memories around here might be very short but mine wasn't. I'd known Gilbert during the war. He was in the RAF. A boy in blue fighting for this country just like Bernard and the blushing Morris. No one else would take him in. I was a little put out when some of Gilbert's friends, fresh off a boat, came begging. I didn't want invading. But he vouched for them. Winston was all right but that brother of his . . . Coming down to my flat with excuses so flimsy I could see daydreams in them. Nosing around. Eyeing up my legs even when I was looking straight at him. Animal, like Morris warned. I told

Gilbert I didn't like him and Gilbert told him to go. He left like a scolded dog without any fuss. At least I think he went – he and his brother being so alike.

But Blanche, or Mrs Smith as she now wanted me to call her, put her house up for sale. Furious with me. Told me it wasn't so much her as her husband. 'This is not what he wanted, Mrs Bligh. He's just back from fighting a war and now this country no longer feels his own.' What was it all for? That's what it left Morris wondering. And she told me she had her two little girls' welfare to think of. Gilbert raised his hat to her one morning. She rushed into her house like he'd just exposed himself. Out came Morris who stood on the doorstep to protect her honour. And Gilbert had only said hello. After that she never spoke to me again – crossed the street to avoid walking in my path. She sobbed as the removers shifted her out.

'That house had been in her family for generations. Her mother, her grandfather, his father,' Mr Todd told me. Forced out, she felt. All those coons eyeing her and her daughters up every time they walked down their own street. Hitler invading couldn't have been any worse, she declared. Moved to a semi-detached house in Bromley. Never even said goodbye to me. People were talking about me, that's what Mr Todd told me. Friendly and smiling like he was only telling it for my own good. People were wondering if I was quite as respectable as they once thought.

'They're only lodgers,' I told him.

'But these darkies bring down a neighbourhood, Mrs Bligh. The government should never have let them in. We'll have a devil of a time getting rid of them now,' he said.

So here is Mr Todd once more standing on my doorstep, wanting to talk to me about my paying guests. I thought he'd come to complain about the racket they'd made taking in that blinking trunk.

'Right,' I said. 'What is it now?'

'My sister had a very unfortunate incident today...' he starts.

I would have invited him in but I knew he wouldn't dare step inside.

'Oh, yes?' I said.

Turns out she'd been walking along the pavement. It was raining and she'd got her umbrella up. It was crowded up near the butcher's at closing time. She's walking along when two darkie women start coming towards her. Walking side by side. Anyway, they reach her and there's not enough pavement for all of them.

I smiled. I'd like to have seen that. I knew the type — black as filth with backsides the size of buses. Surprising they could fit on two together.

'And the unfortunate thing is, Mrs Bligh,' he went on, 'that my sister was made to step off the pavement and walk into the road to get by them. These two had no intention of letting her pass undisturbed.'

'Oh dear,' I said. His point, though he was a long time making it, was that I should see to it that my coloured lodgers are quite clear that, as they are guests in this country, it should be them that step off the pavement when an English person approaches.

'You could tell them yourself, if you want,' I said. I opened the door wide for him.

'No, no, that won't be necessary,' he told me. 'I'll leave that to you. But I just thought it might help relations around here if all our coloured brethren understood how to behave.'

Ten

Hortense

At least the fool man, Gilbert, had had the decency to place himself on to the armchair to sleep for the night. In this rundown room there was no private corner for me to change into my nightclothes. 'Use the bathroom,' the man said. But I had no wish to climb that mountain of stairs in my stocking feet with only a nightdress to keep out the cold and eyes that might pry. 'Tell you what, I will turn my back so you can undress,' he said. 'I will not peek.' But twice I caught his greedy eye perusing me. This man could not be trusted and I told him so. 'Cha,' he said. He took up a scarf to place it over his eyes. And all the while he is sucking on his teeth so fierce I feared he might swallow them. 'Happy now?' he asked me.

My toe immediately fell into the hole in the sheet as I got into the bed. But it was not the fault of my foot that the sheet was so flimsy it ripped in two as easy as paper. 'Cha, that is the only good sheet I have.' I shielded my ears from the cussing that flew from the man's mouth as he began to undress.

'Excuse me,' I said, 'but would you be so kind as to please turn off the light?'

'Wait,' he told me, 'I just get undress.'

Any man of breeding would have realised that that was why a woman such as I might require the light to be off. I did not wish him to stand before me in his nakedness as puffed as a peacock, as he did that night in Jamaica. 'That is why I should like the light extinguished,' I had to inform the fool.

And he laughed. 'So you can't trust yourself to keep your eye away from me?' But I paid him no mind. Even with no light in the room, the street-lamp glowed luminous through the window. Any poor Jamaican would have been proud to have so much electric light reach their night-time eyes. I could feel the man standing by the bed when he had finished changing. Jiggling up himself and skipping with the cold. I decided then that if one of his fingers so much as brushed the cover on the bed I would scream so loud that ears back home in Halfway Tree would hear me. It was hard to tell who groaned more – the silly man as he wrestled blankets around him or the tumbledown armchair as he restlessly fidgeted for comfort.

At first I thought the scratching was Gilbert – he was rough enough for such bad behaviour. But then I heard a pitter-patter running above my head across the ceiling. 'You hear that?' I asked him.

The wretched man was asleep. He wake up saying, 'What, what?'

'Can you hear that scratching?'

It was matter-of-factness that said, 'It's just the rats.'

'Rats!'

'Well, mice . . .'

'You bring me to a house with rats?'

'No, they are mice. And every house in London has mice. They bombed out too, you know.'

But this scratching was coming so loud. 'You sure it is mice?' I asked.

'Well,' the man told me, 'you see mice in England like to wear boots.'

I could feel him smiling to himself at this silly joke. 'You must get rid of them.'

'Okay,' he said.

'Now, Gilbert.'

'How you expect me get rid of rats now?'

'You say it was mice.'

'Mice, rats, it's still the middle of the night. What you wan' me do?'

'You must tell the landlady.'

'Cha, you wan' me go wake her to tell her something she already know. Come, Hortense, please, go to sleep, it is only noise they are making.'

I tried to sleep but the mice had decided to push a piano across the floor of the room above. I could see them in my mind's eye as clear as if I was watching their furry figures labouring in their boots.

'Gilbert?' I said quietly.

'Oh, cha,' he yelled. He took up his shoe and threw it at the ceiling. I heard the vermin scatter just before the shoe landed, 'Ouch', on top of Gilbert. Buffoon!

'What goes up must come down,' I told him.

'Oh, in the name of God, please, go to sleep, Hortense,' he begged. 'I promise it will all be different in the morning.'

Before

Eleven

Gilbert

My mirror spoke to me. It said: 'Man, women gonna fall at your feet.' In my uniform of blue – from the left, from the right, from behind – I looked like a god. And this uniform did not even fit me so well. But what is a little bagging on the waist and tightness under the arm when you are a gallant member of the British Royal Air Force? Put several thousand Jamaican men in uniform, coop them up while, Grand Old Duke of York style, you march them up to the top of the hill and then back down again, and they will think of nothing but women. When they are up they will imagine them and when they are down they will dream of them. But not this group I travelled with to America. Not Hubert, not Fulton, not Lenval, not James, not even me. Because every last one of us was too preoccupied with food. The only flesh we conjured was the sort you chewed and swallowed.

This was war. There was hardship I was prepared for – bullet, bomb and casual death – but not for the torture of missing cow-foot stew, not for the persecution of living without curried shrimp or pepper-pot soup. I was not ready, I was not trained to eat food that was prepared in a pan of boiling water, the sole purpose of which was to rid it of taste and texture. How the English built empires when their armies marched on nothing but mush should be one of the wonders of the world. I thought it would be combat that would make me regret having volunteered, not boiled-up potatoes, boiled-up vegetables — grey and limp on the plate like they had been eaten once before. Why the English come to cook everything by this method? Lucky they kept that boiling business as their national secret and did not insist that the people of their colonies stop frying and spicing up their food.

I was brought up in a family with ten children. At that dining-table at home one lax moment and half my dinner could be gone to my neighbour. I learned to eat quickly while defending my plate with a protective arm. But with this English food I sat back, chewed slowly and willed my compatriots to thieve. I had not yet seen a war zone but if the enemy had been frying up some fish and dumpling, who knows which way I would point my gun?

Now, I am telling you this so you might better understand what a lustless and ravenous Jamaican experienced when he arrived, guest of the American government, at the military camp in Virginia. The silver tray had compartments so the food did not get messed up. Into each compartment was placed bacon, eggs (two proper eggs!), sausages, fried tomato, fried potatoes, toast, a banana and an orange. The cereal with milk was in a little bowl to itself. My arm was round that plate of food before I had even sat down. Only when I was assured that the rumour of second, third or fourth helpings was not the reverie of a deranged mind did I relax. I swear many tears were wept over that breakfast. Paradise, we all decided, America is Paradise. A bath with six inches of water that rivalled the Caribbean sea in my affection and more meals of equal, no, greater satisfaction than the first, had the word Paradise popping from our mouths like the cork from champagne.

'Okay, boys, now listen up here,' was how he began, this officer from the US military. Perched informal on the edge of a desk he was relaxed, the only white man in this room full of volunteer servicemen from the Caribbean.

'Pay attention, you lot,' our British NCO, Corporal Baxter, had warned us while we waited for this American officer. 'He's got something he has to say and you're guests here, so you listen to him politely. All right.'

This American officer's head was angular — a square jaw is not unusual especially on an officer, but a square skull! Lenval whispered, 'Him mummy still cross eye from giving birth,' and my smile made this officer pin two penetrating blue eyes on me and me alone.

'You are now the guest of Uncle Sam.'

Resting easy – some of the boys even smoking – our bellies full, looking forward to a few days in the land of the free, some of us, as Jamaicans are prone to do, concurred verbally: 'Yes, sir – umm umm.'

This momentarily took the officer by surprise, his back stiffening before carrying on. 'While you are here, all facilities pertinent to your rank will be open to you.' He stopped here, waiting for a reaction more animated than just the nodding and grinning he received. 'You will be able to use the movie theatre, the playing fields, all mess facilities, et cetera, et cetera.'

'Where is this et cetera?' the small island boys whispered to each other.

'While on the camp you will be under the command of your own NCOs and following British military law.'

Who cared about law as long as the British were not cooking the food?

'But . . .' I was not the only one waiting for this first catch '. . . you will be, for the duration of your stay, confined to the camp.'

Oh there was much sucking of teeth and moaning, 'Cha . . . cha . . . cha . . .' snapping round the room like firecrackers. There was no eyebrow left unknitted.

The officer had to put up his hand to settle the room. 'The reason . . .'

'Cha . . . cha . . . cha . . .'

'Your attention, please. The reason for this decision, which your own NCOs can go into in more detail – but the reason for this decision is to minimise the risk of contracting disease. The British military authorities are quite clear that any serviceman contracting a disease while here will not be allowed to travel any further and will be returned to his country of origin forthwith.'

This did not settle us. With stomachs full, our thoughts had all returned to women. Although I did not want to be turned round having come so far, this war business was getting me down. No one knew how long we would be immured on this camp without seeing a curvaceous bosom, a rounded hip, a shapely leg. How long without female company? A week, a month? No American girl was to see me in uniform – oh, boy, this was serious. The room hummed – this officer had put his finger in and stirred up the nest.

'I know, I know, you're all disappointed. But while you are at this military establishment,' his voice was rising, 'and guests of the Government of the United States of America you will have the run of this camp. Everyone here has been ordered to see that your stay with us is the best welcome Uncle Sam could give to the negroes of an ally.' He was shouting now. 'You will mix with white service personnel. Have you boys any idea how lucky you are? You will not be treated as negroes!'

Perhaps my cousin Elwood was right. 'Man, this is a white man's war. Why you wanna lose your life for a white man? For Jamaica, yes. To have your own country, yes. That is worth a fight. To see black skin in the governor's house doing more than just serving at the table and sweeping the floor. A black man at Tate and Lyle doing more than just cutting cane. That is worth a fight. I join you then, man. But you think winning this war going to change anything for me and you?'

Anthropoid – I looked to the dictionary to find the meaning of this word used by Hitler and his friends to describe Jews and coloured men. I got a punch in the head when the implication jumped from the page and struck me: 'resembling a human but primitive, like an ape'. Two whacks I got. For I am a black man whose father was born a Jew.

My father said one thing to his nine children over and over – so often that we mouthed the words as they came from his lips. 'Remember,' he'd say, 'you could have been Jewish.' This to him was the worst curse that could befall anyone. He was, with his black curling hair and pale olive skin, 'a circumcised member of the Jewish faith'. He would tell us this when the words he spoke still made sense – which was about four rums into his drunkenness. Six rums down he was tearful about his bar mitzvah. Eight, and we heard tales of his ancestors trading salt. It was towards the bottom of the bottle, slurring and gesticulating crazily, that he would berate his estranged Jewish mother, father, the Torah, the synagogue and the silly hats. 'Thank Jesus Christ that I saw the light,' he'd cry. It was during the First World War, in the fields near Ypres, my father first saw this light. He met Jesus on the battlefield. He insisted on the truth of this. Jesus shared a tin of fish with him and lent him some writing paper and no one can tell him otherwise. 'I became a Christian because of that friendship with Jesus Christ,' he would exclaim, just before passing out.

No more Yom Kippur, Hanukkah, Rosh Hashana, and Passover for him. Finally banished from his family, this gold-cross-wearing Jew was cast out from his community in Mandeville. So many backs were turned on him that my father claimed a bitter talent: 'I can know if a man is a Jew from his rear.'

My mother, Louise, took him in, pleased to be parading round this nearly white husband. As a salesman my father supplied shops in the north of the islands with furniture. As a husband he supplied my mother with children – first two sons, my brother Lester and me, then seven girls. Seven sisters!

A fervent convert, my father took Christianity very seriously. He would march his family every Sunday to the Anglican church. Why he never drove his car? 'You must never work on the Sabbath,' he would say.

After the service we children would be lined up with Mummy whispering, 'No cuss words, no blasphemy, no patois.' We all observed as our father skipped round the white people who worshipped there. Taking their reluctant hands and shaking them. Laughing too hearty at jokes that were barely funny. Patting backs just before they turned round from him. Fawning to these white people who stood haughty and aloof in his presence.

The picture in the newspaper was of a German Jew. He wore a cloth star on a dirty coat. He walked along a street, hunched and humbled, while non-Jews eyed him with an expression of disgust Lester and I knew only too well from those Sunday services. With the fervour of a crusade my brother wanted to fight in this war. But when the British Royal Air Force asked him the question, 'Are you of pure English descent?' Lester replied, 'Come take my blood and see.' Nobody believed him when, rejected by the RAF, he returned home burdened with the knowledge that the Mother Country only required members of the white races for this fight. 'Never,' my father, remembering Ypres, shouted. 'Never!' The factories of America claimed my hunched and humbled brother instead.

My cousin Elwood could not understand, 'They turn down your brother when him colour no suit them and now that them change their mind you wanna go licky-licky to them. Cha, you should be fighting the British not joining them. Stay. Their back is turn now – we can win.' There might have been truth in this. But I was ready to fight this master race theory. For my father was a Jew and my brother is a black man. I told Elwood, 'If this war is not won then you can be certain nothing here will ever change.'

Now, from what I could understand, this American officer with the angular head was telling us that we West Indians, being subjects of His Majesty King George VI, had, for the time being, superior black skin. We were allowed to live with white soldiers, while the inferior American negro was not. I was perplexed. No, we were all perplexed. We Jamaicans, knowing our island is one of the largest in the Caribbean, think ourselves sophisticated men of the world. Better than the 'small islanders' whose universe only runs a few miles in either direction before it falls into the sea. But even the most feeble-minded small islanders could detect something odd about the situation. While being shown round the camp a smiling face would tell us, 'You see, your American nigger don't work. If his belly's full he won't work. When he's hungry again then he'll do just enough. Same kinda thing happens in the animal kingdom. But you boys being British are different.' While being shown to our seats in the all-white picture show, handed bars of chocolate and cigarettes to share, men would say, 'I am loyal to my flag but you would never catch no self-respecting white man going into battle with a nigger.' At a dance in the mess being persuaded to boogie-woogie and jive – to let go, man, go! – into our black faces, up against our black skin they said, 'We do not mix the negro and the white races here because it lowers the efficiency of our fighting units. Your American nigger ain't really cut out to fight.'

Apparently our hosts had tried every solution to their nigger problem. 'Only one that works in this country, and certainly in the military, is segregation.' This was apparently how everyone liked it – black man as well as white. They had a name for it – no, not master-race theory: Jim Crow!

I soon realised we were lucky the American military authorities did not let us off the camp in Virginia. We West Indians, thinking ourselves as good as any man, would have wandered unaware, greeting white people who would have swung us from the nearest tree for merely passing the time of day with them.

And my brother Lester? How would they know he was a British coloured man with no uniform to distinguish him? By a badge perhaps worn on his coat? But in what shape? The word Paradise had long since stopped popping from my lips. We might have been returning to that British boiling business but I was not the only boy who was pleased to be leaving America behind.

Frigates, corvettes, warships, troop carriers, destroyers marshalled all along the horizon in Newfoundland. How many ships? Forty, fifty maybe, stretching out for miles like an illusion from an admiral's imagination. All assembled with one mission: to convoy across the ocean. What a sight! Hubert was struck dumb a full ten minutes. When finally he spoke, his voice quivering, he said, 'So beautiful and so deadly.' It was brief, considering the sheer majesty of the moment, but an intelligent comment none the less.

Once we were under sail, under orders and captive on this ship, Corporal Baxter began with his lectures. This man took satisfaction in telling us 'colony troops' everything his twenty-six years as a Londoner had taught him about England. Me, I found it interesting. Did you know that the smog in London can be so thick that it is not possible to recognise your own hand in front of your face? I did not know this. But many of the boys did and yawned wide as crocodiles so Corporal Baxter might realise.

'Don't expect your rice and peas or spicy things or grub like you had in America in England,' he warned us. That I did know and was not pleased to be reminded. 'You're off to a war zone.'

I was yawning now.

'Britain's been at war for a long time, everyone's tired out. There's shortages. You'll have to get used to 'em. You can kiss the idea of a banana goodbye,' he informed us, with uncharacteristic mirth. Then suddenly, without warning, we West Indian RAF volunteers destined for England felt something like an explosion. I was not the only one on my feet ready to fight when I caught its blast. Not the only one with fists clenched willing to kill, when the renk and feisty fool-fool ras-clot Corporal Baxter, belittling us once more with his 'colony troops', told all us boys, 'And don't think you lot are going there to paint the town red. No white women there will consort with the likes of you.'

Twelve

Gilbert

'Wakey, wakey, wakey – let go your cocks and grab your socks.' The man who shouted those oh-so-funny words at six o'clock every morning to awaken we West Indian RAF volunteers was called Flight Sergeant Thwaites. The hair at the front of this sergeant's head was receding. Under the frugal, carefully combed hair that remained, an angry red birthmark blazed on his scalp, which formed the unmistakable shape of a letter B. We all knew, we other ranks, that one day when this sergeant lost all his remaining hair to gravity and the wind, the word 'bastard' would be revealed written over the top of his bald head in that blushing stain. It was the devil who scorched that word on to his skull in case there was ever any doubt as to the character of this puff-up, dogheart man.

We were billeted four to a chalet at the training camp in Filey in the county of Yorkshire. Pure imagination was needed to see how in peacetime English families could actually enjoy a holiday at this woebegone place. Hubert, Fulton, James and I huddled round the hot pipes after every day of indispensable regimen – like running through freezing fields with nothing to keep out the biting sea wind but vest, pants and the order to 'Keep moving, keep moving,' searing from the mouth of Sergeant Bastard. We blocked up the door of this little holiday home with spare clothes, sealed up the gaps in the windows with old newspaper. Every evening we sat close as nesting birds drinking in the heat that wafted from the pipes. Once James took off his scarf but he was the only one. Could this misery be a portrait of an English holiday? One night that bastard sergeant flew open our door and yelled, 'Blimey, it's like the tropics in here. Get those windows open.'

There was no protest we coloured troops could make that would appear to this man as reason. From the first time Oscar Tulloch from Antigua met the sergeant's order to move at the double with an inane gape – provoking the sergeant to moan, 'What the bloody 'ell have they sent me?' – every action we took confirmed to this man that all West Indian RAF volunteers were thoroughly stupid. Eating, sleeping, breathing in and out! Cor blimey, all the daft things we darkies did. We did not know that answering the question 'What is it, Airman, kill or be killed?' with the answer, 'I would prefer to kill you, Flight Sergeant,' would see you up to your neck in bother. And that insolent, annoying Jamaican habit of sucking teeth – so frequent did the custom ring in his ears that Sergeant Bastard ordered that particular noise to be seen as an act of insubordination and treated accordingly. Now ask an Englishman not to suck his teeth and see him shrug. Tell a Jamaican and see his face contort with the agony of denied self-expression. Oh, we were all, every one of us, by virtue of being born in the sun, founder members of this man's 'awkward squad'.

'Warm air ain't good for you,' he shouted. 'It makes you soft. Cold air keeps you alert.' Once all the windows were opened and we were again a group of cold and pitiable black men, he eyed us with scorn before leaving the chalet saying, 'I bet you lot regret volunteering now.' With a good long suck of teeth no longer available to us, we four saluted his back with the silent two-fingered symbol favoured by Churchill but, let me assure you, with its more vulgar meaning.

Now tell me, have you ever seen a dog with a gecko? We had a dog at home – Blackie – my boyhood friend. Wrestling Blackie from the smothering arms of my sisters, removing the baby's hat from his head, the mittens from his back paws and returning to him his scruffy canine dignity, I would find one of those little lizards to deliberately place in Blackie's path. A gecko sensing a dog remains as still as death. Blackie seeing a gecko is suddenly caught by passionate curiosity. Up with his ears, his eyes popping wide. Fearing the unexpected he moves stealthily round the creature, never – even for a second – taking his gaze from it. Carefully, closer, pat the air above it with a paw and jump back. Circling round. Sniff the air. Closer, closer. Skip forward, leap back, wait. That gecko could not even move one of its prehistoric eyes without that dog's awareness. This could go on nearly all day until eventually Blackie would pluck up the courage to slowly crouch down low, wiggle his back end, and pounce at the gecko. Sometimes he almost caught it but usually the gecko ran away, being skilful and faster than my silly dog.

You might want to know why I am telling you this. But patience. Now see this, a fine day: a weak, heatless sun resting in a blue sky. We are out of the camp for the first time, six maybe seven of the boys and me. Walking in our RAF blue through the English village of Hunmanby. No order to follow, no command to hear, just us boys. We are remarking on the pretty neatness of the gardens – a flower still in bloom, which someone, I forget who, insists they know the name of. Shutting his eye and biting his lip he tries to recall it. 'A rose,' he says.

'Cha, that is not a rose,' someone else says. 'Every flower is rose to you.'

'That is a rose.'

'It is not a rose.'

This argument is going on as we walk on past the post office and shop. The display in the window, piled up high with tins and boxes, still manages to proclaim that there is a lot of nothing to buy inside. Hubert is trying to persuade James, a strict Presbyterian and teetotal, to come into the pub. 'You think one little beer gonna keep you outta heaven?'

It was I who first noticed. Leaning urgently into our group I whispered, 'Man, everyone looking at us.'

The entire village had come out to play dog with gecko. Staring out from dusty windows, gawping from shop doors, gaping at the edge of the pavement, craning at gates and peering round corners. The villagers kept their distance but held that gaze of curious trepidation firmly on we West Indian RAF volunteers. Under this scrutiny we darkies moved with the awkwardness of thieves caught in a sunbeam.

'Gilbert, ask them what the problem,' Hubert told me.

From every point of the compass eyes were on us. 'You have a megaphone for me, man?' I said. When I scratched my head the whole village knew. If any one of those people had a stick long enough, I swear they would have poked us with it.

It was some while before the more daring among them took cautious steps toward us, the unfamiliar. A young woman – curling brunette hair, dark eyes, pretty and plump at the hips – finally stood within an arm's distance to ask, 'Are you lot American?' She had her mind on feeling some nylon stockings on her graceful leg. Which, as she stood pert and feminine before us, every one of us boys had our mind on too.

'No, we are from Jamaica,' I told her.

'The West Indies,' the Trinidadian among us corrected.

Like a chink in a dam, a trickle of villagers approached us. Most merely nodded as they passed. An old man with a face as cracked as a dry riverbed shook us all hearty by the hand in turn saying, 'We're all in this together, lad. We're glad to have you here – glad to have ya.'

An elderly couple tapping on James's shoulder asked, 'Would you mind, duck – would you mind saying something? Only my husband here says it's not English you're speaking.'

When James replied, 'Certainly, madam, but please tell me what you require me to say,' her husband shouted, 'Bloody hell, Norma, you're right.'

As Norma concluded: 'There, I told you. They speak it just like us, only funnier. Ta, ducks, sorry to bother ya.'

A middle-aged man, not in uniform, kept his hands resolutely in his pockets before addressing me. Eyeing intently the young woman, who was by now getting on very nicely with a lucky Fulton – consorting with him as we had been assured no white woman would – this man, not looking on my face as he spoke, asked me, 'Why would you leave a nice sunny place to come here if you didn't have to?'

When I said, 'To fight for my country, sir,' his eyebrows jumped like two caterpillars in a polka.

'Humph. Your country?' he asked without need of an answer. He then took the young woman's arm, guiding her, reluctant as she was, away from Fulton and our group.

* * *

Let me ask you to imagine this. Living far from you is a beloved relation whom you have never met. Yet this relation is so dear a kin she is known as Mother. Your own mummy talks of Mother all the time. 'Oh, Mother is a beautiful woman — refined, mannerly and cultured.' Your daddy tells you, 'Mother thinks of you as her children; like the Lord above she takes care of you from afar.' There are many valorous stories told of her, which enthral grown men as well as children. Her photographs are cherished, pinned in your own family album to be admired over and over. Your finest, your best, everything you have that is worthy is sent to Mother as gifts. And on her birthday you sing-song and party.

Then one day you hear Mother calling — she is troubled, she need your help. Your mummy, your daddy say go. Leave home, leave familiar, leave love. Travel seas with waves that swell about you as substantial as concrete buildings. Shiver, tire, hunger — for no sacrifice is too much to see you at Mother's needy side. This surely is adventure. After all you have heard, can you imagine, can you believe, soon, soon you will meet Mother?

The filthy tramp that eventually greets you is she. Ragged, old and dusty as the long dead. Mother has a blackened eye, bad breath and one lone tooth that waves in her head when she speaks. Can this be that fabled relation you heard so much of? This twisted-crooked weary woman. This stinking cantankerous hag. She offers you no comfort after your journey. No smile. No welcome. Yet she looks down at you through lordly eyes and says, 'Who the bloody hell are you?'

'Okay, Gilbert, you have gone too far,' I can hear you say. You know I am talking of England — you know I am speaking of the Mother Country. But Britain was at war, you might want to tell me, of course she would not be at her best.

Some of the boys shook their heads, sucking their teeth with their first long look at England. Not disappointment — it was the squalid shambles that made them frown so. There was a pained gasp at every broken-down scene they encountered. The wreckage of this bombed and ruined place stumbled along streets like a devil's windfall. Other boys looking to the gloomy, sunless sky, their teeth chattering uncontrolled, gooseflesh rising on their naked arms, questioned if this was the only warmth to be felt from an English summer. Small islanders gaped like simpletons at white women who worked hard on the railway swinging their hammers and picks like the strongest man. Women who sent as much cheek back to those whistling boys as they received themselves. While even smaller islanders – boys unused to polite association with white people – lowered their eyes, bit their lips and looked round them for confirmation when first confronted with a white woman serving them. 'What can I get you, young man?' Yes, serving them with a cup of tea and a bun. A college-educated Lenval wanted to know how so many white people come to speak so bad – low class and coarse as cane cutters. While Hubert perusing the countryside with a gentle smile said, 'But look, man, it just like home,' to boys who yearned to see the comparison – green hills that might resemble the verdant Cockpit country, flowers that might delight as much as a dainty crowd of pink hibiscus, rivers that could fall with the same astounding spectacle of Dunn's river. And let me not forget James, perplexed as a newborn, standing with military bearing surrounded by English children – white urchin faces blackened with dirt, dryed snot flaking on their mouths – who yelled up at him, 'Oi, darkie, show us yer tail.'

But for me I had just one question – let me ask the Mother Country just this one simple question: how come England did not know me?

On our first day in England, as our train puffed and grunted us through countryside and city, we played a game, us colony troops. Look to a hoarding and be the first to tell everyone where in England the product is made. Apart from a little argument over whether Ford made their cars at Oxford or Dagenham, we knew.

See me now – a small boy, dressed in a uniform of navy blue, a white shirt, a tie, short trousers and long white socks. I am standing up in my classroom; the bright sunlight through the shutters draws lines across the room. My classmates, my teacher all look to me, waiting. My chest is puffed like a major on parade, chin high, arms low. Hear me now – a loud clear voice that pronounces every *p* and *q* and all the letters in between. I begin to recite the canals of England: the Bridgewater canal, the Manchester-to-Liverpool canal, the Grand Trunk canal used by the china firms of Stoke-on-Trent. I could have been telling you of the railways, the roadways, the ports or the docks. I might have been exclaiming on the Mother of Parliaments at Westminster – her two chambers, the Commons and the Lords. If I was given a date I could stand even taller to tell you some of the greatest laws that were debated and passed there. And not just me. Ask any of us West Indian RAF volunteers – ask any of us colony troops where in Britain are ships built, where is cotton woven, steel forged, cars made, jam boiled, cups shaped, lace knotted, glass blown, tin mined, whisky distilled? Ask. Then sit back and learn your lesson.

Now see this. An English soldier, a Tommy called Tommy Atkins. Skin as pale as soap, hair slicked with oil and shinier than his boots. See him sitting in a pub sipping a glass of warming rum and rolling a cigarette from a tin. Ask him, 'Tommy, tell me nah, where is Jamaica?'

And hear him reply, 'Well, dunno. Africa, ain't it?'

See that woman in a green cotton frock standing by her kitchen table with two children looking up at her with lip-licking anticipation. Look how carefully she spoons the rationed sugar into the cups of chocolate drink. Ask her what she knows of Jamaica. 'Jam– where? What did you say it was called again. Jam– what?'

And here is Lady Havealot, living in her big house with her ancestors' pictures crowding the walls. See her having a coffee morning with her friends. Ask her to tell you about the people of Jamaica. Does she see that small boy standing tall in a classroom where sunlight draws lines across the room, speaking of England – of canals, of Parliament and the greatest laws ever passed? Or might she, with some authority, from a friend she knew or a book she'd read, tell you of savages, jungles and swinging through trees?

It was inconceivable that we Jamaicans, we West Indians, we members of the British Empire would not fly to the Mother Country's defence when there was threat. But, tell me, if Jamaica was in trouble, is there any major, any general, any sergeant who would have been able to find that dear island? Give me a map, let me see if Tommy Atkins or Lady Havealot can point to Jamaica. Let us watch them turning the page round, screwing up their eyes to look, turning it over to see if perhaps the region was lost on the back, before shrugging defeat. But give me that map, blindfold me, spin me round three times and I, dizzy and dazed, would still place my finger squarely on the Mother Country.

Thirteen

Gilbert

'A little birdie tells me you can drive a car, Joseph,' Sergeant Bastard said to me.

'No, sir,' I replied.

You think it would have pleased me to be able to look this man in the eye and say, 'Yes, that little bird was right.' To watch his amazed features assessing this information, to see him gazing upon the heavens puzzling: 'Could it be that not all darkies are daft?' But I had no time for this brotherly generosity. This was a private conflict. It was a desperate liar who said, 'No, Flight Sergeant, I cannot drive.'

Come, let me explain. Louise Joseph, my mother, realising that the husband she married only provided bread for his family when he was sober (which was generally no more than three days out of seven), determined that her nine children would eat cake instead. A business was born. Conceived and nurtured by my mother and her sister, Auntie May. Be it a light sponge or laden with rum and fruit, my mother and her sister made the finest cakes in Jamaica. Only Jamaica? No, probably the Caribbean, even the world. Cakes for all occasions – Christmas, Easter, weddings, birthdays, christenings, anniversaries, and one time, delivered to the governor's house, a cake for the death of a dog.

In front of my sober father, my mother insisted her cake baking was just a hobby. She told him, 'No problem. I just fix up a cake in the kitchen, earn me a little for extras.' Behind his drunken back my mother and Auntie May ran a serious business, with orders, deliveries, overheads, shortages, labour disputes and taxable income carefully assessed. It was a secret that everyone but my intoxicated father knew — that cake business earned more for her family than her husband ever could. And my Auntie May always laughed that my resourceful mother had even bred her own workers. Seven sisters — bickering, shoving and giggling in the kitchens — would mix, bake, ice and pack. And we two boys, Lester and me, were her trusted deliverymen.

I could drive from the age of ten.

'Been driving since you were ten, that's what I've heard,' the bastard went on.

'No, Flight Sergeant. That is someone else.'

It was cake that sent Lester and me to the private school, St John's College, at the age of fifteen. Cake that saw us educated beyond thinking driving and delivering was any sort of suitable work for a scholarly man. Opportunity called Lester to America, which left me, a frustrated prisoner, behind a wheel. I had dreams of attending a university, studying the law and acquiring a degree. But my station was lowly — my ideas soared so high above it I could see them lamenting and waving goodbye.

It was my auntie May suggested night school. 'Gilbert, your face so long it souring me milk. Go, go.'

Night school in the city. Oh, I bit at the hand that fed me. What of sacrifice, what of obligation, what of family? Duty, tell me of duty. I was as ungrateful as my fickle brother. Six days my mother cussed me until, on the seventh, sensing her defeat she suddenly regained her artfulness and said, 'Son, why you no teach your sisters Doreen and Pearl to drive? Then you can go.'

Elwood rubbed his hands together with joyful giddiness at having his boyhood friend back. You see, he lived near Kingston. He told me, 'You can help me and Mummy around the place a little and we feed you up.'

And I told him, 'Yes, and in the evening I would go to night school.'

We toasted the arrangement with the cake my mother had made me. It was a deal, it sounded good. Until early the next morning when Elwood showed me to his truck. Part metal, part rubber but mostly held together with prayer. 'Gilbert, see there, you deliver me produce.' It was a man-eating truck – my head got trapped under the hood, tying, pushing, banging and poking so it might work for another day. I had no time for night school. The only law I learned was that of the combustion engine.

A wireless operator/air-gunner or flight engineer. With my excellent cake-baked education and my exemplary grades in all exams, those pompous men sitting in the recruitment office in Kingston had told me that, when reaching England, I would be trained as a wireless operator/air-gunner or flight engineer. I would be a valuable member of a squadron, second only to a pilot in respect and responsibility. With a service record like that, those military men had assured me, once the war was won, Civvy Street would welcome me for further study.

'It's good authority I've got that you can drive,' Sergeant Bastard insisted.

'Not me, Flight Sergeant. No cars where I come from, sir.' This was an audacious lie and a mark of how grave the situation had become. But with this sergeant believing anything primitive about his West Indian charges, it was worth the try.

Our commanding officer, Flight Lieutenant Butterfield, addressing us West Indians, began, 'Men. The second front is well under way and our greatest need now is for men on the ground. Some of you, in fact most of you, who had originally volunteered for air-crew duty will need to remuster for your trade training. We need ground staff. You will need to remuster for ground-staff duty.' So many of us had to remuster that there was a dimming of the light as our sights were ordered to be set lower. Small-island men, like Oscar Tulloch with his hopes of flying through the sky on metal wings, medals pinned to his glorious chest, found himself as he had left his island, with a broom in his hand. James was to be a navigator, he was to go overseas. 'A navigator!' Sergeant Bastard smirked. 'Well, you should know then, Airman, you are overseas.'

'A posting to the front, Flight Sergeant.'

'This is the front – the home front.'

'A battlefield, Flight Sergeant, sir.'

'Tell them down the East End of London that this ain't a battlefield.' The discussion over, James was sent to train for radar. Hubert got clerical duties. Only the college-educated Lenval was lucky. His trade tests no better than any of us but his skin a little lighter, he became a flight engineer.

You see, there is a list, written by the hand of the Almighty in a celestial book, which details the rich and wonderful accomplishments his subjects might achieve here on earth: father of philosophy, composer of the finest music, ace pilot of the skies, paramour to lucky women. Now I knew: beside the name Gilbert Joseph was written just one word – driver. All endeavours to erase, replace or embellish were useless. I knew that combustion engine was going to get me again.

'I was told wireless operator/air-gunner or flight engineer, Flight Sergeant, sir.'

'This is a war, Joseph, not a shop. Motor transport. Hear me, Airman.'

See, look, watch it come back. Driver. Yes, sir. I was off to be trained to do something I had been doing since the age of ten. Perhaps Elwood was right when he warned me: 'Be careful, Gilbert, remember the English are liars.'

Fourteen

Gilbert

Driver-cum-coal-shifter was not an official trade in the RAF *Table of Trades for Aircraft Hands*, but I had been 'coking' for so long I felt it should appear. Age limit: none. Vision: blurred. Feet: frozen. At countless bleak and wintry railway stations in Lincolnshire I had shovelled more than my rightful share of the wretched black rock from lorry to truck. Coal dust! That rasping black grit seeped down so far into my hair that when I chewed it felt like the Almighty was scouring my head with sandpaper. My nose blew silt. Through five layers of clothing, including a bulky overcoat, that dust, that granular rock, was tickling my bare flesh when I undressed. A group of us complained to the CO. This coking felt like punishment, we told him. 'We're turning as black as Joseph, sir,' someone said.

Until our CO chastened our mutinous zeal with the words, 'Our men overseas are going through much worse than anything you airmen have had to endure.' And a light rain of soot fell from my hair as I bowed my humbled head. But two days later, 'Joseph, you're down to sort the Yanks out.'

A nice long solitary ride, pretty girls waving, old men saluting and the legendary Yank hospitality at the end of it. Charlie Denton assured me I was jammy: 'That's all right that, Gilbert. It's a bit of a comfy chair that run.' Happy he said he was, tickled pink it was me.

My orders were to drive a truck to the US base up near Grimsby. There I was to retrieve ten wooden crates that contained shock absorbers suitable for our Spitfires. 'Spitfires,' the CO emphasised, 'not Mustangs. Make sure they give us the right ones this time.' How our shock absorbers ended up on a US army base – not even air force – was one of the mysteries of war. But blame was flying back and forth like bullets in a battle. The Americans were 'bloody Yanks, arrogant sods, belligerent blighters' for refusing to just deliver the wayward parts to us. No, they insisted someone from the RAF go to their base to identify and certify that the parts were correct before they could be released. This was not the first time this situation had arisen. Charlie Denton went the time before, staying overnight and coming back with enough Chesterfield cigarettes to keep him in best friends for weeks. It was a lucky man who got the cock-up-with-the-American-army run.

'He's coloured, sir.'

'He's what?'

'He's coloured.'

'Ah, shit. Coloured, you say?'

'Black, sir.'

'Yeah, thank you, Sergeant. I do know what coloured means. What the hell are they playing at? Fucking Limeys.'

Now, the building I was standing in had, at a guess, taken only a few minutes to erect. Stuck together with chewing-gum, the only thing separating me from the American army officers was a wall made from a thin piece of board no thicker than the cover of a book. Perhaps if I had been standing in the room with them at the time, the substance of the exchange might have differed a little but let me assure you its audible clarity would not.

'Shall I send him out?'

'You said he's coloured.'

'He's British, though.'

'British! Who cares? British – it's still trouble. If I send a coloured down to that unit, it's trouble. Fucking Limeys.'

'Shall I send him back?'

125

'How coloured is he?'

'Enough, sir.'

'Ah, fuck. That Limey CO is playing around with me. Allies, he tells me. He may be air force but we're all in this together, he says. Allies! Stuck-up Limey bastard. He didn't like me pointing out his stuff's in the wrong place. Our fault, he says. He didn't like me telling him what day it was.'

'Could we get a coloured unit to show the—'

'No, no, no – am I gonna reorder the entire US Army just because some stuck-up Limey sends me a nigger? Not on my watch. He sent that black just to piss me off. Fucking Limeys. I'll get him on the phone. These niggers are more trouble than they're worth.'

'What shall I do with the coloured driver, sir?'

'I don't know. My problem is what to tell this Limey asshole. Truck too small or what? Probably the only truck they've got. No, some paperwork missing? That oughta do it. Tell him to wait or get him something to eat. They always want something to eat.'

'Send him to the mess, sir?'

'No, not the mess, for God's sake – he's coloured!'

Reflex makes you do strange things when you have been bred to be polite, respectful and courteous. I leaped across the room, feigning curiosity out of an almost opaque window so this sergeant might not suppose I had heard their exchange. Chest out, arms by my side, was I to salute a US Army NCO?

'At ease, Soldier,' the sergeant said.

Coloured, black, nigger. All these words had been used to characterise me in the last few minutes. Insults every one. But funny thing is, not one of those aspersions caused me so much outrage as the word 'soldier'! I am not a soldier, I am an airman. 'Airman Joseph,' I said, which made the sergeant reply, 'Yeah, yeah, whatever.' I stood easy as he carried on. 'Listen, ah . . . Soldier, no . . . umm . . . Airman, we're not quite . . . umm . . . umm.'

As he struggled there was my Mother-bred instinct again. Could I in some way help this man out of this unfathomable plight? He looked a shy man. In peacetime, let me see, he would be serving in a ladies' hosiery shop, turning berry-red when big-bosomed women wanted something that would fit.

'You're gonna have to wait a while,' the sergeant finally told me. 'You want something to eat?'

'At the mess, sir?'

'No . . . no . . . not at the mess . . . umm . . . umm. I'll get someone to bring you something out.'

The officer from the other room called out for this sergeant. When the useless door had been closed behind them he said, 'Finch, send the coloured back. I swear that CO Limey bastard was laughing. He was laughing! "Is there a problem?" he says. Ten minutes in Alabama and he'd have a fucking problem. He knew I couldn't use a fucking coloured here. He just sent him to piss me off. He thinks he's fucking won this fight. He was laughing. Thinks he's pulled one over on us. Yeah, sure, asshole. Get the nigger outta here.'

'He was just getting something to eat, sir.'

'Feed him, feed him. Do what you want. But not in the mess, unless you want trouble. Just get him outta here, then get some private to check the parts and truck 'em over. Believe me, this is the first and last time those fucking Limeys get past me.'

When the sergeant returned to me, he smiled. 'They're bringing you something out but you can go back to your base after that, Airman.'

I had not, as far as I could tell, either identified, signed for or transported any crates containing shock absorbers suitable for Spitfires. And yet this man was telling me my job was done. 'My orders, sir, were to pick up some parts.'

'Yeah, that won't be necessary.'

'Sir, I am sorry but I do not understand.'

'Listen, Soldier, it's all taken care of. Just go back. It's okay.'

'What reason will I give for returning without the parts?'

It was at this point that the sergeant's face began to burn its berry-red. But the officer from the other room called out, 'Sergeant, bring him in here.'

The officer's feet were on the desk. Younger than his voice suggested, he smiled steadily on me. His big white teeth standing to attention – each one pressed into the service of putting me at my ease. He swung his legs to the ground, stumped out a cigarette and leaned earnestly forward. Then, relaxing back on his chair, he opened out his arms and said, 'What can I say? I just

127

explained it to your CO. You see we had a coupla trucks up your way so we stuck the parts on. Save you the bother of picking them up. We checked them ourselves in the end. Who cares whose fault it is? I told your CO. We're allies. The parts in the right place is all that matters. It's all square. Parts should be there . . . today. If not today tomorrow. Wasted journey. There's nothing left to pick up. But the sergeant here tells me he's taking care of you. Yankee hospitality, eh?' Several more teeth were put to work before he said, 'Dismissed, Soldier.'

I had heard every word the officer had said to his sergeant, but it was not until that bashful man brought out my food to me like I was a dignitary come to visit that I began to appreciate the situation.

Was it the square-bashing at Filey, the trade-training in Blackpool, the posting to the airbase in Lincolnshire that made me forget? Perhaps it was my crew – white men every one – Charlie, Bill, Raymond, Arnold. Or the white women in the town – Enid, Rose, that other one with the roving eye. Was it the comely Annie from the Swan? Or was I now so used to England that it just escaped my mind? Of course! If a coloured man finds himself on an American army base surrounded entirely by white people, then, man!, he is in the wrong place. How could I forget? 'I am loyal to my flag but you would never catch no self-respecting white man going into battle with a nigger.' No, not master-race theory – Jim Crow!

A coloured man in their stores. Let me set the scene. Astonished mouths gape like children at their first picture show. Wide surprised eyes flashing from one to another. Pens, paper, tools, anything their hands held tight, would clatter to the floor. Huffing-puffing chests would have arms resolutely folded across them. 'What are you doing in here, nigger? This ain't your place.'

'Hello,' I say. 'I have been sent by the RAF to find our plane parts.'

Man, I would be lucky if I could finish that sentence before I was chased from the place. How could a nigger work with American white boys? See them running to their CO demanding justice. No fear of rank would stop them. They will not, they tell him, they will not work with a nigger, British or otherwise. No Chesterfield cigarettes for me. The tale I would take back? The day a mild-mannered Jamaican man caused the US Army to riot.

128

* * *

An hour later and I would not have seen them. The vague silhouettes of these two coloured GIs would have vanished into the blackout. Company was what I saw. Alone and feeling a little nauseous — my stomach revolted by the quantity of rich food I had gorged at the American base. Roast beef and fried potatoes. Bread so plentiful the five thousand could have invited family and all would have been fed. Real butter and peanut butter and so much coffee it slopped inside me like water lapping on a shore. Was it gluttony or politeness that stopped even one mouthful being wasted? Perhaps it was the distress on the sergeant's face as he continued to check my progress. 'When you're finished, Soldier, you can go,' he told me, two times. On both occasions I was unable to respond owing to the bread and peanut butter having sealed my mouth as effectively as wattle and daub.

But a long journey in blackout is not something to savour, it is something to share. Whose surprise was greatest? Mine, at seeing coloured men once more — the first since hearty back-slapping farewells in Blackpool, prior to the postings that peppered us West Indians around the country? Or theirs — for the astonishing good fortune that had them chancing upon a coloured man with an empty truck going their way? They jumped up into the cab and both men examined me as if witnessing a vision of the Virgin Mary.

'You British?' one of them finally asked.

'Yes,' I said.

'I hope I don't cause offence if I tell you that to my eye you don't look British. You must be rare as a sunbeam in a cave.'

'I am from Jamaica.'

'Jamaica, England?'

Had no one outside the Caribbean ever heard of Jamaica? I did not yell or cry out in pain, although I should have. 'No, Jamaica is in the Caribbean,' I told them. But this made no impression on their look of puzzlement. 'The West Indies?' I tried.

'Well, you could have landed from a twinkling star, I'm still pleased to know you. Name's Isaac Hunt but no one calls me that unless they're mad and yelling. To a smiling face I'm called Levi. Don't ask me why unless you're ready for a long story. And this here is Jon – christened Jon, called Jon, been Jon all his life. Both of us born and bred in Florida, USA. But Florida is the reason we know each other not *how* we know each other if you get my meaning. And who have I had the pleasure of addressing, Soldier?'

'First,' I told him, 'let me make it clear that I am not a soldier. I am a volunteer with the British Royal Air Force. The RAF.'

'A flying man.'

'Perhaps. My name is Airman Gilbert Joseph.'

'Pleased to know you, Airman Gilbert Joseph. May I ask which name people who call you a friend usually use?' I said Gilbert but he said, 'Then, Joseph, I hope you won't mind if I call you by that name.'

Throughout this whole discourse the man called Jon sat like an idle puppet staring straight ahead. Nudged into life by Levi, the two held their hands up for me to shake. Impolite as it was to make them wait, I was at the time concentrating on driving the truck. In twilight you can trust nothing your eyes see because your mind believes this half-light to be a dream. And this on a small country road in blackout where manufactured light had no permission to guide me. Is that a tall man in a black cloak or a tumbling wall? See that phantom, could that be a tree? Did a rabbit run or did I blink my eye? All was quiet, waiting for this handshaking civility to be executed before conversation could carry on. Once on a familiar straight road I relaxed enough to take their patient hovering hands in turn. As soon as this was achieved Levi began to talk again, which left me to wonder whether company was indeed a good idea.

'First leave off the base in months,' he said.

Of course, I must explain that at the time I did not realise Levi had only just begun.

'Three months, I believe. Although Jon here may say different on account of he keeps a little book where I figure I can remember but then I do forget. But, Joe, all I know for sure is that I've been desiring to see a pretty-dressed English woman for a long time.'

'No, you have my name wrong there – Joseph is my—'

'Joe, don't pay no mind to Jon here – he don't go in for no drawn-out tales but his mind's busy thinking. When he does speak it's usually worth the wait but I don't know that he can promise you conversation.' He giggled as Jon continued to stare straight ahead – smiling maybe, it was hard to tell in the half-light. 'Get off the base, that's what I said to Jon. Military as changeable as a summer breeze. One minute you got a pass, next all leave is cancelled. Well, if a mule can't hear it ain't disobeying. Truth of the matter is, Joe, we got a pass and two pretty women waiting for us. Lincoln girls. That's going your way, I believe. I have to say, Joe, you're a sight made me rub my eyes. A coloured man in a British uniform. You're British, you say?'

'British. Yes,' I answered.

'But not English?'

'No, I am from Jamaica but England is my Mother Country.'

Was it the half-light or were their baffled faces really contorting into the shape of two question marks?

'Joe, I don't altogether understand what you're saying. Jamaica is in England and who is your mother?' Levi asked.

'No, Jamaica is not in England but it is part of the British Empire.'

'The British Empire, you say. And where would that be, Joe?'

'There are plenty countries belong to the British Empire.'

'And you say your mother lives in one of them?'

'No, Britain is Jamaica's Mother Country. But we are all part of the Empire.'

'Oh.' Both nodded, both had not one clue what I was talking about. 'The Empire, you say. That wouldn't be the place in London where there was a picture show?'

I tried explaining: 'The British own the island of Jamaica, it is in the Caribbean Sea and we, the people of Jamaica, are all British because we are her subjects.'

Nothing.

'Jamaica is a colony. Britain is our Mother Country. We are British but we live in Jamaica.'

'Well, Joe, I think I get it now. This island, Jamaica, is in the Caribbean Sea.' Jon nodded, pensively turning to his friend. They understood. 'So,' Levi carried on, 'the British have all their black folks living on an island. You a long way from home just like us.'

'Yes, I suppose I am.'

'So you're not from America?'

'No, I'm British.'

'Yes, sir, British, and so is your mother?' he mumbled, in a hesitant way that made me wonder whether anything I was saying was going into his head or merely circling around it searching for somewhere solid to land.

'So, what you doing here?' Levi asked.

'I am a volunteer for the war effort. Here to help the Mother Country.' Oh, I sounded so pompous, I know I did. As I said the words I wanted to breathe them back in but I had heard and answered that question too often. What? Did people think I was lost on my way from the canefield?

'Now, Joe, I think you're misunderstanding my meaning. My question is more what were you doing at that US Army base you've just come from?'

'I was sent to retrieve something that had been lost in transit.'

'From that base? Someone sent you to that base?'

'Yes.'

Levi paused for a moment. Then, frowning like a clever man who sees for the first time that the person he has been talking with is a fool, he said, 'Now, Joe, I know you are a British man. And I understand that the British do things different. But – and I am picking my words as careful as a thief before a judge – but, Joe, I am presuming you do know you are a negro. And a negro on that base 'bout as welcome as a snake in a crib.'

Look on my empty truck, I wanted to say. You see any parts there, man?

'You want to come round to us. We're out near a place called ImmingHam.'

'But the parts were on that particular base,' I squeezed in.

'Now, Joe, I don't know if what I am telling you is something you already know but seems to me someone is playing around with you. See, the American army is very strict about keeping black folks apart.'

'There was a misunderstanding with my CO,' I said.

'Well, you may be right, Joe, you may be right. But the way I see it, tangled strings always got someone pulling them.'

I had no time to contemplate who was pulling whose strings, travelling as I was through a landscape that could not be trusted.

'So, will I drop you two in Lincoln?' I purposefully asked.

'No, we ain't going to Lincoln, though it's good of you to offer, but just before you reach there will be fine.'

'But I thought you said you were meeting two Lincoln girls. I am going through Lincoln.'

'Brenda and Peggy, Lincoln born and bred so they tell us. But Notting Ham is the place we will be meeting them.'

'I am not going as far as Nottingham.'

'We appreciate that, Joe.'

'Nottingham, why Nottingham?' I asked.

'Notting Ham is where we is headed. It ain't our day in Lincoln.'

Our day. You see, I thought I understood those words – simple as they are. It was not their day in Lincoln. Said so matter-of-factly, only a half-wit could not follow. But a curious silence hung in the truck between us amplifying that little phrase. Soon all I wanted to know was what, in God's name, could 'It ain't our day in Lincoln' possibly mean! So I asked.

'Lincoln,' Levi began. 'It being Wednesday, Lincoln is a white town. Lincoln is for white GIs only until next week. Now, me and Jon here don't have a pass for next week when Lincoln would be for coloureds. So we gonna meet our Brenda and Peggy in Notting Ham. 'Cause you see Notting Ham is a black town. No whites going to be resting in Notting Ham unless they're looking for trouble and then they're going to get a whole heap of it 'cause Notting Ham is a black-GIs-only area. But me and Jon here, we ain't looking for trouble – we're looking to have a nice time with our ladies. A little dancing, something to eat and who-knows-what-else, if you get my meaning, Joe.'

'But Nottingham is far away.'

'Now, that's true, but if we were in Lincoln we gonna be niggers in the wrong place. Niggers in the wrong place spend all their time watching their backs. There's white boys and MPs just waiting to jump on our broad shoulders. No, we ain't looking for trouble, me and Jon, we're fixing to have a good time. I know you British do things different but US military has it all figured out.'

'Your Brenda and Peggy don't mind to travel so far?'

They both laughed a little. 'Now, they could rest in Lincoln. Me and Jon ain't so come-lately to think they don't have no white boys dangling from their chain when we ain't there to escort them. But we coloured boys figure we must give good satisfaction and I ain't just talking about dancing, if you get my meaning. Only our money's the same as white boys but they'd travel anywhere for the pleasure of dangling from any part of us.'

'You mean,' I asked, 'you are going all the way to Nottingham so you don't mix with white GIs?'

'Like I say, the military got it all figured out – Notting Ham is a black town.'

I did not ask whether the good people of Nottingham knew their town was black or whether the quiet folk of Lincoln realised their town was only for whites. It was too ridiculous! No, what I asked instead was 'Don't you mind being treated like that?'

'What d'you mean there, Joe?'

'Treated bad.'

'How's that?'

'Segregated.'

'Well, Joe, I know you British do things different, but where we come from it's the way of things . . .'

Suddenly the puppet master awakened – Jon was wriggling in his seat. Opening his lips – a little at first then wider – his bass voice, deep as mahogany roots, steadily said, 'But things gonna have to change when we get home.'

At which Levi, turning to his friend, responded with 'Maybe they will, Jon, and maybe they won't,' before carrying on. 'See, you British are different, you see things different. Take Jon here – he don't mind me talking for him 'cept around women. Jon never talked to a white person 'fore he come here. He knew plenty of 'em to give him orders – take out the trash, sweep the yard – but that ain't conversing. So – and I'm cutting this story as short as I can, Joe – me and Jon and some of the other boys get invited to this English lady's house for tea. Not coffee, tea, always tea. 'Pour it back in the mule' is what I say about tea, although not to this white lady who is friendly enough to request the company of negroes. Now, she lives in a house fancy as a church. Coloured glass, big wooden doors, rooms so big your voice still running round the walls long after you spoke. We sit down on her finest chairs and this lady is asking all of us in turn how we like England. Most of us are just saying the polite thing, which is yes-very-nice-thank-you-ma'am. Only Earl thinks to say something like a complaint 'cause that is his character. He says the climate is a bit too cold, but this lady just laughs so we all laugh along too. Then she turns to Jon here and asks where his family is from. Now, at that same time as she is asking him that simple question, this pretty little white servant girl is placing the tea – in a little cup on a little saucer – into Jon's hand. Well, Jon is so feared having a white woman waiting on his conversation that that cup began to shake on that saucer like the earth was trembling under Jon's rear side. It was clicking and clacking, wobbling and rattling and the hot tea was spilling over the top. This lady she's making like she don't see anything and we boys could do nothing but watch. It was the white servant girl who moves over to Jon. She takes his hand with the little cup and the little saucer and closes her hands around them till it's steady. Jon being grateful looks up to her and smiles and she smiles back. Well, the lady sure notices *that*. 'Thank you for coming,' she tells us, and quick as a crooked dealer with his deck she has that tea back from us. We was out of that house looking at that closing door before any of us had got a drop of that damn brew to our lips. But we was invited. A white woman invited us coloured soldiers to her house, to sit with her on her furniture, to drink with her her tea. Don't get that where we come from. You have anything to do with white folks here, Joe?'

'Yes, I share a billet with seven white men.'

If silence ever spoke, it spoke to me then. Levi's breath stopped. Whereas Jon came to life once more, twitching tormented in his seat, wiping a hand first across the back of his neck then dragging it slowly down his face. Studying me like he saw me for the first time, he asked, 'How can you sleep with them in the same room?'

'What do you mean?' I asked him. But both stared silent on me, convinced I was the strangest apparition they had ever beheld.

With Lincoln approaching, Levi told me, 'Just about here will be fine, Joe.' Assuring me they would be catching a train, they wanted to be left in what seemed to me to be the middle of nowhere.

'You been good company, Joe. Now we sure would like to show our appreciation for the ride but we don't want to offend you.'

'I was going your way. No problem.'

'Now, you sure that is enough for you? Only you've been kind. And you can be sure me and Jon here are gonna eat plenty of chicken when the folks back home request the tale of the British coloured man we met. The British Empire – I'm gonna remember that. And all their coloured folks on an island in the sea.' Both offered their hands for me to shake before they would leave the truck.

'Been a pleasure meeting you, Joe,' Levi said, for both of them.

As I started up the truck again I found deposited on their vacated seats, six packets of Chesterfield cigarettes. Waving goodbye they pulled up the collars of their coats before finally disappearing into the lonely stretch of dark road.

Fifteen

Gilbert

At first I thought, No, no, no, no, you are losing your mind, man – your imagination is deceiving you. But an hour passed and him still there. I had bought my newspaper, walked up the road past the church where the cemetery gate was half eaten with rot. I had sat on my bench noticing that two more lovers had carved their names in the wood, so deep I could feel the indentation of the love ST had for CM through the thickness of my trousers. And still him there – just in my view. Sometimes I swivel my eye to see him and sometimes I turn my whole head. Whatever, this sombre-looking man made no attempt at concealing himself. This was no infiltrator of His Majesty's Services. If he was a spy he was bottom of the class. No Nazi man of espionage would look so conspicuously like a badly dressed Englishman – his old raincoat, plus-four trousers and tartan socks would have sent him straight to jail. But whoever he was, there was no doubt him was following me.

But for what reason? I asked myself. Maybe he wanted to feel the hair of a coloured man. Or rub the skin of this darkie to see if rubbing it could make it turn white. Or maybe he wanted to touch me for luck. (Man, if that were true coloured men would be the luckiest men on the planet just for wiping their backside.)

I gave him the runaround. Who knows how many times we passed that old rotting gate and that carved bench? Not me, I got too giddy to count. I took him through an empty field – just me with him ten feet behind, trailing me like a dog. This was too comical to be real. The ground was freshly ploughed; it was difficult to walk on the tumbled earth. I could hear his chest wheezing with the effort of keeping up. And hear this: soft-hearted man that I am, I slowed so he might follow me at a more stately pace. You ever hear anything like that? But not too slow because I needed to puff this man out. I wanted to leave him with no strength to bash me in the face or pull a knife or run at me. I wanted him so weary he could not even raise the vapour to cuss me. When I was sure I had him breathless, I stopped. Turning full-circle round on him I asked, 'Is there something I can do for you, sir?'

Politeness has always been my policy. It makes the good people of England revise what they think of you, if only for a second or two. They expect us colony men to be uncultured. Some, let us face it, do not expect that we can talk at all. 'It speaks, Mummy, it speaks,' has been called after me. Oh, yes, Mummy, it speaks and when it speaks it usually speaks with courtesy. So I asked this man, 'Is there something I can do for you?' adding a note of respect, which is usually implied by the word 'sir'.

I thought I had turned him to stone he looked so startled. He made no sound, nothing. We just stood, the two of us alone in a field waiting for the other to explain themselves. Then up came a rumbling – a low-flying plane, resonant as an earthquake. A Lancaster, I thought, that is a Lancaster coming home. From the uneven sound of an engine it was coming home injured. It flew so low I held my breath, scared it would not clear the trees at the edge of the field. One inch was all, I swear there was one inch to spare. Man, I could see holes in the side of the fuselage as big as my fist. 'Go, boy!' I shouted. 'Go, boy!' as it passed into the distance.

When I looked back the man had gone, or so I thought. I looked to the ground and there was the man's coat. Now, what you think of this? For a moment I thought the ground had opened up, swallowed this man and left his coat over the hole. And I am considered a sensible man. No. Slowly the man raised himself from the earth where he had thrown himself down.

138

Lifting himself up his face was as black as mine. Of course I laughed, he looked funny this minstrel man, his white eyes blinking at me. But he was shaking, like electric volts quivered through his body. 'Calm yourself, nah, man,' I said. He was gyrating like a bad dancer who couldn't find the beat. Again I said, 'Calm yourself,' but as those stupid words left my mouth I realised this man was not quite right in the head. He did not want a fight, he wanted a nurse.

The aftershock of another plane boomed in the distance. The man covered his ears, his face contorting to a soundless scream. But it passed over us further away. Two thoughts went quickly through my mind. One: I was lucky there was no one else around – anyone seeing us might make a conclusion that I was attacking this man. And two: that this fool-fool man had just escaped from somewhere. He was not a young man but neither was he old. His grey hair did not match the bushy dark of his eyebrows. He could have been handsome, I suppose, if he had not looked so fearful – this fear gave him the look of a simpleton.

But men who are soft in the head are unpredictable, I knew this. I was on my guard when this man placed one of the shaking hands in his pocket. He could still have a knife, he could still have a gun. Mark you, he was so weak and pathetic with his trembling it would have been entertaining to see how he would use them to threaten me. His hand, wriggling like a rat in his pocket, was there so long I feared he was touching up himself for luck. But then just as I was about to call him 'a dirty, dirty little man' he pulled out a piece of paper to show me. Now, paper is harmless – we all know this – but sometimes what is written on it is explosive. So I approached this paper with trepidation. Once he had handed me the paper this man then jumped – and I make no exaggeration – jumped five feet back away from me.

'Wow, I will not bite you,' I told him, which sent the man jumping another two feet further back. I said nothing else in case he hopped out of the field as I read the words on the paper. It said, 'My name is Arthur Bligh. If you find me please return me to 21 Nevern Street, London SW5.'

Now, let me set the scene: me and this man of limited sense were standing in a field in Lincolnshire. It may even have been Nottinghamshire but this was not the point. The point was we were neither of us anywhere near London. There are times so perplexing that the only thing to do is scratch your head. This was one of those times. Luckily, this scratching made me see the writing on the other side of the paper. The same Arthur Bligh business was written there but the address was changed. It was a farm nearby. I knew this farm: I had passed it many times when coming from the base.

'You want me take you home?' I asked this man. I said it too loud, I know I did, and too slow, as if talking to a child, but somehow it seemed right to shout at this jitterbugging half-wit. But he stayed expressionless. Blinked at me twice. I stepped closer to him with the intention of taking his arm to escort him. He stepped back. This happened a few more times before I gave in and accepted his love of the parallel. I walked and he followed ten paces behind.

I did not have to look to know that he was still there, his wheezing breaths told me I was being chased. I kept an ear sharp in case the wheezing got worse. By the time we reached the lane to the farmhouse I was walking Jamaican slow — one foot down and the other foot soon come, what the hurry, no rush — so this man could keep up with me.

I had been in England long enough to know that my complexion at a door can cause — what shall I say? — tension. When I was new to England all the doors looked the same to me. I make a mistake, I knock at the wrong one. Man, this woman come to the door brandishing a hot poker in my face yelling that she wanted no devil in her house. 'Since when was the devil in the RAF?' I asked her. Stand back — I had learned that day — stand back, smile and watch out!

The door to this farmhouse was answered so quickly I was sure we had been seen approaching. The woman who answered the door was Queenie Bligh, although obviously I did not know her name then. All I knew was that a pretty woman looked at me for the count of two seconds with an excited recognition. Two seconds before she realised I was not whom she'd thought I was. Two seconds before she knew I was a stranger. Her first words to me, as she pointed at the man who had followed me, were 'Where d'you find him?'

Just that. No 'Hello, can I help you?' Or 'Good day.' Just 'Where d'you find him?' No politeness, no pleasantry. She wasn't even worried that this once white man's face was now black.

'He appeared to be following me,' I told her.

Her eyes rolled around in their sockets. She was as pretty as a doll – pale hair, very blue eyes, a thin but firm waist and lovely legs.

I, like all servicemen from my country, was adept at taking in the whole spectacle of a woman without her knowing. Every feature was assessed, categorised and compared in the blink of the unsuspecting eye. For the Jamaican man – expert in this art – it is hard to say whether it is a training or a natural-born gift. This woman was so lovely I wanted to rub my hands together, kiss the crazy man who followed me and thank him heartily for bringing me to this house. But instead I held my arms to my side like a gentleman and told my mouth not to give away any unwholesome intention.

'He followed you?' she asked.

'Yes, from a while back. We have been together most of the afternoon. Him just a few paces behind me except for the moment when he threw himself to the ground.'

'Was there a loud noise? Was he shaking?'

'Yes, ma'am, to both.'

'Don't worry – it was nothing you did.'

'My question is, why him follow me in the first place?'

'Oh, I know why he followed you,' she said. 'He thinks he knows you. He brought you back for me.'

I looked again at this man, who had an expression on his face that, if looked at carefully – perhaps with some measuring device – could be construed as a smile. At this point the man passed me, walking into the house with no recognition or gratitude to me at all.

'Does this man speak?' I asked.

'Did he not say anything to you?'

I shook my head as she, addressing him over her shoulder, said, 'Go on, you daft beggar – it's not him.' Then looking to me she added, 'He thinks you're someone else.'

'Don't tell me, Paul Robeson.'

141

'Paul Robeson. You think a lot of yourself, don't you?' she said, frowning. 'Anyway, he wouldn't know Paul Robeson if he fell on him.'

'Madam,' I told her, 'if Paul Robeson were to fall on him there would have been no need for you to come to the door, I would have just posted the gentleman underneath.' This was a very good joke. You see Paul Robeson is substantial and this man was puny. He would be flattened like a hut before a tank. But this woman appeared not to see the amusing side.

'Get washed, Arthur,' she called to the man, 'your face'll frighten people. And get those mucky clothes off.' And turning to me she said, 'Well, thank you for bringing him back,' before moving to close the door.

So I asked, 'Excuse me, but is the gentleman all right?'

'I don't think so, do you?' As I had already asked the question I had no reply for her. She went on, 'He hasn't been right since the last war. He hates loud noise. I brought him here to get away from those blinking buzz-bombs in London, but you lot make such a racket I'm thinking of taking him back for some peace and quiet.'

I was not ready to leave such a pretty woman yet. 'So, if not Paul Robeson who him think I was?' And, oh, boy, she blushed. She blushed so bad I felt the temperature rise around me.

'Oh, just someone else I knew – like you.'

'An RAF man?'

'A coloured chappie like you.'

'Oh, I can assure you, ma'am, there is no other coloured chappie like me.'

'No. You look like him – a little bit.'

'May I ask which bit that is?'

'No, you may not, but thank you for coming and bringing him back. I'm sure you'll want to be getting off now.'

Man, was she wrong!

'Is he your father?'

'Who?'

'The man who is now washing his face.'

'No, he's my father-in-law. I was given him as a wedding present.'

'A wedding present! You're lucky, your husband a generous man. Where I come from a new wife is usually given a toothless rancorous old mother-in-law.'

Suddenly this woman laughed. A laugh from nowhere. No smile or build-up titter. Just one minute solemn, the next a honking laugh, the noise of which could make a pig sit up and look for its mummy. My instinct told me to run or stare. I stared. Then holding out her hand, she managed to say, 'Queenie Bligh. That's Mrs Queenie Bligh to you.'

'Gilbert Joseph,' I said, as I shook her hand delicately. 'That's Airman Gilbert Joseph to you.'

And the laugh came again.

'That's some laugh you have there,' I said.

'I suppose I better make you a cup of tea seeing as you've come all this way.'

'And I finally make you laugh.'

'Oh, you were trying to make me laugh, were you, Airman?'

'Laughter is part of my war effort.'

'Well, I'd better show you some local hospitality, then.'

'What – your husband won't mind if you entertain me?'

'Now you mention it, hang on a minute. I'll just go and write to him. He's in India. Should get a reply within the year. D'you mind waiting?' She stood aside for me to pass. 'Come in, then, Airman Gilbert Joseph, before I change my mind.'

Sixteen

Gilbert

At the time I did not worry. Just white American soldiers – GIs out on the town. I might have wondered whether the swagger in their step was drunkenness or just that national arrogance all allies had come to know.

'Hey, you!'

'Me?'

'Yeah, you. Don't you know to salute your superiors?' As this man's friend was hanging on to his arm trying to steady himself giggling all the while like a silly schoolgirl, I did not believe this to be a serious question.

'I don't know you, man.'

'I am your superior,' he told me. The badge on his arm proclaimed him to be no more than a private in the US Army. Perhaps I should not wipe my boots on him but no more respect than that was required.

'Salute your superior.'

'Fuck you, man,' I told him, before moving on.

He called after me, the giggling one, he shouted, 'Off the sidewalk, nigger.'

I turned round to face them again but they were walking away, strutting towards some other sport.

It was then I heard, 'Airman', being called feminine on the breeze. And I knew it was she. But not until she used my name – not until I knew she remembered me as Gilbert – did I turn round to where she stood on the street. With the sun behind her the silhouette of Queenie Bligh's shapely legs was delivered like a saucy picture show on to her flimsy dress. Oblivious to this intimate display she waved at me like we were old friends. Ugly GIs instantly forgotten. Man, I thought, your luck has just changed!

'Gilbert, have you seen Arthur?' She hurried towards me on the street, enchantingly breathless.

'Don't tell me you lose him again.'

'It's not funny, Gilbert.'

'But you too careless with this man.' Not since I had asked Auntie May if she had ever been kissed had a face looked on mine with such inscrutable blankness. I had gone too far. Man, I was losing me touch.

'You're a cheeky beggar,' she said. But what a relief when in answer her eyes flashed levity instead of the whack round the head I got from Auntie May.

'You need a lead for that man.'

'You're right, I could string him up by it.'

'Such a pretty woman could never do such a thing.'

There was the trace of a blush at her neck as she said, 'Don't try me.'

'So how you lose him this time?'

'Same as always.'

I having met Queenie and her father-in-law on only one occasion, 'same as always' meant little to me. But the familiarity of that phrase was so sweet I made no further enquiry. 'He will come back.'

'He tries my patience.'

'He'll probably bring you someone for tea.' Queenie looked so dismayed I had to say, 'That was a joke.'

'If it was, Gilbert, I would have laughed. Ruddy little sod.'

'Who me?'

'Not you – him.' Her face relaxed, anxious to adorable in one move.

'Well, seeing how your father-in-law has brought us together again, can I offer you a cup of tea?'

'You got one in your pocket?'

'No, but I would be honoured to escort you to the tea-shop.'

145

'It was a joke, Gilbert.'

'A joke? But, Mrs Bligh, if it had been a joke I am sure I would have laughed.'

I swear I could still feel the fingertip touch of Queenie's hand on my arm from that afternoon when we first met. Sitting at the table in her mother's kitchen she had served me with a cup of milky tea. I had gratefully taken it from her hand but declined to add the sugar she offered even though, as everyone is aware, tea is disgusting without it. She had then presented me with a large delicious-looking hunk of crusty pork pie. Despite my mouth watering so that my drooling was visible as a dog before a bone, I refused this repast. Why? Because of Sergeant Baxter. It was this man who taught me, and all his colony troops, that owing to shortages and rationing in Britain if invited for food into someone's home the polite response was to say no, thank you – perhaps with the excuse that you had eaten already. 'They can't go giving the likes of you all their precious food,' this sergeant reasoned. 'So act like you don't need it.'

'No, thank you. I have already eaten,' I had said.

'Are you sure?' Queenie asked me.

'Tell me of pork pie?' I then asked. 'Is it an English delicacy?'

There came that laugh from nowhere – an alarming sound, which suddenly filled every corner of the dull and dour room with dazzle. 'Well, I think we're the only ones daft enough to eat it, if that's what you mean?'

I hoped my envious eyes were not protruding too obviously as I watched her take the first mouthful of her slice. But as she chewed, this pretty woman began to smile. It was then that she had gently laid her hand on my arm. Looking mischievous wide blue eyes into mine, she'd said, 'A word of advice, Airman Gilbert. Never be polite in a butcher's house. You eat as much as you like.' Oh, she was so charming that afternoon. With Sergeant Baxter ignored, I just had to surrender.

For the sake of Queenie, if I had seen them before we stepped into the little tea-shop I might have made an excuse for moving no further inside. But I had just finished seating Queenie into a chair and was half-way into my own when they became apparent to me. Three white American GIs. As I took my seat, Queenie joking loudly to me said, 'You're a gentleman, Airman.' She slipped off her cardigan, placing it on the back of the chair. The three GIs noticed us, as I knew they would. One nudged the other's arm, nodding towards our table while another stared directly on me with a blinkless gaze that did not falter. Queenie, with her back to them had no reason to feel their curiosity. Oblivious she began reading the menu, 'I bet that scrambled egg's not real egg,' while I, knowing fear can animate a face, returned to them an expressionless stare.

Everyone fighting a war hates. All must conjure a list of demons. The enemy. Top of most British Tommies' list would be the army that hated them most – the Nazis. They were, of course, men who would smile to see a Tommy's head blown into mush. But from that first uneasy hospitality at the American base in Virginia to this cocky hatred that was charging across the room to yell in the face of a coloured man whose audacity was to sit with a white woman, I was learning to despise the white American GI above all other. They were the army that hated me most! Out of place in the genteel atmosphere of this dreary tea-shop these three aggrieved GIs twitched with hostile excitement, like snipers clearing their aim at a sitting target. Surrounded by grey-haired old ladies – cups tinkling like bells as uncertain hands placed them on saucers, the clip of cutlery on floral plates, a gentle gurgle of pouring tea, a little slurping, a hushed conversation – these poor GIs were in murderous mood watching a nigger sitting with his head still high. If the defeat of hatred is the purpose of war, then come, let us face it: I and all other coloured servicemen were fighting this war on another front.

'Would you like something to eat with your cup of tea?' I asked Queenie, louder than was required.

'I don't mind if I do.'

'Now, that is one long tortuous way of saying yes,' I commented. 'Why English people say all this "don't mind" business when a simple yes will do? Is it to confuse we Jamaicans?'

'You know, I've never thought about it. It's just something you say. I've always said it. Don't mind if I do. But now you mention it . . .'

Queenie was unaware that our polite conversation caused these GIs to flex their fists. One of them whispered an urgent word into his friend's ear. Another, smoking a cigarette, lips pinched, holding it with his finger and thumb like a shrunken Bogart – blew his smoke in our direction.

I don't know why the fusty waitress posed with a pad and pencil. This woman, looking anywhere but at us, said, 'That's off,' to the teacake, the toast, the muffin, the crumpet, the drop scone.

'What, they all turn bad?' I asked.

'No,' she said, lazily raising her eyebrows. 'They're finished. We haven't got them.'

'I always thought when something was off it gone bad.'

'Well, I dare say. But here we say it's off. Off the menu.'

'But it is written here.'

'Yes, but it is off.'

I looked to Queenie who was giggling into her hand. 'So, Queenie, would you like tea?'

'I don't mind if I do, Gilbert,' she said, and the poor old ladies jumped as she began to laugh.

Meanwhile those GIs were concentrating on us like we were an exam they must pass.

'We've got rock buns,' the waitress said.

One of them had tight black curly hair – man, this white boy should never dig too deep in his past: who knows what strangeness could be uncovered?

'Oh, thank you,' I said. 'Then may I have two rock buns as well, please.'

She wrote this down on her pad while telling me, 'There's only one left.'

'One then, for the lady, thank you.'

The third GI was an ugly brute – look like the Lord above had put him face on in the dark: nose flattened to one side, eyes sitting too close. A boxer, maybe.

Queenie was talking about her father-in-law. 'We're going back to London. We'll take our chances. You see, he's getting on Father's nerves. You know, the way he is, Father can't stand it, says he acts like a girl.'

The rock bun landed on her plate with such an almighty thud – hear this

— I thought the GIs had thrown a grenade. Queenie picked it up and turned it in the air, leaning forward to me to whisper loudly, 'This has seen better days.' And one of the GIs rose from his seat only to be restrained by one of his buddies.

I beckoned Queenie to lean even closer towards me. I could feel her hair on my chin, her breath warm on my cheek as I said, 'Dare we taste it?' Sitting back I looked directly on the three. Man, they were snorting like beasts, looking around this cage for justice. Two MPs strolled by the window and the ugly brute motioned their presence to the other two. More furtive discussion passed between them as we calmly sipped our tea.

'Rock by name, rock by nature,' Queenie said, trying to break the cake into edible pieces.

'Tell me, this rock bun, is it an English delicacy?'

'Well, I'm daft enough to eat it. Excuse me, but there's a war on,' she said, as she dipped the bun into her tea to soften it. Then this beautiful blonde-haired woman held up the bun across the table for me to take a bite. And all the time Queenie had no idea that every move she made, every gesture towards me, every friendly word and now this — allowing a black man to bite food from her hand — was reddening the necks and boiling the blood of those GIs. The hothead GI had to be restrained again. I was captivated by the impotent rage in their eyes. What sport!

'Are you all right, Gilbert? What are you looking at?' she asked, glancing around. But to her, of course, there was nothing menacing that she could see in this room.

I placed my hand on her arm to say, 'Oh, it's nothing.' When the ugly brute, sure I was watching his threatening move, slowly drew his hand in a line across his throat.

I had to get Queenie out of the tea-shop fast. I knew I could not pass these men to get to the door without a punch being thrown from somewhere. Three against one, I still fancied my chances. But Lady Luck is a fickle woman and I did not wish to be humiliated in front of my impressionable companion. She was talking and, let me admit, I did not know what she was saying so busy was I trying to plot our escape. She was not safe from their animosity. Oh, no. GIs as vulgar as these would have no consideration for a white woman whose afternoon is spent with a nigger.

It was then I saw him in the fading light. Arthur – the wonderful man who had brought me to Queenie's door – was walking across the road looking, as always, a little lost.

'There is your father-in-law,' I said.

She ran from the tea-shop and over to where he stood without even an 'Excuse me'. There was something indecent about the way Queenie wagged her finger in this grown man's face while he, head low, kicked at imaginary stones on the ground.

I stood to leave. And so did the GIs. Paying the waitress I tipped her so handsomely she almost smiled on me. The GIs were blocking the door. I needed a plan. It was too late to don a disguise – they would still know me in a blond wig. All my mind could conjure was squeezing myself through some back-entrance window. 'Do you have a WC?' I asked the waitress.

'No, but down the street . . .' the waitress began. Then, turning to point, she stopped her instructions when she saw the GIs making themselves ready to leave.

'Excuse me, I've got eggs here for you three. You can't go just like that. You've ordered.' She hurried over to them. 'In this country you have to wait for your order.' She shooed them back into their seats, and those Mummy-fearing boys grudgingly submitted. 'It's just coming, now sit down. We haven't got food to waste like some. There's a war on, you know.' With she, standing over the table of these pitifully cowed men I, with a kiss for Lady Luck, slipped out of the door. All three GIs eyed me through the window as if vermin were escaping. So I gave them a little wave. Come, who were the pantywaists now?

But still I worried to leave the road quickly. I hurried to Queenie and her father. 'Gilbert,' Queenie began saying, 'Arthur and I were wondering about going to the pictures.'

Lady Luck was still smiling. Linking my arms through theirs, 'Good idea,' I said. 'Come, let us go.' And, with them bamboozled by my enthusiasm, I managed to frogmarch them away.

Seventeen

Gilbert

How Clark Gable make every woman swoon so? *Gone With the Wind*. Queenie was so thrilled she jump in joy, 'Oh, Clark Gable's in it!' Forgetting all sense she squealed delirious at the thought of being in the the dark with this puff-up American star. How Clark Gable turn every woman's head so? Foolish young English girls would see a movie star in every GI with the same Yankee-doodle voice. Glamour in US privates named Jed, Buck or Chip, with their easy-come-by gifts and Uncle Sam sweet-talk. Dreamboats in hooligans from Delaware or Arizona with fingernails that still carried soil from home, and eyes that crossed with any attempt at reading. Heart-throbs from men like those in the tea-shop, who dated their very close relatives and knew cattle as their mental equal. Thanks to Mr Gable's silver tongue, this bunch of ruffians mistakenly became the men of Englishwomen's dreams. The picture had already started, we had missed the music and the Movietone news. Yet still this Gable star – even with him face six foot high and luminous – could not light up the room enough to guide us as we walked.

'Tickets?' the uniformed usherette asked. 'Follow me.' Even in the dark she was scruffy – her ample bosom having been configured for a larger garment. As if trying to escape her, the gleam from her torch wriggled frantic on the floor before resting on some empty seats. Queenie patiently guided Arthur by the elbow into the row. Him mesmerised as a baby sat before he should, while Queenie nudged him along two more seats. As I went to follow them the usherette tugged at my sleeve. I turned to her and she momentarily dazzled me, flicking the torchlight up on to my face.

'You have to go up the back,' this woman said, lighting the ground to indicate the path I should take. I had misunderstood. I tapped Queenie to whisper, 'The usherette say we have to go to the back.'

The girl shook her head as Queenie backed out from the row. 'Not her. You. You have to go up the back.'

'But we are all together,' I said, beckoning Queenie to take her seat again. I followed. But again this usherette caught my arm. Enunciating as if speaking to an imbecile, she said, 'No, you. You have to go up the back. She and him can stay there.'

'But there are plenty seats for me to sit here.' I was whispering so as not to disturb the other people's enjoyment of the film.

'But it's the rules,' she said.

'Rules, what rules?' She had me confused now. The orchestral music from the film was howling as wind does on a runway. Queenie, looking to me, was half in and half out of her seat. The woman behind her told her to sit down. From somewhere I was told to shush. I apologised. Instead of sitting down Queenie once again backed along the row to where I stood with the quarrelsome usherette.

'What's the problem, Gilbert?' she asked. So tumultuous was the music she looked to Arthur, fearful he might have thrown himself to the ground.

'He has to go up the back,' the usherette said.

'But there are seats here,' Queenie responded.

'I just tell her that – she say it's the rules.'

'Rules, what rules?' Queenie asked.

I quieted her with a hand placed gently on her arm – I would take care of this myself. 'You sit, Queenie – I soon come.' Then, turning to this usherette, I asked the same question, 'What rules?'

It was then she took her torch to shine its searchlight beam up to the back rows of the picture house. For the briefest moment she ran her light along the faces sitting there. Queenie would not have seen: she would have asked, 'What? What are you showing me?' But I saw. As startling as exposing a horde of writhing cockroaches, that light, although searching for only a second, gave me an image that seared indelible into my mind's eye. It flashed across lines of black faces, illuminating the heedless and impassive features of a large group of black GIs enjoying the film.

'You have to sit with them.'

'Madam,' I told her, 'I am not an American. I am with the British RAF.'

'You're coloured.'

Queenie was back. 'What are you talking about?'

'Coloured, he's coloured.' She shone the light once more to the back rows, this time holding it there so Queenie, puzzled at first, would gradually come to see. Caught by the beam, some of the men seemed to awaken with the light.

'This is England,' I said. 'This is not America. We do not do this in England. I will sit anywhere I please.'

'Well, we do it here. It's the rules. All niggers—' She stopped and began again. 'All coloureds up the back rows.'

'Why?' Queenie asked.

'Because that's their seats.'

'No! Why do coloured people have to sit where you say?'

'Our other customers don't like to sit next to coloureds.'

'Who are these other customers? Yanks?' I asked.

'They won't sit next to you.'

'What other customers? Who?' I was shouting now.

'They don't like to be all mixed up.'

'Americans?'

'Not just Yanks. Anyone.'

'We'll sit next to him – he can sit between us,' Queenie offered. I wanted so to be pleased that this sweet Englishwoman was speaking up for me. But, come, Queenie's good intentions were entirely missing the point

'In this country I sit where I like.'

'Then you'll have to go. It's up the back or nowhere.'

153

'Madam, there is no Jim Crow in this country.'

'Who?'

'Jim Crow.'

'Well, if he's coloured he'll have to sit at the back.'

'Segregation, madam, there is no segregation in this country. I will sit wherever I like in this picture house. And those coloured men at the back should have been allowed to sit wherever they so please. This is England, not Alabama.'

Like air escaping from an overheating machine, the sound of shushing came at us from all around. Along with the impatient 'Be quiet, some of us want to watch the film.'

'You'll have my job. I don't make the rules. Other coloureds don't make such a fuss. It's up the back or nothing.'

And I told her, 'Madam, I will neither go to the back nor will I leave. My friends and I intend to enjoy the film from this spot.' My heart thumped so I feared the toe-tapping beat would be told to shush. Cha, nah, man – is bareface cheek! We fighting the persecution of the Jew, yet even in my RAF blue my coloured skin can permit anyone to treat me as less than a man. I turned my back on the usherette, indicated for Queenie to sit and went to take my seat next to her.

It was an American voice – solid as thunder – coming from a few rows in front that called out to me, 'Sit where you're told, boy.'

I ignored it.

'Hey, nigger, I said sit where the lady tells ya.'

I sat myself beside Queenie. This GI stood up – his silhouette rising like a mortal tempest before the screen.

'Look, we don't want any trouble,' the now tearful usherette pleaded.

'Nigger, do as you're told,' the GI shouted.

'And you can put a sock in it,' Queenie replied, standing up. Her fierce finger wagging.

'Nigger, move.'

'And you can shut up with your nigger,' Queenie said, 'I prefer them to you any day.'

A woman's voice called, 'You tell 'em, love – ruddy loud-mouth Yanks.' I did not have to look, I could feel the edgy stirring in the back of the picture house as someone shouted, 'Shut up, whitey. We ain't taking that no more.'

The air trembled with the muttered grumblings from the rest of the audience while a white GI yelled, 'Stand up, nigger.' From the back came a harmony of voices shouting, 'Who you calling nigger? Who you calling nigger?'

'Jigaboo suit you better?' another voice called from the front.

'No, it ain't,' came the volley of reply.

The usherette fled, calling, 'I'll have to get the manager – we don't want trouble,' while Queenie, still ranting at these white men, said, 'You can sit down, what's it got to do with you?'

'Shut up, nigger-lover,' the man answered.

'Please sit down, Queenie,' I tried, but she had long ceased to hear me.

'Any time over, you lot,' she shouted.

And again a female voice said, 'Tell 'em, love.'

Two GIs from the front began to shift along their row, forcing others to stand to let them out. I was ready for them.

A woman called to the GIs, 'Hey, leave him alone. Big bullies, the lot of you.' There was chuckling from the back. 'Man, the woman gonna whop ya.'

Another white GI stood up to tell me, 'Just move, boy, and we can all get back to watching the movie.'

'Stay, man, stay,' came a chant from the rear.

'Where's the blinking manager? I've not paid to watch this.' Many people were on their feet now – I could no longer see the screen. Until, without warning, the film went off and the lights came up.

As if painted by a master, this technicolour tableau of a room simply froze. Why? Because everyone saw. Rows of black GIs at the back. Rows of white GIs at the front. And a rump of civilians in their dowdy clothes sitting guileless in the middle. Now there were a few women sitting with the white GIs and some uniforms in with the civilians but, as sure as Napoleon and Wellington before Waterloo, that usherette had drawn us up a battlefield. And every GI was now on his feet.

155

Black shouting: 'Who you calling nigger? We ain't taking that from you no more.'

White screaming: 'Fucking uppity niggers. Shut your mouths.'

'You gonna make us, whitey?'

'Fucking right we'll make ya.'

While the locals, with the trepidation of picnickers before a stampede of bulls, looked one way then the other. The manager came running on to the stage arms waving like a drowning man. Trying to be heard above the din he yelled, 'Everyone is to leave the theatre. Please leave this theatre in an orderly fashion now.' Adding when no one seemed to be listening, 'We'll have no trouble here – the authorities have been notified.'

A white GI galloped over seats towards the back. He tripped and fell into a row pushing two women who, domino effect, stumbled. Two black GIs jumped the rows to reach where the man lay. Women crying, 'Get off,' mixed with the savage hollering of male battle cries. As the fool manager enquired if everyone might just 'Please calm down and leave by the exits at the back.'

Queenie put her hand in mine, nails clasping tight as talons. She held Arthur the same way – him baffled, looked to be wondering if he was still watching a film.

'Come on, come on, you want it, nigger?' A black man was running from four whites while several more black men chased them. The ground tremored under their big boots. I found myself envious – man, I was ready to bash someone today! Only when I tried to release Queenie's aching grasp a little did I recognise that this woman was not seeking my protection. No, Queenie Bligh believed herself to be safeguarding me. Over on the far side a white GI had a black man by the scruff, yanking this bent-double man round, beating upwards into his face; the two men growled, zealous as warriors. A woman set about this brawl, her handbag flailing. Soon both these burly army men were ducking her blows. Until she found herself tripping and falling as three more GIs – one black, two white – waded in. Man, how her friend screamed! People came running, 'Get off her! Get off!' till all were caught up in this thrashing.

For the rest of us panic was pulling us along – an irresistible tide dragging everyone to the doors. Even black and white GIs struggled through the opening together in a brief moment of wholly unwanted integration. I lost Queenie in this crush, my hand torn from her grasp.

Ejected into the not-quite-dark light of a cold evening, everyone in the street looked to be wondering how in the devil they find themselves outside. I was pushed. Struggling to keep my balance, fist ready to whack the culprit, I turned and found a little woman – reaching only to my waist, I swear. 'This is your fault,' she said. 'You're nothing but trouble.' She pushed me again.

'Madam!' I blew with as much authority as my size could muster – if she pushed me again how was I to stop a very small, feisty woman humiliating me?

'It's you that started this.'

'Madam,' I began, but she was gone, rattling through the crowd like a laxative. Man, it was hatred raged in these men's eyes not anger! Tell me, if you build a bonfire from the driest tinder, is it the stray spark you blame when the flames start to lick?

But, oh, boy, what a strange battle this was. The pavement held women putting on headscarves, pulling at small boys to stay close, looking around for friends calling out, 'Vera, over here, come on, love, let's go.' Others moaning in huddled groups, 'It's a bloody disgrace . . . You don't see our boys behaving like that . . . Should save their energy for the Germans . . . War's not won yet and never will be with this lot.' While straggling down the centre of the road groups of GIs – strictly segregated black and white – stood shrieking taunts at one another. 'Come on, nigger you want it, come on . . . Kill the goddam son-of-a-bitch . . . This ain't Mississippi, you gonna have to come shut my mouth . . .' The black GIs, outnumbered a little by whites, sounded to be short of insulting names. How could the harmless 'whitey' heat the blood and jangle the nerves as the established 'nigger', 'jigaboo', 'sambo', and 'jungle boy' did? 'You wan' it, nigger? You gonna get it . . . Fucking son-of-a-bitch you're a dead man . . .' These US comrades buttoned into the same green uniform for a fight against foreign aggression were about to start their own uncivil war.

Perhaps it was the sobering cold in the night air or maybe the locals observing this Yankee feud. Who knows what ferment had been raging inside the picture house but out here it was clear the passion for this fight was gone. These hothead men were now throwing punches that reached no one. Lashing out only into the no man's land between them. Sticks and stones flew, parting the group where they fell, but only vicious words hit their mark. A white man was grabbed. Struggling fierce as if caught in a crocodile's jaw he freed himself to run back behind his lines. Receiving a kick on the backside and taunts of 'We kick your ass. We kick your ass, white man.' The black men laughed. This clash was becoming no more than a venomous ballet. On both sides men had begun to walk away. A small boy even ran between the groups. 'Any gum, chum?' he said, thinking only, GIs and chewing-gum. I, looking around for Queenie and Arthur, thought to offer to escort them home.

But then the whistles started. Sharp as needles, an orchestra of whistle, whistle, whistle ripped at the air. Galloping horses, I thought it to be galloping horses so many boots ran on the stony ground as the American Military Police, their white caps bubbling like foam, gushed on to the street. Surprise caught many men open-mouthed – stunned motionless. Batons raised, these fearsome MPs assailed the group of black GIs. Defenceless skulls cracked like nutshells as panicked black men had nowhere to go but stagger towards the furious boots, fists and elbows of the white GIs. Oxygen to a dying flame, these MPs soon had this fight blazing again like an inferno.

Someone jumped on my back. The wet stone ground rose to smack my head as this sack-of-coal weight toppled me. The blow to my ear rang like church bells. A powerful hand gripped rigid at the back of my neck ground my face on to the stone floor. My cheek scraping raw against wet grit, I struggled as I had never struggled before. This was no Elwood playing rough on me – no one would soon jump up, laugh and declare it my turn. Rage lent me the force to free myself. Lurching over, I took a belt full in the mouth but still I toppled this man from me. Losing his balance, the ugly white GI fell backward – spite buckling up his face. My whack to his head landed so hard his eyes crossed comical with the blow before we two, rolling now, embraced as intimate as lovers. Tearing away I aimed a punch for the soft of his belly – hitting the solid of his ribs instead. Striking once more his belly sank like a cushion as air expelled from him with the force of a fart. Him, still not beaten, lunged to bite my ear. That piercing pain lifted me straight to my feet. Shoving him back down I kicked where he clutched his stomach and stamped on his foot.

As spores to the wind everyone was scattered before the MPs. GIs, black and white, pitched missiles with the force of athletes. And still the MPs came. A white man drooling bloody spittle was slumped against a ladies' outfitter's window. A woman stooping before him was shooed away as three MPs yanked, tugged and poked at this leaden man to stand. Two small girls, clinging to each other as tight as the two halves of a peanut, stood shivering and crying. As an older boy yelling, 'Mum, Mum!' pushed wild at anyone who came too close to them. A white GI whacked a black man's head against a wall. This black man leaked blood – it spilling as dense as crimson cloth down before his eyes. Him ran blind – bumping the wall to avoid an MP's baton blow. A white GI pushed to the ground felt four pairs of boots running over his back before two black men kicked him. Like rags on the ground this fallen man bounced with every blow.

A flying bottle shattered at my feet – me, hopping graceless, felt its splintered shards patter my cheek. My uniform filthy and ripped at both shoulders, my shirt collar sticky, my tie missing – an MP overlooking my RAF blue, concerned only with the colour of my skin, raised his baton ready to charge me. It was a shot that stopped him. One shot from a gun. Did I hear it with my ears or just sense it as every uniformed man ducked low – the trained reflex crouching us all? Another shot. Civilians this time caught still. Like the call of an approaching mother that destroyed the frenzy of my boyhood games, all players in this nasty pastime examined each other in a moment of complete, resounding hush that summoned the question: What is coming next?

Come, let us face it, it was curiosity that saw me walking fast down that street to where a crowd was gathering. No thought of valour, no thought of gallantry and, let me tell you, no thought of Queenie pulled me to where the shot had sounded. Hear this. Only when I heard Queenie's voice yelling, 'Arthur,' did I once again recall that I had had companions that day.

An MP was howling, terrified for everyone to 'Stay back! Stay back!' This runt of a man, eyes mesmerised to the ground, gun still smoking and careless in his hand, flicked it to hold people away from the sight. A man lay shot at his feet. And I knew it was Arthur Bligh even before Queenie began beating at this MP's back – slapping round his head, tearing off his cap. Screaming, 'Arthur! Let me get through . . . it's Arthur! What d'you do that for? It's only Arthur!'

He had been shot in the jaw, his head burst an obscene inside-out by the bullet. I tried to move closer to Queenie – scared this fool MP she was berating could again prove careless with his gun. But the white caps and the galloping boots of the Military Police once more flowed in from every side. This time their batons raised in a line across their chests, they rammed us with this makeshift barrier. 'Back, stay back – everyone stay back. Move on. Come on, get back there!'

Our inquisitive group was impelled, slipping and tripping, backwards. I could no longer see her but I called out to Queenie as an MP, his baton thrusting hard into my chest, his face pressing close to mine, hot breath breaching my cheek delivered the words, 'Get away from her, nigger.' Only now did I experience the searing pain of this fight – and not from the grazing on my face or the wrench in my shoulder. Arthur Bligh had become another casualty of war – but come, tell me, someone . . . which war?

Eighteen

Gilbert

A group of boys jumped lively from the dock into the sea. Gangly arms and legs black against the fine blue sky they soared for a moment like an explosion of starfish. They dived to catch the coins thrown for them from the side of the ship by the first-class passengers. A uniformed band from the First Jamaican Battalion played we returning West Indian RAF volunteers down the gangplank and on to the dock. Who knows what tune they were performing for a thief of a breeze carried this welcome off into less deserving ears. Some of the men wept to feel home under their feet at last. The Blue Mountains folding on the horizon, Kingston dappling in sun and shade. Heads turned, drinking in the curiosity of this well-known vista now unfamiliar to them. Standing to attention for the last time the governor, dressed in his colourful finery, wished us all well. He promised us two months' pay and our discharge papers, then thanked us for our valuable military service. We were demobilised.

I carried home with me the tatty yellowing cuttings from the newspaper. 'London Man Killed in US Army Incident', the headline proclaimed. Letters in the paper asked how many of these ructions the British people were meant to suffer before the US military authorities took their boys in hand. It was a big story — thought a terrible accident. Picture of a distressed Queenie —

mistakenly considered the victim's daughter. Another of Arthur: composed, pipe in hand, this old photograph showed a young English gentleman. At fifty-four I had thought him an old man. Arthur Bligh, it was reported, had been unfortunate to receive a bullet fired with the intention of quelling a vicious brawl. According to several newspapers, GIs about to be posted overseas were angry when the film show they were watching broke down. On evacuating the picture house a fight had ensued. The MP, carrying out his duty, fired a warning shot into the air. The second shot aimed likewise at no one was accidentally diverted when the MP stumbled. It hit Arthur in the head – to be precise in the left jaw – killing him instantly. The funeral was attended by immediate family and a representative from the US Army. An obituary stated that a son, Bernard, was in the forces overseas under the SEAC command. There was no more word about what happened to the MP; there was no reporting of a trial. A letter appearing in a newspaper hinted at the segregation and bad treatment black GIs received from their fellow countrymen. It went on to congratulate we British for being more civilised.

I was posted the day after the incident – moved to Cornwall that very next morning. Then Scotland. Then Filey. Then Cornwall again. I had written to Queenie – several letters, each one taking me care to compose. How was she recovering? Was she well? Might I not be allowed to visit with her? No replies came. If, in my wildest imaginings, I believed that the military authorities ever puzzled over this West Indian RAF volunteer, then I would conclude that my postings were intended to keep me as far from Queenie Bligh as was possible.

I had waited two years since the war's end for a ship that could carry me back to the island of Jamaica for a hero's return. Standing through victory parades in England, countless men had slapped my back, joyfully telling me that I could go home now. No more shivering with winter cold – my teeth would have no reason to chatter. Let me forget the dreadful sausage and boiling potatoes. The barracks and the Naafi. And, no, thank you, I do not want another cup of tea. Bring me back sun and lazy, hazy heat – curry goat, spice-up chicken, and pepper-pot soup. Let me meet pretty black-skinned women, round and shapely, ready to take my arm with pride. Let me look upon faces who knew me as a small boy. Come, let me suck me teeth again among kin.

But instead of being joyous at this demob I looked around me quizzical as a jilted lover. So, that was it. Now what? With alarm I became aware that the island of Jamaica was no universe: it ran only a few miles before it fell into the sea. In that moment, standing tall on Kingston harbour, I was shocked by the awful realisation that, man, we Jamaicans are all small islanders too!

As if Mummy had been shaking out her apron strings I found that all my sisters had been scattered, four of them married and journeying to America before the wedding flowers had even lost their bloom. The three with no rings on their fingers had found Canada beguiling – one nursing, one teaching and one a hopeful who-knows. In Chicago Lester was a big man in construction. Excited as a child before Christmas, Mummy was eager to make plain that Lester had no reason to return to this small island. For despite the young boys who came hurrying from all over the district – eager to set their eye on me, a real soldier, returning from war, to have me bark fierce commands that they, enthusiastic, struggled to obey while parading round with their makeshift guns – Mummy and Auntie May looked pity on me for the misfortune of finding myself once more back in their yard.

The shortages of war and money for celebration took a monstrous bite out of their business. Mummy and Auntie May no longer spent their days on cakes but had now turned their talents to the decorating of their hats. These hats were being readied for a journey that would see them visiting all their exiled offspring in America and Canada. Flowers and fruits, bows, feathers and net were expertly attached to plain and old hats so these two blessed women might attend christenings, church services, graduations, house parties or weddings in full hatted dignity. Cheerful, they declared that this lovingly prepared-for trip around North America was a mission that could take them a long, long, long time. While Daddy, frail and old, rocking on the veranda, sipping a sorrel drink laced so potent it could kill a bull, dozed drunkenly, unaware he was about to be abandoned.

✳　✳　✳

'So what, you no study the law yet, man? Me think you come back a judge.' Despite his words it was obvious Elwood was pleased to have his boyhood friend home. 'You no tell me the Mother Country no keep their word? Cha, nah, man, you wan' me believe the English are liars?' He laughed so hearty at his own joke, I observed that he had lost several teeth since I last looked down his mocking mouth.

Now, what taunt would my cousin have found if I had told him what had occurred when I had endeavoured to study the law while in England? The Colonial Office had rehabilitation courses designed to see us West Indian RAF volunteers prepared for Civvy Street. Man, I know a chance when it is before me and here was one ripe for picking. Come – the law was on the list. I did not place it there, they did – up there among accountancy and medicine. I made my application. But, let me tell you, so many heads shook I began to think all at the Colonial Office had a nervous tic. Tongues tutted that this common aircraftman should have ideas so high above his station. 'The law!' Their eyes laughed as they looked this Jamaican dreamer up and down. My cousin Elwood's wicked giggling would have done him a mischief if I told him what they offered me instead. Bread-baking. A good profession, plenty jobs. Cha! Bread-baking! How could I tell Elwood this tale without this returning RAF man appearing a complete jackass?

'You come back at the right time, man,' Elwood told me. 'You stop run round to those fool-fool English – we gon' lick them. Nothin' gon' stop us now.'

As a growing boy, I thought Elwood my brother. Cricket in the dirt, climbing in trees, fishing in the river – no childhood memory appears without him. We were ten when his mummy, Auntie Corinne – trailing sweet perfume and dangling the deeds to a little plot of land near Kingston – arrived, telling everyone she now had the money to take back her son. It was a long moment that had me, Elwood and Lester worrying which one of us she had come to snatch. Elwood cried a puddle to find his mummy was not his mummy but his aunt, his brothers were his cousins and instead of the seven sisters he had none. Only Daddy had a word of comfort for the poor wailing boy – he told him that he could now rest easy because he was certainly not Jewish.

'They think they keep us happy with this pickney constitution,' Elwood told me. 'We grown men. No more likkle crumbs from the table. We sit and feed ourselves now, man.'

While I was busy with war Elwood had lost most of his coconut, banana, guava, ackee and pimento to a hurricane. This tempestuous wind carried off his livelihood to land its harvest in who knows where? Cuba? The stumps of banana trees still left secured in the earth caught Panama disease. The coconut trees whose leaves still stretched in the sun developed lethal yellowing disease. During the days his mummy watered these feeble plants with an obeah woman potion, while Elwood sat an evening vigil over them among the rat-bats. But still they died.

'Manley get us the vote,' Elwood said. 'But him know you caan eat a likkle cross on some paper. To put food on de table we mus' govern ourselves. Gilbert hear me nah – no more white man, no more bakkra. Me say get rid a Busta too. Him too licky-licky to the British. Jamaica mus' have jobs. Man mus' work.'

Elwood had had to find work, any sort of work, to keep him and his mummy from the devil's jaw. Burying cattle, digging gullies, fixing up damaged houses, loading ships. And hear this – even serving the English tea and dainty sandwiches at the cricket club. Bedecked in white uniform my cousin had had to incline his head in submissive civility while raised hands clicked their fingers for his service. Yet nothing could shake Elwood's obstinate faith in Jamaica. Nothing could infect his dogged delight in his beloved island.

'Man, you come back at the right time,' he said. 'You ready to work? Let me tell you, Gilbert, forget the law. Come, I have a likkle business notion for you, make us plenty money.'

He handed me a ragged, worn-out copy of a book, Lawson's, *Honey Craft for Pleasure and Profit*, its title in faded gold almost unreadable. Elwood's exhilaration dimmed only a little when I eager said, 'Man, good idea! Jamaica will need this – publishing and printing our own books.'

'No, man – tending bees.'

'Bees?'

'Plenty money in honey,' he told me.

165

Oh, how the words tripped from Elwood's impassioned mouth. Tumbling and twisting over each other they juggled to cajole me that this was a chance that simply could not be missed. Demonstrating his one hive, which sat lonely behind the house, its wooden walls vibrating with a dark cluster of quivering bees, 'It more of a business expansion,' he explained. 'I know where me hand can lay on plenty more.' Urging me to dip my finger into a little jar of golden honey, he said, 'Taste – tell me it not the sweetest nectar ever pass your lip.' Arm on my shoulder, mouth close to my ear, he tell me, 'Me have a man not far – everyt'ing him sell. Him gon' live in Scotch land or some fool place. Him have twenty hive – brood chamber and plenty frame each. Everyt'ing there – bottle feeder, smoker, veil. And every one bursting a bees. Young queen and everyt'ing. And so many jar it look like factory. Him make 'nough money get him backside far from here. Gilbert, I can see the Lawd smiling on us and pointing Him finger on those hives.' He gripped me tighter with one arm while the other he used to point at the air. 'Come, money flying around us, all we mus' do is catch it.' I looked on nothing as he told me he would need my demob money to make the purchases. 'Man, it jus' for all the likkle bits and pieces.' Elwood was to look after the bees, Auntie Corinne was to take care of the cleaning and filling of jars, and me? 'You do the business, man. First it pay you back plenty time over, then everyt'ing split between you and me. Me teach you everyt'ing me know. Soon we build up. This only a beginning, you see – soon we sell to all the shop on the rock.' And he nodded gravely when adding, 'An independent Jamaica will need men like us.'

Come, tell me, how long did it take him to win me? 'Is a businessman you will be, Gilbert. Not a lawyer, no, sir, not a judge – but, mark you, not a farmer. A businessman – done up in fine suit and everyt'ing.' You would think I gave Elwood the keys to life itself when I handed him the money. Were they tears in his eyes or was it just the smarting of the woodsmoke in the evening air? 'Me no mess with ya, Gilbert, you me brother. Me gon' see you a prosperous Jamaican man. Come, nah – soon we click our finger and a white man come running.'

Sitting high on a cart being pulled by a mule it occurred to me that perhaps I had accidentally woken to find myself back in the dark ages. It was

Elwood suggested, 'We can take the mule to pick up the hives. Save us money, man. More profit for you and me, eh?' Old women bent on leaning-sticks were waving as they overtook us on the road, while this wretched mule, under a glory of flies, found something tasty to nyam on the ground before it, or dally undirected to take in a view or just stopped to muse perhaps on the meaning of life. A year before my return Elwood had swapped his old truck for this draggle-tailed creature. He was pleased with the deal – a whole mule for a broken-down truck that had to be removed from the farm in several hundred rusting pieces. However, it soon transpired that this one mule was in fact two creatures. At the front end, by its slow blinking eyes and black fat nostrils, you could pet its placid, docile head and feed it from your hand. But should you find yourself at its rear end you would meet a kicking, bucking wild beast there. Auntie Corinne was convinced a fiendish duppy had made its back legs its home. But perhaps its duplicitous character was because this mule, who I took to be male, had been given the name Enid. So while I sweet-talk Enid's front end, Elwood attached the cart before the back end realised. But we had been gone two hours and could still see the roof of the farm we had left, before Elwood yielded, saying, 'Come – me have an idea. We go see Glenville to get a use out of his truck.'

In the RAF in England I had shovelled coal with hands itching with chilblains until my palms were raw meat; I had pushed, pulled and dragged whole aeroplanes through mud; I had lifted mechanical parts that were bigger than a man yet still I had breath in my body to hum a song as I worked. But here I huffed and puffed like an old crone and grumbled, peevish and petty, like a lordly city boy, because, man, I had never known hard work like it. I was fooled by Elwood – I thought my gangly, skinny cousin would snap in two if the load was too heavy to lift. But any exertion made his stick body swell, rounding and erupting with robust muscle sturdy as a stallion. I had no chance to keep pace with him when every bone in my body just cried, 'Gilbert, come nah, man, let us lie down now – we hurt.'

We lashed all the hives with rope to move them. Careful as lifting a bomb we delicately placed these flimsy, weighty wooden boxes on to the borrowed truck. Elwood whispered, 'Hush, hush, soon come – not long now,' to the curious bees inside. Unloading them he shouted rude at me, 'Careful, man, watch it, easy, boy, easy.' Any time, he warned, any time the bees could swarm. We laid out these buzzing boxes – Elwood heedful to make every last one lay straight on the stony land, bending low like an artist to test the angle of each against his thumb. 'Bring me wood, Gilbert ... get me stone nah ... lift ... hold it ... hold it ... no ... back ... stop.' Twenty-two hives were placed with the same care. It took us hours and Elwood, looking on the rows of shabby grey weather-worn hives, proudly proclaimed them a kingdom of bees, (come, I thought them more a shanty town). Veiled as a bride, Elwood lifted a frame from a hive that squirmed with a confused layer of black bees. While I, defenceless and nervous, stood still as death, desperate to believe his assurance that an unmoving body will not be stung. Blowing smoke to calm the tormented ones, he checked that none were too crowded, none were too hot and a queen still ruled over every box.

In the evening light I sat to eat a mango alone under the refuge of the guango tree. Worn out – most of my muscles still twitching from the unaccustomed activity and yet too tired to sleep. Luminous white smoke from fires drifted ghostly through the dense green. Enid chomped loud on his favourite crabgrass. I could hear Aubrey in the neighbouring farm whistling to call his cows to take them to their night meadow. A black dash of crows flew home against the sky. A tree lizard scuttled up the bark licking grubs with its lightning tongue. Cicadas hissed rhythmic as cymbals. The sparks of fireflies buzzed my head like thoughts escaping, while dots of bees returned to the hives, oblivious they were now working for me. This was a beautiful island. As sweet with promise as the honey that would soon flow from the combs. I stuck my fingers into the soft earth that yielded under them. If I held them there long enough, surely this abundant country could make me grow.

Tell me, who could blame Enid? My belly had been grumbling impatient for some time – tormented by the sweet fragrance of the chicken Auntie Corinne was frying and the cornbread she was baking. Elwood glanced up from his newspaper when the mule, smelling the food, brayed with the pierce of a baby's cry, to be fed. Useless, he slowly said, 'Enid, soon come, nah, man.' The fence that confined the mule was flimsy. How many times had Elwood and I looked to each other to promise, 'We must fix up that enclosure'? Tomorrow, the next day, perhaps the day after that? Let me tell you, it was Enid's furious back end decided this neglect was enough. How long did it take Enid to break down the fence? We did not hear as Auntie Corinne had just laid before us a plate of succulent, spiced fried chicken. She slapped both our hands from the meat and followed that with a grumpy order for us to wait before returning to the kitchen. Elwood and I were quietly busy: a wing each of the too-hot-to-hold-chicken in our hands, we were pulling at the flesh using only our teeth, fanning our mouth to cool while all the time watching for Auntie and telling each other to shush. We only heard Enid when Auntie Corinne screeched crimson for us to come. The mule had entered the field with the bees.

As if dislodging an imaginary rider the mule's back legs thrashed uncontrolled at the air. The first hive crumbled like a biscuit under the falling hoofs. And a fuzzy balled dust of black bees rose from the debris.

'The windows – come, close all the windows!' Elwood was alive with panic and command. 'Gilbert – move nah, man, close the doors, the windows!' One, two, three more hives just dissolved under the mule's blows, leaving the hovering homeless bees to seek out the culprit. Attacked by enraged bees eager to defend, the mule's eyes rolled white and wild with the pain of the stings. Crazed now, it rampaged through the field unwittingly flattening each hive like skittles. The angry bees, amassing to a black smoke, trailed the bucking mule before entirely enveloping it. I was standing still because if you stand still you cannot be stung. 'Gilbert, you wan' see us eaten alive, man?' Elwood shook my shoulder as he struggled to pull on his veil and tuck up his clothes with gloved hands. A doodlebug – that's where I had heard the sound: the bees droned resonant as those flying bombs.

On slapping the windows shut this morbid hum died a little. But the bees, unsure who to blame for being rudely thrown into the light, became popping black spots against the window glass. Auntie Corinne fell to her knees praying very loud, 'Lord deliver us from this plague of bees . . . Lord deliver me son from this . . .' While with the same pleading tone that makes heroes of men whose hearts rip at the agonised sound, the mule howled so all for miles around would know that it was slowly being slaughtered. All the while its unwitting hoofs still found bees to vex.

Elwood was outside. Avoiding the mule he lit a fire with the frenzy of a speeded-up film. All the hives were now crushed and their fleeing contents, like soot, rose up to attach themselves surely to all parts of the mule. Auntie Corinne, awakened from her lament, was now ready to kill. Those bees that found themselves buzzing lost inside the house she whacked at with her broom. Knocking pictures from walls, ornaments from shelves, she chased them round like they were burglars, while the mule's squeals bounced its agony from every wall. I stupid hit about me with the rolled up newspaper as Elwood — the fire wafting sheets of white smoke he hoped would pacify — fanned his arms, demented. Enid was no longer a mule: the writhing bees covering him made him furry as a grisly bear. He squealing, circled the field round and round, kicking and shaking his head to flick the stinging bees from his ears, his eyes, his mouth. Was it an hour or was it a day that I stared while him, tortured, stumbled? A million bees piercing his flesh to fill it with poison. How long did I hear those heartbreaking strangled brays before the mule eventually fell, almost graceful, on to one knee? Then the other where he stayed awhile as if praying before he slumped, his whole body falling leaden on to the ground. Whining now, an occasional violent jerk shuddered his frame, his hoofs kicking as if still riding along the stony floor. Crawling with the savage bees, if it was not for his chest that still rose and fell you would think him an old louse-ridden fur coat lying discarded.

Not daring to go outside, useless, impotent, feeble as the frail, I watched as Elwood warily circled the dying carcass of his mule. And all our bees gone. Most dead and spilled on the ground, their tiny bodies ripped apart by the murderous stings. Others flown away. In swarms of black fury they launched themselves off on the breeze.

I laughed. What else could I do? I laughed when Elwood called this event a little setback. We lose the bees, we lose the hives, we lose a mule. I lose all my money. All that remained were jars full of sunlight. Was Elwood a fool or just plain mad? At that moment I could not tell. 'Come, man, you mus' have a likkle faith,' he said, brushing off the incident with a flick of his hand.

'We lose everyt'ing,' I tell him, 'What you wan' me have faith in?'

'Cha, we no lose everyt'ing. There is still two hive and them bursting a honey.'

I had no words to speak that would not come out as a cuss.

'Cha, nah, man – don't give me big lip. No look on me so downcast – too much fog cloud up your blood in England. Listen up to me now, I have a likkle plan. We get a few of the boys – Aubrey, Glenville and some other – we go look for the bees. They no go far. Some hole in a tree them all fly in or they resting in some bush. We can find them, bring them back. Mark you, I know we no find all of dem, but enough to start again is what I'm saying to you.'

'You want us go find the bees?' I asked.

'You, me and a few of the boys.'

'Elwood, you think I am about to run round this island looking for lost bees?'

'Yeh, man. Then we can fix up some hive again. A likkle nail here and there – good as new.'

'A likkle nail here and there! Elwood, are you mad? Have you lost your mind?' I stunned him and startled myself with the temper of this shout. He looked inquisitive on me, a little boy again, curious to know if this was real anger or just foolery. 'Elwood, I will not run round this island chasing bees.'

'You have a better idea for me then, Mr Soldier Boy – Mr War Man?'

It was then I said, 'We cannot get a break in this place.'

'Cha, nah, man, you no hear me, nah? We can collec' up the bees. This is jus' a likkle upset. Tomorrow will be the day we start again.'

'Elwood, come, tell me, you know this is a small island?'

'What you chattin', man?'

'Listen, man. I have been in England, I have been in America.'

'So what?'

'There is opportunity ripe out there.'

'There opportunity here if you look right.'

'So why so many young men and women queuing up for passport? Why so many striking for job and busting up the place? Elwood, I have seen it with my own eye. The world out there is bigger than any dream you can conjure. This is a small island. Man, we just clinging so we don't fall off.'

'You chattin' nonsense, man.'

'Everyone movin'. The time is right.'

Eyes wide with impact, Elwood said, 'But come, now me see – you gon' go licky-licky to the British.'

'I need opportunity, Elwood. I need advancement.'

'You wan' go back a England.'

'I can't get a break here, man.'

'Why you no come to a meeting with me? Me show you the future being suckle and nurture there. An independent Jamaica gon' take care of us.'

I had been to several of his meetings. Angry young men, not enough money to put decent clothes on their backs or keep their teeth from rotting in their heads, fighting with each other over this tiny scrap of land. Squabbling over who will get the fifth quarter. Man, they wrestling over who their next master is going to be.

'When we get rid of the white man—' Elwood began.

'Stop! Elwood, you no see? When you get rid of the white man is a coloured man you will have to fetch for instead.'

'I fetch for no one. Black man will rule.'

'You a dreamer, Elwood.'

'And you a Jamaican. You born a Jamaican. You die a Jamaican. Jamaica mean nothing to ya, man? Why you wan' leave?'

'Why not?'

'Oh, and I am the dreamer. How you gon' get England? You need money. You gon' swim or maybe you slip in some rich-lady bag make her carry you?'

'I don't know – but I mus' try.'

'Why? Why you wan' the whole world when ya have a likkle piece a hope here? Stay. Stay and fight, man. Fight till you look 'pon what you wan' see. Man, fight for your own country this time.'

'Elwood, I tired of fighting.'

Looking on me like I was a stranger who had just appeared in his yard, he said nothing while he leisurely shook his head and sucked his teeth. Then lifting his eye away from mine, he quietly began, 'Ah, Gilbert, me know you would do this. Me know you would wan' go live Babylon. Me know you nah stay here. You wan' ask me how I know? Come, let me tell ya, Gilbert. You may look like one of us but not'in' gon' change the fact your daddy is a white man.'

I was a giant living on land no bigger than the soles of my shoes. Everywhere I turn I gazed on sea. The palm trees that tourists thought rested so beautiful on every shore were my prison bars. Horizons my tormenting borders. I envied the pelican, I envied the crow – with wings they could fly easy from this place to rest in some other. I became a big-talk man – even when the clinking of small change in my ragged pockets accused me of being a fool. Oh, there were plenty men like me, wandering this small island, their head cluttered with the sights they had once looked on. If you would listen then we would talk – widen your eyes with stories of war and the Mother Country. Tell you of bombs, planes, bullets and guns. Fog and snow and autumn mist. Come, ask a question you have always wanted to know. The King – oh, a fine man, and Shakespeare too. Paved with gold, no – but, yes, diamonds appear on the ground in the rain.

When my mirror could only return to me a look of disgust, a dainty girl like Celia Langley, who would gasp excited at my traveller's tales, puffed me proud as a prince. I had no thought of courtship, my only need was her adoration. Entrance her, dazzle her. Come, let me tell her those truths, those lies, those half-baked dreams.

But with Hortense my feet landed on solid ground with such a thump my ankles nearly snapped. How come this woman who was inches shorter than I could look down at me from so high a height that I felt like a dwarf? Oh, she was pretty – a golden complexion that left a faint blush of pink at her rounded cheeks. Eyes flashing alive – brown and wide with lashes that flapped like butterflies' wings. And her lips could have been soft and charming if not always pinched tight with vexation or lifted haughty about the corners to show her disdain. Man, when she doubted the truth her eyebrows would raise so high on her forehead they looked to be blown there by the wind. How did this woman learn to sneer so? Was it through bad odour or was she always smelling her top lip? Even her ears could cuss you. Come, let us face it, my big talk just shrivel in the face of her scorn.

She did not like me. My face distressed her, my jokes confused her, my tales of war bored her and talk of England made her yawn. So I thought she was messing with me when she offered me the twenty-eight pounds and ten shillings I needed for a passage to England. 'I can lend you the money,' was all she said. She followed it with no explanation. Man, I do not recall that she even smiled. I laughed – a sort of giggle you make when someone is having a joke you do not find funny. But she just stare on me in so serious a way it led me straight to wondering how I might pay her back. Excited now, I decided that every week I would send her money. A little at first until I find me feet, then I would build it up. Sometimes more, sometimes less, but regular until this woman was paid. I would write it down in a little book so no argument would occur. My honour would see the debt was paid. Hear this, I even thought to slit my finger to seal the deal in blood. But she had not finished with me yet. With no persuasion, with no fancy words, with no declarations of love, she let me know that I would have to marry her for the money. This woman was looking for escape and I was to be the back she would ride out on.

When I walked away from her that day I went to sit under the refuge of the guango tree. Tree lizards still scuttled up the bark and the cicadas still hissed like cymbals. But the ground was now parched and dry – too hard for me to push my fingers down into the earth. And it was there that I wept. I am not too proud to tell you I sobbed like a boy lost. I was beaten. There was no choice before me except one. If Hortense had money to buy me then, come, let us face it, my price was not too dear.

Nineteen

Gilbert

You see, most of the boys were looking upwards. Their feet might have been stepping on London soil for the first time – their shaking sea legs wobbling them on the steadfast land – but it was wonder that lifted their eyes. They finally arrive in London Town. And, let me tell you, the Mother Country – this thought-I-knew-you place – was bewildering these Jamaican boys. See them pointing at the train that rumbles across a bridge. They looked shocked when billowing black smoke puffed its way round the white washing hung on drying lines – the sheets, the pants, the babies' bonnets. Come, they had never seen houses so tall, all the same. And what is that? A chimney? They have fire in their house in England? No! And why everything look so dowdy? Even the sunshine can find no colour but grey. Staring on people who were staring on them. Man, the women look so glum. Traffic turning their head this way and that. Steady there, boy – watch out. Look, you see a white man driving a bus? And over there, can you believe what the eye is telling? A white man sweeping the road.

But this old RAF volunteer had seen it all before, during the war. So I was looking down, unlike them big-eyed newcomer boys. I just arrive back in England and there on the pavement before me I spy a brooch. What a piece of good fortune, what a little bit of luck. Lying lost, this precious oval jewel shimmered the radiant iridescent green of a humming-bird caught by the sun. My auntie Corinne would have raised her hands to the heavens to call it a sign.

Now these were the thoughts that passed through my head in the three steps it took me to reach that brooch. One: perhaps it fall from a young woman's coat. Cha, so my blessing was another's misfortune. Two: it was an old woman that lose it from her purse; maybe the police station was the proper place to take it. And three: Hortense — this deep-green brooch would look so pretty on her. I conjured an image in me mind. See me take the sparkling brooch to pin it to her dress, near her neck, against her smooth nut-brown skin. And look, see her touch the pin then tilt her head to charm a smile on me.

So all this rumination is taking place as I move closer. I was about to bend my knee so I could reach the brooch when hear this . . . it flew away. Black flecks suddenly pitting the air. That jewel was no more than a cluster of flies caught by the light, the radiant iridescent green the movement of their squabbling backs. My eyes no longer believed what they saw. For after the host of flies flew they left me with just the small piece of brown dog's shit they had all gathered on. Was this a sign? Maybe. For one of the big-eyed newcomer boys walk straight along and step right in the muck.

Sleep in a room squashed up with six men and you will come to know them very well. Not because they tell you why they leave Jamaica or pine for the sweetheart that stay behind. You learn nothing of mummies, or schooldays, and hear no hopeful dreams for their life in England. No. What you come to know more intimate than a lover is the sound of every sleeping breath they make. Take Winston: every night him call out the words, 'Gimme nah.' His twin brother Kenneth sleep slapping his lips together as if sucking on a melon. Eugene and Curtis snore. Both sound to your ear like a faulty rumbling engine. But if you shout, 'Hush nah, man,' Eugene will obey while Curtis will rev up. The breath from Cleveland's open mouth smell as if it come from his backside, and Louis spend his night scratching himself and his morning wondering why his skin raw.

This old RAF volunteer had slept in barracks with many more than six men and everyone know war is as hard as life can get. But sleep in this tiny malodorous room, step over three beds to sit on yours, watch as one boy jumps out of his bed to go to work and another returning from work jumps in to take his place, have this man shush and cuss you because he needs to sleep while you try to dress to look respectable for another day, try shaving with no water and sucking cornflakes so the crunching does not disturb and you will swear those days of war were a skylark.

But still breezy from the sailing on the *Windrush* these were the first weeks for we Jamaicans. And every one of us was fat as a Bible with the faith that we would get a nice place to live in England – a bath, a kitchen, a little patch of garden. These two damp cramped rooms that the friend of Winston's brother had let us use were temporary. One night, maybe two. More private than the shelter. Better than the hostel. Two months I was there! Two months, and this intimate hospitality had begun to violate my hope. I needed somewhere so I could start to live.

So how many gates I swing open? How many houses I knock on? Let me count the doors that opened slow and shut quick without even me breath managing to get inside. Man, these English landlords and ladies could come up with excuses. If I had been in uniform – still a Brylcreem boy in blue – would they have seen me different? Would they have thanked me for the sweet victory, shaken my hand and invited me in for tea? Or would I still see that look of quiet horror pass across their smiling face like a cloud before the sun, while polite as nobility they inform me the room has gone? Or listen as they let me know, so gently spoken, 'Well, I would give it to you only I have lots of lodgers and they wouldn't like it if I let it to a coloured.' Making sure I understand, 'It's not me – if it was just me I'd let you,' before besmirching the character of some other person who, I was assured, could not bear the sight of me. Man, there was a list of people who would not like it if I came to live – husband, wife, women in the house, neighbours, and hear this, they tell me even little children would be outraged if a coloured man came among them. Maybe I should start an expedition – let me trace it back and find the source of this colour bar. Go first to that husband, then to that wife, the woman in the house, the neighbours, the children. When each of them tell me it not them but the next man I move on. Eventually the originator of this colour prejudice would have to stand there before me. And I could say to their face, 'So, it is you that hates all niggers, I presume.'

It was desperation that made me remember 21 Nevern Street, SW5. From that little scrap of paper I first read in a field in Lincolnshire many years before. And from envelopes carefully addressed in my neatest hand. Who knows? That house might have been nothing more than a gap in the road where neighbours still talk of the rocket hit. A stranger might have come to the door to ponder long on who lived there before. A vexed husband's fist might have been all that I would see. But it was not just my feet that were too sore to care.

Trepidation trembled my hand as I rang a bell that did not work. I knocked. It was Queenie Bligh who answered. And again she looked on me as she had done when we first met. For the count of two seconds she thought I was someone else. Then she called my face to mind and said, 'Well, if it isn't Airman Gilbert Joseph. Now, what the bloody hell happened to you?'

1948

Twenty

Hortense

He woke me rude, this man, shaking on my shoulder. 'Come,' he said, 'I make you a cup of tea.' It was not the rousing that most alarmed me but the white smoke that came puffing from his mouth like he was the devil himself. 'I must get to work now,' he said, as smoke wafted from him as sure as if his inside was fire. I seized the cover to me. 'I no touch you. I am going to work.' As I raised my head from the pillow I saw breath come as a curtain of vapour from my own mouth. Only as I felt the pinching of the cold on my exposed cheek, sharp as acid, did I remember that I was in England.

'Cold today, eh?' he said. Awake now, the covers too flimsy, my body began to shiver. 'Come, drink the tea – warm you up. I must get to work now.' He put the cup on to the table. A glance to the window told me it was still night time. This man never said he worked during the night. He pulled back the ragged curtain but it made no difference to the light – only excite a draught of chill to nibble on my other cheek. 'It's morning,' he told me.

'Morning?' I said.

'Yes, it is nearly seven o'clock.'

But there was no sun – not even a feeblest shadow. How the birds wake in this country and know when to sing? Gilbert rouse them with a cup of tea? 'It's too dark,' I said.

'It is winter. Always dark on winter morning,' he told me. The man sat heavy in the armchair to lace up his shoe. 'It get dark early too,' he said, although he was not addressing me but thinking loud. 'Most of the day dark. Sometimes if you blink you can miss the whole day.' I stretched out my arm for the tea but the cold threatened to take the skin from it, so I replaced it quickly back under the cover.

'I put on the fire for you,' he said, wrapping himself in this big dark coat. 'But if it go out you must put money in the meter. You think you can do that?' I did not give the man an answer, merely turned my head from him. It was not I who was the fool. 'I will be back at six o'clock. You think you can fix me up a little something to eat? There are some eggs and potatoes in that cupboard by the sink. You can make some chips for me?'

He said it so plaintive I almost felt sorrow for him. 'Of course,' I told him. Then he was gone.

Twenty-one

Gilbert

It was with trepidation that I had learned to pass by Queenie's door. That last flight of stairs saw me like a criminal stepping lightly in my socks. Balancing, I swear, on one toe alone so I did not make noise enough to rouse her. It was early morning – not even the birds had sensed a new day – and I am approaching her door so light, my feet are feeling no floor, just hovering above lino.

'Gilbert,' I heard her call. Man, this woman's hearing so good she must catch the sound of the stitching rustling in my socks. 'Is that you, Gilbert?' To avoid her I would have to float down from my window on angel's wings.

'No,' I called.

'I can tell it's you,' she told me, her face now at the door.

How? I wanted to ask her. Tell me how, in God's name, she always knows when I am near? 'Queenie, I am just off to work. You wan' me be late?'

'Won't take a minute.'

Luck is a funny thing. To some only a large win of money at the pools is luck. Or finding a valuable jewel at your feet on a London street. That surely is luck. But during the war luck take another turn. The bomb that just miss you is luck. Only your leg blown off and not your head is luck. All your family die but your mummy is spared – congratulations, you a fortunate man.

So, let me tell you what luck is for a coloured man who is just off a boat in England. It is finding Queenie Bligh. It is seeing she has a big house and is happy to take me and a few of the boys in as lodgers. Greater than sipping rum punch from a golden bowl – that is luck England-style.

Early days and Queenie was still that pretty blonde woman who friendly leaned across a table to share a rock bun with me. And though no longer dressed in uniform, I was still, even in my plain suit, one of the boys in blue. Happy to have me around her house, she made me tea. We, sipping the drink, would talk. All that business with her father-in-law: 'That's all in the past,' she told me. No need for me to worry. And her husband: 'I don't know what's happened to him but I've got to get on with my life, Gilbert.' She needed my help – a woman on her own. She wore me out. Jumping steps and laughing like a girl as we moved furniture around the house so she might let the rooms. Let me tell you, every night in those early days I slipped to my knees to give thanks at my good fortune and cuss those hastily taken marriage vows. Meeting up with Queenie Bligh was the best luck this Jamaican man had ever had.

Then Winston and Kenneth moved in. The rent Queenie charged us made me clean my ear to ask again. Three pounds a week each for these rundown rooms? Winston and even Kenneth gaped dumbfounded as she assured us she had no choice but to charge that sort of money. Then with the first week's rent I delivered to her on Saturday morning she told me someone kept the door open too long. The next day she wanted me to know someone shut the door too loud. Something smelling up a room. Someone making too much noise. I must tell the boys not to leave on the light. Have I told the boys to keep their room clean?

'Cha, me thought you say she your friend. So why the woman act like bakkra?' Kenneth wanted to know.

We must not come in too late. There must be no one in the rooms without permission. Can we step over the second step on the first flight because it creaks? 'Gilbert,' she told me, 'I'm relying on you to keep them all under control.'

Was I her caretaker now? This woman start vex me so I think her husband a sensible man to lose him way between here and India. Man, if there was a way I could disappear before her, come see me grasp it.

'Was that Kenneth who helped you with that big trunk last night?' she ask me.

Once I could not tell a lie. But to this new Queenie, and my abiding discouragement, I had now become skilled in the art. 'No,' I tell her.

'I don't want that Kenneth here, Gilbert. I don't mind Winston. But I can't tell which is which. I don't want Kenneth here. I don't trust him. He's sly. And I've had Mr Todd round complaining about this and that.'

'No worry. That was Winston help me with the trunk.'

'You sure?'

'Of course – why would I tell you a lie?'

She look in my eye. Then, 'How's your wife? Why didn't you meet her?'

'I am late for work now. I must go.'

'Hang on a minute, Gilbert, there's just one thing . . .' she say. This one thing could be 'Come dig up the garden for me.'

'I must be off,' I tell her, presenting her with my back.

'Won't take a minute . . .' she call out.

Discourteous it may be but I am gone.

Twenty-two

Hortense

I hoped that Celia Langley could no longer see me. Where was she now? Sipping fruit punch and fanning herself in sunlight. While here was I on my first morning in England, shivering with goose bumps rising large as hillocks and my jaw aching with the effort of keeping my teeth from chattering. I never dreamed England would be like this. So cheerless. Determined, I held my breath but still I could hear no birdsong. The room was pitiful in the grey morning light. I thought it tumbledown last night but daylight was happy to show me more of its filthy secrets. Plaster missing from a bit of the wall. Jagged black lines of cracking everywhere. A missing handle on the chest of drawers. No basin in the sink. And there were lacy white patterns on the windowpane. Frost. I was taught by my headmistress, Miss Morgan, that frost is to be found on the outside of a window in England, but my curious finger got fastened to this stuff. Sticky with cold it melted under my warm fingertip on the inside of this room! For the useless fire roared with fierce heat only when I stood right on top of it. One inch, that was all, one inch back and the heat no longer reached me. Two inches, and I was in need of my coat. Three and it was as wintry as on the street. This room would not do. I could hear Celia Langley laughing on me. 'The Lord surely moves in mysterious ways, Hortense,' her mocking tone exclaimed.

186

But I paid her no mind. I opened my trunk. The bright Caribbean colours of the blanket the old woman had given me in Ochi leaped from the case. The yellow with the red, the blue with the green commenced dancing in this dreary room. I took the far-from-home blanket and spread it on the bed.

Miraculous — it was then I heard a bird sing. Oh, so joyful. Finding colour through a window its spirit rose to chirrup and warble. 'Don't laugh on me, Celia Langley,' I said. 'Just watch me, nah.' I determined then to make this place somewhere I could live — if only for this short while. For England was my destiny. I started with that sink. Cracked as a map and yellowing I scrubbed it with soap until my hand had to brush perspiration from my forehead. Pulling the stinking tin potty from under the bed, 'You next,' I told it. But then there was knock on the door.

I ceased all movement — not even my heart dared a beat.

'Anyone there?' a voice said.

I made no reply. However, my held breath was preparing to choke me. The knock came again.

'Anyone in there?' It was the woman from downstairs. The landlady who had the evening before looked on me in a very rude manner. 'Just like a word. Can you open up?' Politeness and good breeding left me no choice. I opened up the door a little way.

Her face, coming close to the opening, smiled. 'Just came to see if you're all right.' Her hair so blonde put me in mind of Mrs Ryder. That woman driving a car in her feathered hat as Michael watched her pass. But at once I put the thought from my head. I was in England now. That day was over.

'Gilbert gone to work?' the woman asked me. Her head was straining like a curious cat's, moving this way and that trying to get a good look into the room. 'I'm from downstairs. Remember me? I let you in last night? Hortense, isn't it?'

I did not wish to appear rude to this woman on my first day in England so I acknowledged her questions with a small nod of the head.

'Cat got your tongue?' she said. What cat was she talking of? Don't tell me there was a cat that must also live with us in this room. 'My name's Mrs Bligh,' she carried on. 'But you can call me Queenie, if you like. Everyone here does. Would you like that?' The impression I received was that she was talking to me as if I was an imbecile. An educated woman such as I.

So I replied, 'Have you lost your cat?'

And this woman's eyes rolled as if this was a question I had asked of her several times before. 'No,' she told me, too forcefully. 'In English it means that you're not saying very much. Everything all right, though? I just thought I'd come and have a word with you.'

I did not wish to appear ungrateful as the woman was obviously trying to be kind, even though she had me confused with this cat business. I opened the door wider for her before she thought me impolite. I merely meant for us to talk through a larger opening. But she walked straight through, even though I had not formally invited her in!

'Oh, you're tidying up a bit. Men, eh – they've got no idea.' She perused the place as if this was her home. Pushing her nose into corners, she walked the room as if inspecting some task she had asked of me. Alighting upon the sink she said, 'Bit cracked, isn't it? Still, you're keeping it clean, that's good.' Now, as she was the landlady and at that moment viewing the sink, I thought to take the opportunity to ask something of her. 'Excuse me,' I said, 'but would you perchance have a basin that I might get a use of?'

'A what?'

'A basin,' I repeated.

'Sorry.'

'A basin to put at the sink.'

'A bee – to put what?'

'A basin.'

'I'm sorry but I don't understand what you're saying.'

I thought to say it again slower but then remembered an alternative that would work as well. 'A bucket,' I said.

'A what?' she started again.

It was useless. Was I not speaking English? I had nothing but the potty to point at instead. But she would surely misunderstand that. And who knows where that confusion could take us? So I hushed my mouth.

'Where did you get that thing?' she said, pointing at my blanket. 'It's so bright. You need dark glasses for that.' It obviously amused her. She began a giggle. 'Did you bring it over with you?' Moving past the blanket she went to warm her hands on the fire. She bent over closer to the flame. 'It's perishing today. I bet you wished you never left somewhere nice and hot?' When I made no reply she looked to me and mouthed the words, 'Cold today,' as if I might have lost my hearing. 'When it's cold,' she went on, 'we say it's "perishing". Perishing cold. It's a saying, like the cat got your tongue.' She turned back to her hand-warming while telling me, 'You'll soon get used to our language.'

I told this Englishwoman, 'I can speak and understand the English language very well, thank you.'

And she said, 'No need to thank me.' But I had not meant it to sound grateful. Still she carried on: 'I'm sure there's a lot I could teach you, if you wanted.' And then she sat down on a chair and invited me to come and sit with her. But this was my home, it was for me to tell her when to sit, when to come in, when to warm her hands. I could surely teach this woman something, was my thought. Manners! But then I questioned, Maybe this is how the English do things when they are in England? So I sat.

'That's right – sit down.' Did this woman think I did not understand the injunction, sit down? 'You don't say very much, do you?'

I held my tongue. Forbearance prevented me informing her that what I do say she does not appear to comprehend.

'So how long have you and Gilbert been married, then?'

The barefaced cheek of the question sucked all the breath from me. Did she want to know all my business? I just look on her and wait. Soon this white Englishwoman must realise she is talking ill-mannered to me. But she say it again. This time in that slow way, as if I did not grasp her meaning the first time. But she tricked me. If this woman was to realise that I am an educated person then surely I would have to answer her enquiry. Cha.

'Gilbert and I have been married for nearly six months,' I said clearly.

'Six. Six months?'

'That is what I said,' I told her, with vowels as round as my cheeks would allow.

'What, altogether? You've only been married six months?' I nodded. 'But Gilbert's been here about five months.' Then, tipping her head, she looked on me playful. 'Ah. You're newly-weds, then,' she told me.

'I suppose so.'

'Did you say "I suppose so"?' she asked, amused. 'You don't sound too pleased about it. But Gilbert said you hadn't known each other long.'

Oh, he did, did he? How typical of that rogue man to spread our business for everyone in England who want to hear. But I said nothing.

'I knew Gilbert during the war,' she went on. 'Did he tell you?' She might want to know everyone's business but I was taught prudence – especially with a man who believes a gold tooth to be appealing. She began shifting on her seat, which caused the chair to creak so I thought it would collapse under her. But she paid this shabby furniture no mind. She folded her arms, then unfolded them. She took a breath then gave out a faint 'Ohh' as if a pain had stabbed her. A dainty pattern of red patches flushed on her cheeks and neck. I worried she would want a drink of water next for I was not sure there was a glass. But she was not distressed. She just brushed a blonde curl behind her ear and carried on as before.

'He didn't say, then?' she asked me. I did not reply. I was weary of this conversation and I had work that I had only just begun. At last the woman raised herself slow from the seat. 'Well,' she said, 'if you want anything I'm just downstairs. Just call down.' Politely I stood to follow her to the door. Suddenly she looked on my face as keen as a child who needs you to join in their game. 'I could show you round the shops, if you like. Show you where to get things.'

Pity had me soften. 'Thank you,' I said.

But this excited her. 'No, don't thank me. It's no trouble. Be nice to have some company.' I was nodding and smiling like a half-wit while all the time opening the door so this woman might leave me in peace. 'Do you have pictures . . . films . . . where you come from?' she wanted to know. What, this woman think Gilbert spill me from a bottle?

'Of course we have films – cinema,' I told her.

'Do you like them?'

'I have always enjoyed the films of Shirley Temple,' I said.

The woman laughed so raucous I swear the window rattled. 'Shirley Temple, I haven't seen one of hers for a bit. Imagine you getting Shirley Temple where you come from!'

Again I did not reply. 'Well, we could go if you like – to the pictures.' And again she took my breath from me. Is this woman wanting to be friendly or is she wanting a friend? I was confused. What class of white woman was she? 'Well if you want to go to the shops or anything I could show you how to use your ration book. It's easy but takes a bit of getting used to.' Then she looked upon me, puzzled. 'Can you understand what I'm saying?'

'Of course,' I said, quietly.

'Good. Well, give me a knock and I'll let you know when I'm ready to go out.' She then took her hand and placed it on my arm. She leaned in too close to me to whisper, 'It's all right. I don't mind being seen in the street with you. You'll find I'm not like most. It doesn't worry me to be seen out with darkies.'

Now, why should this woman worry to be seen in the street with me? After all, I was a teacher and she was only a woman whose living was obtained from the letting of rooms. If anyone should be shy it should be I. And what is a darkie? I held the door polite for her and once more said, 'Thank you,' in the hope this would move her more promptly through it.

'You don't have to keep thanking me.'

She had misunderstood again. But then I remembered there was an urgent thing I needed to ask. Something that had been troubling me since Gilbert pulled the door behind him that morning. Now was my chance. But I waited until she was outside my door in case she had a mind to turn and sit back upon the seat. I said, 'Excuse me. I will ask you something if I may? Can you perchance tell me . . .' I raised my head to look upon her in the eye and asked, 'How do you make a chip?'

Before

Twenty-three

Queenie

I was christened Victoria Buxton. My mother had wanted me to be christened Queenie but the vicar had said, 'No, Mrs Buxton, I'm afraid Queenie is a common name.'

'Common!' my mother had replied. 'How can it be common? It's a queen's name.' The vicar had then given an impromptu sermon, which my mother, father and their gathered guests had to listen to as they stood round the stone font in our bleak local church. The vicar went on at length about monarchs having proper names like Edward, George, Elizabeth while everyone, dressed in their pinching church-best shoes, shifted from foot to foot and stifled yawns behind their scrubbed hands. 'Take our late queen,' the vicar finally explained, 'her name, Mrs Buxton, was not Queen but Victoria.'

So that was how – one thundery August day in a church near Mansfield, dressed in a handed-down white-starched christening gown that wouldn't do up at the neck – I, the first-born child of Wilfred and Lillie Buxton, came to be christened Victoria yet called for ever Queenie.

My mother, Lillie, was an English rose. Flaxen hair, a complexion like milk with a faint pink flush at her cheeks and a nose that tipped up at the end to present the two perfect triangles of her nostrils. She was a farmer's daughter and had hands that could clasp like a vice, arms as strong as a bear's and hips that widened every year until even the old men on the village green agreed they were childbearing.

My father, Wilfred, was a butcher – the son of a butcher, the grandson of a butcher and the great-grandson of a butcher. Father was ten years older than Mother and not very good-looking. Some said it was his good luck at courting and winning the hand of a lass who had once won a village country maid contest that had left his face with that startled 'You don't say' expression. The front of his hair was cursed by a 'cow's-lick' which meant that every day it fell in eccentric wild swirls over his forehead. His bulbous fat hands were like great hams. Broad, pink and fleshy with stubby fingers. He wore leather straps round each wrist to protect them from the sharp blows of his butchering knives. I thought those straps held his hands on to the ends of his arms. Leather and three inches wide, they only came off when he had a bath on alternate Saturday nights in front of the range in the kitchen. I had to bring the hot water that rolled black grime down his skin like mud washing off a wall, while the leather straps would be on the floor, still in the shape of his wrists. Blackened manacles – worn, battered and bloody. I never looked at the front of him in the bath in case I saw stumps where his fat ham hands should have been.

There was a shed on our small farm, out of the back door, across the yard and round a bit, where Father did his butchering. Carts from the cold store, driven by young boys whose aprons were splattered and smeared with dried blood and who smelt acrid like vinegar made from rotting flesh, would come into the yard and dump the carcasses of slaughtered cows, sheep and pigs. Father carried them over one shoulder into the shed. And with sharpening, slicing, chopping, grunting, slopping noises, cattle were turned into topside, rump, sirloin, best rib, chuck, shin, brisket, silverside, lambs into leg, loin, best end, neck, breast, shank end, chump chop, cutlet, scrag end, shoulder, and the pigs were turned from snuffling muddy pink porkers that had been fed every morning on swill boiled up in a copper into heads, feet, hind, loin, knuckle, fillet, belly, spare rib, blade bone. Or salted, cured and smoked in an outhouse for bacon. The bits that had no name were squeezed into sausage skins, extruded and twisted as Buxton's finest pork sausages. All the offal –

the liver, the kidneys, the hearts — was packed on to trays. The fat was rendered down in a cauldron and set into lumps of lard. And anything left after that was stuffed into a mincer. The bits that had fallen on the top of the table were finest beef mince and the bits that were swept off the floor were not. Father always dreamed of having sons. Sons who could sharpen, slice, chop and carry. Sons who would replace the stupid boys he had to hire who stole cuts of meat when they thought he wasn't looking, stuffing them under their caps and down their shirts.

When I was born the midwife came out of the upstairs back bedroom, wiping her hands, saying, 'Well, Mr Buxton, I'm pleased to say you have a lovely daughter.'

At which Father slapped his forehead, slumped on to the stairs and groaned, 'God, this'll be the death of me.'

Mother had wanted a daughter, someone who could help her out just as she had done with her mother. She got out of bed at four every day, sprinkled clouds of flour over the kitchen table and prepared the hot-water-crust pastry for her pork pies. She kneaded it on the scrubbed wooden table, rolling and slapping the dough into shape, her knuckles pressing pastry the colour of babies' bottoms until it was made malleable, adding more flour, banging and stretching it round a wooden form, then thumping it into the baking tins ready to take the pork meat that Father handed her every morning in a bucket. When the pies were baked, steaming and golden, the rich pork-bone stock was poured through a hole in the top of the crust and left to set into a marble jelly.

Mother could craft her pies without looking down at her hands. This left her time to watch the dozy girls who came up from the village to help her. She could direct them to open the oven quicker, wash up the pans cleaner, pass her the flour faster, without losing a moment of pie time. 'Hurry up, I'll need to put the tops on these pies,' Mother told the dozy girls every morning, no matter how fast they went. Then, after that, tea was made — for the stupid boys and Father, who came in rubbing his bloody hands down his apron before cupping them round his old chipped mug. After two mugs of sugary tea Father directed everything to be loaded on to the van. He and Mother ran a shop that sold everything they produced on our small farm. The pies, the meat, the sausages, the bacon were all driven down to the shop where Mother and Father spent the day serving their 'blinking fussy' customers.

Years before I was born an envelope was pushed through the door of the butcher's shop. 'Wilfred Buxton', it said, written in a child-like script with capital letters where they shouldn't be. Father thought it was someone paying their bill. They all owed him. Most of his customers had stuff on strap that they paid off at the end of the week. Mother said he was a soft touch but he liked to think that he understood his customers – if he didn't give on strap they'd go elsewhere, he'd say. So Father casually opened the envelope and a white feather fluttered out and circled gently down to the ground.

He was alone in the shop but he was being watched. He'd never thought of joining up, of fighting in the war. He was a butcher. If he joined up who would supply the meat? The war seemed so far away, nothing to do with him, just names in the paper, pictures of young lads and a lack of good men to work round the place. But his customers – probably the fancy ones who bought the topsides on Sundays then ham *and* turkey at Christmas, or was it the miners who ate scrag end and pigs' heads? – obviously thought that fat butcher's hands like his could be put to better use strangling the Hun.

Mother complained when he went away to the army that the two boys he'd hired to replace himself were skinny and ill. 'Too young for Kitchener, and too young to be any good to me,' she said.

Father went south. Three weeks later there was a rap at the back door of the farmhouse. Mother opened it to see Father standing there. 'The army won't have me,' he told her. Turned out he was too old and had a weak heart. Three bouts of childhood rheumatic fever left it murmuring loudly. 'I'm not bloody fit enough to be shot,' he moaned. That night, Mother prayed that if she ever had a son he'd get rheumatic fever because, she reasoned, it might keep him alive a little longer.

I was looked after by an assortment of girls while Mother wrapped sausages, sliced bacon, cleaned blood from counters and chatted over a pound of black pudding in the shop. These girls were daughters of miners who worked for a few weeks, then argued with Mother about a job not done or something gone missing. They were sent packing and another one hired. These girls would wake me up and get me out of bed, feed me warm milk and biscuits, wipe a damp cloth round my face, dress me. One of them used to pinch my arm hard – she liked to hear me squeal. Another refused to wipe my bottom after I'd done a number two. A spotty girl with cross eyes used to slap me when I laughed and squeeze me when I cried. And the big lass with breasts like two stolen cushions used to scare me to trembling with her tales of the small boys she said Father cut up in his butchering shed. I never learned these girls' names. 'They're only miners' daughters,' Mother told me. She called them all 'Girl', and they were that stupid they never seemed to notice.

I was six when Mother became pregnant again. She'd held off having 'bothersome childbirth' by breast-feeding me until I was old enough to ask, 'Mum, can't I have milk from a cup?' Or she'd flush herself out with a mixture of water and vinegar, which she squirted inside her using an old rubber forcing bag that looked like a cow's udder. But then one day she was sick over the smell of her pork meat and said that the jelly stock looked to her like scum on the top of a blocked drain.

The midwife was delighted when she came from the back bedroom to tell Father, 'You have a son, Mr Buxton.'

But Father just said, 'About bloody time.'

The next year mother gave birth to two more sons – twins.

That birth had Father moaning to the midwife, 'Twins! Bloody hell! They'll castrate me.'

There were three sons now: Bill, Harry and Jim. And by the time I was twelve I was my mother's little helper – the filler of pies, the ladler of jelly, the person to whom Mother snapped, 'Hurry up, I'll need to put the tops on those pies.' After pie duty I got my three little brothers out of bed. I wiped a cloth round their faces, fed them warm milk, cleaned their bottoms, combed their hair with water – one by one daubing down the cow's licks they'd all inherited from Father. Then I changed the sheet that little Jim always seemed to wet in the night and slapped all three of their heads just in case. Then one morning I went to wake little Jim and found the bed wet, not with his usual wee-wee but with sweat.

Mother got her wish. Rheumatic fever the doctor pronounced. Little Jim turned scarlet and complained that his wrists hurt. Mother screamed, 'I didn't mean it,' as the body of my little dead brother was brought out of the room in a wooden box.

He was buried in the churchyard, and as the coffin was lowered into the ground Harry, his twin, shouted, 'Queenie, we can't leave Jim down there, it's all dark. Jimmy don't like the dark.'

And I told him, 'Don't be daft, he's dead.'

The doctor gave Father a bill for three visits and a death certificate. Father slapped his forehead as he read it and groaned, 'We'll all be in the workhouse by Christmas.'

I knew from the first day that I ever walked into Bolsbrook Elementary School that I was a cut above the miners' children. Miners' children had snotty noses and grime round their faces that was so worn in they would need to be soaked in a bucket overnight to get it out. And a lot of them didn't even have shoes. Reginald Watkins came to school in girls' boots with paper stuffed inside instead of socks. And there was another boy, Wilfred Allcock, whose dad had been killed in a pit accident. This was obviously sad, him losing his dad and the body not being found for days. And I joined in when all us children sympathetically tapped Wilfred on the back during playtime. But I couldn't see how it entitled him to turn up for school every day wearing a pair of his dead dad's old football boots with the studs taken out.

They used to follow me round the playground, these miners' children, wanting to know if I had brought one of my mum's pies in for dinner. When I had I'd show it to them. I'd turn it round in the air – the brown crusty pastry, the pink jellied meat. Then I'd take a bite and lick the crumbs from my lips. 'Ooh, it tastes lovely,' I'd say. I liked to see them all unconsciously miming chewing, closing their teeth round air as I ate. And then they'd plead for a bite, 'Go on, Queenie, give us a bit, go on. Be your best friend.' When I saw my soft brother Harry sharing his pie with Wilfred in his dead-dad's-boots I hit him round the head and told him not to do it again. And Harry whimpered, 'But he were hungry, Queenie, he were hungry.'

Our school teacher's name was Miss Earl. It was only behind her back we called her Early Bird. Early Bird slapped children for scruffy work and appearance. She whacked the backs of hands twice with a ruler for daydreaming. Three times for opening your eyes during prayers. She shook children for dawdling or not knowing their times tables. She knocked heads together for talking out of place and used the cane liberally for answering back.

Our classroom had neat rows of dark wooden desks and was heated by a coal fire that often had a motley assortment of steaming wet boots lined up in front of it. Early Bird used me for all her errands: I was the tallest in the class and a butcher's daughter. I collected the register from the headmaster and took it back when Early Bird had ticked all the names present and correct. I gave out the pens, the nibs and filled all the inkwells with watery blue-black ink. I led every queue for dinner and playtime. And I fetched wool from the village shop when Early Bird had us all knitting blankets and scarves for missionaries and starving black babies. When a message needed to be taken to the headmaster, Early Bird's twitching finger always beckoned me out to the front.

'You're a sensible girl, Queenie Buxton,' she'd say, before she handed me the message on a folded piece of paper. Sometimes I ran for most of the day performing errands – missing out on sums, copying from the board, grammar, spelling, even hands-on-head time.

'What's the point of the lass being at school when there's work to be done around here?' It was three weeks after Father had said that to Mother that I left Bolsbrook Elementary School to work on our farm as a skivvy – the outside-inside-three-bags-full girl. I was fourteen with a large bust that my brother Billy always yelled, 'Crikey', at when I had a bath. I knew how to read and write, add, subtract and divide but, in all honesty, not much of anything else.

After Mother and Father put me to work any fun I used to have on our farm came to an end. My brothers could still run down to the slaughterhouse and beg the slaughterman for the pig's bladder. They could still blow it up, kick it like a ball and watch it flop and fall all over the yard. They could jump around in the clouds of white down when the geese were being plucked or run into the fields when the beasts were chased and rounded up for slaughter. They could still hide their eyes as the pigs' throats were slit, coax the turkeys out of the trees before bedtime or follow the hide-and-skin man round taunting, 'Beardy, beardy, you're barmy – can't you join the army?'

But I wasn't a child any more. I was maid-of-all-poultry – scruffy apron, tatty headscarf with a scraper and bucket. While other girls were waving their hair and admiring their Cupid's-bow mouths in mirrors I took my bucket and scraper round poultry pens. Fat chickens eyed me up as they sat round squawking, pecking at the ground or tap-tap-tapping at wood. Feathers, sawdust and muck. I scraped the droppings boards to get rid of the revolting black and white crust the fowls left. My instructions were to scrape the boards clean, sprinkle them with sawdust, and change the water in the pens. And while other girls read love stories and dreamed of having a best boy, I had to find eggs – perfect, delicate, oval white forms sitting in the middle of all that filth.

The fertile eggs I hatched into fluffy yellow chicks. They arrived all shaky and curious into the incubator light, then their first faltering steps would drop them down into the under-half. I separated out the little bundles with beaks: the lanky cocks I set to one side to be fattened for Christmas, the females I led off for egg laying, which started the whole process again. I was pleased the year they got fowl pest. It was something different. I had to collect up all the scrawny dead birds with their swollen blind eyes, throw them into a barrow and take them to the boilerhouse for burning. Even though I woke up some mornings to find my eyes stinging and sealed shut with pus and no one to help me find my way to the kitchen so I could bathe them open with warm water, at least with most of the birds dead there were fewer eggs to find, fewer chicks to separate.

'Watch out for them miners, Queenie,' Father warned me every morning.

Miners came to the farm gates, bought half a dozen eggs then hatched them. They didn't pay the extra for a proper sitting of fertile eggs. Eggs to eat were cheaper than eggs for hatching. But I could tell by the way they carried them off. Little kids would be sent for eggs to eat. But grown men and women, carrying a sack with a warm lining, came up our path when robbing us Buxtons of our livelihood. They'd hatch our eating eggs, then keep their own chickens, collect their own eggs in their own backyard and stop calling at our farm gate. But Father soon put a stop to the thieving. He added another job to my list: pricking freshly laid eggs with a darning needle. 'Let them try hatching those,' he told me.

Even though the miners stole our eggs, Father still gave them Sunday meat on strap. Some of them ran up bills that could never be paid. And when the marches and the bad times came, little kids, like the ones I'd been to school with, would come to our back door and ask me if there were any scraps. Skinny, dirty children, with eyes sunken and skin as grey as a February sky as near as begging me for something to eat. I'd have chased them away and did sometimes. 'Go on, hop it,' I'd say. And they'd look at me with the same pitiful eyes as when I'd gobbled Mother's pork pies in our school playground.

Mother told me, 'They're hungry, Queenie, they're hungry,' before she found another chore for her maid-of-all-drudgery. I had to make soup. Over the fire with the copper that usually fed the pigs, I had to boil up bones and vegetables. I made soup for unemployed men who shuffled to the door in their dirty collarless shirts. Shivering in the cold, stamping their feet up and down in the yard, blowing hot breath on to their hands. Or waiting with their heads bowed not saying a word. One man ate right there in front of me, spilling fatty juice down his chin. The women that came said, 'God bless you, lass, and your mother and father.' But mostly it was children that were sent. Little kids without shoes who carefully carried their full cups and mugs and jugs back up the stony path. When Wilfred, who once wore his dead dad's boots, turned up he handed me his jug grinning, showing me yellow-stained teeth that pointed in any direction but down. 'All right, Queenie?' he said. He then had the cheek to ask me if I wanted to go for a walk with him. Not on your life. Any boy I was going to walk out with would have to court me in a collar and tie, with a freshly scrubbed neck and a wage packet about him.

I should have been going to dances, larking with men who had Clark

Gable hair and whispered in my ear that I was as pretty as an English rose. My legs should have been caressed in silk stockings, a pointed toe and a delicate heel on my shoe as I stepped from a car. I should have trailed lily-of-the-valley scent, my hair waved, my face powdered to porcelain perfection. I should have been a lady. But I was stuck on a stinking farm. Muck. Muck. And every day the same. Until one day Mother said, 'Queenie, go and fetch Father from the butchering shed.'

'No,' I said to Mother. 'Send one of the boys.' I never went into the shed where Father did his butchering. The shed where the sharpening, slicing, chopping, grunting, slopping noises broke in the air. Not since the big-breasted girl made me cry with tales of the small boys hacked up into pink paste. I kept my eyes shut tight and my ears covered when I was anywhere near the place where Father and the stupid boys went in clean and came out covered in blood. After all, it was no place for a lady.

But Mother made me go. 'And don't shut your eyes or cover your ears,' she said. 'You're old enough to know what goes on. Remember you're a Buxton.'

I could hear the noises before I could smell the sweet vinegar of meat and blood. When I opened my eyes I was looking at Father's back – broad and strong as a wardrobe. And by his side a small boy – but not any small boy, it was my brother Harry. Both of them wore boots, bloody boots, standing in a sludge of sticky gore. On the slab a beast's head was lolling, mouth open, lonely and dismembered. Feet away, its raw-red skinless carcass was mangled and split with clods of yellowed fat tumbling to the floor. Blue-white splintered bones, almost beautiful, were piled up in a ghastly heap. And there was Father, knife raised like a dagger. He was going to smash Harry. Splice the knife into his head and rip him in two. I screamed. Father turned round suddenly and nearly chopped his hand off. The leather strap saved it – skidding the blade away from the skin and bone. They both stared: Father saying something angry, Harry wide-eyed. It was then that I was sick all over my shoes. And the last I remember is Father rushing towards me with his knife still in his hand.

'Queen B', that was what Father started calling me. He liked to tell everyone about the day Queen B fainted in the butchering shed at the sight of blood. 'Soft lass,' Father said to Mother. 'How did you raise such a soft lass?'

After that I became a vegetarian. 'A what?' Father thundered at the table, 'A ruddy what?' Who'd ever heard of that? A butcher's girl who won't eat meat. A blithering turnip head. They did everything to get me to tuck away some bacon, to swallow the chicken's breast. 'Pull on the wishbone, Queenie?' But I wouldn't. Not even a pork pie when Billy turned it round in the air — the crusty brown pastry, the pink jellied meat.

'Our meat's not good enough for Queenie B,' Father roared, nearly every mealtime. He even banged his fist on the table, sending his dinner slap-sliding down the wall. And he whacked me hard around the head the day I tossed an apple core on to the fire. 'There's stock out there wants feeding,' he shouted, as he flicked the smouldering core back on to the hearth.

And I swear I heard an angel singing a celestial note as I looked up at him and told him, 'I don't bloody well care.'

It was not long after I'd shouted at my dumbstruck father that Aunt Dorothy came to visit. Mother's posh sister from London, who pronounced her aitches with a panting breath even when there were no aitches to be pronounced. She had come, she told me, with a whisper and wink, to take me away and better me.

Twenty-four

Queenie

In Herefordshire, Hertfordshire and Hampshire hurricanes hardly ever happen. My elocution teacher said the problem was that my mouth was too quick to stretch into a smile when I spoke. 'You'll never get on in polite society like that, Miss Buxton.' Tulip, dandelion, buttercup – I said them all wrong. Bottle, cup, saucer were not much better. My mouth was too weak, it needed discipline and Mrs Waterfall was the woman to give it.

'You won't go wrong with her,' Auntie Dorothy told me. 'She'll throw in deportment if she thinks you're worth it.' Head up, shoulders back – heel-instep-toe, heel-instep-toe. I had been walking all wrong since I was a baby. No sooner had she shown me how to do it properly than I started stumbling across the room like a cripple.

'How come bath should be said barth but fat is definitely not fart in high society?' I asked Auntie Dorothy.

She laughed but cautioned, 'Just do as she says, it'll come out all right.'

'And bank's not barnk and Mansfield not Marnsfield.'

'Oh, Queenie love, just do it. She'll see you married to a prince.'

I brought tears to Mrs Waterfall's eyes when I finally managed to extinguish the candle while breathing out the word 'what'. 'Hope,' she told me then. 'Miss Buxton, there is at last reason for hope.'

206

Auntie Dorothy swore the pink bit on coconut ice tasted different from the white – she knew everything about sophistication. She served coconut ice on a china plate, cut into neat squares, and ate it with a fork. Her feet up on a chair she called a French lounger, with her little poodle Prudence – coiffured into fancy shapes like a posh privet hedge – she delicately stuffed ounce after ounce into her oval mouth as I watched.

She'd inherited the sweet shop from her late husband Montgomery when he died in the Great War. Not in a battle – he was run over by a tram on his way back to barracks. Auntie Dorothy was still upset about the half-pound of treacle toffee that had mysteriously disappeared from his pocket by the time his dead body reached the hospital. 'Who could do such a thing, Queenie? Would you credit it? We live among barbarians,' she said.

She'd run the shop on her own for years. 'With Prudence, Queenie. That dog kept everyone in line for me. Didn't you, my little poppet?' But to get out of the French lounger for some little boy with a lazy eye and hair flying up like iron filings, wanting a chew that barely cost a ha'penny, began to try Auntie Dorothy's patience. 'Don't get me wrong, Queenie, it knocked baking pork pies day in day out, like my sister, into a cocked hat. But it's not what Montgomery would have wanted for me. I was his Duchess.' With no children of her own to help her, this was where I came in. In the big city, Auntie Dorothy had wanted to start calling me Victoria – it had more elegance as a name. I had my own bedroom, my own wardrobe and a dressing-table with three mirrors. If I angled those mirrors just right, hundreds and hundreds and hundreds of Queenies would appear, all smiling smugly at their good fortune. But not one Victoria was waving at me among that crowd. 'Don't worry, love, we'll stick to Queenie – it'll do till you're more genteel.' Auntie Dorothy loosened her corset the day I came to London to live with her. 'Oh, Queenie, I'll make a good catch of you,' she said, tightening mine.

Elocution and deportment lessons twice a week – Bourne and Hollingsworth or Selfridges for a new outfit every Saturday afternoon. At first Auntie Dorothy had come with me to Oxford Street, reclining on the shop seat telling the assistants how I took after her side of the family, all Lees being exceptionally graceful. But when the assistants began to scratch their heads trying to find things in her size – moving buttons, taking out seams – she stopped coming. She started pressing money into my hand instead, only bothering to get off the French lounger to put up the closed sign and measure out some more coconut ice.

I worked in the shop, woken every morning by Prudence attempting to scare off the newspaper delivery with a growl as terrifying as an old man clearing his throat. Men, rushing on their way to work, cast their eyes over my display of papers – neat with all the headlines on show – before choosing which horror they wanted to read about that day. After that it was mostly little kids, two or three coppers sweating their palms green, wanting some liquorice or a quarter of humbugs. As I got the bottles down and shook their favourites into a bag, I was followed round by eyes which, in that moment, loved me better than their mum.

I noticed him at first because he went for the *Mail* but then picked up *The Times*. 'Is it *The Times* you want?' I asked him. And he looked round like I'd just bellowed at him from the stars and blushed as pink as bacon.

'Did you say it right, Queenie?' Auntie Dorothy asked. 'Only, men for *The Times* will want to be spoken to properly.'

I was ready for him the next time. It was my best breathy voice, which would have plumped Mrs Waterfall proud, that said, 'We have *The Times*, if that is what you require?'

He gulped as loud as a stone down a well before saying, 'Thank you, I will take *The Times*.'

'What does he look like?' Auntie Dorothy wanted to know.

'Tall, skinny, not bad-looking,' I said.

She was watching for him the next time.

He tipped his hat at me as he left, 'It's a lovely day today,' he said.

That was enough to convince Auntie Dorothy, 'He has an eye for you, Queenie. I knew it as soon as you said he blushed.'

A lot of men came into the shop trying to make me blush. 'Aren't I sweet enough for you?' most of them got round to joking. Blowing me kisses and winking. Calling me their sweetheart, or their sugar-baby. Offering to show me how sweet they could be if I went with them to the pictures. Auntie

Dorothy just shook her head at those advances. 'The cheeky ones,' she told me, 'will be Cockneys. You'll want nothing to do with Cockneys, they're all jellied eels and knees-ups. No, that one's a gentleman. No spivs or ne'er-do-wells ever read *The Times*.'

He started coming in twice a day. Before every one of his visits – *The Times* in the morning and a half pound of something or other about quarter past five – Auntie Dorothy got off her lounger long enough to see me dressed right. 'What about that yellow cardigan, Queenie love? You look like an angel in that.' She'd check my face for newsprint smudges, taking her hankie and spitting on it to wipe my forehead or a bit off my cheek. You'd think I was going on stage the way she winked at me for good luck as she opened the door from the back room into the shop.

'Good morning,' says he.

'*The Times*?' says I.

'Thank you. A lovely day today.' Or variations like 'rather cloudy' or 'a little inclement for the time of year'. And I'd agree, no matter what his weather forecast. His gaberdine coat was always done up, every button, and the belt too. His shirt collar was always white. And when he lifted his hat, for that brief moment of hello or goodbye, his hair was shiny as liquorice. Auntie Dorothy thought him the nearest thing to a prince she'd seen since the day her late husband Montgomery adoringly looked up at her from one bended knee.

'Has he asked you yet?' she teased me, like a best chum at school.

'Asked me what?'

'You'll soon find out.' And I did.

A little boy, Sidney, was playing with some tin soldiers on the counter. They were all being executed by Sidney's firing squad, which was his two straight fingers, a squinting eye and a bang. My job was to flip the dead one over.

'It ain't 'im I shot. You killed the wrong one.'

I was just asking Sidney whether his mother wouldn't be wanting him home for his tea when the man came in. It was neither morning nor quarter past five and he had no gaberdine coat on. Sidney was lining up his victims again.

'It's time to go home now, Sidney. You can come again tomorrow.'

'I ain't finished yet.'

I swept up his blinking soldiers into a bag, threw in a piece of aniseed twist and said, 'Go on, hop it.'

After the sulking Sidney had slammed the door the man took a step forward. 'I wonder if you would care to come for a walk with me tomorrow afternoon, in the park – I've been assured it's to be a lovely day.' Straight out with it like he'd been practising and had to say it in a rush or his tongue would tie. My mouth was just dropping open with the surprise so it wasn't me who said yes, it was shouted from the back room by Auntie Dorothy.

'Good. I'll call for you at one.' And he went to leave but then said, 'I'm sorry but I don't believe we've ever been introduced. Bernard Bligh.'

I said, 'My name's . . .' and he smiled for the first time ever when he interrupted with 'Queenie – yes, I know.'

We'd been stepping out for about four months – every Thursday early evening, Saturday night and a walk on Sunday if it was nice – when I began to hate the back of his neck. It was bony and scrawny, looked more like the back of a heel with his ears sticking out like a knobbly ankle. And there was a vein on his temple that wiggled like a worm under his skin when he ate – just a little but enough to put me off my sandwiches, which we often packed up to eat in the park, by the fountains or under a tree. He had this way of screwing up his face as if he was wanting to dislodge a tickling hair from up his nose. He did it first when he met Auntie Dorothy. I had to ask her, 'Is it normal?'

'Didn't see it, love,' was all she said.

I don't know how she missed it – it made him look really queer. And he dithered over change. He was paying for a pot of tea and two pieces of Simnel cake at Lyons, going through his coppers, putting them in lines on the table, then counting them off into his hand. Then doing it again to make sure, while the waitress was standing looking at him like he was backward. Did it at the pictures too, holding everyone up while he rummaged in his trouser pocket, jiggling it to hear the change then counting out his ha'pennies and threepenny bits. A man from the back of the queue complained that he and his wife would miss the sing-song.

But Auntie Dorothy said he was a gentleman. She spent most of our evenings together explaining to me why. Did he or did he not open doors for me? Only a gentleman would do that. He walked on the outside of me when going down the road. 'You'll not get splashed by a carriage,' Auntie Dorothy told me.

'Auntie, when did you last get splashed by a carriage?'

'Well, a motor-car, then, or a tram. And don't be cheeky.'

He stood up if I stood up and wouldn't sit down until I sat down. And for two months all he did was shake my hand when we said goodnight. And when he did pluck up the daring to kiss me, he puckered his lips so tight it felt like kissing a chicken's beak.

'He don't talk much, Auntie.'

'That's good – you'd not want a chatterbox.'

But, crikey, he lived in Earls Court with his father, he was a clerk at Lloyds Bank and he liked fresh air. Surely after four months there was more to know about him than that?

He spoke more with Auntie Dorothy than with me. First time he came for tea there she was sitting upright on her lounger, her corset back on but not doing much, wishful-thinking red lips painted on way past her natural mouth and an inch of grey roots on her hair that gave the impression that the rest of it, which was dyed black, was hovering, waiting to land. All three of us were listening to the dog licking its private parts when Bernard piped up to tell Auntie how his great-great-grandfather changed their family name from Blight to Bligh in the hope of reversing a run of bad fortune.

'Did it work?' Auntie asked. And he laughed all jolly. I just sat with my mouth open. He'd never said anything near half as interesting to me. 'Do you think there'll be a war?' Auntie asked him. And he talked for a good ten minutes on how, unfortunately, he thought it unavoidable. Alone with Bernard I only ever heard my silly voice, making no more sense than when my teeth chattered with the cold, but the silence was just too loud for me.

'He's shy with you, love, and that's as it should be,' Auntie assured me.

'You're lucky there, Queenie. That man is a brick – you'll be safe as houses with him.'

So I asked her, 'Do you think we're courting?'

'Of course you're courting,' she told me.

'Is that all courting is?'

And she said, 'Well, what did you think it was?'

I'd seen girls who were courting. They looked dreamy-eyed on the world, floating on feet that never felt the ground. They plucked at daisies for most of the day, sighing, 'He loves me, he loves me not, he loves me'. When they danced, their best boys held them so close you couldn't pass a paper between them. And when they kissed, it was rapture that made their legs buckle, delight that made it taste of nectar. Courting girls thought their best boys to be fashioned by the hand of God Himself.

I moved the dressing-table mirror to see what all the other Queenies thought of courting Bernard. Not much. They were all a bit down in the mouth about it.

'Bernard, I've enjoyed our little trips but I don't think we should see each other any more.' I said it on a park bench, as a drizzle of rain was just starting to polka-dot his coat. Like a baby who's just been slapped but doesn't know it smarts yet, it happened ever so slowly. His face went from plain-day, through quizzical, then headlong into hurt. I never thought Bernard could be caught by feelings but there they were. Unmistakable it was, the quivering lip, the watering eye. He was about to cry. It was the most exciting thing he'd ever done.

'No, Queenie, please don't say that. I've grown very fond of you. Our walks mean a lot to me.'

'I didn't know you'd be so upset,' I said. I thought only women felt emotion – all men far too practical for such silliness.

'Yes, Queenie, I really am very fond of you. I know I'm older than you and perhaps not as gay as you'd like. But over these months . . .' He stopped, turned his head away from me and there it was, the back of his neck.

'It's just, Bernard . . .' I began, but he spun back fast, held my hands tight in his.

212

'Please, please don't say any more. Just give me another chance. Please, please, Queenie . . .' And he was crying, only one tear but crying none the less when he said, 'I was hoping to persuade you that we should get engaged.'

Oh, blinking heck, I thought, which is not what you should think when your best boy's just proposed. 'Well, never mind, then, I'll see you again on Thursday, Bernard,' was what I said. And that was how it was left.

We'd been for a walk along the river up to Big Ben. It wasn't late when Bernard and I reached the sweet shop. I couldn't get the door open. I thought it was just stiff – we'd had a lot of rain. It cracked an inch but then wouldn't budge. There was something behind it. Bernard had a go using his shoulder as I called out for Auntie. I was about to yell again when Bernard said, 'She's behind the door on the floor.'

And I teased him, 'That rhymes – you're a poet, Bernard,' before I'd quite realised what he'd said.

She was laid out on the floor clutching the closed sign to her breast. Pale as sorrow apart from her wishful-thinking red lips. And as out of place as a fallen tree trunk on a road. I thought if I could just return her to her natural position on the lounger she'd be all right.

'Auntie, get up?' I said, as Bernard knelt beside her feeling her pulse and putting his cheek right to her nose.

'What are you doing?' I asked him, but I got no reply. It was then I noticed the two coiffured back paws of Prudence sticking out from under her like the wishbone on a chicken. Bernard jumped when I screamed at her, 'Auntie, you've fallen on the dog!'

And then I'm not quite sure what happened. But Bernard was there, pulling me away from Auntie, taking me into the back room, sitting me down on the lounger and saying twice, maybe three times or more, 'Queenie, are you listening? Just stay here. It will be all right. Just sit here until I come back.' I could see him through the window glass in the door putting a blanket over her. Then leaving the shop and coming back in with Mr Green from the greengrocer's next door. Some other people came in, I know they did –

whispering and shaking their heads while Bernard was trying to make me drink some foul sweet tea.

'What's happened to her?'

'There'll be an ambulance coming soon.'

'Will she be all right? What about the dog? Should you fetch her in here? Only she'll fret and bark when they come.'

'Mr Green's kindly taken the dog,' he said. And then he sat by me to hold my hand.

Auntie Dorothy had had a stroke. They assured me at the hospital that she was killed outright and, honestly, truly, wouldn't have known that when she fell she crushed poor Prudence flat. She'd only got off her lounger to put the closed sign up and measure out some of her blinking coconut ice.

At her funeral, burly, broad-shouldered, fat-handed butchers – Father and four of Auntie's brothers – were gasping and sweating to lift her in her coffin. They had to rope in Bernard, who stepped forward without a word to put his skinny clerk's shoulder under one end. Our singing of 'Abide With Me' was accompanied by their grunting and grumbling as they carried her up the aisle. She would have laughed. Her Montgomery, Auntie Dorothy would have told them, would have had no trouble lifting her because she was his Duchess.

Mother's funeral outfit looked to be last worn for King Ted's or his late mother's passing. With her hand on my arm, which still clasped a damp, tear-stained handkerchief, she said, 'Don't worry, Queenie. You can come back home now. There's plenty for you to do around the farm.' And I'm not sure if I said it out loud because my elocution teacher would have despaired, but I know I thought it – Not on your nelly, Mother! You'll not get me back there. I looked over at Bernard, smoking in a huddle with Father and the other men.

'No,' I told her. 'I've some good news for you. I'm getting married, Mother, to Bernard Bligh.'

Twenty-five

Queenie

Bernard would untie his pyjama bottoms, loosen the cord then bunch the fabric into his hand so they didn't drop and spoil the surprise. 'Darling . . . ?' It was said as a question but the rest of it was never uttered: the shy missing words hanging between us were too lewd to show themselves. I'd stop reading to loosen my nightdress while he got into bed. He'd kiss me, in the early days, full on the lips with a timid tongue slipping gingerly into my mouth. Later it was the peck from a chicken's beak. His hand would slide under the covers tracing my nightie until it could go no further. He would ruckle up the material, pulling it up and up until he slipped his hand between my legs to part them. Then he'd roll himself on top of me. In the early days his eyes gazed down on mine – his soft, warm breath panting. Later he looked into a distance in the headboard, the corners of his mouth filling with two spots of spit as white as breadcrumbs. With the concentration of searching for a light switch in the dark, he'd fumble about until eventually, located, he'd stick it in. Slippery as a greasy sausage sometimes but mostly it was the bark of a tree. And he'd sigh as if lowering himself into a hot bath, his hand creeping up my nightie to lie awkward on my left breast. A held breath that turned him pink, then a grunt that slathered spittle all down my neck, and it was all over. In the early days he

215

kissed me before he rolled off but later he just left me with the indent from his pyjamas buttons.

All that lily-of-the-valley scent. Hours spent waving my hair and powdering my face to porcelain perfection. Silk stockings, red lips, and hands as soft as lah-di-dah. And I was married to a man who wouldn't have noticed if I'd come to bed in my gas mask. If I could have asked Auntie Dorothy, 'Is that all sex is?' I know what she would have said: 'Well, what did you think it would be?'

Babies, that's what I thought! All those warnings of things that could leave me in the family way. I'd been scared simple from the time my breasts first poked up in my jumper. Kissing at the garden gate, canoodling at the pictures. If he stuck his tongue in your mouth that was definitely a baby. If he touched your breast, well, that was twins. And what girl didn't know you could fall pregnant sitting on a toilet seat? So sex every Saturday, Sunday and sometimes twice in the week for over a year should surely have left me with child.

'Do you take pleasure in conjugal relations?' the doctor asked me.

'I'm not sure,' I said.

'You're not sure if you find it pleasurable, Mrs Bligh?'

'Not sure what it is, Doctor.'

I was the most bothersome thing he'd had in his dingy surgery since he last squashed a buzzing bluebottle against the glass. If I didn't partake fully and enjoy relations with my husband I would never get pregnant, he assured me. 'A young, pretty, healthy woman like you cannot have a problem. My advice to you is to go home and try harder.'

The vicar at St John's Church wondered if it was wise to want to bring a child into the world when there was almost certainly a war coming. Told me to go away and think very carefully about it. So I went to the Roman Catholic church instead and lit a candle. I knew they wouldn't mind.

'I would like children, Queenie,' Bernard told me more than once. Accusing me or near as. He thought I didn't realise that he searched in my chest of drawers to see if the packets of sanitary towels were open or still shut. He always knew when it was my time of month. But what he didn't know was that with every curse that came and went I cried over those bloody rags.

216

* * *

From the basement to the top there were sixty-five stairs in the house in Earls Court. I told Bernard after I'd counted them. 'Indeed,' he said. And that was not counting the five up to the front door. Sixty-five stairs and endless rooms. But Bernard and his father, Arthur, lived like a couple of unwelcome mice in the few rooms in the basement. All the other rooms, except one, were empty. They used to have lodgers – men, mostly, who came to London for work, stayed a few weeks or months and then moved on. With every vacated room Bernard closed the curtains, covered the chairs and beds with newspaper and shut it up.

The wedding confetti had hardly finished floating to the ground when Bernard told me, 'I don't want my wife to go out to work.'

I'd hugged him. Who wouldn't after so many years as a skivvy? I was to be a housewife. I could hear Auntie Dorothy: 'Oh, Queenie love, you've landed on your feet there.'

'Let's open up the house,' was this new bride's suggestion. Wielding my lavender polish and duster all day I tried to show Bernard how it could be. I put flowers and a cloth on the table. Changed the heavy red brocade curtains for modern ones with roses climbing up. 'We could have a sitting room for ourselves.' I persuaded Bernard to move out some of the enormous old-fashioned bookshelves and cupboards that lurked like the ghosts of families past. 'You could have a study, Bernard, use one of the rooms for somewhere to read.' Let in some light. Open the windows. 'It could be a proper home again,' I said. But most things I suggested were met with Bernard's shaking head. 'Why not?' I'd ask him.

'I've got my reasons.' But I never really got to hear them. Didn't I have enough to do to look after him and his father, what with the shopping, the cooking, the cleaning? And, silly woman that I am, didn't I know that there was a war coming? Or sometimes he'd mutter something about wanting to move to the suburbs.

Twenty-six

Queenie

That blinking grandfather clock went off every fifteen minutes. I'd near as begged Arthur not to keep winding it up. Bernard said it was his father's clock and it had always been kept wound even when he was away in France. I think those two were deaf to it, it being so familiar to them. So with those ruddy bells tolling for me again I nearly missed Chamberlain's speech. I was knitting. Bernard kept looking over to my needles as they clacked away. I could see they were annoying him. He pulled his chair a little closer to the wireless. Then slyly looked over at them again. You'll have to say, I thought. You'll have to open your mouth and make conversation. Queenie dear, could you please stop knitting for a little while? I can't hear what is being said properly. But I knew he wouldn't. He'd tut, maybe, but that would be it. I'd knitted this wool three times. 'This morning the British ambassador in Berlin handed the German Government the final note . . .' Every time I finished I unravelled it and knitted it up in another style. '. . . withdraw their troops from Poland or a state of war would exist between us . . .' He did ask once, 'You've been knitting that garment for a long time?' which made me smile. '. . . I have to tell you now that no such undertaking has been received and that consequently this country is at war with Germany.' So that was it, just ding-dong, ding-dong, clack, clack, clack, and there you go, we were at war.

Then blow me if the air-raid siren didn't go off! For a good few seconds all three of us stared at each other. We'd heard it before, taken no notice of it. But that was before the war, which was only a few minutes ago. Now it was the war, so there was every chance that we were going to die.

Bernard moved first – not towards me: he lunged for Arthur's gas mask, grabbed it from the sideboard and threw it at his father. I waited for him to throw me mine but it was his next. I had to grab mine myself and Bernard was yelling, 'Gas masks! Gas masks!' And any loud noise made Arthur shake. So 'Gas masks! Gas masks,' and the siren made Arthur tremble so much his fumbling hands could make no sense of the box let alone the mask – even though we'd practised it often enough. And I was wondering, Will he start coughing, choking, spluttering with the poison while I'm putting on mine?

Bernard was still shouting although his voice sounded like it was coming from a deep hole with his mask over his face. And for the first time I had to tell him, 'Oh, please, shut up,' which was a bit of a turn-up considering they might have been the last words I ever said to him. But he didn't hear, too busy unlocking the back door. I couldn't breathe with the gas mask on – no air let alone poison gas was getting through. Arthur's was round the back of his head, the straps pressing down over his nose and he was shaking so much that anyone else seeing him might have thought he was trying to make us laugh.

Then I heard, '*Schnell, schützen Sie sich!*' being yelled. And I thought, the war's on for, what? no more than five minutes, and there's Germans coming down our stairs. I was trembling then. 'Bernard,' I shouted, as he heard it – '*Schützen Sie sich!*' and some other foreign words. And I swear he looked startled, which is odd because he had a gas mask on. It was me that remembered, 'It's Mr Plant!' just before our lodger, a refugee from outside Berlin, ran into the room. I let out such a long breath it steamed up my mask. And Mr Plant's arms were flapping like someone was pulling them on a string from the ceiling.

'Gas mask?' Bernard asked him. And he looked at us one at a time, then slapped his hand to his forehead muttering something nobody could understand – except Hitler if he was here. 'You'll be gassed alive, man,' Bernard shouted at him. And this gent started to walk out of the room, to go up the sixty-five stairs to get his blinking mask.

I grabbed him. 'No, get in the shelter, there's no time now.'

Bernard shouted at me then: 'He'll need his mask.'

He was not a young man. 'It'll take him till next Tuesday to get it,' I said. 'There's no time.'

With the door open I looked up at a blue sky. Dazzling sun threw the shade of next door's tree across the garden, while a blackbird on the wall held its head up to let out its song. Until, that is, it saw the four of us scrambling across the yard. I thought the sky would be blackened with the gently floating wings of parachuting Nazis. But nothing. Just the bird watching us silently from the safety of the tree.

So much for women and children first: Bernard helped Arthur on to the steps of the shelter, whispering for him to 'get a grip', while I was still hurrying along Mr Plant, who was grumbling away in German. Then I stepped on to the ladder of the shelter and that was when I looked down. Blow me, Arthur had been out there day in day out and he'd not dug us a shelter: he'd burrowed a tunnel. I swear I couldn't see the bottom. I climbed out again as Mr Plant passed by me, and Bernard managed a look of confusion behind the mask.

'I'm not going down there – we'll be buried alive,' I told him.

'Come on, Queenie,' he said, all agitated.

'Not on your life. They're not meant to be that deep.' I knew it had taken Arthur a long time to dig it, coming in night after night mucky and excited as a boy from a sandpit. Bernard would help at weekends. 'How's it coming along?' I'd ask him. 'Fine,' he'd say. I didn't know they'd dug half-way to Australia. 'I'm not being buried alive, Bernard. I'll die up here, if you don't mind.'

And I thought I heard my husband say, 'Suit yourself,' but it might have just been the mask. He started to climb in but then the all-clear sounded. The half of him still sticking out of the ground reminded me of a worm. I took my gas mask off to giggle.

When I got back inside I talked to no one. I went straight to our bedroom, shut the door and turned the key in the lock. That raid was the most exciting thing that had ever happened in this house. Tingling with life, that was how

I felt. I took two steps and leaped up on to the bed. There was no doubt about it, I was looking forward to this war.

When the real war started Mr Plant was gone.

'That's better all round,' Bernard said.

'What do you mean?' I asked.

It was all that ministry stuff Bernard complained about, although he was always at the bank and never at home to deal with it. The sinister government man with his notebook and sly looks over my shoulder, wanting to know who visited Mr Plant. Where did they go, what did they say?

'He sits in his room,' I told him. Sometimes he would come down and sit with Arthur on the step looking out on to the yard. He'd tell Arthur, in English with an accent better than Lord Haw-Haw's, about the things he and his wife used to grow in their garden just outside Berlin. So when this ministry man visited to check up on our refugee, all I had to do was tell him, 'Nothing and no one.'

But Bernard said, 'These Jews are more trouble than they're worth.'

They came really early in the morning to get him. 'Where are you taking him?' I asked. Internment for his own protection. He wasn't the only one who went from the street. There was a woman, too, and a family with little children from further down the road. They were put in the back of a lorry, although they were only taking them to Olympia. Mr Plant just had the little leather case that he'd first arrived with when Bernard couldn't find an excuse quick enough not to give him the room. Just before leaving, Mr Plant tipped his hat at me. On seeing the lorry, he had stopped, frozen, for a second then shrugged.

'He was German, you can't be too careful,' Bernard said, before going upstairs to lay newspaper down in the room.

'You devils, you devils!' I yelled, when I heard the first bombs exploding. 'You devils.' Those terrifying noises. They were hardly real – I had no image in my mind that went with a racket like that. It wasn't wardrobes falling down the stairs. It wasn't a lorry full of cans spilling over a road. It wasn't the coalman dropping hundreds of sacks on the pavement outside. Our neighbours weren't all slamming their doors at once. But somewhere people were learning about that din. Someone now had a vivid picture of what went on with all that commotion.

Bombers arrive like thunderclouds. Can you see them? Maybe not. But the threat sits on you like an ache. Majestic almost, those dark formations grimly determined on their target. Acks-acks shouting, 'Over here, over here!' trying to distract them but making no difference. We couldn't get Arthur into the shelter when the real bombs came. No amount of coaxing or pushing could get him into another trench during a bombardment. He was off. Into his room and under the bed as if a bayonet was prodding his backside.

So it was just me and Bernard in the shelter, which was now a regulation four feet down. A little bunk each. A chair that Bernard usually sat on, it being next to the little table with the lamp. His knees seemed to be everywhere I turned, knobbly as a hammer-head even through his trousers. He read his paper, sniffing and making that queer dislodging-a-tickling-hair face. He'd clear his throat with such a phlegmy noise I thought he'd have to spit but then he'd blow his nose pushing his crumpled hankie up each nostril in turn to scour it out. The shelter started with the smell of damp earth, sharp as manure, and I felt like a daffodil waiting for spring. But after a few hours it became his breath — tobacco mixed with whiffs of digesting potato from dinner. Then the stale, under-the-blanket smells of a lifeless mouth. And there was me saying, 'What was that? Did you hear that one? Oh, God, someone's got it tonight . . . I hope Arthur didn't hear that . . . Do you think he's all right? That was close. Was that closer?' and hearing absolutely nothing in reply. That shelter was so blinking noisy and so bloody quiet all at once.

Bernard became almost animated talking with the next-door neighbour, Mr Todd. 'They'd be happier among their own kind,' he said. The two of them, arms folded, heads practically touching and shaking sombrely. 'Putting them here really isn't doing anyone any good.' I thought it must be Hitler outside our door. Or perhaps the entire Third Reich was moving in down our street. There was such a rumpus. Curtains were lifted to look, some stood in their front doors, windows were opened, endless disapproval was being tutted. But it wasn't an invasion – it was a sadder sight than that. It was a family. A mother wearing a brown coat with one sleeve hanging off, carrying a baby wrapped in a shawl made of an old sheet. Her face not so much blank but unreadable as a corpse. And straggling behind her were four kids. Filthy, grimy mudlarks – sootier than any miners ever got. Their hair matted to string and flying this way and that. And they're all staring around, looking up one minute at the houses, mouths gaping enchanted. Then in the next moment, feeling the tutting grown-ups watching them, they're looking down at their feet. One of the children – could have been a boy or a girl it was that hard to tell – was pushing a pram. One wheel was buckled, and it wobbled so much another child stretched up trying to hold a couple of shabby boxes on to it. Then there were two little mites who were holding hands – one, a girl, carried a gas-mask box, the other, a boy, a little stuffed toy. The boy was wearing trousers too big for him – short trousers that were tied at the waist with string and came down to well below his ankles. And these two little ones were trying to keep up with the pram. And the pram was trying to keep up with the mother. And the mother was trying to keep pace with a rather smart woman dressed in a wool suit with a fake rose in the lapel, who was marching resolutely forward.

They were not the first such family, so Mr Todd told all the other neighbours. This was the third lot he'd seen and he hoped there would be no more. They'd been bombed out round Rotherhithe and someone high up in some ministry had decided they should be rehoused in the empty rooms down our street. Mrs Newman at number thirty was taking this lot.

'I don't want to,' she told anyone who'd listen. 'I've been made to. And, let me tell you, there are many people in this street that have more room than me.'

'Is every waif and stray to end up here?' Mr Todd asked. 'I mean, we've got enough Poles living here to start their country anew. Now these Cockneys. I ask you.'

We weren't getting that much bombing, not like in the East End. Some clown in the butcher's said it was because if Hitler invaded he'd want somewhere nice to live. 'Treasonous,' that's what Bernard said about that comment.

The little boy in the giant trousers tripped over the hem. He looked like a sack all splayed out on the pavement. He didn't cry. Got picked up by his sister and carried on. I don't know if he realised he'd dropped his stuffed toy. He looked back for a second but then had to rush to keep up. It lay there in the road, and got run over by a car, becoming camouflaged in muck. I picked it up. It was a soggy, wet, filthy little dog or horse made out of someone's old sock with eyes sewn on in black wool.

'What on earth are you doing with that?' Bernard asked me, when I'd washed it and pegged it out on the line by its spindly legs that looked to be cut from an old glove. It came up quite well – made fluffy by the breeze. One of its legs needed a repair where it had started to unravel and I put a bow at its neck to make it look a little less forlorn.

I swear the attic room Mrs Newman had that family in was no bigger than our Anderson shelter. She looked to be storing them in a cupboard, not giving them somewhere to live. The mother had to push the little boy forward to take the toy from me. He didn't recognise it. 'It's yours,' I told him. 'You dropped it.'

He turned it round in the air, then his face opened like a shiny present. 'It's Neddy,' he said.

He showed it to his mum who said, 'Say thank you to the lady, Albert.'

But he couldn't quite manage it even when his sister hit him round the head and his mum said 'Oi, you, stop that – if there's any hitting to do, I'll do it.'

Mrs Newman complained to me as I left that she couldn't let the family in the bathroom because they smelt and were too filthy. 'Well, what do you expect, if you won't let them at a bath?' I said. And she said, 'I know you have plenty of rooms in your house, Mrs Bligh. You take them instead if you think you would do better.'

He'd got stubble on his chin, Bernard, almost a beard. Hadn't been in the house long enough to get a shave. His eyes were red-rimmed, his hair ungreased and ruffled, skin pale as a potato root. I probably looked as bad. I'd been in the same clothes for days, my hair only combed with a quick flick from my fingers. We'd spent every night in that blinking shelter for what felt like for ever. Sleep? Wasn't that something we used to do during a peaceful night?

When they're close, bombs whistle. Their melody is a sharp descending note that only sounds right when it ends with a bang. Then everything you thought was solidly fixed to this earth suddenly takes flight, for just a second, and then is put back down – if you're lucky in the same place. Breath is ripped from your lungs, your eyes bulge, your stomach squeezes its contents up or out, and your heart races so unfamiliar you think it a clockwork toy. I remember fairgrounds – the helter skelter, the switchback – paying good money to make my face blanch, my knuckles whiten. In those days, before the war, I thought it fun to be scared witless.

I knew it would be close by the whistle – clear as the kettle on my stove. Bernard turned the page of his paper, lifting his chin to read something at the top, his lips involuntarily parting with the effort. I couldn't say I heard the bang, I was just weightless for a moment, my arms swimming in air. He was still reading when I landed back down. Still concentrating on the news when everything that used to stand silent around us burst with clatter. Shrapnel and who-knows-what pelting the shelter like hail. Only his upper lip stood firm. And I swallowed back the sick that came up into my mouth.

When his newspaper started to rustle I looked round for the source of the breeze. When it began flapping, as if it was trying to bring a fire to life, I realised Bernard was trembling. His fists, tight as a baby's, were gripping the pages, screwing up the words so they were unreadable.

'Are you all right, Bernard?' I was expecting no more than a grunt in reply.

'Queenie,' he said, softly. 'That's the house.' He gulped then, and grabbed for another breath that wasn't there. 'Father . . . Father . . . Father in the house . . . That's the house . . . gone . . . Queenie . . . Queenie . . . Father . . . in the house . . .'

A drowning man could breathe easier. I went to take the paper from him but his grip was so tight I had to rip it from his hands. And he was left with fists still clenching bits of torn paper. 'Calm down, Bernard.'

He was gasping now, his chest jumping hiccups, 'We're going to die . . . die . . . here . . . Father . . . that was the house . . .'

'Bernard, listen, calm down. It's not our house. It wasn't that close. Listen, let me have a look,' I said.

I was on my knees and only turned round to open the curtain at the entrance when he howled a mighty, red-blooded, full-bodied 'No!' He lunged for me, flinging his arms round my waist to drag me back, then he swaddled me in his arms popping any last breath out of me.

'No . . . no . . . not you . . . no, never . . .' He buried his head in my neck, shuffled his knees up round me until I was totally captured by him. And I could see the house as he held me there. A hulking black mount against the sky. Intact. I ran my eye over all its corners – every one present and correct. Arthur was under the bed – probably dirty, scared, but all right.

'I can see the house,' I said. His gasps were pumping warm breath into my neck. 'Arthur's all right. It's still there, Bernard, the house. Look – look for yourself.' But he wouldn't lift his head up, he just clung to me for safe-keeping like a toddler. And there I was, protecting my husband against those big bad incendiaries, that nasty flying shrapnel, and the horrid, horrid bombs from the naughty, naughty German planes. And the funny thing was I felt so peaceful being embraced by him and gently whispering, 'There there, Bernard, there there.'

It was quieter outside by the time I felt his grip slowly release me. He shuffled away like he had shuffled towards me – sitting on his backside, his knees up. He didn't look at me. Wiped his nose. Gathered up the paper from the floor, folded it and placed it on the table. He righted the toppled chair. Coughed, cleared his throat, smoothed his hair and sat down. And all the while I was watching him. There was a bitter smell of burning and whiffs of smoke were foggy inside the shelter. From outside there was shouting, feet running, crunching along on broken glass. And water was trickling somewhere. Bernard at last looked at me and I nodded to say, Hello, so you're back. But his eyes didn't hold my gaze for long. He looked to his hands, to his slowly intertwining fingers, and he licked his lips twice before murmuring, 'I want you to know, Queenie, I do love you.'

Number thirty looked like a blinking skull. The bomb had come in through the roof of the house, down through the floors to explode on the inside. All the windows were gone, so was the front door. Which just left the shell, an empty head in the middle of a terrace. This skull was crowned with the crumbling jagged walls of what was left of the attic rooms. Open to the sky with the green wallpaper of one room and the brown paint of the other, the skull looked to be wearing a gaudy Christmas hat. Everything that was on the inside was now on the outside – the smashed wreckage of this home spilling over the pavements in great mountains of rubble, blocking the road and crunching underfoot. 'You'll be safe as houses,' Auntie Dorothy had been very fond of saying. Anything solid she thought to be safe. Even Bernard. I was glad she wasn't alive to have to face the fact that even solid can crumble.

Everyone was out to stare. Enraged at the devastation but relieved it wasn't them and theirs. 'Lucky they were in the shelter . . . Lucky no one was at home . . . Lucky no one's buried alive in there.' Mrs Newman, whose house it was, was left uncharacteristically speechless. Shock, the warden said, as someone took her away. It was only number thirty, nowhere else was touched. What the hell did that house have to do with this war? Was Hitler sleeping easier now he'd turned it into a heap of junk? Like all the other houses either side, we'd lost a few windows and some little bits of number thirty's chimney went through our roof. But that was it.

'That bomb had their name on it,' Mr Todd decided.

We were all being kept back by a tin-hatted warden shouting, 'It's not safe to come too close. That lot could come down at any minute.' While firemen with black faces and dreadfully tired eyes were gingerly peering inside, pushing at walls, looking up, looking down, looking around.

'Oh, fucking 'ell!' That's what the Rotherhithe woman said when she came home to see her tiny attic room now open to the sky.

'There's no need for language like that,' Mr Todd said.

'It's understandable,' I told him. 'She's just lost her house.'

'It was not her house, Mrs Bligh.'

'Oh, how would you like it?'

'Could be me tomorrow and, let me assure you, I won't be using language like that.'

The woman took no notice, slumping down to sit on a wall saying, 'Has anyone got a fag?' After more silent, disdainful rolling of eyes she was given one. She only had the two little mites with her, the others were still down in the Underground. And these two kids, scuttling like rats, disappeared over the rubble and into the house with the warden chasing them, shouting, 'Get out of there, it's not safe.' The next minute the little boy, still in his overlong trousers, was being dragged out of the house by the warden who had him by the ear. His feet were nearly off the ground. And the warden was telling him, 'Give that back. I saw that. That's not yours.'

The mother was on her feet, 'Oi, put 'im down.'

'He's got something, saw him pick it up. He's put it in his mouth.'

'Get off 'im.'

'Not until I know what he's got in his mouth. You shouldn't be round here.'

'They live here,' I told him.

'Here? They live here? You sure?' the warden asked, while the mother was still shouting at him, 'Let 'im go or I swear I'll land you one. I've had enough – all right? Jus' let 'im go.' The little boy puffed out his cheeks then spat something on to the ground. It was a brooch.

'There – little thief,' the warden said, triumphantly.

'He ain't a thief!' the mother shouted. She picked up the brooch.

'Oi, leave that. That belongs to this house.'

'It's mine,' she said.

'Give me that. I'll keep it until we've cleared this lot up.'

'It's mine – it belongs to me,' the woman was shouting. It was just a little brooch, no better than one you'd find in a Lucky Bag. The woman was pitifully pleading now – a kid clinging to each of her legs. 'It's mine. I swear, honest. It's mine.'

'Give it to her,' I said to the warden.

'Not until I have ascertained whose property it is,' he said.

'What does it matter? It's just a little tuppenny-ha'penny brooch,' I whispered to him.

'It is my job to make sure . . .' he began, for all to hear.

'She's just lost everything. And this is not her first time. Can't you just give her the benefit of the doubt?'

'It is my responsibility to see no looting takes place in this . . .'

So I said to him, 'Oh, fuck off.'

Bernard didn't say, 'Over my dead body,' because we'd all become a little superstitious during the past year. Instead he said, 'Under no circumstances . . . it's out of the question . . . Queenie, have you gone quite mad?'

'They're people,' I said. 'They've got nowhere to go.'

'They're not our sort.'

'But they need helping.'

'They can't stay here. There are places that will take care of them.'

'They'll be no bother.'

I wished the little mites were being quieter at this point. But they weren't. They were running round our living room, jumping off furniture, playing planes and bombs and making the appropriate racket. Their mother, feet up on a chair, sipped tea and smoked Bernard's cigarettes.

'Just for a few days.'

'I've made myself perfectly clear.'

'Oh, come on, Bernard. Have you no pity?'

'They're filthy, Queenie,' he whispered. He had a point. Their heads were infested. If I turned the little boy Albert on his head the lice would have carried him away.

'We've got all this room. How can we when so many have nowhere?'

'The authorities will deal with them. You can't help everybody. There's a war on.'

'I know – that's what I mean.'

I took that poor bombed-out family to a rest centre. We collected the other two kids and the baby from the Underground. And when I came back to our house later, I walked in to tell a thunderstruck Bernard that I didn't care what he said, I didn't care what he thought – I had got myself a job. So there!

229

Twenty-seven

Queenie

Sometimes they were still smouldering like a burnt pie pulled from an oven. The pungent stench of smoke, the dust from rubble steaming off them. Shuffling in or being carried. Some wrapped in blankets, their clothes having gone flying off with the blast. Blackened, sooty faces, red-rimmed, sunken eyes with whites that suddenly flashed, startled, to look around them agog like they'd stumbled on to another planet. And shivering, there was so much shivering.

Population, we called them at the rest centre. The bombed-out who'd had the cheek to live through the calamity of a world blown to bits. Leaving the cardboard coffins empty but filling up the classrooms of the old school building with their tragic faces and filthy clothes that made miners fresh up from the pit look like Christmas fairies. They came in as a crowd like you'd wade through on the Underground or elbow during a department-store sale. And that's how some saw them — population, not people. Not mothers called Mavis who, stunned speechless, clutched two small children crying for their mum to make the banging stop so they could get to sleep. Not a ten-year-old son called Ralph, trousers soggy with wee, who tried to save bunks with carefully placed socks, jumpers and a fierce face. Not a husband called Sid, whose bloodstained arms held each one of his family in turn to tell them he'd go back to recover what he could from their bombed home. Not a young woman called Christine, who clawed at a warden's back begging him to find her fiancé who was lost under a toppled wall. Just population. A mass whose desperation made them seem like the feckless, and whose drab presence drained the classrooms of all colour until even the white potties in the corner glinted like diamonds. I would never forgive Hitler for turning human beings into that.

And it was my job to find out who they had once been and where they had once lived. Even the ones who couldn't remember or couldn't hear because a blast was still ringing in their ears. It was raucous some days at the rest centre, me straining to hear those weary fragile voices. Other days were so frighteningly silent I wished someone would scream or even start a chorus of the dreadful 'Roll Out The Barrel'. And sometimes when there were just too many – when even I had to fight my way in – I'd forget a queue, just turn round to the first person I saw and say, 'Do you need helping? Good, then I'll start with you.'

Twelve-hour shifts, fourteen sometimes, I had to do at Campden School rest centre. And when I got home Bernard would complain that there was nothing on the table except dust. It wasn't for himself that he was worried, he took an unusually long time explaining, it was for me. 'I'm just worried that this job is proving too much for you, what with everything . . .'

Meanwhile at the rest centre two women were sitting there grinning gratefully at me. Violet and her sister Margery. Both husbands were away. One in North Africa, the other in Northampton. They'd got three children between them – twelve, eight and another who, they told me, was a bit slow.

'The house is completely gone,' Violet said. They'd lost everything but they giggled. Hysterical euphoria, I was warned, what with the relief of them all being safe. Dug out of their Morrison shelter when Margery tapped on the ceiling rose, which was just in reach, with a teaspoon. 'Our ration books are still there in the sideboard, you see.' Another chuckle. 'It's under there somewhere but it's not a priority, they told us, to find things like that. People and persons, that's their job, they said.'

'Right, well, to get replacement ration books,' I began, 'you'll need to apply to the administrative centre at the town hall. Or your local food office. Just go to one of those places – I can tell you what bus to get – and fill in a form for yourselves and each of your children . . .' Both of them were staring vacant as shop mannequins.

'Shall I write that down?' I asked.

'Write what down?'

'What I just said.'

'What was that?'

'About the ration books.'

'We lost them with the house. They're in the sideboard, you see. We need to get new ones.'

I should have been asleep on my days off. Lulled drowsy by ordinary daytime noises I'd thought so loudly disturbing before the war – postmen, delivery lorries, kids playing cricket in the street. But as often as not those precious days were spent craning my neck trying to calculate how long a queue could go on. Six sausages and a loaf of bread later and I'm still trying to work it out. If I cooked the dinner and Bernard and Arthur ate it sharpish, I could wash the dishes, and a few clothes from the basket, iron my dress for work, a shirt for Bernard, then maybe get an hour and a half sleep in my feather-pillowed, clean-sheeted, highly sprung bed before they started – the bombers – and I had to go to the Anderson to kip in Armageddon.

Didn't seem any point being at home for just a few hours when in the morning I had to fight my way through an upside-down world. Roads that should have been familiar turned to wastelands strewn with mountains of wreckage, the displaced intestines of buildings spewing everywhere. Coughing in the fog of rubble dust. Stepping lightly over this, teetering over that. Forced round corners to avoid a factory still ablaze. Gushing streams of water lapping at my heels. Glass crunching under my feet. One morning, looking up a road near home, I recognised nothing. I was a foreigner to this newly modelled place. I had to ask a warden, 'Have you seen Longbridge Road?' And even the warden was puzzled, looking around him as if he'd mislaid his hat. 'It used to be around here somewhere,' was all he could offer. I had to start spending nights in the rest centre, too, because those few miles to work were taking me hours! But Bernard didn't like it. He turned up at the centre more than once, standing in the doorway on tippy-toes, scanning the classroom until he'd found me.

'I just need to know you're alive,' he'd say.

'Oh, yes,' I'd tell him. 'Very much so.'

'You say you lost all your clothes in the fire,' I said now, 'and your coupons.'

'Miss, what I'm standing up in is all I've got, is what I'm telling you.' And that was no more than tatty rags. The man's son was wrapped in a blanket with no shoes on. 'My boy here was in bed. I was making a quick cup of tea. I only had time to grab him when I see the thing falling out the sky. Then suddenly nothing and we're on fire. My neighbours are screaming, I can hear them through the wall. I get him out. My wife, she was in the shelter – well, she's in the hospital now. Dunno what happened to next door.'

'There's clothes in the other classroom. You could go in and get something for your son and—'

'We tried that, miss. One of your colleagues pointed it out to us when we came in. But there weren't any trousers left, well, not to fit 'im, and my boy really don't wanna wear a dress.'

'Okay,' I said, looking for advice in my little book. 'To replace your clothing coupons you'll need to get the form CRSCI from the administrative centre. That's CRSCI. Fill it in, then forward it by post, to the Customs and Excise office at the Board of Trade in Westminster. That's in . . . SW one.'

'Right – is that it, then?' he asked.

And I had to tell him, 'Yes, I'm afraid it is.'

'Well, I suppose we could have another go in the classroom next door.'

There were just not enough bunks. People were having to sleep on the floor.

'But my house has gone. Surely there is some compensation I can have now so I can find another property?'

'Well, madam, you could try writing to the Assistance Board or send to the War Damage Commission for a form CI but they don't usually pay out until after the war.'

'Usually! What are you talking about? How many wars have we had where this has happened? And please, miss, don't get me wrong but what exactly will they do with my claim if, God forbid, we don't win?'

Sometimes the food ran out and all we had to offer anyone was a blinking cup of tea.

'Have you no other relatives that could take you in?' I couldn't stop this woman crying and why should she? Her husband, her mum, her dad had all been killed at the mouth of a shelter. She was at least eight months pregnant. Her only reply was a very slight shake of the head.

'Tell you what, I could get you evacuated if you like?'

'The road to hell,' my mother would tell Father, after he'd given another miner something she thought he shouldn't, 'is paved with good intentions.' He'd shrug. The only paving left in London was that sort. And me at my desk diligently deferring to my pamphlet for Loss or Damage Services was laying every last blinking stone to hell and back. My job was no more than to send the still shaking and stunned round London – once, twice, three times – to answer more questions, fill in more forms so they might get back some of what, through no fault of theirs, had just been rudely taken from them.

Mrs Palmer insisted I call her Dora. She'd been bombed out round Hammersmith way, with her husband, three sons and a very manky cat. 'I just looked at the house and there it was, gone.' Returning from the billeting officer she skipped towards me fresh as a girl. 'They've found us a lovely place, Queenie. I can hardly believe it. Guess where it is? Go on – you'll never. Connaught Street. Can you imagine? My husband's always wanted to live somewhere posh like Connaught Street. It was like a dream for him. And here we are being offered a flat in a house down there. Ordinary people like us. It'll take his mind off losing his foot. So, I've been sent back to you to see about getting some furniture.'

'What happened to all yours?' I asked her.

'Oh, it was all lost, Queenie – every last stick.'

'Did you make a claim for it at the time?'

'No, I don't think so. My husband sees to things like that and he was in the hospital until couple of days ago.'

'So you haven't filled out a PC54?'

'I think I can safely say no. But I can do it now if it would help.'

'When was your furniture damaged, Mrs Palmer?'

'Please call me Dora – you make me feel so old. Now, let's see, it'll be about two months now. 'Cause Jack was in the hospital six, seven weeks. Me and the boys were at my sister's until that took a hit. Been here a week or so. Yeah, about two months.'

'Oh,' I said. My little book was telling me that with the PC54, the claim had to be forwarded to the District Valuer within thirty days of the damage or loss occurring.

'Is there a problem, Queenie?' she asked. My head became such a weight that I could not lift it to look her in the eye with that news. 'Is it something Jack will have to do?'

'For furniture, Dora,' I began hesitantly, 'you should have put in the claim within thirty days of the loss.'

Clear as a silent-movie star, her face ran through an assortment of expressions – roughly corresponding to a baffled how, what and when. Then her eyebrows rose briefly to spring apart with understanding before sinking back down to a confused anxiety, while she said a quiet 'But . . .'

Bernard was so furious with me that the vein on his temple that used to annoy me when he ate was standing up pumping like it had a heart of its own. 'Queenie, for the last time, it is not our furniture to give away. It belongs to my father.' I'd arrived at the house with a van and two men, who prudently kept their eyes down as they passed carrying a table and another chair.

'I'm not giving it away – I'm lending it.'

'It's still not ours – even to loan.'

'It's doing nothing upstairs, just sitting in those rooms covered in newspaper. It's just a couple of beds, a table and four chairs. We'll not miss them before they're back.'

'Where are they going? Who are you giving them too?'

'Mrs Palmer – Dora and her family.'

'Who on earth are they?'

'They're from the rest centre.'

'Absolutely not, Queenie! We don't know these people. How can you be sure you'll get the furniture back?'

'I know I will. I promise I will.'

'Are these people our sort?'

'What do you mean?'

'Queenie, for God's sake, have some sense. You can't help everyone. Isn't it enough that you work all hours at that place? Look at you – you're tired. You look awful.'

'Thanks, Bernard.'

'I'm just thinking of you.'

'They're just borrowing the furniture until I can get them some. Otherwise they've got a requisitioned flat with nothing in it. Nothing at all.'

'That's not our problem.'

'Oh, no, sorry, that's where you're wrong. Bernard, there is a war on.'

'I'm very well aware of that.'

'Oh, yeah? Well, let me tell you something, let me give you a fact – there's thousands of people having much more of a war than you are.' And as soon as I'd said it I wished I hadn't. He reeled from me as sure as if I'd spat in his face. Swallowing hard to guzzle up those words he nodded at me – just a little – then turned to walk into the gloom inside.

Dora found it hard to stop thanking me. 'I don't know what we'd have done, you've been such a help, Queenie, you really have . . .' Out on her precious Connaught Street she didn't appear to want to stop waving goodbye. I was quite a way down the road and could still hear her calling, 'How can we ever thank you enough? Don't be a stranger. Come any time.'

''Bye, then,' I was saying when I noticed a woman running after me down the street. Well dressed with delicate heels that clopped on the pavement like a thoroughbred.

'You there, you there,' she called. 'Are you responsible for this?' I stopped for a moment until she said, 'I want to know on whose authority those people have been put into that property.' I began walking again, fast, as she chased after me saying, 'I want to know the name of your superior. I want to make a complaint. I'm not happy to have those people living here. This is a respectable street. Those kind of people do not belong here. Let me tell you, there will be a great deal of trouble if they stay because I am not happy about it, not happy about it at all.'

Twenty-eight

Queenie

It was my fault that Bernard volunteered for the RAF before waiting to be asked. Men not in uniform began to look out of place in streets rolling in blue and khaki. With us having to import Yanks and him still wearing what he liked, he was self conscious, apologetic, even. But it wasn't that – it was all that catastrophe that dodged in behind me every time I came home from the rest centre. And when he tried to turn away he'd look straight into another war – scarred into the face of his own father. He had to join up. And the RAF wanted him. A skinny bank clerk who always blew on his tea before he drank it. A man who had trouble finding enough rage to scare next-door's cat out of our shelter. And it wasn't just that the military could see his wiry frame fitting into any desk space no matter how small: Bernard was to become part of their fighting machine – they were sending him overseas. Mr Todd slapped his back, saying, 'Good show, Bernard, good man.' People who would never before pass the time of day with me asked after my husband. And when I talked about him I plumped almost as proud as Auntie Dorothy with Montgomery. I swear his shoulders got broader, his hands more manly with every leave. Even the back of his neck looked fearless with the collar of his RAF blues pressing against it. I was almost jealous now someone else wanted him. He's my husband, where are you sending him? Training in

Skegness and Blackpool, he was home more often than he used to be. But overseas! Where overseas? How far? We live on an island, for God's sake, everywhere is blinking overseas.

He left with no more ceremony than if he was going to the bank. I wanted to hug him, whisper into his ear to be sure to tell me what he was doing, to show me what he was seeing in all those foreign places. But he stiffened like a plank of best mahogany, then bent to kiss my cheek. Watching him walking down our road – his forage cap sitting at an angle on his head, his kit-bag lolling like a corpse over his shoulder – I thought, He is so thin that any enemy soldier would have to have a ruddy good aim to hit him. It was a strange thought, not one I'd have shared with anyone, but funnily enough I found it comforting. The pity of it was he wouldn't have known that I was watching him through the window, let alone that I was worrying. And when he was finally out of view, the road screamed with emptiness. I couldn't help what came to my mind next – it just sneaked up behind me to sigh over my shoulder: he'll not be able to post it home so you'll never get pregnant now, Queenie.

Early Bird, my teacher at Bolsbrooke Elementary School, taught us all in English grammar that an apostrophe is a mark to show where something is missing. And that was how I'd always seen Bernard's father, Arthur: a human apostrophe. He was there but only to show us that something precious had gone astray. When Bernard said he was being posted overseas I asked him who was going to look after his father now. A bewildered expression was all I got to tell me that I was.

Arthur never spoke. He shook his head, he nodded, he grunted, he sighed, he even tutted. But no word came through his lips – not even his sneeze would accidentally say, 'A tissue.' But gradually I came to notice his eyebrows. Two dark, thick, bushy lines roving over his forehead. I forgot about waiting for his lips to move and started reading those hairy brows instead. They were more expressive than Bernard's mouth had ever been. Two upward flicks and he was asking if I'd like a cup of tea. One up one down, and he wanted to know if I was sure.

And it didn't take me long to appreciate that Arthur was a magician. Out in the garden all day he could pull carrots, cabbages, potatoes, turnips, swedes, parsnips out of rubble and stone. One day I came home to find him holding up an onion for me. Big as a ball, a perfect specimen, its skin golden brown and crackling. He laughed when I asked, 'Where in heaven's name did you get that?' Then slowly he revealed another one in his other hand. What wonderful things – I could have gone into the street and sold them for twenty guineas each. No one had seen an onion for months. But Arthur had two. And it was him that lovingly cooked me the sausage and mash with onion gravy.

He would queue for hours for food. Lines and lines and lines of women and then Arthur – this ageing gentleman trussed up in his gaberdine with his little cloth bag – standing still and silent as a monument to patience. They'd let him in the queue in front of them sometimes, the women: they felt sorry for him just like I once did. He looked broken, trembling at the slightest noise, his face changing from plain-day to wild and hunted at the drop of a pin. But he wasn't. Without Bernard fussing about him, pulling, coaxing, he began to unfurl as sure as a flower that finally feels the sun when the tree is gone. And in the evenings the rotten beggar always beat me at Monopoly. His metal boot silently hoarding the board until the only course of action left to me was to declare war, sound a siren, then bomb all his blinking hotels and houses to bits.

'None of your rubbish.' That was how Franny, who worked with me at the rest centre, described them. 'Flyers. 103 Squadron. Lancasters. God's honest truth. Go on, Queenie, they deserve a bit of home comfort.' Three officers on leave for a couple of days in London before going back on active duty at their airbase in Lincolnshire. 'It's a favour to me, really. And to my sister, who's very keen on Kip. Go on. Just for a couple of days. I know you've got the room.'

If Bernard had still been there it would have been a stony no, bomber crew or no bomber crew. Arthur was so amazed that I asked his permission, his face went blank as white bread. Then one ponderous eyebrow lifted before he nodded, yes.

The tea was too weak – both officers looked down at their cups distrusting, not wanting to swallow what they had in their mouths. They were the last leaves we had left and, in all honesty, I had used them before. I hoped this third officer was going to turn up before the pot got cold otherwise I'd have nothing to give him except some boiled-up dandelion leaves, which Arthur, and only Arthur, thought a refreshing alternative drink. The redheaded officer had skin so pale it looked to be dusted with flour. Still a boy, he giggled nervously before and after anything he said. He introduced himself as Walter but said everyone called him Ginger. I didn't ask why. But I did ask the other one why everyone called him Kip.

'Because it's my name,' he said. 'It's short for Kipling.' He was dark with a thick moustache and a deep blue chin, a growth of beard just itching to get out. He went on to explain, while carefully placing his untouched cup on the table, that his mother was an ardent admirer of Kipling. 'So it could have been worse – she was also fond of Brontë and Trollope.'

'Right . . .' I said, and was just going to ask what happened to the other chap when there were three sharp knocks at the door.

'Ah, there's the other member of our party,' Kip said.

The RAF man's hand was raised almost in salute, ready to knock at the door once more. But that wasn't the first thing I noticed. I was lost in Africa again at the Empire Exhibition, a little girl in a white organza frock with blood rising in my cheeks turning me red. He was coloured.

'Are you Mrs Bligh? Have I got the right number? Only I try three houses and they tell me this the right one.' He looked up the street again. 'I am Sergeant Roberts,' he said. His face awakened to smile a grin so broad and white you could have projected a film on it. 'You have Ginger and Kip here? You expecting me? May I come in?'

Arthur didn't even try to hide his surprise, his eyebrows rose so startled they got lost in his hair. I thought I was going to have to shake him as Kip said, 'Michael Roberts – well, well, well, late as usual.'

A direct hit from a fifty-tonner, that was what it sounded like. The house was rumbling and on the landing I was faced with a big blue bottom sliding towards me down the banister. It landed with a painful thump against the newel post because another of the officers had followed on behind and slid into his head. They were both laughing. It was Ginger who fell off on to the floor rubbing his skull. The coloured one, Michael, was jumping down the stairs three at a time. He leap-frogged over Ginger's head shouting, 'I win me bet. Stairs are quicker, boys. Come on, pay up.' I swear he flew off the last step, landing right in front of me then tripping. I put my hand out to steady him. Before I knew it he was holding me up, one arm on mine, the other round my waist saying, 'Mrs Bligh, please forgive me. So sorry.'

On hearing my name Ginger began straightening himself while Kip, doing the same, said, 'Ah, Mrs Bligh, just testing out your banisters. Very strong.' He hit it with a fist, miming 'ouch'.

I felt so old standing there in my ugly headscarf and my apron, a half-peeled potato in my hand, with these three young men, my age, shuffling about in front of me trying to stifle their giggles like I was their scolding mum. I used to lark once. 'Beardy, beardy, you're barmy – can't you join the army?' But the pity was I couldn't remember when I last choked back the giggles or jumped steps three at a time.

'We needed to have a word, Mrs Bligh,' Kip began, trying to be more sober. 'We may be late coming back. Will that matter?'

'No, Arthur can let you in. I'll tell him.'

'Thank you, that's very kind of you,' he said, looking to the others. He was obviously used to talking for them. 'Well, I hope you have a pleasant evening.'

'And you,' I said.

No sooner was the front door open than Kip grabbed Ginger's cap from his head, and leaped down the stairs while Ginger managed to kick Kip's departing backside. But Michael, the coloured one, walked out slowly, then turned back round and gave me another of his picture-house smiles.

Only Michael appeared in the morning. Standing at the kitchen door his shirt collar open, his sleeves rolled up, he waited for a moment before saying, 'Good morning.'

And I don't know why I jumped – I knew he was there. All I had to say was 'Good morning' back, put the kettle on the stove and light the gas. But I held the kettle in front of me and said, 'Would you like some . . . ?' then completely forgot the name of that brown stuff we're always drinking.

'Tea?' he said.

I giggled, tea, then poured the cold water from the kettle into the teapot.

'Yes, thank you, that would be nice. You have big house here.'

'My husband . . . well, Arthur . . .'

'Arthur is your husband?'

'No, no, *no!*' I almost screamed.

He held up his hands — his palms were pink and slashed with deep brown lines. 'Oh, pardon me,' he said.

'No . . . no . . . It's all right. My husband is in service overseas.'

'Army, navy?'

'Yes.'

'Which one?'

'No. Sorry. RAF.'

'RAF. You sure?'

That blinking silly giggle again. 'Yes,' I said, pouring the tea from the pot to a cup. I could see it was clear cold water with a few brown specks floating on the top, but blow me if I could think of a sensible thing to do about it.

I took the kettle and put it on the stove. I tried to strike a match. The first one broke, the second flew out of my hand across the kitchen floor. The third I just dropped before he said, 'Let me help you there.' As he took the matches from my hand his fingers glanced against mine. Once the stove was lit he was standing so close to me I wasn't sure whether the heat I could feel was coming from the gas ring or from him. He smelt of his night out — cigarettes, beer and a faint whiff of female cologne. He looked at the cup of water I'd made, then back at me. The corners of his mouth creased just a little — hardly a smile, more like pity. I stepped back, away from him.

'Where are the others?' I said, fussing with my hair. I was sure there was something wrong with it. Or my face. I'd taken care that morning for the first time since I can remember. I'd curled my hair but a bit of fringe still flopped all straight. I had such little lipstick left I had to push my fingernail right down into the tube to get any out. No powder, no rouge. I pinched my cheeks for pink but maybe I'd done it too much – scratched my face, made weals come up. Because even if he wasn't using his eyes he was examining me. Or maybe I'd overdone my lily-of-the-valley.

'Ginger's still asleep. He had a good night. But Kip? I cannot tell you a lie, Mrs Bligh . . .'

'Queenie, please call me Queenie,' I said, then regretted it as his eyes, lively as fairy lights, ran the wrong way all over those words as sure as if I'd written them backwards on a page.

'Queenie,' he said slowly, then added, 'Kip did not return with us. His young lady had something else in mind for him.'

'What was that?' I asked.

He sat down, lifting his face to look at me before I realised what a daft question it was. But, being a fool, I still waited for his reply. 'I'm sorry, I don't know what it was,' he finally said.

I went to the sink, turning my back to him. My legs were bare, my feet a little apart. I closed them together. I knew my dress had an odd button at the front. I put my hand up to feel it. The button was undone! I quickly did it up. Blinking fringe kept falling over my eye as I picked up the teapot. The dress I had on was a little too short and a little too tight. I knew he was watching me. I tried to relax my pose – lifting my weight on to one foot. But I worried that it made the dress look shorter and pulled across the hips so I stood back straight. I was aware of what every single part of me was doing. Bits that used to work on their own suddenly needed my control. Move hand and don't shake. Come on, Lungs, in and out, in and out. Stop swallowing, Throat! I couldn't pour the precious tea away: it was unused and Arthur had queued for hours for it. I took the strainer and poured the water out through it – the puddle of leaves collecting. All the time I was thinking, I bet he's wondering what the blinking heck I'm doing. The plughole started to slurp loudly as the water went down it. I put my finger in the hole to try to stop the disgusting noise in case he believed it was me. I could smell burning as he said, 'Queenie?' I turned round so fast I knocked the tea strainer off the draining-board. The tea splattered on to the floor, bursting a shrapnel of black spots up my leg. I know he saw but he was busy taking the kettle off the stove – so carefully, his hand wrapped awkwardly in his pulled-down shirt sleeve. 'Perhaps,' he said, shaking the kettle a little to show me, 'we should put some water into this.'

I only noticed he had a moustache later that evening when he was standing at my door. I'd thought it a black shadow against his lip. But in the dull electric light of the hallway I could see it was the thinnest line of stubby hair. Leaning casually against the door-frame, his jacket slung over his shoulder he asked, 'Would you perchance have a tin-opener?'

'Why do you want a tin-opener?'

'So I may open a tin.'

I found that answer a little rude. I'm not that daft. 'I thought you had all gone out for the evening.'

He stood up straight, lifting his arm to rest high on the door-frame beside me. 'They both have companions they are going to meet and I am a little tired.' He started to rummage in the pockets of his jacket and pulled out a tin of ham. He handed it to me, saying, 'It needs a tin-opener.' Still feeling in his jacket he produced a bar of American chocolate and, I hardly recognised it, an orange. 'And these need someone to share them.'

I hoped I wasn't too eager when I said, 'Well, why don't you come and join us, then?'

'Are you gambling?' I asked. I'd not been out in the kitchen that long but when I got back Michael and Arthur had cards fanned in their hands and the table between them was piled with little stacks of coppers.

'No, I am gambling,' Michael said, without looking at me. 'Your father-in-law here knows he is going to win.'

'How d'you mean?'

'Because he is cheating.'

Cheeky beggar, I thought. He may have brought the food but he was still a guest. 'Arthur does not cheat,' I told him.

'Oh yes he does. I don't know how he do it but he does.'

'I think that is very rude of you.'

'Queenie, if he is not cheating then let me assure you that your father-in-law here is the luckiest man on this earth.'

And I was saying, 'I really think you should apologise . . .' when Arthur looked up at me and winked. It was meant only for me but nothing could get past this RAF man – he was a rear-gunner, after all. Or was it that all of his kind were so sharp-eyed? He glanced from me to Arthur and back again. 'So, I am right. But no problem. You know why? Because you are a skilful cheat, Mr Bligh. Give me one more game, nah, see if I can learn your secrets.'

As Arthur shuffled the pack, his hands dealing so fast they blurred, Michael said, 'So now, Queenie, if I am not mistaken it is you who must owe me the apology,' adding, 'but later will do.'

He kept flicking at the edges of his cards, making deep-throated umming sounds. He'd slowly shake his head, tip it to one side, then the other, as he watched Arthur, who sat as still as a sunny Sunday afternoon. Michael was the colour of a conker – not ruddy and new from the shell but after it had dulled in your pocket for a bit. As he leaned forward to pick up a card his shirt gaped to show that dark skin all over his chest. Would you know he was naked when he was undressed or would he look like he was clad all over in leather?

'Mr Bligh,' he said, 'you willing to teach me your secret?'

'He doesn't speak,' I told him.

'I know – I am watching those eyebrows,' he said.

Did his hair feel like hair or something you'd scrub a pan with? Would it chafe against your skin or would it brush gentle as an angora jumper?

'You win again,' he said. The inside of his mouth was pink as a powder puff. His lips plump as sausages – would you bounce off them or would they soften when kissed?

'Come, Mr Bligh, you take all me money, you wan' show me something in return?'

But Arthur got up. He packed away the cards and counted the coppers on the table as efficiently as Bernard would.

'You can't leave me so arouse – come, tell me how you do that?'

Slipping the clinking coppers into his pocket, Arthur nodded good night – first to Michael, placing a finger to the side of his nose, and then to me with another wink – before leaving the room. Michael lifted his eyes to me. I thought he was going to say something so I held his gaze. But he didn't. One of us had to look away first. And it had to be me, I was burning up.

'I didn't know he did that – he's a constant surprise to me,' I said. Michael was still staring, still silent. 'Well, I should be getting to bed,' I said.

'Won't you stay awhile with me?'

'It's late.'

'I will be gone tomorrow. Why don't you ask me all the questions you have been thinking about sitting quiet there?'

'What questions?'

'I don't know – you tell me.'

'What makes you think I've got questions?'

'So you no curious about this coloured man in your house?'

He wasn't reading my mind, it was me – I was too obvious. 'Okay . . .' I said. 'Where are you from?'

'Where am I from?' He repeated the question two more times to himself. 'Is it too hard for you? Should I ask you something easier?' I asked.

'Jamaica.'

'In Africa?'

He made a strange noise, as if he was sucking out a bit of trapped gristle from between his front teeth. 'Why every English person I meet think Jamaica is in Africa?'

'Is it not?'

'No, it is not. It is an island in the Caribbean.'

'Oh, well, I've never been anywhere,' I said quickly.

'A person who has never travelled still believes their mother is the best cook. Do you like your mother's cooking?' His face warmed with a smile.

'Not much.'

'Then you must have made a journey somewhere.'

'Don't you miss your family?'

'I have no family in Jamaica. My mother and father are dead. There is no one else.'

'No sweetheart?' His gaze once again turned to mine. Feeling awkward I said, 'You must miss being among your own kind.'

'My own kind?' He frowned but his eyes never left me.

'I mean you're a long way from home.'

He came and knelt on the floor beside me resting his elbow on the edge of my armchair. I felt his leg gently touch my foot. 'We have bird in Jamaica,' he said, softly as a bedtime story. 'A humming-bird – our national bird.' His breath was on my cheek. 'It is very small but beautiful – blue, green, purple, red – every colour you can see in its tiny feathered body. And when it flies, its wings flicker so fast your eye cannot see them. It hovers – its wings beating to hold it still – while, steady as a man with a gun, it sticks its long yellow beak into the flower to feed . . .' His hands made tender movements close to my face – his fingers the fluttering wings, his pinched lips the still beak. 'One time in London during the Blitz, everywhere I look is devastation. But then you know what I see?' His hand floated up high. 'A humming-bird. In the middle of rubble and bricks, a humming-bird. In the buses and bustle of a city, a humming-bird. Piccadilly and Trafalgar Square and a humming-bird. I thought my eye was playing trick on me – too long flying in this war. But not only I saw.' He was mesmerised – staring at our ceiling as if that pretty bird was flying near our cornice and coving, and pointing so I might see it too. 'A humming-bird in London. I watched that bird like I see an old friend. It looked dowdier in this grey British light – no sun to sparkle it up. But there it was so far from home and so happy to have the chance to sample the nectar of English flowers.' And as his hand fluttered downward, his fingers delicately caressed my hair.

Twenty-nine

Queenie

It wasn't me. Mrs Queenie Bligh, she wasn't even there. This woman was a beauty – he couldn't get enough of her. He liked the downy softness of the blonde hairs on her legs. Her nipples were the pinkest he'd ever seen. Her throat – he just had to kiss her throat. This woman was as sexy as any starlet on a silver screen. The zebra of their legs twined and untwined together on the bed. Her hands, pale as a ghost's, caressed every part of his nut-brown skin. She was so desirable he polished her with hot breath – his tongue lapping between her legs like a cat with cream. It wasn't me. This woman watching his buttocks rise and fall sucked at every finger on his hand. She clawed his back and cried out until his mouth lowering down filled hers with his eager tongue. It wasn't me. This woman panted and thrust and bit. And when he rolled her over she yelped wickedly into the pillow. Mrs Queenie Bligh would never do such a thing. That one, Mrs Bligh, usually worked out what she could make for dinner during sexual relations with her husband. But this woman, if it hadn't been for the blackout, could have lit up London.

I'd felt him leave me in the night. With me naked under the slovenly bedclothes, the side of the bed that he'd heated so nicely gradually grew stone cold. I knew Michael, and the other two, were all down to catch an early train in the

248

morning – they'd asked about the best route to the station. It wasn't long before they were all jumping the stairs and slamming their way out, back to their squadron for more active service. But there was a gentle knock on my bedroom door before they left – once, twice. It even opened a crack before it was carefully shut. It seemed so feeble to me just to say a simple goodbye. Truth of it was, Michael Roberts deserved a fanfare with trumpets and dancers. But with Arthur waking me so urgently it did occur to me that perhaps I was wrong – that there was still a woolly-haired black head or a foot with five nigger toes where my buttoned-up, pyjamaed husband should have been.

'What is it, Arthur?' I asked. There are times when his eyebrows just will not do. Like a dog trying to get his master to come to rescue the kid down the well, I had to guess what these grunts and pointing fingers and head-flicking movements meant. 'Oh, for pity's sake,' I finally snapped. 'There's nothing wrong with your voice, Arthur – can't you just bloody well say it for once?' A blank curtain dragged across his eager expression and I immediately regretted what I'd said. I was so sorry.

He'd found a battered leather wallet that Sergeant Michael Roberts must have mislaid or forgotten in his rush to get away. There were photographs in its tattered inside. One of an old negro man standing formally in front of a house. Looking to all the world like a chimpanzee in clothes, this lord of the manor stood behind a seated black woman with white hair and a face as grumpy as Monday morning. Another was of a little darkie girl with fuzzy-wuzzy hair tied in ribbons as big as bandages. They were like any airman's photos, dog eared and fading with sentiment. The wallet must have fallen from his jacket when he was rummaging for his war-time weapons of seduction – his tin of ham, his orange. But there was something about its tattiness that let you know this wallet had been places. Stuffed into a pocket, jammed into a kit-bag, sheltered in a hat. It was so beloved its preciousness warmed my fingers as I held it. It might even have been his good-luck charm. I was told that most flyers had them – that they weren't safe flying without them. This was Michael Roberts's fortune and it had no place lying in my hand. So I dressed quickly with the idea of catching him at the station, handing it to him before it was too late. And, anyway, it was easier to find a coloured man in RAF uniform at a station than it was to spend the morning looking apologetically into Arthur's face and finding his wanton trollop of a daughter-in-law could no longer stare him in the eye.

I was not far from the station when I heard my name being called with the urgency Bernard used when he needed a towel getting out the bath. Looking around me I swore someone was taking my photograph – the flashlight's spark burnt spots on to my eyes. But then my legs were lifting off the ground. I could see the pavement lowering under me, feel a whoosh of air, a roaring waterless sea rushing my ears. Then everything was quiet except for a note that sang sharp and high in my head. I wasn't the only one flying. Over there a woman, a bundle of rags, was rolling over – a cardigan, a skirt, twisting and flapping. A man, or was it a boy? making an arc, diving off a swimming-board. A silent ballet so beautiful my eyes were sucked from their sockets with the sight. Something hit me hard across the back taking all the wind from me. And then I was coming back down. Sliding down the slide near our school. Wilfred in his dead dad's boots screeching like a girl. 'Shut up,' I told him, 'you'll wake the dead.' Landing with such a thump – the ground is so hard in winter. 'It's dark. Look at the fog. What a pea-souper! Go home. I don't want to slide again, Wilfred, and I'm out of puff now. You find your own way home. Go on, hop it. I'm going to stay here and have a little sleep.'

When I woke up, Wilfred's sharp screeching had stopped. He must have gone home. No, Queenie, he was never there. And that wasn't fog, that was bricks and glass and wood and soot billowing in thick folds of dirty cauliflower smoke. One of my shoes was gone, my coat was ripped, and my skirt was up round my waist, knickers on view for anyone who wanted a look. Crunchy slivers of glass were in my hair. The taste of blood was in the corner of my mouth.

Perhaps I was dead. My back was against a wall, slumped where I'd fallen, unable to move, watching silently with an angel singing in my ear. A doll falling slowly from the sky towards a tree: a branch stripped of all its leaves caught the doll in its black spikes. A house had had its front sliced off as sure as if it had been opened on a hinge. A doll's house with all the rooms on show. The little staircase zigzagging in the cramped hall. The bedroom with a bed sliding, the sheet dangling, flapping a white flag. A wardrobe open with the clothes tripping out from the inside to flutter away. Empty armchairs sitting cosy by the fire. The kettle on in the kitchen with two wellington boots by the stove. And in a bathroom – standing by the side of a bath, caught by the curtain going up too soon on a performance – a totally naked woman. A noiseless scream from a lady who was gazing at the doll in the tree that dangled limp and filthy in a little pink hat. The lady landing hard on her knees started to pray, while a man in uniform turned slowly round to vomit.

But surely the dead don't feel pain, that's the whole point. Population, that's what I was. Smouldering like a kipper, I was one of the bombed. If it was a doodlebug I hadn't heard its low moaning hum. Hadn't had time to plot where it was going to come down. But surely I'd been walking among houses? A woman had called out from a window, 'Herman, get in here,' and I'd thought, How common. The boy running past me had made a face as he went by. And a tabby cat was stretched on a step. Too everyday to remember but surely there were people walking, looking at watches to see if they were late for a train, arm in arm, carrying bags? There was an old man reading a paper and a pub on the corner with a sign that swayed. Where had they gone? Now it was all jagged hills of wreckage, crumbling, twisting, creaking, smoking under far too much sky. There was only this bleak landscape left.

'Can you get up, love? Can you hear me? Can you get up, missus? Are you all right? Can you move?' A man's face was very close to mine, breath as foul as a dog's. I could only just hear him but I knew what he was saying – I'd said those sort of things so many times myself. I pointed in case no one but me had seen the naked woman in the bathroom. He looked round. 'Don't you worry about that, we'll take care of that young lady. Let's see if you can move. Tell me your name. Can you tell me your name?'

I said, 'Queenie,' at least I thought I did.

'Can you hear me, love? What's your name?'

'Queenie.'

'Right, Queenie, let's try to get you up. You don't look too bad. I've seen worse turned out of pubs on a Saturday night. Up you get.'

Three men were putting up a ladder, trying to find a footing for it in the quicksand of rubble. While the naked woman – her dark pubic hair a perfect triangle – stared out from the shattered room as if a bit puzzled as to why she was now so cold.

'Can you walk to the ambulance? Course you can.'

Bits of me that should have slid easily together cracked so painfully I needed oiling. Glass sprinkled down from me as constant as a Christmas tree shedding its leaves. One of the men started up the ladder – he trod each rung as dainty as if it were mined.

'Come on, Queenie, can you walk? Don't you worry about what's going on there, that's being taken care of. You just watch where you're walking.'

The man was with her now, up there in the once-private bathroom, beckoning her to come to him, to step to the ladder. But she stood like stone, unwilling to admit there was anything amiss. He tested the sheared floor, bouncing on it gently, then stepped off the rungs. When he reached her he wrapped his coat round her urging her to put her arms into the sleeves. She obeyed like a sleepwalker.

I took four steps, the man helping me along. I knew it was four steps because every one was as difficult as for a newborn. At first my ankle wobbled. My shoeless foot was lacerated. On the third step I almost tripped. It was on the fourth that my torn naked foot landed on something soft. Looking down, I saw I had stepped into the upturned palm of a hand – the fingers closing round my foot with the reflex of my weight. I could feel its warmth coming up through my sole. 'Sorry,' I said, expecting to hear a cry of pain.

'Just keep your eye on that ambulance, that's where we're going. Queenie, can you hear me? Can you hear me? Come on, love – not far now. We'll soon have you nice and safe.'

The hand was wearing a gold ring, clothed in a blue woollen sleeve, but lying there attached to no one. My foot was being cradled by a severed arm that merely ended in a bloodsoaked fraying.

* * *

So many people at the hospital told me I was lucky. A nurse, a policeman, even a little old woman with an oversized white bandage over one eye said, 'Never mind, it could have been worse.' Some cracked ribs, a sprained wrist and a cheek swollen to the size and colour of an overripe plum. After a rocket attack — yes, I suppose that was blinking lucky.

'I'll be all right, I'll be all right,' I kept telling Arthur. He fretted round me like a mother. He fetched tea, then sat close, watching my hand trembling the cup up to my chin. I had to put it down before too much was spilt. He brought a cloth, gently wiped it round my face. He then placed the cup in my hand again. This time his hand, for once steady as a rock, enfolded mine, bracing it until the warm sweet drink was safely in my mouth.

'Bit of a turn-round, eh, Arthur?' I said. I wasn't lucky, I was pathetic. Years of war, all those bombed-out people who could joke and smile at me with a steady gaze just after they'd had everything wiped out, and here was I, shaking so much that an old shell-shocked veteran had to help me get tea to my lips.

'Trust me, eh, Arthur, to get killed when the war's nearly won. Funny, really, when you look at it like that. Don't you think it's funny? Eh, Arthur, do you think it's funny?'

He had to help me to bed, walking me up the stairs — I was an invalid.

'I heard someone call my name. Just before the blast someone called me. Who was it, d'you think? Do you think it could have been Auntie Dorothy or my little brother Jimmy, warning me, you know, from beyond?' I didn't ask him if he thought it was Michael seeing me in the street, although I wanted to. But Arthur was tucking in the bedclothes and plumping pillows that still had an improper whisper of Michael Roberts on them. I couldn't do up the buttons on my nightdress, my fingers were all quivering thumbs. 'Come on, Queenie, pull yourself together,' I said. Arthur, sitting me on the edge of the bed, carefully did them up for me. 'Thank you,' I told him. He tucked me in, swaddling me tight enough for an anxious baby. Then, lowering his head, he slowly moved towards me. And I knew he was going to kiss me. But he was going to kiss me on the mouth. I turned my head to the side. He hovered, fearful as a lover gone too far. Softly, slowly, his lips opened.

'I would die if anything happened to you,' he said, one careful word at a time.

'Arthur, you spoke.' His voice, deep like Bernard's, was posh as the BBC. I was as stunned as if the wardrobe had told me it could take no more clothes. 'You spoke. You can speak.' I waited, wanting him to say something else. Talk to me. All those things he'd seen he could tell me now. Explain how it was for him. What he felt, what he thought. Recite me a poem, perhaps. But he didn't – he just leaned forward again, this time to kiss my forehead. And I couldn't help it – I started to sob. Bring me back the blinking chiming clock, the knitting needles going clack, clack, clack, and Bernard pulling his chair closer to the wireless before giving me a tut. I had had enough of war. Come on, let's all just get back to being bored.

'Don't leave me,' I told Arthur. I opened the covers for him to get into the bed with me. But he tucked them back, then pulled the chair up beside me and sat down. Silently.

1948

Thirty

Gilbert

If the Almighty, perusing that list in the celestial book, was to have told me, 'One day, Gilbert Joseph, you will be pleased that by your name, in the list of achievements, is written only the one word . . . driver,' I would have had to tell the deity, delicate but firm, that He was mad. But, as ever, the Almighty in His wisdom proved to be right. Come, let me tell you how. See me now. I am dressed no longer in my RAF uniform of blue but still, from the left, from the right, this West Indian man is looking just as fine in his best civilian suit. In my hand I have a letter of introduction from the forces labour exchange concerning a job as a storeman. I take it to the office of the potential employer.

I enter and am greeted by an Englishman who smiles on me and shakes my hand. 'Come in. Sit down,' he tell me. A cup of tea is brought and placed before me. All good signs – I have the job, I comfort myself. The man takes up the letter to read the contents. Everything is in order. 'So, you were in the RAF?' he ask.

'Yes, sir.'

'I was in the RAF. Where were you stationed?' There then followed a short conversation about those days, before the man said, 'Myself, I was in Falmouth.' For the next hour I am having to shift delicately on my seat and pinch myself so my eyes do not close, while this man acquaint me with his time on radar.

In a pause between his breaths I shrewdly remind him of the job I had come to see him about. Was it to be mine?

'No, sorry,' he say.

His explanation was that there were women working in the factory. Not understanding his meaning I said that I did not mind. He smiled at this and then told me, 'You see, we have white women working here. Now, in the course of your duties, what if you accidentally found yourself talking to a white woman?' For a moment the man sounded so reasonable, so measured, I thought him to be talking sense.

'I would be very courteous to her,' I assured him.

But he shook his head. He wanted no answer from me. 'I'm afraid all hell would break loose if the men found you talking to their women. They simply wouldn't stand for that. As much as I'd like to I can't give you the job. You must see the problems it would cause?'

Once my breath had returned enabling me to speak again, I asked him why he could not have told me this an hour before when I still had feeling in my backside. He tell me he wanted to be kind to an ex-serviceman.

Another office I am invited into, the man ask me if I am a Christian. Let me tell you, after a few weeks back in this after-the-war England, God slipping from me like a freshly launched ship. But I say yes. The man start praying among the telephone and blotting-pad. He invite me to join him. I need the job so I lower my head. At the end of praising the Lord together he tell me he cannot employ me because his partner does not like coloured people. I nearly knock him into an early meeting with the Almighty when he called on God to bless me as I left.

In five, no, in six places, the job I had gone for vanish with one look upon my face. Another, I wait, letter in my hand, while everyone in this office go about their business as if I am not there. I can feel them watching me close as a pickpocket with his prey but cannot catch even a peeping twinkle of an eye. Until a man come in agitated. 'What're you doing here?' he say to me. 'We don't want you. There's no job for you here. I'm going to get in touch with that labour exchange, tell them not to send any more of you people. We can't use your sort. Go on, get out.'

The girl at another office look on me with such horror – man, I swear her hair standing straight as stiff fingers – that with no hesitation I walk right back out again. Was I to look upon that expression every day? Come, soon I would believe that there was indeed something wrong with me.

After a few weeks of this benighted behaviour it was as the Almighty had foretold. This ex-RAF man had come to love his full and permanent driving licence. Man, I was as jubilant as a boy on his birthday when my hands finally caressed the cold of a steering-wheel as a postman driver for the Post Office. Ah, that celestial book. I may not have been studying the law in this Mother Country but, let me tell you, for a Jamaican man a job as a driver was great luck – if only luck England-style.

'Oi, you,' the foreman said at the sorting office. As far as I can remember this man had used my name on only one occasion. When I first stood before him his gaping mouth had mumbled, 'What's all this?' Looking confused he rifled through pieces of paper from his seniors. Then, finding that I was indeed the driver he had requested, he said, 'Humph. You're Joseph, right?' However, since that early, almost courteous encounter, 'Oi, you', had become his preferred way of addressing me. Scraping ice from the windscreen of a van, I did not answer in the hope it might force him to use my given name as he did to all his other drivers.

'Clarke's sick,' he told me.

Bert Clarke. I had been delivering and collecting with Bert from Victoria for weeks. On every run, there and back, he insisted on telling me the way. Left here . . . right now . . . round the roundabout. He believed I, as a foreigner, did not know or could ever learn the route. Every day the same way, and every day the same instruction. He had been working for the Post Office since men still rode the mail across the land on horseback, he assured me. But his drilling had lately become accompanied with an unruly cough. 'Oh, sorry, Gilbert, bit of a frog today but you're doing all right.'

'Sick?' I said.

'Yeah. Don't you know what sick means?' The moustache on this fore-man always seemed to have a little bit of egg yolk clinging tenacious to it. And the bothersome ice had so numbed my fingers I was unable to make a fist.

'There's someone else on the run with you. Get going.'

The foreman pointed this young man, who was to partner me, in the direction of my van. I watched this man. Strutting along, his hands in his pockets. He wiped his nose with his sleeve. Took the cigarette from his mouth with his thumb and first finger. Smoke wafted from the side of his lips. He coughed and spat on the ground before replacing the cigarette. He saw someone he knew and, smiling, he waved: 'All right.' And at that moment I longed to be once more in Jamaica. I yearned for home as a drunk man for whisky. For only there could I be sure that someone looking on my face for the first time would regard it without reaction. No gapes, no gawps, no cussing, no looking quickly away as if seeing something unsavoury. Just a meeting as unremarkable as passing your mummy in the kitchen. What a thing was this to wish for. That a person regarding me should think nothing. What a forlorn desire to seek indifference.

Seeing me, the young man approaching my van stopped dead. I greeted him with a smile. But suddenly his forehead was frowning – two sharp parallel lines dramatically creasing on his head. He pulled the cigarette from his mouth to allow it to open wider. Throwing it down he screwed it into the ground with his foot while looking around him to make sure I was not a joke played on him by his mates. He lifted his finger to point at me and only then did he shout, 'What the bloody hell is going on?'

Some jeers carried through the air from the other men looking on at this comical situation. Oh, it was so funny – their friend has got the coon. I had got no time for this. 'Come on, man,' I tell him, 'we have to go.'

'I ain't going nowhere with you,' he say, before starting off back to the foreman.

The foreman took me off the run.

'Why?' I ask him. 'I have been doing this run for weeks with no trouble.'

'Because I said so. He don't wanna work with you.'

'But it is his job.'

'And I don't bloody blame him. I said you'd be trouble.'

'I am not the one giving the trouble.'

'One more word out of you, coon, and you're out. You can pick up from King's Cross on your own. Or get your cards. You got it?'

This was the first time I had been to King's Cross. And standing by the trolleys of sacks that had been taken from the train it was not obvious to me which were for Post Office sorting. I did not want to mistakenly take railway parcels as this would cause great commotion.

'Which ones are post?' I ask a group of workers – four men – who were standing watching me.

'Did I hear someone speak?' one of them say. They looked as idle as layabouts, leaning on a wall scratching themselves. All began chuckling at this man's funny joke.

'Will you help me?' I ask again. I got no reply but all looked to me mischievous like I was sport. Rolling their eyes around pretending they cannot hear where my voice is coming from. Ignoring them, I move to lift a sack.

'Look, a darkie's stealing from the railways,' one of them shout. I put down that sack and go for another. As long as I take the right thing that is all that concerns me. As I pick up another sack I hear, 'Oh, my God, what's the coon doing, now?' How many sacks I pick up and with all they jeer that I am wrong?

'Can you please help me?' I have to ask them.

'Speak English,' one of them say.

'It is English I am speaking,' I tell him.

'Anyone understand what this coloured gentleman is after?' More laughing.

But, man, I could not afford to get into trouble. 'Could you please tell me what I am to take?'

'All right,' one of them say. This man pushing himself from the wall moved closer to me. One of his eyes looked at me while the other roamed in the socket like a lost marble. I am thinking maybe they had tired of this sport – after all, they had been playing with this coon for a long time now. But this cross-eye man just say, 'I'll tell you, if you answer something for me.' His friends start chuckling again in anticipation of a nice piece of humiliation.

But I answer him civilly, 'What?'

'When are you going back to the jungle?' Oh, man, this is the best joke these four men had heard today. They all laugh at this. A coon. The jungle. What a lark. Two of them light up cigarettes. Man, I am better than a tea-break. While the hands on the clock keep moving. I pick up another sack. 'Oi, darkie, you ain't answered me. When are you going back to where you belong?'

And I said straight into this man's one eye, 'But I just get here, man, and I not fucked your wife yet.'

'What did you say? What did he say?' He turned to his pals but they had not heard. 'Fucking wog. What did you just say?'

'Nothing,' I tell him.

Then this man grabs a handful of my Post Office uniform to pull me to him. 'Go on, hit him,' his chums encourage. But this is one fool man. My arms are free. So, let me see, I could have whacked his nose until it cracked and bled. Or punched his stomach so his breakfast choke him. I could have pulled his head back, grabbed his throat and wrung breath from him. Knee him in his balls. Wind him with an elbow. Smash my forehead into his mouth to dislodge a few teeth. And all before his friends had time to reach me. His grip was not strong. This man was skinny from rationing. Come, let us face it, I could have just blown on him to push him to the ground. But if I was even to friendly tweak this man's cheek, or matey pat his back, I knew I would lose my job. Three white men looking on would have the story – the day the darkie, unprovoked, attacked this nice gentleman. Savages, they would say. And all would agree, we must never employ any more of these coons: they are trouble – more trouble than they are worth. What else could this Jamaican man do? I dropped my head.

'I said nothing, man. Nothing.' And then I cringed craven until my submission cause this man to leave hold.

'I'll have to wash my fucking hands now I've touched you,' he told me, pushing me from him. I stood pitiful as a whipped dog while this man said, 'There's decent Englishmen that should be doing your job.' I kept my eyes at his feet while he indicated with his chin, 'Over there, that trolley. Now get packed up and fuck off.' And I went about my business with a gunfire of cuss words popping and pinging around me, while the postal sacks and an aching shame stooped me double.

Come, let us face it, I had forgotten all about Hortense by the time I arrive home from work that evening. All I am dreaming of as I climbed the stairs was to lie down on the bed and sleep. Perhaps dream of walking in the heat of the sun nyamming a mango. Or sipping sorrel with Elwood on the veranda. But I am woken rude as I opened the door of the room. Hortense was on her hands and knees there before me on the floor.

'Get up! Get up!' I shout. The anger so loud the force bounce from the wall to slap me back. She is startled. She jump and spill water from a bucket. She fuss to mop at it but I grab her arm. Enclose my hand round it and pull her from the floor. With the shock her feet make no struggle to stand upright. 'Get up from off your knees,' I tell her.

Suddenly she is looking in my face. Fear rounding and watering her eyes. She leaps away from my grip, her chest gasping for breath. 'What is wrong with you?' she say.

'I am sorry,' I tell her. 'I am sorry.' I back away from her to show her I am not a madman. To let her know she is safe. 'But I cannot stand to see you on your knees, Hortense.'

'But I have to wash this floor. The floor need washing.'

And I say, 'I cannot see you on your knees so soon. I did not bring you to England to scrub a floor on your knees. No wife of mine will be on her knees in this country. You hear me?'

'How you wan' me clean the floor, then?'

'Any way,' I plead. 'Any way, Hortense. But please, please, not on your knees.'

Thirty-one

Hortense

'This is not chips,' Gilbert Joseph say to me. 'Your mummy never tell you how to make chips?'

'My mother,' I tell him, 'taught me to be thankful for the food the Lord provide.'

'But your mummy not here to eat this.'

The man was fussing again, looking on his plate as if all that was odious rested there. Everything I do in this sorry place he find fault. I move his suit from the wall. All day it hang flimsy there – this jacket and trouser like the trace of a man. And it watch me. Each time I catch this empty suit in my view, I swear, an arm would move or a leg would wiggle. But when I turn on it sudden it would stop. I placed the garments in the chest of drawers so it could no longer menace me. Why I touch his suit? His suit will crease. That is his best suit. So vex is he his bottom lip stick out far enough for me to wipe a postage stamp on it.

'I have to tidy the place,' I tell him. But I cannot even wash the filthy floor without raising his wrath. 'Get up, get up!' The Lord will be my witness – this fool man was unreasonable.

'How you don't know what is a chip?' he ask me. He pick up the potato with his finger to hold it up to show me. Any fool could tell it would burn

264

him. He drop it again and blow on his hand. I tell him the Englishwoman downstairs assure me this is a chip. His eye is wide awake now. 'You been talking to Queenie?'

It was she that inform me that a chip is a potato cut up small. Reminding me twice that it must be peeled first. So I cut up the little Irish potatoes as instructed. I have only the one little ring to cook on but I place the chips of potato in a pan of water so they might boil.

When Gilbert Joseph came in from work the cold clung to him so fierce the room shivered in his trail. He proceeded straight to the fire, not even stopping to remove his coat. He pulled up the chair in front of it and lordly placed himself down on it, blocking all the heat as sure as a stormcloud before the sun. And it is in this fireplace where I am having to cook his wretched chips. The ring of blue gas flame I am to cook on snake just in front of the fire in the hearth. I cannot get round this brute of a man to carry on my work.

'You must move,' I tell him.

'Why?' he say.

'So I might make the food.'

He move his foot a little way to the left and say, 'You can get by me here.'

'No, I cannot,' I say. 'Can you please go somewhere else?' But the man just suck on his teeth then lift up his legs to rest his feet on the mantelpiece above the fire.

'You can sit on the bed until I am finished,' I tell him.

'I am cold,' he say.

'But your leg is in my way.'

He shut his eyes so he could no longer see me but his lips still pout ill-tempered. 'You can get under my legs,' he tell me.

'What?' This man cannot bear to see his wife washing the floor on her knees but is content to have me limbo back and forth beneath his legs to make his food.

'I have just come in from outside. I must warm myself up.' He show me the path I can take under his big leg, waving his hand back and forth. 'Plenty room to get by,' he say.

'Move yourself,' I tell him. But the buffoon pay me no mind except to budge his leg to rest a little higher. Soon he is snoozing there on the chair – his head lolling on his hand, his mouth gaping. While I am left crawling under his legs like a cringing dog, carrying a pan of water. Ducking beneath his foot with the chip potato. Crouching to stir the pot. And twisting misshapen to see it is cooking right.

I had to shake him awake when the food was ready. And as he stirred he gaze on me as if he had never before beheld me.

'You will take off your coat now?' I ask him.

'No,' he say. And again he say no when I ask him to come to the table to eat.

'The proper place to eat your food is at the table.'

'You can eat where you want, Miss High-class. I am too cold to move.' He just hold out his hand for the plate. Then looking on the dinner before him he say, 'What is this?' But I paid him no mind. 'Hortense, what kind of meal you call this?'

The Englishwoman downstairs tell me that the English like to serve chip with egg. This was pleasing to me because I had learned at college to cook an egg like the English do. Four minutes in boiling water. So I had served up Gilbert the chip potato with the egg. I thought to take the shell from the egg but I had in mind to watch how this man I had married would eat the egg. It was in domestic science that Miss Henry had showed we girls the proper way to eat an egg. Sliced across the top with a knife. On no account were we to tap the egg with a spoon to remove the shell, and only the uncouth could be found dipping a slice of bread into the yolk.

'What is this?' he say again. All the while this egg is rolling round on the plate.

'It is chips with an egg,' I tell him.

He gaze on me inscrutable for a long while, only his breath in motion. 'You can't cook at all, can you?' he finally say.

'Eat up,' I tell him, 'before it gets perishing.'

He lower his head, stroking his hand down his chin before saying, 'What?'

'How long you been in this country and you don't know what is perishing?

Cold. Eat up before it get cold.' The man start to mumble and I know it is the Lord's name he is taking in vain.

'You can't even cook a simple thing like chips.'

'You are ungrateful, Gilbert Joseph.'

'Chips is fried,' he say, flicking angry at the potato on his plate.

'Well, how can I do anything with your big leg in the way?' I tell him.

'Look,' he shout. 'I take away me leg. You know how to cook chips now?'

I averted my gaze from him, left my plate at the table and went to sit on the bed. This vile man would not make me cry. This uncouth ruffian would see no tear in my eye. And he cannot even see how I tidy up this wretched little room. How I make up the bed with the pretty bedspread. How I clean the sink, wash the walls. He does not notice that his precious armchair is resting on a wood box and not the Holy Bible. He does not see the plates cleaned and tidied away. The rug beaten. Or the cloth on the table. Just his big body blocking all the heat of the fire with steam rising from his coat like a dragon. It was I who should complain over this intolerable situation. But it was he that look over on me to sigh long and hard.

'I can show you how to make chips,' he say.

'I do not need any help from you, Gilbert Joseph,' I tell him.

'Have it your way, Miss Can't Cook.' He start to crack his egg as I had imagined he would. He smash the shell into little pieces to pick it off. But as the heat began to rise from the egg even I can smell it is bad. It renk like a gully in the heat. He jump up. 'Man, this egg gone bad!'

'It is not my fault you have a bad egg. I did not buy the egg,' I tell him. He throw the plate to the floor spilling the potatoes and the stinking runny egg over the beaten carpet.

'I can take no more of this!' he yell, for everyone in the house to hear. And he charge from the room slamming the door so ferocious the armchair collapse sideways off its box.

Thirty-two

Gilbert

Perhaps Elwood was right. 'Stay in Jamaica,' he had begged me. 'Stay and fight till you look 'pon what you wan' see.' My boyhood friend, what was passing before his eye now in that Caribbean island? Sitting on the veranda, he was watching the Jamaican sun as, lowering, the sky glowed purple orange blue pink. Sucking on soursop, the juice sticky on his chin, the flesh fat between his teeth. The cicadas singing, he raise his legs on to a foot-rest and sigh. In the cooling evening heat his hand flop down to take up a glass of his mummy's honeyed ginger juice while he calls for his friend Aubrey to join him. And the two men share a joke sitting there resting on the veranda after a long day. Chatting while supping, soon they are shaking laughter into the sweet Jamaican night air.

And you know what the joke was that they share? Gilbert Joseph. It was I that was their merriment. See me walking in the London street with the rain striking me cold as steel pins. My head bent low, wrapping my arms round me to keep the cold from killing me. With nowhere to go but away from a wretched room and a woman I marry so I might once more sail the seas to glory in indignity and humiliation in the Mother Country. But it is not only I that make them chuckle. All we ex-RAF servicemen who, lordly in our knowledge of England, had looked to those stay-at-home boys to inform

268

them that we knew what to expect from the Mother Country. The lion's mouth may be open, we told them, but we had counted all its teeth. But, come, let us face it, only now were we ex-servicemen starting to feel its bite.

Take Eugene. This mild-mannered man was going about his business when an old woman trip on the kerb and fall down in front of him. He rush to her side, his hand out for her to hold. On his lips were soft words spoken. 'Let me help you up – come, are you hurt?' This nice old English lady took one look at him and scream. She yell so bad the police came running. Eugene was taken away. The charge? Attacking an old lady. In the police cell Eugene sweat himself scrawny before this old woman clear up the matter.

A devout Christian, Curtis was asked not to return to his local church for his skin was too dark to worship there. The shock rob him of his voice.

Louis now believed bloodyforeigner to be all one word. For, like bosom pals, he only ever heard those words spoken together.

And Hortense. Her face was still set haughty. But how long before her chin is cast down? For, fresh from a ship, England had not yet deceived her. But soon it will. All us pitiful West Indian dreamers who sailed with heads bursting with foolishness were a joke to my clever smirking cousin now.

Regret had its hand clasped to my throat as I walked that London street, my desire smothered and choking. Then I heard someone call after me. I took no notice. A shriek of surprise: what coloured man in England would look to stare when they heard that? But it came again this time with words, 'Excuse me, excuse me.' And the clip clop of a woman's footfall along the pavement. I stopped and, turning slowly, I saw a tiny woman approach me. Out of breath, smiling, she looked up in my face. Not a young woman – forty, fifty, it was hard to tell in the street-lamp glow. But her smile was wholehearted. 'You dropped this, I think,' she said. It was a black glove. I was not sure it was mine but beguiled by the gesture I took it from her.

As I parted my lips to thank her no words came. Trying again I could only mouth the gratitude.

'Are you all right?' she asked me.

A tear was on my face. I could feel its damp, itchy path creeping down to my chin. I wiped it away.

Watching me, she took her hand and laid it on my arm. 'Are you all right? You look cold. It's a cold night.'

'Yes,' I said. The place where her hand was on me was melting with the warmth of that gentle touch.

'Here,' she rummaged around in her pocket and pulled out a little bag, 'have one of these.' The bag was full of sweets. She pushed it towards me, 'Go on.' I put my hand in this little bag. The contents was one sticky hard lump. She pulled the bag away again. 'Oh, they're all stuck together. Sorry.' And she started fiddling with the bag – cracking and poking it with her fingers. 'It's cough sweets, they always get stuck together. Sorry. But they warm you up.' Once more she handed me the bag. I took one. 'Have one for later if you like.'

'No, one is fine,' I told her.

'Right, I'm going home.' She put her own hand into the bag, then the sweet into her mouth. It bulged in her cheek. 'It's the only place to be tonight,' she said, with some difficulty owing to the confection. She touched my arm again, saying, 'And cheer up, it may never happen,' then clopped off down the road.

How long did I stare at that sweet in my hand? Fool that I am, I took a handkerchief from my pocket to wrap it. I had no intention of eating that precious candy. For it was a salvation to me – not for the sugar but for the act of kindness. The human tenderness with which it was given to me. I had become hungry for the good in people. Beholden to any tender heart. All we boys were in this thankless place. When we find it, we keep it. A simple gesture, a friendly word, a touch, a sticky sweet rescued me as sure as if that Englishwoman had pulled me from drowning in the sea.

I carried two portions of fish and chips back to the room for Hortense and me. There she was, still sitting on the bed. Her face, even after this time, remained set in an ill-tempered frown. 'See here, Miss Mucky Foot,' I said. 'I have fish and chips for you and me.' Only her big eyes swivelled to my direction while her arms folded tighter across her chest. I got out two plates, which were neatly stacked in the cupboard. Unwrapping and placing the fish and chips on the plate I tell her, 'You know what the English do?' Of course she did not reply but I did not expect her to. 'They eat this food straight from the newspaper. No plate. Nothing.' I knew this high-class woman would not be able to keep her face solemn in the presence of such barbarity. Scandalised, she could not stop herself staring on me in disbelief. 'Yes, from the newspaper! So lesson number one, Miss Mucky Foot. This is a chip.' I offered the chip to her on a fork. She took it from me and popped it greedy into her mouth. 'And now lesson number two. Are you listening to me carefully.' I leaned in towards her to whisper the secret. She had her big eye on me, mesmerised as a gossip. 'Not everything,' I tell her, 'not everything the English do is good.'

Thirty-three

Hortense

Mrs Bligh, or Queenie, the familiar name she desired I use, came to her door, wrapping herself in a dowdy woollen coat. I presumed she had changed her mind about the arranged excursion to the shops, for I believed this dreary coat to be her housecoat. Wishing to allay any anxiety that I might be disappointed by this alteration of plan, I told her, 'Do not worry yourself on account of I. I shall find my way around the shops with no problem.'

I was astounded when, closing the door behind her, she said, 'What? What are you talking about? I'm ready.' For this dismal garment, which I had taken to be her dressing gown, was her good outside coat. Could the woman not see this coat was not only ugly but too small for her? She determined, wrestled herself in to do up the button. When she was finished this fight, she look on me distasteful, up and down. I was dressed as a woman such as I should be when visiting the shops in England. My coat clean, my gloves freshly washed and a hat upon my head. But Mrs Bligh stare on me as if something was wrong with my apparel, before telling me once more, 'I'm not worried about what busybodies say. I don't mind being seen in the street with you.'

And yet it was she, this young Englishwoman, and not I who was dressed in a scruffy housecoat with no brooch or jewel, no glove or even a pleasant hat to lift the look a little.

Imagine my astonishment when, reaching the bustling street, every Englishwoman I look on is also attired in a dowdy housecoat. And as if the Almighty had stolen the rainbow from this place not one person was dressed in a colour bright enough to cheer my eye. All was grey. But walking through this drab, my eye began to detect colours that did amaze me. The surprising colours in the countenance of all the English people. In no book or tutoring that I had acquired did anyone tell me that so many different types of English people could be found. In Jamaica all English people had looked as my tutors at college had appeared. Their hair fair, the colour of baked bread. Their complexion red and ruddy from the sun. It was with great ease that an English person could be distinguished walking along the road from even the most high-class of Jamaican. But here now, in England, so many different complexions were placed before me that my mind became perplexed. This walk to the shops with Mrs Bligh had me looking about in confusion.

'These are shops,' Mrs Bligh told me.

I paid it no mind that this woman believed I could not tell that the place before me, with its window of food displayed, was a shop. Because my mind was puzzled by the woman standing beside us. Her hair was black as ink, her complexion not much lighter than my own – the colour of honey. She held the hand of a small boy with the same dark hair. Seeing me gazing on them, the boy nudged his mother and both of them turned blue eyes to stare back on me.

'This shop is called a grocer's,' Mrs Bligh told me.

I nodded. It had groceries in the window, what else could it be? But I was waiting for this blue-eye-yet-black-hair woman to speak. Was she English, or foreign?

'Come on, let's go in,' Mrs Bligh said to me.

As the dark woman and her son had gone in before us I was happy to follow. The dark woman perusing the counter asked the shopkeeper, 'Have you got cheese today?' Impeccable English, rounded and haughty. My mouth could do nothing but gape. I had never seen an Englishwoman so dark before. At home her countenance would leave many elderly Jamaican men looking about them abashed.

Mrs Bligh, seeing my gaping mouth, said, 'In a grocery shop, you can get milk, biscuits, sugar, cornflakes, eggs, that sort of thing. Do you need eggs? Bacon? A lot of it's still on ration but most things are here. So remember that, it's a grocery shop.'

Now the man serving this dark woman had hair that was red. His face was speckled as a bird's egg with tiny red freckles. Scottish. I believed him to be Scottish. For in Jamaica it is only Scottish people that are so red. But no, he too was English.

'What can I do you for?' he asked me directly. A red Englishman!

'He wants to know if you'd like anything,' Mrs Bligh told me.

I obliged her concern by making a purchase. 'A tin of condensed milk, please,' I asked him.

But this red man stared back at me as if I had not uttered the words. No light of comprehension sparkled in his eye. 'I beg your pardon?' he said.

Condensed milk, I said, five times, and still he looked on me bewildered. Why no one in this country understand my English? At college my diction was admired by all. I had to point at the wretched tin of condensed milk, which resided just behind his head.

'Oh, condensed milk,' he told me, as if I had not been saying it all along.

Tired of this silly dance of miscomprehension, I did not bother to ask for the loaf of bread – I just point to the bread on the counter. The man enclose his big hand over the loaf, his freckled fingers spreading across it. I stared on him. Was I to eat this bread now this man had touch it up? With his other hand he wiped his nose as he held out the bread for me to take. I did not take it, for I was waiting on him to place the bread into a bag to wrap it.

'There you are,' he said to me, pushing the loaf forward enough for me to see a thin black line of dirt arching under each fingernail. It was Mrs Bligh who came and took the bread from him. Her dirty hand having pinch up my loaf as well, she placed it into my shopping bag.

Then she tell me loud for all to hear, 'This is bread.'

She think me a fool that does not know what is bread? But my mind could not believe what my eye had seen. That English people would buy their bread in this way. This man was patting on his red head and wiping his hand down his filthy white coat. Cha, why he no lick the bread first before giving it to me to eat?

I whispered into the ear of Mrs Bligh, 'He has not wrapped the bread.'

But she paid me no mind, so busy was she joining this shopkeeper in rolling their eyes to the heavens as I paid my money over.

Mrs Bligh was a punctilious teacher. The shop with meat in the window she tell me is a butcher. The one with pretty pink cakes is the baker. And each time she tell me she want me to repeat the word. Instead I tell her, 'I know, we have these shops in Jamaica.' She nod. She say good. Then seeing a shop selling fish she tell me this is the fishmonger.

But when we reach the shop selling cloth, it was I that had to ask of her, 'Is this where you buy your material?' For all the cloth seemed to be spread about the floor. There was little room to tread. Bolts and bolts of cloth thrown this way and that all about the place. Some of it dirty. Some of it ragged and fraying. And two old women looked to be crawling on their hands and knees through this mess of cloth while the assistant just daydream behind a counter. How the English treat their good material like this? In Jamaica, I told Mrs Bligh, all the cloth is displayed neatly in rows for you to peruse the design, the colour. When you have chosen you point to the bolt that the assistant will then take up for measuring. She understood what I was telling her but still she look surprise on me, saying, 'Oh, do you have drapers where you come from?'

Three basins! Mrs Bligh shout for all to hear in the hardware shop, why I want three basins? So I tell her softly, one to wash the vegetables, one for the cups and plates and one for washing. No, she tell me, I only need one. 'One will do you – just rinse it out.' How can an Englishwoman expect me to wash myself in the same place where I must clean up the vegetables? It was disgusting to me. Surely it was distasteful to this Englishwoman? I stared dumbfounded. But one was all the shopkeeper delivered me even though I had requested three. But I paid it no mind. I thought to make note of the position of this hardware shop so I might return when this busybody woman had removed her nose from my business. But my eye was diverted by the countenance of a woman pushing a child in a pram.

Never in my days had I seen such a white woman. The hair curled upon her head put me in mind of confection – white and frothy as foam. Her complexion so light, beside it paper would look soiled. Eyebrows, eyelashes, even her lips appeared to have no colour passing through them. So pale was she her blood must be milk. I could not keep my surprise within my breast. 'That woman is so white,' all at once came gushing from me. 'Is she English?' I had to ask Mrs Bligh.

'Stop staring, it's rude,' Mrs Bligh whispered to me urgent. Then, looking to the woman with a sly eye, she told me, 'Yes, of course she is.'

'But she is so fair.'

'Don't be silly,' she told me.

Beside her Mrs Bligh's complexion appeared swarthy. From the pram that this unearthly woman was pushing, a small blond child sat forward. His finger, a little chubby dart, pointed straight at me. He attracted his mother's notice by yelling, 'Look! She's black. Look, Mum, black woman.'

The white woman then turned a glassy gaze on me. Who was the most astounded? For we both stared, certain we were viewing an apparition before us. She nearly pushed the pram into a lamp-post before leaning forward to admonish the pointing child. 'Don't point, Georgey. She's not black – she's coloured.'

While from the other side of the road came shouting. Loud, uncouth and raucous. 'Golliwog, golliwog.' It was three young men. Holding up a wall they yelled through the funnel of their hands, 'Oi, sambo.'

'Take no notice,' Mrs Bligh said.

'Are they talking to me?' I asked her.

'Just keep walking, Hortense.' But I wanted to see these men's faces. What sort of English person could call out so coarse?

'Yeah, you, darkie. We're talking to you.' They moved away from the wall to stand at the edge of the kerb, waving their arms like buffoons.

Mrs Bligh was very agitated – she pulling on my sleeve as I called back to them, 'You are rude!' A half-eaten bread roll flew from the hand of one of them and hit Mrs Bligh on the shoulder of her ugly coat.

'Just keep walking, hurry, please,' Mrs Bligh pleaded. A little patch of oil was now staining the coat.

'Look, they have dirtied up your sleeve.' I tried to brush it but Mrs Bligh grabbed me in so firm a grip I could do nothing but follow.

We were nearly at Nevern Street – about to pass round the corner. Mrs Bligh, after regaining some composure she had lost to the ruffians, was instructing me on what she assured me was good manners. I, as a visitor to this country, should step off the pavement into the road if an English person wishes to pass and there is not sufficient room on the pavement for us both.

Not believing what my ear was hearing I asked, 'I, a woman, should step into the busy road?' She nodded. So I enquired of her, 'And if there is a puddle should I lie down in it?' She was, I believe, considering the efficacy of this suggestion when, looking up along Nevern Street, she suddenly stopped. The breath she took was so sharp it struck her chest and staggered her back. For a moment she was lifeless, the pink draining from her cheeks as if she had bled it away. Perusing the street my eye could conceive of nothing that might give so cruel a reaction. Except there was a man with his back towards us standing at the door of the house. Mrs Bligh slowly began to raise a pointing finger. But the effort of this gesture caused her to fall hard against me. I caught her but this woman was surprisingly heavy. My arms could not hold her. I had no choice but to lower her gently down on to the ground. The man now turning round was screwing up his eyes, looking to where Mrs Bligh was sitting upright on the pavement mumbling softly, over and over, 'Bernard? Bernard?'

Thirty-four

Queenie

I'd have recognised it anywhere, the back of Bernard's neck. Bony and scrawny like the back of a heel with his ears sticking out. Seeing me there on the pavement he came towards me. A hat. A white collar. A gaberdine mac – every button done up and the belt too. He lifted his hat when he reached me, formal, courteous, as if this was a casual meeting. And I was collapsed, sitting on the pavement because my husband whom I hadn't seen for near five years had just approached me. And I said, 'Bernard. You've been away a long time.'

And all he said was, 'Indeed.'

Just that. In-bloody-deed.

The last time I had seen the back of my husband's neck it had had RAF blues pressed against it. Walking down our street, off for service overseas in India. A war had been fought and won since then – the world turned topsy-turvey. He'd been missing for so long I was ready to have him officially declared dead. But there he stood, hat raised and smiling. I mean, blinking heck. So I told him, 'Unless you're a ghost, Bernard Bligh, I'll be wanting more of an explanation from you than that.'

278

Before

Thirty-five

Bernard

We were packed like cattle on to the train in Bombay when we first arrived in India. Hundreds of troops. We walked three abreast into the station but were quickly outnumbered. Brown people all around. At my back, at my front, under my arms. Hands out. White palms begging. 'Baksheesh, baksheesh,' in my ear. Some held up wares – colourful cakes, drinks, trinkets of all kinds. Others had no pride, wanted something for nothing. Behind me someone was shouting, 'Please, sahib, my mother and father dead, rupees.'

To my right a father was trying to sell his daughter to a Tommy, 'Pretty girl – very clean, sahib.'

Children, who should have been in school, ran at my feet, hardly clothed. Eyes as black as apple pips. Some so young they could barely walk. No parents there holding them back from being trampled under a large man. Nothing for it but to walk on through. Shrug it off as best I could. No thought of causing offence. These people stank. Body odour was masked by sweet, sickly, spicy scents.

Confusion had me bewildered. Our chaps calling out, wanting to know which way to go, 'Oi, oi – over here.'

Groups of carnival-coloured natives gesticulating with arms as skinny as sticks. Jabbering in mysterious tongues. 'Good worker, sahib. No trouble. Please, job, please, sahib.' Natives' spittle breaking on my cheek.

English cries, 'Fall in, fall in. Move on through there.' The squeaky wheel on a cart. The screech of a train's hooter. The dirty laugh of an erk. 'Her? You're joking! Maybe with a bag on her head.'

The station was familiar. A concrete building with vaulting roof. Could have been back home – St Pancras or Liverpool Street. There was even a man in a black bowler hat bobbing through the crowd. Looked like Pa on his way to work. Except he wore a long shirt and his legs were wrapped in baggy white cotton pants. He smiled bright red teeth as he passed. Thought someone had punched him in the mouth for his cheek, impersonating a gentleman. But he was too carefree – chewing and spitting globules of red on to the floor.

'Sahib, nice oranges, juicy.' We'd been warned about their oranges. Boiled in filthy water to make them big. The cakes spoke for themselves. Gaudy as Christmas and speckled with black – not raisins but flies. Some chaps bought them. Flicked off the insects and tucked in. Couldn't blame them – never sure when we'd eat again.

A native man in a uniform, transport not service, hurried us on, muttering in a language of his own. He piled kits on his back. Five, sometimes six. They bent him double as he struggled to climb the steps of the train. Offload, then back for more. Face like thunder. 'Chatty wallah,' chaps jeered, as he hobbled away.

The train might have been in Bombay but the footplate I stuck my boot on said it was made in Crewe. The sooty stench of steam had me thinking of childhood holidays in Dymchurch. A sudden blast of grey smoke caused everything to disappear. As it cleared, through the mist, a cow wandered along the platform. Nobody shooed it or tethered it. A mangy beast with ribs you could count. It clopped, docile, through the crowds, parting a group of women who were carrying coal in bundled rags for the train's engine. Some struggled with a hump of a child on their back and a fat belly of coal on their front, while the able-bodied native men jostled and begged from British troops. That had us all tutting and shaking our heads.

They came through the train windows. Faces. Fingers. Hands. Arms.

Hustling and shoving. Clutching useless items. Yelling to be seen. 'Sahib, take – you like? Take, sahib.' Most things were no more than a shape to me. Should I eat it, play it or rub it on my prickly heat?

At last the train started to move off. The natives began running. Still hopeful. Until we picked up too much speed, and hands, arms and trinkets were grabbed back.

Two minutes out of the station I spotted grown men squatting by the tracks, defecating on the ground. For a moment there was silence in our carriage, like we'd just come through a raid. Out of the window, wobbling in the heat, I saw an elephant slowly dragging a car. I nudged the chap beside me. He just shrugged. There were hundreds of men on this train. Our toilet was a little hole in the floor with two handles to keep you upright. The silence was only broken when a well-spoken man shouted, 'Wasn't there a poet who once wrote about India's spell?'

Answered by a Cockney calling back, 'More like India's smell, mate.'

Queenie didn't want me to join up until I was conscripted. 'You can wait until you're asked,' she kept saying. I'm not sure that women understood how it worked. We all knew, the men who met in the Feathers, we all understood. Harold, Arthur, Reg and George all signed up years earlier. RAF too. Harold flew Spits somewhere in Kent. Arthur and Reg became wireless operators but I lost touch with them after their posting. George was a gunner. Shot down over France. Missing in action. He'll probably walk home one day and demand to be bought a pint, which he'll down in eleven seconds, his speciality. That just left Frank and me. We were older, you see. Old hands at the bank – we understood what needed to be done. The other boys were young. They had no family of their own and their country needed them.

Frank suggested it. After two halves of watered-down beer in the Feathers, he flicked his cigarette out of the door. It flew in an arch of sparks and Hilda, the barmaid, yelled, 'You'll start a fire!'

He blew her a kiss, which I thought was a touch uncouth for Frank. But he was fired up. 'Right, Bernard, let's go and join up or it's the PBI for us.'

The poor bloody infantry. Everyone knew, except Queenie, that if a man was conscripted, he went straight into the army. Gun under his arm, tin hat on his head and a bullet in his back. I didn't need persuading. It was the RAF for me. If I was going to go, I wanted to go as a boy in blue.

'You think you're going to be like Biggles, don't you?' Queenie said, when I told her. I shook my head and said no. But I suppose if I was honest I would have liked to be a hero of the skies. A Brylcreem boy with the sun on my quiff. The enemy coming at me, rat-a-tat-tat at three o'clock. Diving swiftly. Hiding in a cloud. Emerging. Giving the enemy machine everything I'd got. Glorious deeds valiantly achieved. Queenie, tearfully joyful at my return.

But I wasn't accepted for flying duty – eyesight failed me. Neither was Frank, which, I'm ashamed to say, I found a relief. We were both channelled as aircrafthands, known to everyone as erks. Ground crew. Options given were airframes or engines. Frank chose frames so I took engines.

'You're going to do what?' Queenie said. 'I thought at least they'd teach you to fly.'

She would have liked to live with a hero. I knew that much for a fact.

I was thrown from the truck when we finally reached the base out east, my face landing in the dirt. A mouthful of parched dust had me spitting and choking. Someone stood on my leg. No time to yell before another tripped over me. Stood on my hand as he staggered and fell, cursing. Everyone was running. The ground rumbled with pounding boots. Men shouted, 'Move! Move! Cover!' I soon got to my feet. Ran with my head low, the dirt kicking up into my eyes. I could barely see, just followed other moving legs.

There was the screech of a low plane. One, two – more, perhaps. Had no time to look before gunfire was hitting the ground. Dust erupting in a line, its debris belting me in the chest. I screamed (I admit). My boots skidded along the ground to change direction. The dust was like fog. I was blind. Lost. No idea which way to go. Then someone grabbed me. Ripped my shirt as he pulled me towards a trench. It was full of men, there was no room. I know I shouted, 'Budge up,' before I was pushed over.

'Get in,' yelling in my ear. I landed on top of someone. My forehead cracking against the back of his head. 'Watch what you're fucking doing,' was screamed into my face.

Everyone was shouting, 'Get your fucking head down, you stupid erk.'

The plane passed low again. Had us all wriggling, ducking, swearing. Bullets pelted into the dust which flew high into the air, then fell, covering us like a suffocating blanket.

I watched the planes. Two Japanese Zeros. Swooping and strafing the ground. Their gunfire sometimes pinged and popped like harmless fireworks. But so close. I could see the pilot. Thought I saw him laugh.

Then someone landed on me. A mountain of a man crashed into my back. Winded me. I gulped. Couldn't yell. There was an explosion, an almighty bang that left everything silent for one brief second. Until stones and earth fell in on us like hail. Everyone was choking and coughing, their arms over their heads and mouths. The dust surrounded us like a London pea-souper. I couldn't breathe, as sure as if someone had clapped their hand over my face. I scratched at the air trying to inhale. Involuntarily grabbed at the man beside me, who shrugged me off. Gulped mouthfuls of thick unbreathable yellow filth. My mouth was dry, my tongue fat.

The noise of the planes soon faded to a buzz, like distant bees. And I breathed. I breathed a smelly lungful of the sweetest breath I have ever tasted. Suddenly it was over. Japs were gone. The relief had the whole trench sighing as one man.

'Get off my fucking arm – you've broken it, you clumsy bastard.'

Someone was talking to me. I moved off him. Said I was sorry but he'd stopped listening. We began clambering out of the trench, all of us coughing and spitting like tubercular cases. I lost my balance and slid back down. It was then I noticed an unmistakable bulge in the front of my shorts. I had an erection.

'Come on,' I heard above me. I looked up to see a hand being held out. Tried to wave it away but the chap insisted. I grabbed his hand hard as a handshake and scrabbled up.

'Just off the boat?' he said. Tried to hide my shame as best I could – twisting round, arm in front. Chap looked about eighty. We all did, with our pantomime ageing of dust. I wondered if he'd noticed, seen the bulge. I shook myself loose, dusting down the baggy ill-fitting shorts. Decent again. I started to tell him how long I'd been in India but he'd already walked away.

I breathed out. That was the closest I'd come to real war. I'd been bombed in London. Houses, shops, factories, streets – everyone shaken silly by the destruction. Queenie and I hid like rats. Bailed out the water in the garden shelter. Sat with our candle listening as the planes droned above us. A matter of being unlucky if we got in their way. I was useless to her. But now, with bullets breaking the ground inches from me, I was being aimed at because I was dangerous.

'Move! Get those kites off the strip. Move! Move! Get it cleared.'

Men started running again. I ran with them. There were two Hurricanes on the runway. Shot to pieces. It was a sorry sight, like birds fallen from the sky after a shoot. Undercarts twisted. A wing lying dismembered. Nose buried in the dirt. Buckled metal. Flapping cloth. Limp, lifeless.

I couldn't see the rest of my unit, the chaps I'd travelled with. My kit was still on the truck, which was abandoned – tipped at an angle, one wheel in a shallow monsoon ditch.

'Come on, move it! Get those kites moved.'

I found a place in the gang, thrusting my hands out to join the many others on the stricken kite. The metal burnt. I yelped and pulled my hands off for a second. I quickly put them back before anyone noticed. There were dozens of men round the plane. Grimacing with effort. Trying to keep their foothold on the dry earth. Slowly the kite moved – graceless as a corpse. Soon the sweat we created dripped on to the dusty ground, turning it into a thin layer of mud. I lost my footing. Slipped. Found myself with my face in the warm man-made muck. I got up, my damp hands fizzing as they hit the hot metal again.

First one kite then the next. Pushed off the strip into a graveyard of planes. A despair of kites. No wings. No wheels. No windows. No hope of flying. Pierced with bullet-holes like colanders. The golden powder of rust shaken all over them. Animals had made a home in some.

Seconds after the strip was cleared a plane landed. Vibration like an earthquake. Bouncing along the ground. Dust swirling a sandstorm. Its thunderous engines the only sound. A Vulti Vengeance.

'That's lost,' a chap next to me said.

The pilot got out, jumped down sweeping his hair back. He was no more than a boy, hands on his hips as he looked around. Word was soon out. Jap plane had crash-landed half a mile away. A cheer went up from the tight circle of men round the pilot.

'Gurkhas will get him,' same chap said. 'Just arrived?' I realised he was talking to me. He was looking down at something on my bottom half. I crossed my arms over the front of my shorts (just in case). Then saw it was my knees that interested him. They were bleeding. Dribbles of blood running down my leg. Couldn't feel a thing.

'Just a scratch, nothing serious,' I said.

He laughed. 'No. White knees – dead giveaway.' Looked anything but white to me. 'You've just arrived.'

'Been in Worli,' I told him.

'As I said.' He stuck his tongue into the corner of his cheek. 'You've just arrived. Don't worry, you'll get used to it.' I must have looked puzzled. 'The slit-eyed bastards,' he went on. 'You'll get used to their funny little ways. They come every day. Bit early today – must be a public holiday or something. Every day though. Could set your watch by the nip in the air.' He stuck out his hand. 'Maxi. George Maximillian but everyone calls me Maxi.' His hand was calloused, felt like knotted wood.

'Bernard Bligh.'

'What do they call you, then?'

I didn't answer. Last name I could remember being called was miserable beggar.

They brought him through the camp, down the strip, through the dozens of natives dressed in straw hats and rags. Men and women who'd appeared from nowhere with makeshift shovels, who were smoothing over the freshly made craters. They stopped, along with the men and officers of the RAF, and watched. A Japanese pilot. Hands on his head. Two army men with rifles –

fixed bayonet – pointed at his back. Nudging him along. Shouting. Not in English. Foreign themselves. Black. Indian. 'Gurkhas,' Maxi said. 'May not look like one of us but they're good sorts. You don't mess with the Gurkhas.'

He was young, this Japanese pilot. This 'unintelligent slum dweller with nothing worth fighting for except the fanatical belief that his emperor is God'. Looked twelve or thirteen. One side of his face was smashed and bloody. No shoes. No trousers. Bare skinny legs. One foot dragging as he walked, turned at an impossible angle, scraping the ground. He wore just a vest inscribed with their picture writing. Chaps spat at the ground as he passed. Some jeered. Some cheered. Some turned their back. He walked on. Looked at no one.

'Where are they taking him?' I asked Maxi.

He shrugged then sighed. 'Listen, Pop, you know what it says on his vest? The writing on his vest. They all wear them. It says: "I will fight for my country. I will die for my country. I will not return." We can't take prisoners, nowhere to put them.'

'Well, what will they do with him, then?'

Maxi put two fingers up to his temple and said a quiet 'Bang.' I felt like a fool. A white-kneed fool who was expecting war to be polite. 'Quite frankly we're doing him a favour,' Maxi told me. 'Least he'll have the dignity of an enemy bullet.'

Thirty-six

Bernard

I'd not wanted a war. None of us had. And I never wanted to be out in India. But (I admit) it put a rod in the back and spring in the step of this middle-aged bank clerk who'd thought his life was set. Even started whistling (nothing fancy) now I was part of a team: 298 Repair and Salvage Unit. RAF trained and tested – mechanic (engines) – and proud to be an erk.

Maxi needed someone sensible with him on this salvage trip. Me, his first choice – that bit older, you see. Orders were to find a downed kite (Spitfire). Reports claimed it had come down somewhere in the hills. Vague, but an army unit nearby knew where. Maxi was after some piece of equipment it was carrying. All very hush-hush. Security too tight to tell this lowly aircraftman. Draw some supplies (including a Sten each), then into the truck. Glad to get off my duties on the base. Sense of freedom. Mission, even.

Maxi wasn't as silly as some – senior clerk on the railways back home. A wife, two boys (one he hadn't seen yet), waiting in Brighton. We had a good-natured argument all the way, like brothers.

'Underestimate your enemy, lose your war. Show me someone who thinks a Jap a fool and I'll show you someone who's sun-happy.'

Maxi had all the stories. Collected them in a scrapbook in his head. Pulled them out to scare the white-kneed. 'If you bring one in wounded then you better strap him down because if you don't he'll pull out a grenade and blow everyone up while you're nursing him. Or, failing that, you'd better tie his hands 'cause a Jap will open up his own wounds – his own wounds! – to die for his emperor.' They were relished – savoured, even – these stories. Everyone had them. Tales running round the camp blanching even the most sunburnt faces. Maxi's were not quite as fanciful as some. One chap swore that with twenty bullet-holes a Jap could still run. Others were truly convinced these little men could rise from the dead. But I was having none of it.

'It's not that I don't believe everything the chaps say,' I said.

'You should, Pop,' he replied (that bit older, you see, hence the name). 'You haven't been out here long enough to tell us all different.'

He'd misunderstood (my point, finer).

'You can teach a dog to attack anything to the death. Any dumb animal will keep coming at you with no thought for themselves. That's not intelligence, that's obedience. But that doesn't win wars. Our superior wit will win through,' I said.

'I hope you're not referring to your sense of humour, Pop?'

Deliberately misunderstood (again). 'The Japs are just clockwork toys,' I told him, 'they'll eventually run out of wind.'

The army CO turned out to be useless. His idea of pinpointing was to wave his arms about in the general direction of the hills. 'Have you got a more precise bearing, sir?' Maxi (diplomat) asked cautiously.

One indecisive finger flicked instead. 'You'll need a mule,' he told us.

'Have you got one we could use, sir?'

'No.'

Maxi threw me a look I quickly caught. Sometimes it was hard to understand we were fighting a war together, side by side with these khaki chaps. He left us with a curt warning, 'Watch out up there. Jap patrol was spotted earlier,' before waving us off.

Looks like curly cabbage from afar, the forest on the hills. Harmless. Playful. Think you could fall and bounce on it. Soon change your mind. Slashing through dark, wet, stinking undergrowth. Painfully slowly. Ticks dropping bloody inside my shirt. Flies sipping on the moisture in my eyes.

Mosquitoes massing thick as cloth. The relief at seeing the track the fallen plane had made had Maxi and me hugging like goal scorers. Not too far away, we both agreed. Still took us hours, though. Tunnelling through the undergrowth – each step as hard won as a miner with his coal. Would Queenie have recognised her husband now? Molten and brown as a warm bar of chocolate. Intrepid as Livingstone. Not that pallid bank clerk, fretting when the tube got too crowded.

It was dark by the time we reached the prang. No chance of struggling back without the light. 'We'll have to camp here,' Maxi said. We were ready for a spot of McConachie's stew, a cigarette, a dry place for backside and gun. Maxi, settling down, wrapped himself tight into a blanket. 'You'll need your blanket, Pop.' Had noticed when we stopped that it was cold, had almost forgotten what it felt like. Couldn't get the shivers at the base even under cold water. Hot day and night. I even slept under a towel just to mop the sweat. I had laughed when the chap at the stores pushed across this hairy thick blanket. Heavy, dusty, filthy thing. Just looking at it had excited my prickly heat. I left it behind and took extra biscuits and water instead.

'You have got a blanket, haven't you, Pop?'

'Couldn't see the need.'

'Couldn't see the need? I told you you'd need a blanket up here.'

'Seemed a bit unnecessary . . .'

'Jesus, Pop, that's typical of you.'

Uncalled-for, I thought.

Maxi shook his head. Tittered at my expense. 'You always think you know best, don't you?' he said. It was only a matter of time before he brought up the business with the thunderboxes.

'Remember the thunderboxes?'

'Not that again,' I said. The chaps wouldn't let me forget it.

I still insist it was a good idea. Timing was wrong, that was all. The latrines at the base were disgusting. Hundreds of men defecated into a trench of old thunderboxes with a roof on. The stink, the flies, the maggots. Who knows what diseases were incubating? Bowels in India open more than most. The wallahs do their bit. But every so often only fire can clean, to sterilise it until the next time. A gallon or two of petrol is poured in. Chap approaches with a long match made of a pole topped with a piece of burning four-by-two. Ignite, then run like hell while it burns. To me it was elementary. Pour in the petrol and run a line of it like a fuse. Then sit back to watch the fire trip along the ground before cleansing the trench. No running, just intelligence. Chaps shook their heads – won't work, can't be done (Maxi included). It was grist to my mill. There was quite an audience watching.

Poured in the petrol. Ran the line carefully along a prepared grooved track. Sat in a chair to light it casually with a match. Fizzled off as predicted. But it fell just short. One, maybe two feet. Much laughing and merriment. 'Now what, Pop? Any ideas left?' The problem was I'd spent too long explaining why the fuse had not reached its target. Petrol had evaporated too quickly on the hot ground. 'Go on, get the pole,' the chaps taunted. Of course, by the time I'd reached the latrine with the burning pole that two gallons of petrol had also evaporated into the air. There was one almighty explosion. Roof flew off to Kohima. Threw me into the air as well. I landed with a shower of thunderbox contents raining down on me.

'It could still work,' I told Maxi.

'Oh, give it a rest, Pop.'

'Granted, I didn't take enough account of evaporation. But next time . . .'

'Next time! You think anyone's going to let you do that again? We're still finding shit in places it shouldn't be. You just have to know best, don't you?'

'Well, maybe.'

'Well maybe,' he taunted.

'But I know a snake when I see one, Maxi,' I told him.

'Don't change the subject. That could happen to anyone. I was asleep!'

Hardly fair to remind him but he'd started it.

Maxi had woken us all in the *basha* in the middle of the night. 'Snake, snake,' he's yelling. Struggling about on his *charpoy*. 'Big bugger,' he's telling us, thrashing this way and that. We're all up, knives, guns at the ready. Snake. Big snake. Maxi going at it like Tarzan to get it out of his bed. The legs of his *charpoy* collapse. Everything falls on the floor, including Maxi. He screams he's been bitten and runs off to the MO clutching his leg.

Leaves us all turning over this, prodding at that. Scared as hell, we all admit, hunting this big snake in the *basha*. Turns out Maxi fell asleep on his arm. Woke up, grabbed it, felt nothing. Concluded it was a snake. Cut himself on a piece of sharp bamboo in the struggle to throw his own arm out of bed.

'Look,' Maxi said, 'we're not discussing that now. What I want to know is what you're going to do up here all night without a blanket.'

'Cold air can rid you of prickly heat.'

'For once you're right, Pop. What's the word you always use? Elementary. It gets so cold up here prickly heat is not a problem because exposure rids you of your life.'

'Come on, it can't be that bad.' I was pretty chilled but no point admitting it. I lit a cigarette. Queenie never liked it hot. She would undo the top two buttons of her blouse, soak a handkerchief in cold water and put it on the back of her neck. Water would trickle down her front, the droplets disappearing into the pleat of her breasts. 'It's like living in an oven,' she'd complain, lying back in a chair fanning herself with the newspaper. I'd tell her I liked it hot. The endless summer days when I was a boy. Sleepy afternoons of birdsong. Sitting out on the steps in the sun. The warmth on my bare legs waiting for Pa to come home. His smile as he sauntered up the road in his shirtsleeves. 'Phew! It's a scorcher today, Bernie.' Cricket in the backyard and Ma's lemon drink with four sugars. But a few months in India's eternal heat had me dreaming of snow. Wintry mornings when lacy ice crazed the inside of windows. Misty breath condensing in the cold. The shocking dash from bed into clothes. Stamping up and down, nose numb and running. Blowing hot breath on to freezing fingers. Cracking ice with the heel of my shoe. Shivering. I missed shivering. But be careful what you wish for out in this godforsaken place. I was shivering now, cupping my hands round the cigarette tip. Clenching my jaw so my teeth couldn't chatter.

That's when we heard it. Coming out of the black night. Clear and piercing.

'Johnny, come and help me, Johnny.'

'Hear that?' I said.

'It's Japs,' Maxi whispered. Both of us were crouching now, grabbing for our guns. Useless. Pointing them around like boys in a game.

'Don't fire,' Maxi said.

'Johnny, my leg is broken. I'm over here, come and help me.' Perfect English. 'Johnny, Johnny.'

'Sure it's not the pilot?' I asked.

'It's Japs. They're just jittering us.'

'They know where we are.'

'No. If they knew where we were we'd be dead.'

'Johnny, help me. Please help me.'

I pointed my gun. I was sure I could tell which direction it was coming from. Maxi put his hand on it, bringing down the barrel. 'Don't fire,' he whispered, urgent. 'They'll know where we are if you fire.'

'Help me. I'm over here. Come quick, Johnny.'

'We'll just sit quiet. Put out that cigarette.'

A moonless forest. Dark. Alien. Crowded with the unfamiliar. Phantom shapes. Peculiar sounds. Strange creaking, twittering, fluttering, squawking. Funny that the strangest and, I admit, most terrifying sound was the most familiar. A human calling for help. An eerie, resonant voice coming as clearly as if it was piped. The cold obliged me to shiver. Insisted my teeth chatter. But that voice – 'Johnny, come here, Johnny' – that voice trembled my hands.

Maxi sidled up to me. Shifting along our makeshift camp on his bottom. Quiet. Eyes alert as prey. Lifted out his arm to wrap his blanket round me, then back round him. Two vigilant heads swivelling. Our bodies wrapped as one, sticking together where bare flesh pressed.

'Johnny, help me.'

Our guns were quickly erect, poking through the gap in the cloth, pointing different ways. 'It's all right, Pop. They don't know where we are. They won't bother coming.'

'Can you be sure?'

Maxi tittered. His warm breath on my cheek, smelling of tobacco. 'Sure as you can be with a Jap.' Wafts of body odour were puffing from the blanket. Rough fibres scratching our cheeks. Our body heat gradually warming the air in the cocoon.

'Johnny. Johnny.'

The muscles of Maxi's arm pumped against me (tense again). His knee nervously rubbing mine.

'Johnny, come quick. Can you hear me, Johnny?'

Maxi's chest rising with a held breath unexpectedly sighed relief. 'It's all right. They're not getting any closer,' he said.

The calling stopped coming so often. But neither of us felt like sleep. In all honesty we needed each other upright so the blanket would fit round. Maxi rested his gun on his knees.

'I wish you'd brought a bloody blanket,' he told me, close in my ear.

'Sorry.'

'I told you you'd need one.'

'My fault I know. Sorry.'

Sitting in the desolate dark, we couldn't even light a cigarette in case the glowing tip gave us away. Maxi began telling me about his plans for after the war. Couldn't imagine going back to being a clerk on the railways. 'I've got this idea. See what you think.' He wanted to breed rabbits. Got it all worked out. A rabbit farm. Reckoned it would only take two to start. Not much initial outlay. Male, female, then sit back and watch. 'Because,' he said, 'you know what they breed like?'

'No.'

'Like rabbits.'

'I see.'

'That was a joke, Pop.'

'A joke, yes, I see.'

By the time the light came up we'd got it all worked out. I was even a partner. Doing the ledgers, profit and loss (taking care of the business side). Set up in Kent (just outside Ashford's nice). Main line: rabbit for food (with ancillary products – pies, stews). Sideline: lucky rabbits' claws. We decided against the rabbit stoles (like fox furs). Maxi didn't think English housewives would like a dead fluffy bunny round their neck even if the floppy ears would make a lovely bow.

Sunrise – the most delightful sight. Ghostly mists hanging in the far hills gradually burned away. Those warming rays were as welcome as a first breath. Back to the job in hand. Rabbit farming folded up with the blanket. Still cautious, though. Whispering out of instinct. Shoulders stooped. Guns at the ready in case the Japs could see us better now.

The wreckage was hardly recognisable as a plane. Pranged into the hill and cartwheeled down taking the vegetation with it. A wing gone. Fuselage half the size it should be. Engine ripped out and fallen further down the hill. Propeller vanished. No bullet-holes that we could see. Fuel tank empty – evaporated, maybe. 'Someone's got to this before us,' Maxi said. There were signs of a fire in a burnt clearing nearby.

'Perspex, wheels, they've all gone.'

'Another RSU?'

'No.'

'Japs?'

Maxi shrugged. 'Locals probably. Get a good price for them.'

Such an inhospitable place. Hard to imagine anyone living nearby just ready for a Sunday stroll. No sign of the pilot. 'Could have bailed,' I said. Maxi looked doubtful – showed me why. Sleeve of a bush jacket was hanging in a tree. Jagged, bloody like some beast had just bitten it off. Although the three stripes on it were still clean and intact. I noticed my hands were sticky where I was touching the tree. Turned them over to find them covered in congealed blood. The side of the tree was dripping with it. Nothing said, but my job to look for remains. Only found the blackened edge of an identity card. Name, number burned away. Then another patch of blood. Maxi, inspecting the fuselage, shook his head. Tutted. Removed a few instruments, which he secreted about him.

No point hanging around, Maxi decided. Nothing more to find. I bowed my head to say a prayer before we left just in case this was a graveyard. Maxi was annoyed at first, itching to get away, but he soon joined me.

'Shall we sing a hymn?' I asked.

'Yes, why not, Pop? How about "Over here, Japs. Sorry you missed us last night." '

Point taken.

We were walking for a few hours, neither of us wanting to say the word lost. 'That looks familiar. Yes, this is the way,' more in order. Just about to breast the hill when we heard voices. Foreign. Close. Very close. Both of us were soon on to our bellies. Low in the grass (but there for anyone to see). Maxi signalled to be quiet, hand to his lip. My finger was on the Sten's trigger – trembling again. I wondered if I looked as scared as Maxi. He was as bloodless as a corpse. I could feel the urine warming my pants before seeping into the ground. Powerless to stop it. I was a coward, I knew, but I didn't want to die. Shot flinching on the ground, quivering like a girl. Could Queenie be proud of that? At least Maxi had sons who would gild their father's story into something worthwhile. Maxi started mumbling to himself (prayer, perhaps). Voices, again talking gibberish. A cackling laugh. Maxi and I dared a quick glance at one another. Our last, perhaps.

I caught sight of the top of a head first. Suddenly Maxi came back to life. 'Nagas,' he shouted, and jumped up like a jack-in-the-box. Those three brown skinny natives were not surprised at seeing us. They knew we were there. Wily lot. Euphoria had Maxi negotiating (sign language). The blanket, four packs of limp cigarettes, a few rupees, and these toothless old men were happy to lead us back to the army camp.

The army CO looked surprisingly relieved when we got there. 'Thought I'd have to send someone out to find you. You RAF chaps aren't cut out for combat,' he wanted us to know. Maxi was quietly furious – jaw tight as a cage. Until the CO handed us a beer each. We could hardly believe it. Christmas in May? 'Good news,' he told us. 'The war with the Germans is over. Hitler's dead.' Poured himself a whisky from an almost-full bottle. 'They'll be sending us everything they've got now.' Lifted up his generous glassful and told Maxi and me, 'Didn't fancy your chances against that Jap patrol. But thank God. Maybe you fellows aren't such clots after all. Cheers.'

Thirty-seven

Bernard

It was a relief for everyone to know loved ones back home were now safe. Free from those unimaginable things we heard the Nazis were throwing at them – doodlebugs, rockets. I stopped picturing Queenie huddling in the shelter, with Pa under the bed. Brought her out into the light again. Standing by the kitchen stove reaching up into the cupboard for flour or salt. Her blouse pulling taut against her breasts. Her fair hair flopping in front of her eyes before she pushes it behind her ear where it curls obedient as thread. Everyone cheered at the war in Europe's end. Every back felt a pat on it. A job well done. But none of that made our long road ahead feel any shorter. It would take us years to wrest back Burma from those little yellow men. Everyone agreed with me. Inch by inch we'd have to go. Just look at the Yanks in the Pacific – island by island, and each battle bloodier than the last. Maxi wagered me two years. I'm not a betting man, I told him. Four, some other chaps said. While the thought of 'never' dulled the eyes of some.

So the Japs' sudden surrender was a startling shock to all. I had a dose of dysentery. I'd been ordered by the MO that day to hold on to an enema. Seven hours he said I was to keep it warm. Only had it in two when Maxi's face appeared at the basha door.

'Have you heard the news, Pop?'

298

I told him to go away. The chaps tried those tricks all the time. I expected some airman to come in and slowly pour his tiffin tea into a mug in a deliberate, long trickle – an old ruse. Auto-suggestion that saw the fainthearts biting their lips and crossing their legs. Only those with an iron will and the stamina of a bull could stay the distance with this particular medicine. I was determined to be one of them.

'The Japs have surrendered,' Maxi informed me.

'Pull the other one,' I told him. Everyone knows Japs don't surrender.

But his face lit like he'd won the pools. 'Honest, it's God's truth,' he said.

Shock had me running straight for a thunderbox, which gave Maxi a laugh.

News of the new-fangled bomb had everyone curious. They all wanted to know what I knew – that bit older, you see. But there was little I could tell them. Even the officers were left scratching their heads. Arguing over what an atom bomb could be. They were clueless. But the Japs surrendering spoke louder than any top-brass explanation. All agreed, it was God's own weapon if it could make the yellow peril turn tail and run.

So the war was over! A day's holiday from duty with three days' beer ration. Maxi, after several beers, gathered everyone round to show them his peace-time plans for the rabbit farm. Painted it on an old parachute slung from a tree. Two bunnies, a cage and several leaping pounds signs. 'One male and one female, that's all you need,' he yelled, 'because you know what they breed like?'

'Rabbits!' came the drunken response.

Maxi led the whole camp practically in a rousing chorus of 'Run Rabbit Run'. Said it was to be the company song. Grabbed me next. 'And Pop here is Chief Bunny.' Got everyone laughing. 'But there's rabbit pie for you all when we get home,' he shouted. Couldn't help thinking he wasn't taking this whole rabbit-farm venture seriously enough. He flung his arms round my neck, hugged me to him for quite a while before I realised he was heavy – a dead weight. It took three of us to get him on to his *charpoy*.

But no matter how sore the head, every one of us on our RSU – probably every chap in the whole of SEAC – joyously wrote a letter home to our loved ones that night. War over, I'll be home by Christmas, it said. Believed it too.

Then we got the order to move. Everyone cheered. Only to find we were moving nearer to Burma. Going the wrong way, the chaps shouted. We were worried we weren't getting out but were on our way to Rangoon. Top brass insisted POWs should get home first. Nobody disagreed. They'd died once already those prisoners. They'd been turned round at the pearly gates by St Peter – might look dead but still too warm to come in. They came through the camp on their way to Bombay. I gave one of them my chocolate ration. Chindit. He'd flown a glider behind the Jap lines. Been in their hands for nearly two years. His bones jangled inside his skin like coins in a bag. Could almost see the squares of chocolate passing down him. Had to watch as he clutched his stomach. He spewed brown liquid back up. Too rich for him. The poor chap cried – openly. 'Sorry,' he said, 'what a waste.' Every man was happy to stand aside to let these flimsy scraps of Englishmen get home. What race of people could watch flesh wither on a man until he was no more than a framework? Left me proud to belong to a civilisation where even the most aggrieved was held back from raising a hand to our Japanese prisoners.

But word was, some men were getting their demob quicker than others. Particular skills, you see. Needed for post-war rebuilding back in Blighty. Britain required a new backbone. Men to reconstruct the ravaged land back into something worthy of the British Empire. Evidently there was a list the top brass had drawn up. At first, every airman on our RSU puffed out his chest waiting for that call. Nobody had actually seen this demob priority list but soon everyone began muttering about it. Reports said they had sent home a ballet dancer. A chap had heard it on another unit. A ballet dancer rushed back to England. Perhaps he had to dance on Hitler's grave, a joker wondered. Maxi knew of a theology student who had been urgently delivered back to his mother in Purley. A bell-ringer. That got everyone tutting. This list worked its way under the skin of nearly every man left out there. Some young goofy idiot, who'd not been out long and spent all that time on mess fatigues, got sent straight back. I asked him what he did in Blighty. He told me he was a plumber's mate. A plumber's mate was deemed more important than chaps who could rebuild a fallen Liberator, piece by piece. Absurd. That had me muttering along with the rest. The mechanics, the teachers, the clerks who were all left out here sat brooding on their worth to a country they loved. Wondering what sort of Britain was being built without us. Forgotten war, forgotten army, forgotten again. Everyone agreed: surely every man out here had earned his say.

Of course, it was the Communists who started it. Uncle Joe Stalin's friends. Wanted everyone in our RSU to down tools. Stop refuelling kites, unloading, servicing, that sort of thing, until we were all promised early demob. I'd wanted nothing to do with those hotheads. Those men who'd cheered the Labour Party victory back home. Ungratefully booting out Churchill after he'd won us the war. They couldn't wait to get back to England, those Communists. Thought there was a new order waiting for them. 'Now things will be different,' spoken with every gesture, every look. Eyeing up Squadron Leader Howarth at Christmas while he (traditionally) served us rankers our meal. Thinking all officer class would be serving them soon. Then moaning about the CO after he'd left. 'Off back to his bearers and whisky,' they'd say, 'and we're here with just a beer.' Even the chaps who should've known better began agreeing with these rabble-rousers.

'Got to do something about this business, Pop,' Maxi said. He wanted me to join in. I told him I had no intention of ending my service days in prison. Think of his sons back in Brighton, I cautioned.

The germ of a rumour about a strike spread to all the RAF out there. Soon everyone had caught it, everyone was dragged in – part of a team, you see. Top brass were jumpy. Squadron Leader Howarth stood on an ammo box, flanked by two Military Police, demanding silence. He called the strike a mutiny, then read out the Riot Act to the circle of disbelieving aircraftmen. Ordered us all to return to duty with immediate effect. Unfortunately the poor CO was the only person in the unit who didn't know that his two Military Police guards were traitors. Part of the strike plot. He looked as dismayed as a lost child when one of Uncle Joe's boys began to laugh.

The silly strike lasted no more than a few hours. No one had the stomach for it. Time enough for a game of cards, a letter home or for those chocolate-drop troops from West Africa to beat our lot at football in their bare feet. But still the troublemakers, the ringleaders, strutted around camp like they'd won

301

us a victory. Top brass were listening now, they said. Boasted about some MP that was coming out from Blighty just to hear our grievances. It had all been worthwhile, they told everyone. Groups home were to be speeded up, all thanks to them. Toasted it in beer – the better this, the better that. Believed it too, for a while. Before, that was, they sent us all to Calcutta.

Thirty-eight

Bernard

It was usually a treat to get a few days in Calcutta. Off to the Bristol for a welcome sleep in a bed with cotton sheets. Always Laidlaw's for a meal. Its best china (after wretched tin cups) tinkling with civilisation. A touch of shopping, perhaps – the Army and Navy or even Hogg Market. A film at the Globe or the Regal. A cold beer for some at the Nip Inn. For those who could, a dance at Firpos. Or just lazing around on the *maidan*, like young chaps, watching girls glide by.

But this trip to Cal was to be more memorable than most.

The men looked puzzled as we RAF tradesmen were issued with a rifle each. 'Fix bayonets,' NCO barked. What about ammo? we all wanted to know. 'No ammo,' he told us. Herded us on to trucks. Told us to stand in straight rows. Then we were driven off through the streets.

The carcasses of shops came first. Burnt out. Smouldering. Flurries of ash blowing like tropical snow. Goods everywhere. Items that should have been inside strewn down the street. Looted. Picked over for value, then tossed away. But not a native in sight. Not even a begging child was left on the road. Even those who'd never been in Calcutta knew that was an eerie spectacle for India.

More than one man gasped at the scene before us in the next street. Same burnt shops and flurries of ash. But among this were the corpses of the dead.

303

They lay down every road we travelled. Some might have been taken for bundles of rags. Or discarded rubbish. Others were unmistakable. Caught in a silly pose. An arm up, a leg raised. Most carried a look of astonishment. Mouths agape. But all stiff with sudden death. The chaps looked to one another. 'Fucking hell,' more than one muttered. This was as savage as anything witnessed during the war. Faces blanched and eyes squeezed shut over some of the sights. Feral dogs worrying at the bloody clothing of the dead. Mouths smeared with blood like a baby's with chocolate. Gangs of vultures (death's lackeys) hunching together to squabble over the flesh. Yanking at sinews. Pecking at eyes.

I've no idea what started it. But nothing to do with us, we all silently agreed. The natives rioting. Bloody coolies at each other's throats for something. Hindu against Muslim. Muslim against Hindu. Even those wretched Sikhs were in there somewhere. Spotted carrying swords and blowing a din on their conches. Everything soon became clear. The truckloads of cheerless RAF erks were there to keep them apart.

The stench was as sharp as toothache. No up-wind or down-wind. There was no direction that gave relief. Fearful to breathe it into a living lung. Some chaps tore cloth from an old shirt to put over their noses and mouths. Sucking at the perfume of an erk's sweat instead. The NCO soon made them take the masks off. 'Get those off your faces. You look like bloody bandits,' he said.

Many of us lost our footing as the truck's wheels wobbled. We stopped. The driver looked behind, out of his window. He'd rolled over a body. An arm was still caught under a wheel. 'You and you, pick that up.' The NCO ordered two men to pick up the body we'd just run over. One of them (troublemaker, Pierpoint, or Spike to his friends), standing square, just looked at this NCO. He put his hand out to his friend to stop him obeying the command.

'Come on, pick it up, you two,' the NCO repeated, then moved off. Pierpoint wiped sweat from the back of his neck. His friend watched him, confused. The NCO turned back to them. 'Pick it up,' he yelled.

'Why?' Pierpoint said.

A few gasps popped in the air. The NCO was as startled as most of the men.

'What, Airman?'

'Why, Sergeant?'

'Because it's an order.' The NCO was sweating so much he looked as if he had been varnished. 'Pick it up.'

Pierpoint flung his arms wide. 'There's hundreds of bodies – why are we picking up this one?'

Many thought he had a point.

'Are you addressing me, Airman?'

'Sorry. Sergeant. What is special about this one . . . Sergeant?'

'Name, Airman?' There was no reply.

'Name,' he yelled into his face.

'Pierpoint, Sergeant.'

'Well, Pierpoint, I can put you on relief duty. You could spend the day with the wogs picking them all up if you want. Now, get down and pick this one up.' He lifted up some sacking and threw it at Pierpoint to wrap the body. But Pierpoint just let it drop to his feet. Then stopped his friend bending down to pick up the fallen cloth.

Maxi whispered, 'Jesus, this is trouble.'

The NCO, blood-vessel red, swallowed hard. 'Are you disobeying an order?'

His answer was delivered military style. Loud. Decisive. 'Yes, Sergeant.'

'Right. You're on a charge. Both of you,' the NCO said.

Pierpoint shrugged. His hapless accomplice was astonished.

'Take those guns off them. Tie their hands. You're both on a charge for refusing an order.'

Pierpoint looked relieved. He sat down where he'd stood on the truck floor, his silly friend now joining him with a defiant swagger. There was nothing to tie their hands with, but both obliged their chums by pressing their wrists together in a phantom bind.

Everyone knew what was coming next. Every gaze dropped to the floor to avoid the sergeant's eyes. I felt him pointing to me and Maxi through the top of my head.

'Come on, you two. Pick it up on the double.'

Maxi threw me a look. Is it worth it? Should we do it? he wanted to know. He knew my answer. We could be going home soon. And an order is an order.

'Hindu or Muslim?' some joker shouted from the truck. How are we supposed to tell the difference? How those coolies recognised one another as an enemy was a mystery to all. After two years in India, they still all looked the same to me. Apart from those Sikhs, that is, with their headscarves.

The body was warm. It gave Maxi a fright. 'Is he still alive?' he whispered. The throat was slit. Neck open in a scabby second grin. Stiff as an ironing-board. Stench thick enough to chew. The truck had cracked its arm into zigzagging pieces. An ear was dangling. Came off in my hand. I held it in my palm. Flimsy as a flap of leather from a shoe. 'Just chuck it, Pop,' Maxi shouted.

I turned away from the truck. Had to vomit.

'You all right?' Maxi said. I waved him away. Didn't need to be seen.

Maxi started covering the body. Tucking the sacking under like bedtime. Ready to lift. Suddenly there was gunfire. 'Come on, you two,' the NCO shouted.

Maxi lifted his end. Couldn't get mine. Wretched *dhoti* on the corpse was still caught under the wheels. 'It's stuck,' I shouted. Maxi dropped his end, which landed on the ground with an almighty thump.

'Leave it,' the NCO said. 'Get back on, now.' The truck started lurching off. Pulled up by the others, we climbed back just in time. Silly, but in the end the body was left where it had fallen.

They came running down the street. Gushing towards us like a flash flood. This horde of men. Jumping out from shabby windows and doorways. Down the alleys between the flimsy buildings that looked to be made of cardboard. Turned over a rickshaw. Tipped up a stall. Spilled the fruit. Pulverised it underfoot. All brandished something — a fist, a stick, the blink of a blade. Loud as a football crowd. Unstoppable. Rushing our lone truck. The NCO yelled for us all to 'Stay calm! Stay calm!' I hadn't fixed my bayonet yet. Hands quivering, I dropped it. Scrabbling round. Maxi found it and handed it to me. I dropped it again. Hundreds of scruffy black-eyed coolies — maybe thousands

— coming for us. We started lunging out with our bayonets. All yelling something. Get back. Fuck off. The NCO shouted, 'Hold your line. Stay calm.' My mechanic's fingers — used to tinkering with kites — were trembling. Pulling on the trigger of the rifle. But no ammunition. Not a bullet between us.

'Bang, bang,' a young chap shouted. Desperate but not forlorn.

They surrounded us like water. Bobbing black faces at every side. But, strangely, once they were upon us they quietened. Crowding round the truck as if not knowing what to do. 'Look fierce,' the NCO whispered loudly. A chap fainted. Unsteadied several as he fell; he was left where he landed. There was a stand-off — us looking at them, them looking at us. Seemed like hours. But it could only have been seconds. Slowly the truck began to rock. We started to lose our footing, grabbing the sides of the truck and each other.

Maxi's hand was squeezing my shoulder. I clutched a bunch of someone's shirt. Everyone splayed their legs ready to stand firm. Jabbing bayonets out of the side of the truck. The NCO shouted, 'Hold on. Grab something.'

Maxi yelled, 'It's a hundred to one here. What do we do, Sarge?' Everyone knew that if the truck went over we'd be spilled under the feet of this rabble and pounded to paste for the vultures. The NCO was banging the side of the truck with his rifle butt, aiming for the black hands and fingers that rocked us. Everyone joined in. Even Pierpoint was on his feet, hanging over the side, lashing out with his fists. His hapless friend was holding his legs. But we were being tossed around like a boat in a storm.

Suddenly there was gunfire. A police truck came round the corner and fired several rounds of bullets into the air. Our truck steadied in a cloud of dust. The rabble scattered like rodents, scurrying off down side-streets. Back through the windows and the doors. Chased by the ping of real gunfire. One dropped over here, another couple over there, tripping, grabbing at a wound, while some of the fallen were hurriedly pulled away. Chaps cheered, watching them go down. Slapping to the ground like a duck shoot at a fair.

'Wait a minute. Were they Hindu or Muslim?' one joker asked.

Breathing relief, quite a few yelled back, 'Who the bloody hell cares?'

Thirty-nine

Bernard

Thousands were killed in Calcutta. Men, women, children, even suckling babies, it didn't matter who. They called it a riot. Those of us who'd been there in the thick of battle with these bloodthirsty little men knew it was more than that. Muslims butchering Hindus. Hindus massacring Muslims. And who knows what side the Sikhs were on? Rumour said the wounded were too many to be counted, the dead too many to be buried. They were fighting for who should have power when a new independent India comes. Made me smile to think of that ragged bunch of illiterates wanting to run their own country. The British out of India? Only British troops could keep those coolies under control. A job well jobbed – all agreed. For our RSU it was back to the airfield. All present if not all correct. Left it to other Indians (and the vultures) to clear the streets of the tragic litter.

But everyone was riled after that turn of duty in Calcutta. Some more than others. Mutterings. Huddles of men. The talk? The stifling hot journey. The train rushing us through to get there but spending the trek back idling away in sidings. The heat. The overcrowding. Too many erks bunked up together in the museum for four days. Only let out in official convoys with no ammo. The endless parades through the streets. The orders to look fierce. The rumours that the fish we were offered to eat came from the Hooghly river, where many of the rancid rotting bodies of the dead were found. The days of nothing to eat but boiled eggs. (Not easily forgotten, the sulphurous burps of hundreds of BORs.) Then there was Pierpoint and his chum, taken off to await court-martial for disobeying that hasty order.

There was to be a meeting in our *basha* after *khanna*. Maxi and a couple of others had suggested it. Wanted to discuss the business of Pierpoint and the charge. I couldn't understand why Maxi wanted to get involved. He was usually more sensible than most. He'd be going home soon, back to Brighton to order a pint in a pub. Pierpoint and his antics would be a bad memory.

'We can't see them on a charge for what happened in Calcutta,' he told me.

'Why, in heaven's name, not? An order is an order, surely.'

'Jesus, don't get on your high horse, Pop. Just stay away if you want.'

There was no love lost between me and Pierpoint. Spike to his friends, Johnny to his mother. We'd shared a *basha* once. Made my life very difficult. I was older, you see, than most of the men. Tried to keep my head down. Had a job to do. Just quietly get on with it. Considered myself a civilising influence. But it was hard when all around me were young men like Johnny Pierpoint. He was a lanky chap. Arms as long as an ape's and an eye that winked (without warning) every so often.

'You're a married man, then, Pop? I thought about getting married but I didn't like the hours.' I suppose it became a bit of a sport trying to get me to join in with his antics. Thought he could make me blush (never). Spike found it hilarious that my only girl was my wife.

'Pop, what have you been doing with your gentleman's friend all these years?'

Spike bragged about what he'd done with women. How many had let him and what they had let him do. 'Two together – twin sisters. I swear as God is my witness.' He got everyone going. It became like a contest, comparing positions (wishful thinking mostly). 'Have you ever done it from behind, Pop? Doggy fashion?' I told him that that was my business and I would not discuss it with him. 'I'll take that as a no, then,' he said, 'but try it next time.' Obligingly got on the floor of the *basha* to demonstrate the position. (Of

309

course, Queenie would have been appalled at the suggestion. She'd have put on her dressing-gown, thick as an overcoat with buttons like padlocks, and made me sleep in another room.)

'You can be ridden like a horse, you know, Pop,' Spike kept telling me. Standing – her legs round his waist – was another of Spike's favourites. Some were obviously ridiculous. The one he called sixty-nine made me laugh. (A minor victory, which made some of the other chaps cheer.) I praised him for his imagination. But he insisted he'd done it many times. There was nothing he could not do with his tongue, he told me.

The *basha* was blacked out, just like in the meetings during that other bother. Same form too. Too many erks sweating in a tiny space. Same rotten smell like a fishmonger's slab. A hand grabbed my shirt, pulled me in and blocked the door. 'Squeeze in there, Pop,' he said.

'No names,' someone shouted, but I knew it was Curly. His *basha* too. Black as the back of an eyelid inside. Men were everywhere. Sitting over the floor, on the *charpoys*, standing round the walls. Couldn't see anyone but could sense it was a crowd by the deadened shuffling and the lack of breathable air. Feeling my way in, I realised I was fondling a face. My hand was flicked off pronto. I felt some fingers spread under my foot as I stepped on. 'Oi, watch it. Christ!' I sat down as best I could. Chaps on either side were clammy as hot baked potatoes. The person speaking was attempting to disguise his voice with a pencil in his mouth. Old trick. But it sounded like he was bubbling up from under water. I couldn't understand a word. Soon realised it was Maxi, once everyone shouted for the silly pencil to be removed.

'I say, we make a delegation to the CO. Explain the circumstance – it was a stupid order, the sergeant wasn't thinking. Ask him to get the charge on Spike dropped.' Some mumbling went off round the room. Bloke beside me shot his hand into the air. His elbow banged my head as it went. The room was pitch black, no one could see it. Fool.

'What if he don't wanna know?' someone asked.

Then a chap by my side shouted, 'Strike!' right in my ear. Moved my head away sharpish. Cracked my skull on the knobbly shoulder of the fellow beside me. The chap said it again, 'We have to strike.' Felt the splatter of his spittle this time. Everyone groaned. I tried to rub my head but my arm was jammed to my side. I could hear the tap of a pipe against teeth. Knew it was Maxi – he did it when he was nervous. Hadn't been using a pipe for long but already his teeth were wearing to accommodate the wood.

'We're being used now,' someone at my side said. 'Prop up the British Empire.' His face was so close I could smell his breath, sweet with gentian violets. One of Uncle Joe Stalin's friends buzzing at my ear. So near I knew he was unshaven. 'The military are just using us now,' he went on. His sweet breath was obscene in the stifling heat. Intimate in my ear, he wanted to know if we'd lost our lives in Calcutta would that be 'killed on active duty' even though the war most had signed up to had been over for a year? He sat up straighter and I had to shift with him, our shoulders sticking together in the crush. 'Some mother,' he spouted, 'would have lost a son, some wife a husband for that. Piggy in the middle of squabbling Hindus and Muslims.' The silly room had quietened down to listen to him. One of Uncle Joe's boys! I was having none of his nonsense.

'Maxi . . .' I said, to get his attention. I knew what direction he was but could only imagine him there.

'No names,' everyone shouted.

The whole meeting was ridiculous. I could feel the rise of a man's chest on the back of my head. His knees digging my kidneys. 'Mr Speaker,' Maxi said from a long way off, 'just call me, Mr Speaker.'

Nothing for it. 'Mr Speaker,' I said, 'what is the point of this meeting? To run down our country?' I could hear breathing behind me. A chap clearing his throat, sniffing up the phlegm. 'I, for one, am proud to be part of the British Empire. Proud to represent decency.'

Everyone started to jeer.

'Trust you, Pop,' someone from over Maxi's side called.

'No names,' Maxi said. 'I don't want anyone put on a charge for having this meeting.'

'So, why are you having it, then?' I asked. A finger poked hard into my ribs.

I brushed it off. 'We'll all be going home soon. We don't need this trouble for someone like Johnny Pierpoint.'

'Why don't you just belt up?' was whispered to me, so close it sounded like a thought.

The man beside me landed a knee on my fingers. 'You're on my hand,' I said. But he didn't move. I pulled away, accidentally cuffing someone who was too droopy to yell. I could hear Maxi muttering something. Soon the whole room was at it like a classroom with the teacher gone.

No sense was going to be talked in this cauldron. I could see two cigarette tips, waving round like sparklers. Shapes, shadows, but nothing else. My fingers hurt like hell. There was no air to breathe – only foetid breath wafting about.

'Put a sock in it, Pop,' I heard, accompanied by a whiff of gentian violets, 'or fuck off.' A knee kicked into my back winding me. The culprit said sorry. But I soon realised I'd sat in the red corner among the Communists. I would have known to avoid them if I'd seen their faces.

There was no point in me staying. 'Excuse me, I want to leave.'

Several men around me jeered. I pushed and shoved to get to my feet. And I was jostled roughly back. One of them grabbed my ankle with a 'Watch where you're bloody stepping.' I made my way like a blind man to the door. Squeezing against clammy torsos and slimy bulks. Grabbing what I could to steady myself. I wished Maxi was coming with me. Away from this rabble.

I felt some fingers again, back under my foot. 'Fuck off,' the chap screamed. Curly had trouble getting the door open. Pushing at it nearly brought the walls down. But the sticky night air soon had me – hitting me fresh as a mountain breeze.

Forty

Bernard

I had a stint of guard duty that night so I would've had to leave the meeting anyway. A three-hour patrol on a hangar out near the edge of the field, guarding gliders that were still stacked up in their crates. Funny thing was, during the war, filters, magnetos, even simple washers you could get new for neither wish nor prayer. Had to scavenge everything from somewhere else. An undamaged wing off one kite put on to another. Use the butchered one for spares. Most of the mechanical training we had back home had been pointless. Stripping engines down to the last nut and bolt. Endless tests and VVs. Out here if it didn't work, take it out and replace it. Engines, props, wheels, anything. We had to ransack a Japanese Oscar 2 after it landed intact. Maxi (disgruntled) said we should have been trained by thieves. Said any loose wallah could have taught us the skills we needed – how to dismantle and carry away in the fastest possible time. Absurd, I know, but he had a point. We even patched up a kite's cloth bodywork with a chap's shirt and then doped it with rice wine – never taught that in Blackpool. Yanks had had it all, of course. All their bent kites tinkered and fussed over in their well-equipped workshops.

But even though the war was over – the Japs having long surrendered – supplies still kept coming out. Stuff we'd dreamed of during the fighting.

313

The explanation: the ships were on their way and couldn't be turned back. Most chaps complained, of course. No crates of roast beef and Yorkshire pudding found their way out. No hangars filled with bacon sandwiches on white crusty bread. No barrels of spotted dick and custard. Just the ammunition COs had begged for. The planes, the trucks, the nuts, the bolts, the spares every erk had wished away his back teeth to fondle. Out they came. The trouble was, now it all had to be guarded. Kept safe from the thieving little black hands that sneaked all around us.

Those loose wallahs could lift anything. Took a man's wallet, more than once, from under his sleeping head. Didn't know a thing about it until the morning. Every piece of Perspex was stripped from a hangar full of kites, while the two armed guards outside pooped off their rifles at shadows. The booty was then carried off into the jungle leaving His Majesty's Forces scratching their heads. A priest lost his entire church: the bell tent that housed it, the altar, the seats. One night there, the next morning an unholy gap. Chaps jeered that not even God had seen that one coming.

But the worst by far were the dacoits. These men were murderers, not sneak thieves. Thugs. Thought nothing of stabbing, shooting, bludgeoning a guard to get their booty. Professionals of a sort. Everyone complained. 'Now the war's over,' they said 'we're fighting these wretched bandits.' Dacoits everywhere. Hell bent on using our ammo against us to tear up the British Empire. Everyone was jumpy. Worse than the Japanese, we all agreed, because we couldn't tell them apart from the coolies.

And there were camp followers everywhere. Nothing those dark little Indians wouldn't do for the precious baksheesh. Char-wallahs wherever you turned (*'Ek piala cha,* sahib') with their urns of foul tea. Dobie-wallahs washing clothes like women. Throw a few coins at a nappi wallah, get a shave, they'll even do it while you sleep. And all around us a plague of untouchables – happy to clean out the toilet cans with bare hands. Miserable creatures. Even other Indians hated them. Several chaps had seen Indian women squirting their own breast milk for a thrown rupee. Shocked even the most worldly.

That night my guard duty was with an Indian. Army wallah. Conscripted, not a bearer. I'd worked with this one many times before. Spent several

314

months with him taking tyres off bent kites and putting them on others. He was keen to learn. Eager to know what to do. Took orders well. Black eyes always watching me quizzically. Put him straight on the proper way of quite a few things. Arun was the name he went by. Last name rather queer (tongue-twister). He tried writing it down for me once, slowly with great concentration, but it was just a jumble of letters in no apparent order. Little chap, but muscly for an Indian. And happy. Not miserable like most of them. I noticed him straight away. He was outside my *basha* where the meeting was being held. A little way off but watching. One chap walked up to him, asked him what he was doing there.

'Please, I am hanging about,' he said. His English was hopeless. I had to jump in quick in case the chap gave him a thump for his cheek. Another Indian had been assigned to our watch. Ashok was his name. New to the camp. Been up in Cawnpur and Cox's Bazar. Guards on duty always walked to their patrol together. Collected their rifles, then out to relieve the last watch. On your own you'd be picked off by dacoits. Murdered – or, worse, found wandering the jungle in your underwear.

Usually I spent a watch with Arun very quietly. A need to be vigilant (of course), but the truth of it was, there was not much to chat about with a native Bengali. Not so with this Ashok. No sooner had we three settled down than he started: 'Tell me, Mr Bernard, how do you like India?'

These people could never get the hang of our names. But I let it go. 'Hot,' I said. 'Too many mosquitoes. You don't get that sort of thing in Earls Court.'

'Earls Court?'

'In London, where I live.'

'You miss London?'

'Of course. Who wouldn't, so far from home?'

'All Englishmen say this. I wonder why you stay in India if your Blighty is so missed?'

'Well, I'm afraid I don't have much choice in that matter.'

'Of course. Forgive me. Are you wanting to get home?'

'We all want to go home.'

'But like the other men – the ones who strike for their demob.'

315

Strange thing for this little Indian to say. 'What do you know about that?' I asked him.

'Oh, nothing. Just that many men – like Johnny Pierpoint and others, are they not browned off? They want to get home do they not? To Blighty. The white cliffs, Vera Lynn, a jolly good cuppa.'

'What do you mean?'

'It is that I am hearing that men are tired of India now the war is over.'

'Everyone wants to get home, of course. See their loved ones.'

'Exactly. Loved ones.'

'What do you know about all this?' I had the feeling he was being a cheeky fellow.

'I know nothing, Mr Bernard, please forgive me. My English is not good. Not pukka.'

'You speak good English,' I told him.

'You are surprised?'

I knew lots of them had been educated. 'Taught by missionaries, was it?'

'No.'

'Where did you learn? In the army?'

'No, I am lucky to learn the language at school. They call me a little brown Englishman there. The British have taught me so many useful things.'

I was glad to hear he was grateful.

'What would we poor Indians have done without you British? I say this to Arun. "Arun," I say, "all the things the British are giving us in India." "The Taj Mahal?" he says,' Ashok whispered to me, breath foetid with garlic. 'Arun is a simple man. Not educated.' Then louder, 'I have to tell him the Taj Mahal was built before the British came. "Who by?" he is asking me. "Indians," I am telling him. And he is looking surprised. "No," I am saying, "not that marvel. But let us think – ah, yes, tax and cricket . . ." '

'Fair play,' Arun adds, grinning like a simpleton.

'Fair play, tally ho, let's play the white man,' Ashok was shouting. Excitable people.

'Keep the noise down,' I told him.

'Forgive me. I am happy when I talk of the British. Like the King. What a great man. Some say he stutters like a devil is holding back his tongue. But I say no. He is a noble man.' He looked up humming and thinking, then slapped his head – a comic movement for an Indian. 'The railways! How am I forgetting? A gift from the British to an ignorant people. Just like your Lancashire cloth. Better than homespun, my mother says. Better.'

I could hear some shouting coming from a way off. I lifted up my gun. 'Hear that?' I said.

'I hear nothing.'

I listened. Told him to be quiet. Our duty was to guard not to chat. But all was still. No sooner had I relaxed than this Ashok was jabbering again: 'Now what am I saying? Oh, yes. The British. The rule of law – let us not forget the rule of law. Look here – are we not defending quality British goods from thieving Indians? Without your rule of law what are we?'

As he spoke I noticed smoke rising from the vicinity of the camp. Could smell it more pungent than usual on the night air.

Still he went on: 'I am not one of those people who wish the English out of India. I like you. Are you not protecting us all this time from the filthy Japs with their slitty eyes? Your British bulldog understands that there is nothing worse than foreigners invading your land. Look how you British fight those Germans. No sausages and language of the Kraut for Englishmen. "Go back," you say. "Leave us or our bulldog will bite." A dreadful thing to have foreign muddy boots stamping all over your soil. Do you not think?'

The horizon was beginning to glow orange. The sun had set hours ago but looked to have popped up again. Something was going on.

'You have seen what we Indians are like when we are being left to ourselves. The Hindu hate the Muslim, the Muslim hate the Hindu. They are fighting all the time. You were in Calcutta. I know this, Mr Bernard. Shocking, was it not? We must learn to live in peace – like you British when you are not at war with your neighbours.'

There was shouting again. This time unmistakable. Something was happening at the camp.

'But, tell me, are you ever wondering why the British are coming here to India?'

317

The chaps will take care of it, I thought. The shouting, the smoke, nothing to do with my watch.

'Mr Bernard?'

This Ashok had obviously asked me something. I wished the blighter would shut up. But it was our duty to get along. 'Did you ask me something?'

'I am just musing why the British are here in India.'

'Are you serious? There was a war on, man!'

'Mr Bernard is angry, I can see. Please forgive me.'

'I'm not angry. Can we just be quiet now? There's some flap going on and I need to . . . No more questions.'

'Of course, of course. I am hearing this noise too. But I am sure it is nothing more than your British high jinks.'

'Really, I would prefer it if you did not speak to me.'

'As you wish,' Ashok said. He turned to Arun. Shifted, moved his body away from me to talk tête-à-tête to him. Thought I couldn't understand but I knew what he said in Bengali to Arun: 'So this is the man you say is your friend?'

Arun shook his head in that snaky way they all have. Looks like a no to the inexperienced – all fresh white-kneed erks confused by it. But it's a yes. Both of them started jabbering away. I couldn't understand a word now. But Arun kept glancing my way. Sheepish. Embarrassed. Then I heard the word 'Lifebuoy' through the babble. Soon I realised he was saying something about me to Ashok. Arun was stroking his own arm as if washing. His brown fingers were tapping the air to show rain. Ashok, wide-eyed, was listening like story-time at school. The penny soon dropped and I knew what he was telling him.

It was the day the monsoon broke. The smell of sodden earth was like perfume to our gritty nostrils. Relief at being rid of dusty heat had all the chaps out. Dripping wet in the rain. Loving it. Frenchie – Claud Winters to his family – told us all of his cure for prickly heat. Lifebuoy and rainwater. Soap yourself up in the monsoon downpour, he prescribed. Got everyone doing it. Stripping off. Lathering up. Passing the soap through many slippery hands. Frenchie was soon nervous – his precious bar of Lifebuoy was getting smaller and smaller. He was yelling for everyone to go easy. 'Come on,' the chaps said. 'Your turn, Pop.' But I was reluctant. Naked in the rain – that's something for the young. But an end to the itching was a super thought. And Maxi, more sensible than most, was doing it. It works, he told me. 'Soap's nearly gone. Come on, Pop,' everyone called out. Nothing for it. Stripped off. Wonderful. The cooling rain beating against my bare skin. Tiny stabs of ecstasy. Lathered up, bubbly as a Hollywood bath. I was ready to wash it off when just then the rain stopped. Quickly as it had started. (Monsoon can do that.) Left me standing there naked as Adam in full lather and not a drop of water coming from the sky. The chaps all laughed (of course). It was a comical sight, I suppose. Palms up. Bewildered. Me in the wherewithal frothing like a sponge.

I didn't realise Arun had seen and had woven it into a tale to tell his friends. This Ashok laughed at the end of the little story, and went out of his way to slap me on the back. 'Forgive me,' he started, 'Please excuse. You do not speak our language, do you? Arun is telling me—'

'I know what he was telling you,' I said sharply.

'You do? It is a funny story.'

'Monsoon is very unpredictable.'

'As you say. But . . . Pop, is it, what they are calling you? . . . How is your . . . what is it you British get when you are too far from home? Prickly heat?'

I stood up at this point. Did he think I'd take it sitting down? I was being laughed at by coolies. 'Come on. On your feet, you two. Someone's coming. On the double. Come on. Shift yourselves.'

The smoke was getting thicker. Something was going on and I longed to know what. Two men soon appeared through the dark. Running. Guns at the ready. I couldn't make them out until they got closer.

'Hold back there,' I told the coolies.

It was Frenchie and Fido. Puffing like bellows. 'The *basha*'s on fire,' they told me. My *basha*. The one that had the meeting in it. The darkened one, stuffed with men over the floor, on the *charpoys*, standing round the walls. The truth is I didn't even think about it when they shouted, 'Maxi's in there. Come on, Pop.' I just ran.

319

Forty-one

Bernard

Every inch of the *basha* raged with flame. The men silhouetted against this blazing dazzle looked to be dwarfs feeding a beast. Throwing on buckets of water, barrels of dust that fizzled useless as spittle on a griddle pan. Everyone was yelling. One chap thrust a bucket into my hand, face contorted with panic, his arms flailing towards the inferno. I ran at the flames. The heat hit me like a wall. Eyelids rasping like barbed wire as I blinked against scorching smoke. Suffocating. Doubled up. Had to stop several feet back along with everyone else. Lob the contents from there. Hopeless. But any closer and the beast would have licked me raw.

We needed order. Obvious to me. Elementary. A line. A chain passing buckets one to the other would soon see the flames quelled, then move in closer.

'A chain,' I shout. 'Into a chain.' No one hears. All running about pell-mell. Headless. 'Come on, you clots, into a chain.' I grab a chap with the intention to hold him, to show him my idea. He drops his bucket on my foot. Water gushes round my boots.

'What you doing? Fuck off,' he says.

'A chain,' I yell, but he's gone. Next fellow struggles just the same. Somehow I end up on the ground. Nothing for it, I grab someone round the legs. Bring him down. Got his attention. Eye to eye he looks at me. I'm panting, 'We need to be sensible and make a—' He punches me in the face, yells at me to get a grip, while the blazing roof on the *basha* collapses with the sound of a gruff sigh, its green afterglow dazzling my eyes. Expected anyone still inside to run out now like the little piggies, hide in another house made of straw.

The walls tumble next, sending out a firework of sparks almost beautiful in the dark night. Skipping on to the roof of another *basha* it flames into life. Still slipshod everyone turns their buckets on that. A chain – Maxi would have got everyone into a chain.

The fire engine arrives. Bumping along the ground. Slow as molasses. Rumour is the men in it aren't the real operators. Those MT firemen got demobbed months ago. Obvious to all, the idiots working it don't know what they're doing. I soon jump up to help them with the hose. Show them how it's done. Seen it used before hundreds of times on pranged kites. Pull the hose off the truck, start rolling it along the ground. There's a chap shouting, 'Leave that – not yet.' I take no notice. 'What you doing, you fucking stupid erk?' But the fool wouldn't let me show him. Pushed me away. Grabs the hose from me and runs at the flames. Should have listened. Dribble of water comes out of the end with as much force as a baby's spittle. Scratching their heads (I swear) trying to work out what's what. While the fire in the *basha* has nearly run out of things to burn.

'Kink in the pipe,' I yell at them. Nothing for it – I push my way in. Man on the tap is useless, looking at it confused as if he'd just found it in a Christmas cracker. Won't budge, though.

I tell him I know what to do, but he just sticks an elbow in my ribs. 'Get him out of here or I'll land him one,' he shouts. Two chaps grab me. Pull me away. One on either side. Won't listen, just yelling, 'Leave it, leave it.'

I know what to do, what's needed. 'That bit older, you see,' I tell them. When the water finally starts to pour they point the hose at the wrong *basha*. Absurd. 'Not that one,' I shout. I struggle away from the clots bracing me.

'Turn it on to the one Maxi's in.'

'It's too late for that one,' one chap yells.

321

'Rubbish,' I tell him. But the imbecile takes no notice. Language as foul as any drain. Pushes me so hard I fall over. Police around me now. One of them's got a gun. Get to my feet but he's telling me to stay back or else. Shoving me. Pushing. Not a care that I'm tripping as he jostles me. 'Get back,' he says. No more than a raggle-taggle boy. Shut my trap, he wants me to. 'Stop yelling,' he tells me. Can't get him to listen to a word of sense.

Someone seizes my arm. 'Come on, Pop. Leave them to it.' It's Curly. Curly the doorman at the meeting. Curly from the *basha*. He was out. He got out. I'm so pleased to see him I hug him. He flinches back. Face wincing with obvious pain. Shows me the burn on the back of his shoulder. I ask about Maxi. Did he get out? 'Don't think so,' he says. Tells me the fire started outside the door. He got out in time by running through the flames along with some others. But it spread all around in the blink of his eye. 'There were about eight, ten I don't know. I thought they'd follow but . . .'

'Perhaps they got out a back way,' I say.

'What back way, Pop?'

The fire truck (useless) trains its water on the *basha* just in time to turn smoking cinders to mud. We weren't allowed in close. Held back by RAF police. Horror seared into the smutty faces of all the onlookers. Men stripped to the waist. Chests still heaving from exertion. Sweat running down them like shower water. All looking on helpless. Except those coolies. Those camp followers stood jabbering calm as if this was market day. They hadn't run with buckets. Not one of them. Did anyone see them trying to help? Not me. Some of them were smiling now it was over. One even found something funny enough to make him giggle. 'What do you know, what do you know?' I confronted him. This coolie backs away from me like a cringing dog. But I'm after him. I can see it on his face. Guilt. He probably set the fire – thought it was a joke. Grabbed the blighter by his filthy *dhoti*. Stinking rag comes away in my hand. 'Who did this? What do you know?'

'Please, sahib, nothing, sahib. Please.'

But I'm having none of it. Not fooled by their craven act. Probably part of some dacoit gang. Murdering thugs would strangle their own mother for money. Shoot us, run us through, and not the first to go up in smoke. Worse than the Japs. All us chaps knew it. Bloody coolies. Wanting us out of India dead or alive. This wretched, simpering little wog was cowering like a girl. But someone held me back. Grabbed my fist with both his hands. Silly coolie is on his knees in front of me, weeping. But I'm pulled off him. Dragged away by three chaps. Bloody fools, I tell them, what were they doing? Stopped me just when the cunning little bugger was about to talk.

Forty-two

Bernard

'You're in trouble, Bligh,' the sergeant told me. I thought he meant for striking a coolie. 'No. You were meant to be on guard duty.'

Asked his permission to explain. Thought it would be best. 'Just ran to help, Sergeant. My *basha*, you see. Knew the men in it.'

Nothing for it, I was ready to take my punishment. Deserting my post. Should never have left it, no matter what the circumstance. The CO would need to be told. But it was worse than that.

The sergeant asked me, 'Where's your rifle?'

My gun. The rifle. I'd fixed the bayonet, I remember, when I heard running. I'd pointed it thinking, Last time I shot one of these off was at basic training. Five rounds that had left my ears ringing. Hoped I wouldn't need a bullet this time because I wasn't sure if it had any. Rested it down when I realised it was Frenchie and Fido. Then what? Then I ran. I remember the buckets, the hose. Their urgency still itched my fingers. But the rifle?

'My rifle, Sergeant?'

'Yes, Bligh. Your rifle. Don't tell me you've lost your weapon too?'

I was brought straight before Flight Lieutenant Moon on the charge. Stood to attention in front of him. Sergeant on one side and a guard at my other. Arun and Ashok were marched in. No, they said. My gun had not been

324

left behind when I deserted my post. They had not seen my rifle except when it was in my hands. In fact, Ashok remembered helpfully, I took the gun with me. Eyes to the front, head erect, he told the CO about the bayonet. He worried, he said, that in my agitation to help my friends I might hurt someone accidentally with it. Impertinent blighter added that tradesmen are not very good with guns. The CO seemed to agree. Didn't question him. Didn't ask him what he knew. Whether he was in league with them. Had hidden the gun to sell it later for a good price to some scruffy countryman who'd end up piercing the belly of a Muslim with it. Just nodded. He was too young, this CO. Fresh out from Blighty. He'd missed the war altogether. A boy when it started. And still unable to thicken his blond moustache by the time it had finished. Hadn't been out east long enough to get used to the heat. Knees chalk white and skin rashed as pink as bully beef. He dismissed Arun and Ashok without a hint of misgiving. They marched out swinging their arms. Smartly. Their backs as straight as tin soldiers. Their legs rigid as wood. Too smartly. Only the experienced would realise these two scoundrels were poking fun at His Majesty's Services.

'Losing your gun and deserting your guard post. What have you got to say, Airman?'

The sergeant spoke up for me. 'Sir, it was Bligh's *basha* that got burnt down.'

'Are you saying there are extenuating circ-circ-circ—' Took me by surprise – he was stammering. Eyes batting as if adjusting to bright light. Put his hand up to cover his mouth. Then looked down at his desk twisting a pen through his fingers, still trying to cough up the word. I looked at the sergeant, who flicked his head for me to eyes-forward again. 'Reasons,' the CO finally said. 'Are you saying there are extenuating reasons for this neglect of duty?'

'Yes, sir.'

'Not you, Sergeant, I want to hear it from Bligh.'

'Knew the chaps in the *basha*, sir. But should have stayed at my post, sir.'

'And the gu– the gu– the rifle?'

'Should have kept it with me at all times, sir. My responsibility.'

'Losing a weapon is a court-martial offence. You do know that, don't you, Bligh?'

'Yes, sir.'

'Were you in your *basha* just before you went on guard duty?'

'Yes, sir.'

'With other chaps. Men you'd chummed up with?'

'Yes, sir.'

'Bad business. But you left not long before the fire started?'

'Yes, sir.'

'What were you in Civvy Street, Bligh, before the war?'

'Before the war, sir? Bank clerk.'

'Bank clerk. Responsible position.'

'Yes, sir.'

'Have you got plans to go back to it? Being a bank – bank – bank clerk?'

'Yes, sir.'

'You'll need a good service record, then, I would think? You won't want to . . . blot your copybook.' The CO grinned to himself, as if this was a joke that pleased him. He looked at the sergeant, who obliged him with a whiff of a smile. 'Well, Bligh?'

'Sir?'

Seemed to have lost his train of thought. Fiddled with his pen while he pulled his face straight. 'The RAF can't have you erks losing weapons. Very delicate time. Could end up in anyone's hands.' He barely paused before asking, 'What can you tell me about the men in the *basha* last night?'

'George Maximillian was in there, sir. He was killed along with seven . . .' my turn to stammer now '. . . along with seven others.'

'What was he doing?'

'Who, sir?'

'This Max . . . this airman.' He didn't stutter over Maxi's name, just couldn't be bothered to remember it.

'He had a wife and two sons. Probably writing a letter home, sir.'

'A letter home. So you men weren't having a . . .' He hadn't started a word. Just the blinking and quick breaths. Knew he was searching. '. . . meeting?'

326

The word had me startled (I admit). Wasn't expecting that.

'Meeting, sir?'

'Come on, there was a meeting, wasn't there, going on in that *basha*?'

'I don't know about a meeting, sir.' Any one of the chaps would have said the same. Part of a team, you see.

'You're in very serious . . . tr-tr-tr-trouble, Bligh. You do know that?'

'Yes, sir.'

'Are you taking me for a fool? Eight men die in a fire in a *basha*. How do you explain that?'

Wasn't sure if he wanted an answer but for Maxi's sake it was time to give it. 'Sabotage, sir. The dacoits, the coolies.'

'Are you saying that someone deliberately started that fire?'

'Indians, sir. They want us out of their country. Fire started at the door. No chance of escape. Sir.'

'No, Bligh. Things are delicate enough. No one here says the fire was started on purpose. Do you understand me? It was an unfortunate accident. Everyone here agrees. What was it, Bligh?'

'Sir?'

'The fire, what was it?'

'An accident, sir.'

'An unfortunate accident, Bligh.'

'Unfortunate. Yes, sir.'

'Good, that's cleared that up. However, what does interest me is the meeting that was going on in that *basha* at the time.'

An unfortunate accident — they were burned alive! 'I know nothing about a meeting, sir.'

'You'll lose your Burma star if you're court-martialled, Bligh.'

'Sir?'

'Come on, Bligh, what was going on?' He was agitated. Threw down the pen. Thumped his fist on the desk. Eyes swivelled in his head as he searched for something large to throw at me. 'You lost a rifle after deserting your guard post. It's a court-martial. Almost certainly prison, man. Unless you can help me out. Top brass don't want a repeat of last time. We can't have strikes. I won't have a strike. Discipline must be maintained.'

'Know nothing about it, sir.'

'I bet you were in it last time, eh? That mutiny. A bloody bank clerk, you'd have been in it up to your neck.' His stammer had gone with his anger.

'No, sir.'

'Look here, Bligh, I've got eight letters to write. Eight families to inform of these deaths. And I want to know whether I'm talking about troublemakers or decent men. Now, are you going to help me or not?'

Forty-three

Bernard

No doubt Maxi's sons will cherish the letter from Flight Lieutenant Moon. It would almost certainly say that their father died on active service. A corporal in the RAF. A boy in blue. For ever remembered that way. A framed photograph on the mantelpiece. A Burma Star in a case. Their father died fighting for his country on active service in India. What better words could there be for a son to cherish? They could be proud of their dad.

There were times I wished I'd died alongside him in that *basha*.

I was the only Englishman left in the prison. Most of the others had gone home or were moved somewhere more secure. The two-week sentence would soon be up, the sergeant had said. Take the punishment, then forget about it. You'll be going home soon, just think about that. Two weeks, that was all.

Then the RAF shut me in a cell with four Indians. Coolies. This leading aircraftman – this Englishman – locked up with the loose wallahs, the thieves, the scoundrels the RAF took such pains to guard against. Every one of my cellmates was a common criminal, caught with his little brown fingers in something. Could even have been the men who murdered Maxi. But I had the same kind of mattress as them, rolled on to a stone floor hard as a biscuit ration. Same tin mug and plate. Same single spoon. Prison wasn't a hardship for coolies. Regular meals. No work. They slept all day. Brushed aside the bugs that crawled over them. Jabbered away in their tongues. The withering heat in the small cell didn't trouble these natives. Or the dust that circled the foetid air like a sandstorm. Used to it. But for an Englishman . . . The gritty sweat rolled down me night and day. Stinging into my eyes. Dripping salty into my mouth. Itching me senseless. Seeping into my mattress until it was as soggy as a biscuit dunked in tea.

Had to stay alert around these larcenists. Couldn't shut my eyes to sleep, not even for the briefest doze. Had a pen and an air-letter, you see. The guard, a Tommy, hearing I'd lost all my kit in the fire, had brought them for me. Kept these two possessions on the floor under my mattress. Away from those eight filching hands and envious black eyes that ceaselessly watched me. Thought to write this air-letter home to Queenie. Nothing for it – I'd have to make up what was happening. Moved to a nicer spot, hoped to be home by Christmas, that sort of thing. No need to mention the court-martial or Flight Lieutenant Moon making an example of me. Or the officer who was sent to speak up for me who could find nothing to say about my service record that would change the court's mind, and avoid the shameful sentence – two weeks in prison among the most heinous cellmates a civilised man could imagine.

Had to rest the air-letter on the floor to write it. Turned my back to the coolies but could still feel them straining to know what the Englishman was doing. Began, as always, 'Dear Queenie'. Then stopped. Think before you write, the paper urged me – printed at the top with two exclamation marks. Think!!

My father had been in the army in the last lot. The Great War, they call it. He was in France. A young lad, barely nineteen, with a wife and small son back at home. In letters he'd told Agnes, his wife, my mother, that he was having a good time. She imagined him sipping wine with the locals and sampling loaves of bread as long as his arm. And fighting the Hun, of course – a pot-shot here, a loud bang over there. 'He's in the Somme,' she'd say on the doorstep, like he'd popped down the road for a swift half. She had no idea he'd been living on mud in a battered gash in the ground for three years. That is, until they returned him. He didn't come on his own, he was dropped off by a truck. Quite a spectacle in the street (everyone out to stare). A parcel being delivered to number twenty-one. Two men, one on either side, marched him up the steps and knocked at the door. Ma answered. Untying her apron, smiling at her hero's return.

They had to give him a little shove to get him inside.

She got his body back – in one piece, whole, hardly touched. A body that defecated every time a door closed too loudly. At night he rocked, sitting on his bed in striped pyjamas done up to the neck. When he slept he screamed as if someone was pulling out his teeth – the buttons on his pyjamas pinging across the room like shrapnel. Ma had to coax him out from under the bed every time a dog barked. 'Your father's lost his mind,' she told me. And I, aged eight, hoped if someone found it they'd bring it home for him.

He got gradually better (a little), coaxed on by Ma. He was fed his food with a bib tied at his neck. Excrement was cleared up from the floor. Trousers changed. He was gently persuaded out. Ma dressed him in a hat and gaberdine coat and took him with us to the shops. A young girl, barely a woman, handed him a white feather. He played with it like a toy, wiping its softness over his cheek. Until Ma saw it. She spat at the girl and would have done her serious harm if a constable had not been called. 'He's done his bit,' she shouted at everyone come to stare.

She made me hold his hand all the way home.

He dug a trench in the garden. I watched him dig it (a straight line). It was his first (he dug another four). Ma gave him geraniums to plant in them. Showed him how to shovel the earth back over the trenches again. He watched them grow, sometimes sitting for hours, his head in his hands, waiting for the shoots to push up into the light. When the first dazzling red flower appeared, he cried. Openly.

But he was never my pa again. Every time he looked at me was for the first time. It didn't matter if I'd only just left the room, when I came back I was a stranger. He used to carry me on his shoulders before. Taught me to throw a ball, overarm, like a cricketer. 'Nice shot, Bernie. You're learning, my son, you're learning.' Brought me *Boy's Own Annuals* even before I could read them

331

without help. When he came home from work (the bank) I'd climb on his lap and ask him to read me a story of derring-do (*Saber & Spurs* or *The Sheik's White Slave*). When he left for the war I wanted to know where he was going. The last thing he ever said to me was, 'Derring-do, Bernard. Your pa's off for derring-do.'

Ma aged sixty years in ten. She sagged and shrank. She would have liked a big family, more than just me. But her husband couldn't do it any more. At least, not when she was there. All she saw were the crusty white stains on the sheets, on his pants. She'd turn away. Call me to clear up that mess.

She had a big house and a small pension. The handed-down silver cruet that sat on the parlour table disappeared, one piece at a time. So did the rings on her fingers. Except her wedding band, which she twirled every time she watched my father in his garden. She let rooms in the house. Spent her time chasing rent and morals up and down the staircase. Listening at the parlour door in case evil came into her home. When I left school she put on her hat and best coat (saved twice from the pawnbroker) and visited the bank where my father used to work as a clerk. She came back with a job for me, starting the next day. 'They owe him that much,' was all she said.

She died aged forty-two. Cancer, they whispered. A lump in her breast that feasted on her from the inside. Before she died she managed to ask, 'Who's going to look after him?' I didn't say a thing. What was there to say? Who'd look after him?

I would.

Pa was quiet when Queenie moved in. Tending his garden, sitting in his chair (no trouble). He knew she was something different. Followed her round with his eyes. She cleaned the place. Said she was adding a woman's touch. Flowers, embroidered runners on the sideboard. Pa started smiling, tapping his foot to the wind-up gramophone. Humming to 'Show Me The Way To Go Home'. She danced with him, one foot at a time, in front of the hearth. Then the war came and the bombs. His excreta flowed freely again. Out came the bib at mealtimes. We couldn't get him into the shelter. He always stayed under the bed, quaking like a girl.

'It would be the best thing if he did go,' Queenie had said once.

It was the first time I realised she could be heartless.

After a raid I'd have to coax my father out from under the bed with bread and jam – the wireless on so loud it sounded like we lived in a dance hall. Sometimes he'd dance round the room on his own, holding his arms up for an imaginary partner when he thought no one was looking.

They were running out of young men in this new war, conscripting older and older men every week. There was nothing else for it. Fire watch and black-out duty weren't enough. And a bank clerk who spent all day writing figures in ledger books would never be essential to the home front. It was my turn for derring-do.

All I knew was that I was going overseas. Embarkation leave – one week with loved ones, then off. Of course I had no idea where I was being posted but Queenie kept asking. 'It must be somewhere hot if they've given you a tropical uniform,' she said. The chaps who trained with me laughed at that – tropical uniform could mean Iceland or Siberia. 'You must know where you're going. Can't you ask them?' She thought I was just keeping it to myself. Of course they wouldn't tell us, otherwise it would be news in every dance hall that ever saw a chap dressed in his best blues. 'They won't tell me,' I told her. I'd shouted in the end, raised my voice.

I hadn't wanted to spend my last day with her like that. We should have been having a kiss and a cuddle. She let me do it to her, of course, but only because I was her husband and going away to who knew where? She let me, but she lay there like a limp rag. Wouldn't even put her arms across my back. And as for kissing – she turned her head away. I had to kiss her cheek. I mean, my mother let me do that. When she waved me goodbye she said, 'Take care and be sure and write.' But she'd shut the front door behind me before I'd got down to the last step.

Liverpool was overcast in those days before I left. Dishwater sky. Wet-weekend-in-Wigan days, Queenie would have called them. I left with a heavy heart (I'll be honest). Wished I'd parted from Queenie on better terms. Seemed to hear the door she'd slammed everywhere I went. Boots on wood, train doors, distant gunfire – all had me turning with a start. Silly, of course.

I'd watched on deck in drenching rain as the coastline gradually slipped into the sea. I'd never left England before. Only once could I recall turning back to look at land. Paddled out too far at Dymchurch. Startled to realise I'd gone so far. Ma, a little unrecognisable figure on the beach, calling me back. Pa wading out, sweeping me up safe in his arms.

England disappeared so quickly. Soon there was nothing but sea. My legs wobbled. Couldn't get my balance, find my grip. I sat down to watch the spot where my country dissolved. It was there, etched on to my eyes like an afterview of the sun. Pa's back as he tended his vegetables. Queenie waving at the door before she slammed it shut. All were left indelible.

I held my pen above that blue flimsy paper on that prison floor. Held it there for so long that the sweat trickled down my arm and dripped off the nib like teardrops. Soon the paper was too soggy to write on. And 'Dear Queenie' had blurred to a blue stain then run until it was just a blot.

Forty-four

Bernard

He said it like I'd won the demob in a raffle. You wouldn't have known the man had put me in prison in the first place. Looked me straight in the eye. Happy to deliver his news. No doubt thought someone with my record would consider it an honour that a CO would tell them personally. 'Bligh. Your number's up. Collect your kit from Cal. You've got a week to get to Bombay. You're going home.'

Rumour had it our unit was one of the last left in India. And, thanks to this CO, I was later than most. One chap had even gone native. Refused a boat home – took his demob in Cal. But only a few of the unlucky were still left counting. Flight Lieutenant Moon, sitting high in his truck, wanted to tell his driver to carry on but stuttered over the command. 'Ca-ca-ca—' he said, before miming it with a flick of his hand.

There was nothing left of the *basha*. The RAF police had cleared every last trace away. Except the scorched marks where it once stood. A sooty black square drawn in the dust. It was impossibly small. Looking no more than the size of a packing case. Hard to imagine where *charpoys* lay, let alone where eight large men fell. Alf Lamb, Bill Bulmer, Nobby Bloomfield, I knew them all. Nobby especially. We'd been on a river salvage together. He'd volunteered to dive into the water, swim under the wreck of the plane to attach cables round it. I was on the party that heaved the Wellington out. So was Alf, I believe. It only took a hint of interest to get Jock Davison to recount the story of the tiger he killed for some natives. Attached a pig to a tree evidently. Sat all night in the branches waiting. Got it with one bullet between the eyes. He was a local hero for a while. Didn't know Gordon Pink or Jack Bark – they'd not been long on our unit. Ron Simpson was an unlucky man even without the fire on his score sheet. Been in Normandy for D Day. Parachuted in. Watched most of his unit shot down before they hit the ground. Got wounded twice himself. Thought he was going home on VE Day. Drunk as a navvy, climbed a lamp-post with a Union Jack painted on his bare behind. Next week he was marched on to a boat out east. The eighth name on that gruesome list was, of course, my friend George Maximillian.

This stripling CO's vehicle drove right across the scorched remains of the *basha*. I watched it as I stood there saluting this officer in the dusty wake of his vehicle while he swerved two tyre tracks over the grave of eight aircraftmen. *Basha* no longer there, it was a bit of a handy short cut for him. I had to spit on the ground after he'd gone – rid my mouth of the grit and dust, you see.

So that was how I found myself once more in Calcutta. Vultures still sat like scrawny hunch-backed hags looking down from the rooftops. They watched me as I walked along. Silly, but their gaze was so keen I imagined they recognised me from the last time I was here. The carnage they gorged on then was now all cleared away. Of course. The piles of putrefying rubbish – the pecked and gnawed bodies of the dead – all gone. But still those ugly beasts seemed to be dallying patiently for some next time. Picked up my blues from the holding centre. Only bit of kit I had left. The forage cap made me look like an old man. One of those coves from the Home Guard, playing soldiers. Trousers were roomy, jacket a little big. Left them there years before, you see, when I was a stouter man.

It was in the *maidan* I saw him walking. Johnny Pierpoint – Spike to his asinine friends. Wouldn't have believed it could be him. Too carefree. Sauntering. A skip in his step. But he stopped me. Hand on my arm. Held me back. To a trusting eye, he was pleased to see me.

'Well, well, well, Pop. You still here? I'd have thought they'd have got you on a boat before this. What you been up to?'

Nothing for it. Had to tell him I was on my way to Bombay.

'What you doing in Cal then?' he said. Then stopped my answer with, 'Don't tell me. You've finally taken my advice. Eh, Pop? Come to get some bint here? See if you can't learn a few things to show that wife of yours before you get home?'

I was speechless. The scoundrel should have been locked away not standing in this sweltering city insulting me with 'I can recommend a few. Not down Free School Street, though. Let me give you an address. They'll see you're all right. All very clean. Very young. Pretty. You know.'

'No, thank you,' I told him.

'Pop, do yourself a favour. Your gentlemen's friend really does need a decent outing. It's withering away in there.'

The scurrilous blighter! He should have been in prison and I told him so.

'Prison! Why? What are you talking about?' he said.

'For all that business.'

'What? Showing a lady a good time?'

'Good God, man, can you think of nothing else?'

'I can, but I don't like to.' He started laughing. His eye winking rapidly as a faulty bulb. Pushed a piece of paper into my hand. When I didn't take it he stuffed it into my pocket. Patted it twice, saying, 'Trust me, you won't regret it. You ask your chum, Maxi.'

'What's Maxi got to do with it?'

'He didn't regret it. Came back a few times for more.'

'Rubbish!' I told him.

'Don't take my word, ask him.'

'Maxi's dead,' I said. That wiped his smug face clean.

'Dead!'

'Died in a *basha* fire. Him and seven others.'

'Jesus. Bad business. Dead. How did that happen?'

'It was your fault,' I told him.

337

He looked at me, dumb as a coolie. Mouth agape. Eyes popping. Who would blink first, me or him? 'Come again?' he finally said.

'I said it was your fault. The fire. The fire that killed them was because of you.'

'I hardly knew him. I hadn't seen him since Cal.' He frowned, his dark eyebrows meeting in a hooded V over his eyes. I almost felt sorry for him. A lot to carry. A lot to bear – the death of eight men. Then his mouth flickered into a grin. Slowly revealing two front teeth. Stained with nicotine they looked to be made of wood. 'I've been nowhere near your unit for ages. What are you going on about now, Pop?'

'They wanted to get you off the charge. They had a meeting in the *basha*. It got burned down with them in it.'

'What charge?'

'That business.'

'What business?'

'Disobeying an order.'

'Oh, that! Didn't you lot hear? They dropped all those charges after a couple of days. I got posted with another unit. The CO couldn't be bothered with it. Said the war had been over for too long. Me and Geordie. We should all have been home anyway, he said. I'd got a good record. He just gave us a bit of a warning. Discipline, blah, blah, blah. That sort of thing. I promised to be a good boy from now on and he forgot about it.' He told his story like I'd be pleased for him. The man was an idiot. 'But it's bad about Maxi,' he said.

'He was a decent man,' I said.

'Yeah, but he knew how to enjoy himself.' He leered again. As ever, commanded to by his loins.

'Oh, for God's sake! Have you no decency? Men died trying to save your skin.'

'Look, Pop. They were your unit, I know. You're upset. Who wouldn't be? But it's got nothing to do with me.'

'Nothing to do with you? It's got everything to do with you and your sort.'

He stared at me for some time, wondering how to respond. Looked over my shoulder. Bit his lip. Down to his feet. Back to my face. 'Fuck off, Pop.' He turned his back to me. Took two steps away. Then stopped, turned on his heel to face me again. 'Come to think of it, didn't a little birdie tell me something about you? Weren't you in trouble? Weren't you in the clink?'

I felt no need to answer him. Adopted a parade-ground stance. Head up. Chest out.

'You were, weren't you? What was it for? Being a miserable bastard? Being the most useless erk on your unit?'

I grabbed him round the throat. Got my whole hand over his Adam's apple. Felt my nails in his skin. But he pushed me off – younger man, you see. He started walking away. I chased after him. I'd never meaningfully punched anyone in my life but, by God, I was ready to try. He dodged me as I whacked at air. Lost my balance. The fool was laughing at me. I came at him again. He lifted up one gangly arm and rammed it on my forehead. Long as an ape's, his arm – my punches could get nowhere near him. He had me struggling, ineffectual, like a dunce with a bully. Whacking the air between us. Passers-by looked amused. Thought these two servicemen must be having some high jinks. But he had a tiger by the tail. I lunged at him when he dropped his hold. But he grabbed me. Spinning my arm up round my back. Thought he would rip it from my shoulder. Mouth next to my ear he spat into it, 'God, Pop, you're just a laughing-stock, you know that? Everyone says it. Maxi was the only one who could stomach you. Go and get yourself fucked properly, Pop. Show that poor wife of yours that you did something useful while you were out here.'

She hardly spoke any English. Just a few words learned by rote from other men who'd passed through.

'Tommy. You are liking me, nice clean girl?'

I told her to shut up.

She lay back on the bed. Rested on her elbows. Examined me while I unbuttoned my trousers. 'Turn away,' I told her. Said it twice. Silly girl only smiled. Obviously never heard those words come from a Tommy's lips before. Carried on eyeing me. Batting her eyelids sleepy slow. I turned my back to her.

'How you are liking it, Tommy?' she asked.

'Doggy,' I said, over my shoulder.

She came up behind me, started wiping her hands down my back. Hadn't a clue what I meant. 'Doggy,' I said again. She brushed a hand over my chest. I watched her tiny brown fingers pushing down over my nipple. Threw her off as I turned round. 'Doggy. On your hands and knees.'

She frowned.

'Like this.' I showed her how just like Spike had for me. Eventually she wriggled up the bed on all fours. The cheeks of her bottom curving tight as a doped kite. Sleek as marble. Breasts dangling like a cow's udder. She looked back cursorily to see if she'd got it right. My erection was fierce. I got on the bed behind her. On my knees, I grabbed her where I could. Rammed her in one. She cried out. Something. Tommy. Something. 'Shut up,' I told her. And she started wiggling side to side like a blasted dancer in a bazaar. 'Stay still,' I shouted.

She was panting, 'Aah, aah.' And writhing the way her Tommies usually enjoyed it.

Nothing for it, I grabbed her hair into a bunch. Held it firm in my fist to keep the wriggling whore still as I thrust at her. Riding her hard – just as I had been promised.

Didn't take long. Yelled out (I admit). Ejaculation was a blessed release, like lowering myself into a cool bath. Leaning back, closing my eyes, breathless. A few moments of peace before I realised I still had her hair wrapped tight in my fist. Her head, wrenched back, was baring its teeth in a rictal gape. I soon let go and she quickly pulled herself away from me. Got up from the bed. Jumped out of my reach. And only then did I see that she was nothing but a girl. Surely no more than fifteen. No younger. Fourteen or even twelve. A small girl. Hadn't noticed before. Just took in a whore's room. The coloured lights, the trinkets on the walls, the overpowering smell of jasmine. The breathy whispered, 'Hello, Tommy.' Her scanty robe, bare breasts, naked behind. And my pathetic need of it all. But now the fear in her black eyes – harmless as a baby's – was denouncing me as depraved. What was I doing?

What would Queenie think of her husband now? Trousers round my ankles in a brothel, defiling someone's daughter. 'Is this what the war's done for you?' she'd say. This war hadn't made me a hero. It had brought me to my knees.

'I'm so sorry,' I told the girl. She didn't understand. I put out my hand to her. 'I'm so terribly sorry.' But she cringed, fearful. She was covering her body as best she could – with her arms, her hands. 'Never done this sort of thing before. I've no idea what came over me.' She was feeling for her robe, obviously too scared of me to let me out of her gaze. 'Please forgive me.' As I moved again, the merest shift off my knees to sit on the bed, she took a startled breath. 'I won't touch you,' I told her. She cringed lower to the ground like a cornered animal. 'I'm an Englishman,' I explained. 'In the RAF. Back home I was a bank clerk. It's a very responsible position. I'm a married man, you see. An Englishman . . . me English-man . . .' But I felt like a beast. It was then, as if from nowhere, a sob fierce as a child's rose in me. I gulped for air. Mouth open – a long, breathless pause ended with the release of an anguished howl. Great spasms convulsed through me. My hands trembled. I covered my face. Gasped for more breath, which came in short bursts of pitiable whimpering.

She came and stood before me. Her face softening back to a girlish sweetness. I doubt she'd ever seen a Tommy cry. She put her hand out to touch my cheek. To wipe a tear. The tenderness of it stung. Shocking as a bolt from a current. 'Terribly sorry,' I said again, my breath coming in puffing gasps. I wiped my face as best I could. She patted my arm. Her hand no bigger than a monkey's paw. And she said, 'Johnny. Johnny. No cry, Johnny.'

It was the name that did it. Not the thought that Johnny Pierpoint had probably been through earlier. It was the way she said the name. It gave me the jitters. Like the Japs calling to me and Maxi, 'Johnny, help me, Johnny.' It soon pulled me together. 'Don't call me that, my name's not Johnny,' I told her, which sent her stepping smartly back away from me once more.

Nothing for it, I just threw the money at the wretched whore, then left.

Forty-five

Bernard

Nothing to do on the sea journey back home. Hundreds of servicemen wandered aimless on the decks. What a change from the adventure of the journey out. Frigates circling. Lifeboat drill every day. U-boat watch. Chaps up on the deck in twos, staring at the sea in case of something odd. Not a clue what we were looking for, most of us having only ever been familiar with boating ponds. But now, returning, mine was not the only dull-eyed gaze that drifted to the horizon as I thought of home. Could I go back to the bank after what I'd experienced? Silly, I know, but I thought of the Wellington bomber. Thirty-six thousand five hundred pounds of metal, Perspex and cloth. Wings that spanned eighty-six feet. Nose to tail in sixty-four. Two engines and room for six crew on board. Bolts as big as my fist on some parts. Propellers that dwarfed me. Wheels wider than an arm span. When she flew, her massive propellers spun so fast they were invisible. She would edge along the ground until thirty-six thousand five hundred pounds of metal, Perspex and cloth lifted into the air as light as a handkerchief. What could compare with that sight for me now? My old bicycle with its dicky chain that I used to fix and fuss over in the backyard? A bus? Tiny miniature creature. A tube train? You could step into a tube train with one hop. You didn't have to climb up seventeen dizzying feet just to get into it. A car? A lorry? Now, all puny as tin toys.

I slept in a lifeboat under the stars. Not in a hammock below the water-line with hundreds of others. Shoving and pushing for space. Arguments. Shocking language. Endless talk of women — Johnny-Pierpoint-style: what they could and would do to them once they got home. I gave my cigarettes to an old sweat who worked the ship. In return he knocked on the lifeboat before the decks were swabbed. Warned me out before I was caught or washed overboard. Swarthy fellow. Came from Argentina. Didn't speak English. Conducted the whole transaction with gestures and mime.

Just as on that ship out years before, two days in, everyone got seasick. A wretched nausea. Head like a sponge. Stomach in my boots. Constant dull tang of salt on my lips. Nowhere to fix my sight. Giddy. Praying for just one settled moment. A minute to stand firm. But nothing stayed still. Least of all the grub in my belly. The old sweat laughed. Slapped me on the back and used his tattoos to insult me. Pointed to something on his left arm — a badly drawn bird of some sort. I got the idea. Couldn't blame him: all day vomiting over the rails of the ship I was a pitiful sight.

Thought nothing of it at first. Too sick to worry. A bite, perhaps, from some rogue mosquito. Could feel it under my fingers as I urinated. Just a small lump. But the next day it was considerably bigger. I borrowed a torch from a chap. Needed to get a clear look. But I could only get the worthless torch to blink on and off. Under this stroboscope in the gloom of the lifeboat it appeared not much smaller than a halfpenny. I convinced myself it was the flashing light that gave it that dimension. In the light of day, locked secure behind a toilet door, the enormous throbbing sore had produced a hat of pus. I felt it pop like a grape in my pants as I sat down in front of another meal of sausage and potato. It was ringed with a blue line clear as if drawn with a pencil. I vomited twice. Once when I saw its seeping pus matted into my pubic hair. And the next time as I wrapped the sore in a bandage. It was unbearably itchy and clammy inside this wrapping. And useless — a small spot of yellow brown muck had soon stained it through. When I eventually unwrapped it, the bandage clung like paper to a sticky toffee. I bit the leather of my belt to stop me yelling out. Nothing for it. I had to face it. I knew what this angry pustule on my penis was.

The medical officer, on the boat when we first came out east, had warned us RAF recruits. Ulcers, inflammations, colourful discharge, swellings. All the result of sexual relations with the wrong type. He'd given us lectures. Colourful pictures were passed round. Lurid photographs. Quite shocking. Parts of the body unrecognisable as human. Turned some of the chaps a sorry shade of grey. Had them worried. Frowning. Thinking back. Stopped their bragging for a while. One of them, I recall, fainted – blamed seasickness. 'Always use this,' the MO had said. Took a rubber sheath out of his breast pocket. Waved it around in the air.

Some joker had shouted, 'Is there just the one, sir?' Got everyone laughing.

Apoplexy, mental failure, nervous disease, blindness. And, of course, eventual death. Syphilis!

The inevitable result of my sexual relations with the wrong type. A small girl with black eyes harmless as a baby's. The wretched whore in Calcutta – still left clinging on me. Syphilis! In the day, I felt this ulcer's presence like a galloping pulse. And at night we both wept. Syphilis! I couldn't imagine what Queenie would say to that. I tried to conjure her admonishment. A wagging finger. A tutting tongue. A turned back, perhaps. All useless when faced with the shame of a husband riddled with the clap.

Clinging to the rail of the ship I looked down into the sea. Only one step would be needed. A big one. Over the rail, off the side of the hull. It would be days before I was missed. No one would see my scrawny figure slip under the foaming wake of the ship. If they did they'd blink twice, thinking the ocean light was playing tricks on them. It was the only honourable thing for a man in my position to do. They would have to declare me missing. And Queenie, like Maxi's two sons, could keep me as I was. A middle-aged bank clerk who'd thought his life was set. Who even started whistling once he was part of a team. An RAF aircraftman fighting a just war. An Englishman proud of his country, right or wrong. Sitting there at the rails of the ship the moonlight was brighter than an English February sky. All night I waited for courage or despair to overwhelm me. To slip me into the navy sea. But neither came.

Would the military now have to drop me off at home by truck? A spectacle in the street (everyone out to stare). A parcel being delivered to number twenty-one. Would two men march me up the steps and knock at the door? Queenie untying her apron, would she smile at her hero's return? Would they tell her that syphilis had made me lose my mind? Would it now be Pa who hoped that if someone found it they'd bring it home for me? And would they have to give me a little shove to get me inside?

1948

Forty-six

Bernard

I expected Queenie to be shocked. Could hardly blame her. Husband back from the dead. But I didn't foretell that 'appalled' would play for quite so long around the corners of her mouth. Sitting there clutching her stomach. Speechless. Pale. Shaking. Eyes rimmed red. She looked older. More careworn. She'd put on some weight. I'd watched her wither away during the early part of the war. Day by day. I was not the only husband who'd felt impotent about that. So a little plump looked well on her.

'How's Pa?' I asked.

Suddenly she was crying. Weeping into her hands. I lifted my arm to caress her head. But she moved. Brushing her nose on her sleeve, she'd never know I was trying to comfort. Thought it an innocent question. Except she walked the room demented.

'Oh, Bernard. I wrote to you . . .'

Letters went astray. Part of many chaps' grievances. We moved so much, you see. In India, it could take months for a letter to catch up with our RSU. Some never made it. Misunderstandings passing unknown in the post. Silly question (I know), hardly worth asking, but I did. 'Has something happened to him?'

'Bernard, you've been away such a long time . . .'

349

Who could doubt I owed Queenie an explanation? But describe snow to someone who's lived only in the desert. Depict the colour blue for a blind man. Almost impossible to fashion the words. How to begin to tell? It had been over two years since my ship docked back at Southampton. A long time, I admit, to get from there to here. After demob, I'd made my way to Brighton. Found lodgings in a seaside boarding-house. Just a room. Landlady was called Mrs Joy Bliss. Miserable woman. But discreet. Or, at least, too ungracious to ask many questions. I just came and went as I pleased.

England had shrunk. It was smaller than the place I'd left. Streets, shops, houses bore down like crowds, stifling even the feeble light that got through. I had to stare out at the sea just to catch a breath. And behind every face I saw were trapped the rememberings of war. Guarded by a smile. Shrouded in a frown. But everyone had them. Private conflicts. Scarring where touched. No point dwelling on your own pitiful story. Chap next to you was worse off. The man over there far more tragic. Silence was the only balm that healed.

I never doubted I was doing the right thing. Even on days when the longing for familiar was as substantial as hunger. To lie with Queenie. To sit with Pa. To gaze on objects that communed in memories. I had no idea how long the awful disease would take to claim me. No thought of doctors or cures. Shame saw to that. My only worry was that I would lose my mind. Do something rash without sanity's firm hand.

But in waiting to die I felt fit. Found employment, cleaning tables in a café. Kept my head down, had a job to do, just got on with it. Proprietor, rather dim fellow, needed a hand with his bookkeeping. He was tickled pink when his worthless waiter turned out to be useful. I helped him out. He told all his chums. Soon I had a few of them calling on my services. Became quite a little business. All very informal but regular. I stopped being a waiter. Double-entry bookkeeping earned me enough for board and lodging.

I found Maxi's house, of course. Up near the station. A modest house. Painted pale blue, its bow-front window hung with thick yellowing nets. I walked his street often, my footsteps marking the pavement where Maxi's should have been going about their business. Rushing to work. A pint or two in the pub. A game of football in the park. Or cricket. Maybe even church with his family on Sunday.

There was a graveyard nearby. I sat on the bench there. Saw his two sons coming out from the house. His wife tying a headscarf against the wind, calling for the boys to wait. Them, boisterous, running up the street. Clambering up walls to walk balancing along their length. As the younger one passed me he dropped his model car. I picked it up for him. Got a faint smile. Little chap staring at me. Spit of his father. A natural successor. He grabbed the car from my hand and ran. Maxi had never seen this younger son. I felt like a thief, stealing a sight that should have been his.

They soon got used to seeing me sitting in the graveyard. His wife would nod to me. Some days she'd raise up her brown eyes to say, 'Lovely day.' Attractive woman, her black hair always hidden by scarves. Short. Not much taller than the elder boy. I only spoke to her in polite greeting. Silly, I know, but I was anxious not to befriend, just to watch over. I never told them I knew Maxi. Scared she'd ask the unanswerable. Want to know what befell us all out east. With the war over, even the truth seemed sordid. Loving memory was the best resting place for George Maximillian.

It was Mrs Bliss who called the doctor. My temperature raged, sweating my sheets sodden as freshly used bath towels. I could feel every bone in my body. Even the smallest of them ached. Any movement – to roll in the bed, even to blink an eye – felt impossibly exhausting. I told her not to bother but she brushed me off with a 'Nonsense.' Couldn't blame her. Must have been a pitiful sight.

The doctor, after examining me, said flu. I pulled him to one side. Out of the keen hearing of Mrs Bliss. Whispered, 'Afraid it's considerably more than just flu.' Got the landlady to leave us before I told him, 'It's syphilis.'

'Syphilis?' he repeated. Quite unsettled.

'Picked it up in India.' He wanted to know why I thought it was syphilis. Told him of the indiscretion and the disgusting pustule. 'How long did this boil last?' he asked.

'A week, maybe two.'

I detected a certain distaste as he said, 'And?'

I didn't quite understand.

'And what other symptoms?'

'And this, Doctor . . . this . . . flu.'

'Right,' he said. He began writing notes. Checked for something in his bag while asking, 'How long have you been back from India?'

'Two years,' I said.

He stopped. Turned slowly to face me again. 'Two years?'

'Yes.'

'You mean it's been two years since you noticed this lesion on your private parts? Two years since the . . . indiscretion?'

Hesitated my next yes. Sensed that answer might be wrong.

He began folding his book away. Said tersely, 'Flu – like I said, Mr Bligh.'

'But . . . India . . . '

'I can do you a WR test if you want – put your mind at rest. But you'll be wasting everyone's time. Two years! You should be mad or dead by now. No. Flu. That's what you have, Mr Bligh. Wretched, horrible flu. But it needs to be taken care of. I'll talk to your landlady on the way out.'

'Are you sure?' I called after him.

'Flu, Mr Bligh. Trust me. Flu. You'll be fit as a fiddle in a couple of days.'

And I was.

Wasn't even a miracle. I never had that awful disease. The pustule had probably been picked up from some straying insect after all. Or something gone septic. Nothing to do with that little madness in India. There was no one to tell of my silly error, of course. 'Feeling better now?' was all Mrs Bliss could ask.

'Much,' was all I could reply. Should have been a relief, I know. A return from the dead. But I had to admit there was release in imminent mortality – it had me transient, a bystander. Now unexpectedly to have my life back. Laundered fresh by a war. Ready to start again. To be thrown back among them. Suddenly to realise this war-torn England before me was now my welcome home. Good God!

Maxi's family moved away. The yellowing curtains were gone. The house empty. The neighbours were useless, looking at me suspiciously. Why was I interested in where they had gone? Who was I to them? I had to walk away. I didn't make a decision to go back to London, just found myself on a train. If it was sleep-walking, I soon woke up at the corner of our street. Hard to believe this had been my home for most of my life. Nothing was familiar. Had it always looked so exhausted? So friable? Buildings decaying and run down. Rotting sashes. Cracked plaster. Obscene gaps where houses once stood. I came a few more times, each visit less startling than the last.

I hoped to be discovered (I admit). Pa running to greet. Queenie laughing with relieved joy. Got closer and closer. But still approached as a stranger.

It was the darkie woman I saw first. What a sight! On our street. Never seen that before. I was dumbfounded to see that the white woman she accompanied was Queenie. What was going on? I was standing over them before I knew it. Then back in our parlour before I'd considered.

'Has something happened to Pa?' I had to ask Queenie again.

'Where have you been? Why didn't you come straight back?' Her terrified eyes demanded the more urgent answer.

'Lost my mind a little,' I said.

'How d'you mean? Did you lose your memory?'

'Yes. Something like that.'

'Where were you?'

'On the south coast.'

'In England?'

'Brighton.'

'Brighton!' She screamed this. 'Blinking heck. Brighton! What were you doing in ruddy Brighton?'

'You haven't said about Pa. Has something happened?'

'I want an answer first, Bernard. I've a right to know. I'm your wife. I thought you were dead. It's been years. And you just turn up and say, "Brighton!" Were you having a blinking holiday with a bucket and spade? Why Brighton?'

She'd changed the sideboard in the parlour. This one used to be in a room upstairs. Ma had it taken out. Quite rightly thought it far too big for this room. Pa's chair was no longer by the fire.

'Queenie, please, tell me if there is something to tell.'

She sat down again, wringing her hands. The noise of dry skin rubbing pricked up the hairs on the back of my neck. 'Your father's dead,' she said, a little too promptly.

I'd known, of course. Soon as I walked into the house. I could feel him gone.

'Oh,' I said.

'Oh. Is that all you can say? Oh?'

That's what war had done to me. Made death a reasonable thing. But she was quite hysterical.

'Don't you want to know how he died? Haven't you got any questions? He was shot you know. Here – through the jaw. His head looked like butcher's meat.' A crueller man might have told her to get a grip. To come to her senses. To shut up, even. 'Shot by Yanks. A Yank shot him. But it was all hushed away. No one was even asked why they did it. No trial. Nothing. His brain all over the pavement. And they just cleaned it up, gave me the pieces and carried on as if nothing had happened.'

The bones in her neck were standing out like scaffolding. She was screeching at me. Then there was a loud knocking on the door. I thought the person would break it down. I answered it to find a black man standing there. He looked straight past me, calling, 'Queenie, Queenie, you all right?' Then the cheeky blighter looked at me and said, 'Who are you?'

' "Who are you?" is more the question,' I told him firmly.

He took no notice. 'Queenie,' he called again, before attempting to push me from his way. I blocked the door. Tried to close it. But he held it open.

'Who the bloody hell are you? This is my house,' I said.

'Don't get me vex, man,' he said. 'I mus' see Queenie is all right.'

Queenie soon popped up behind me. More composed. 'It's all right, Gilbert,' she said to this darkie.

'Who is this man?' I asked her.

'A lodger,' she told me.

'Used to coming in, is he?' I said, while this black man babbled on.

'Who are you? What's all the commotion?'

354

'This is my husband, Gilbert. It's Bernard.'

That shut him up. Eyes popping out of his head like a golliwog's. Stared me up and down. Stepped back to get a better look. Scratched his head, saying, 'Well, well . . .' Then the cheeky blighter put his hand out for me to shake.

I just shut the bloody door on him.

Forty-seven

Queenie

Of course I had to ask Bernard if he was staying. He needn't have looked at me like that. A balloon deflating, slowly sagging on the wall after a party. I wasn't throwing him out. How could I? It was his house. I hadn't forgotten that. Blinking place yawned in my face every morning.

'I'll make you up a bed in the spare room . . . in Arthur's old room,' I told him.

Every day in the paper there were stories of the dead's return. Loved ones who'd already been mourned turning up on the doorstep after years. Not so loved, most of them, by the time they'd found their way home.

'I was rather hoping to sleep in our bed,' he said.

And I said, 'All right.'

He smiled at me then. Took another sip of his tea. The cup trembled as he put it to his lips.

'I'll sleep in Arthur's room. You take your old bed,' I told him.

'Queenie . . .' he started, urgent. But I was out of the door to fetch sheets for me and a towel for him from the cupboard.

My dressing-table mirror soon caught me. Hundreds and hundreds of terrified Queenies. Scared stiff every one of them. Shrieking silently, what the bloody hell happens now? He came in behind me.

356

'Is there something wrong?' I said.

'I was just wondering . . .'

'Yes, what . . . what? What is it, Bernard?' I was trying not to shout.

'. . . if I can be of any help. With the bed?'

'No, I'll just be minute. Go and finish your tea.'

Wounded dogs walked with more joy. And my eye caught them again – the Queenies, all wondering now whether Bernard didn't deserve a better homecoming than this. A kiss and a cuddle like Gable and Leigh. 'Hop it,' I told them. None of their blinking business.

With every awkward silence I'd offered him tea. And he'd taken it. How many cups did we have? Twenty, thirty, or near as. I was out of milk and preciously low on sugar. He was just as finicky as before he left. Lifting the sugar into the tea like it was gold. Stirring enough to wear a hole in the bottom of the cup. Tapping the spoon to dislodge the stray drops like a clanger on a bell. And then, of course, blowing on the tea before he drank it. I thought he'd take it hot like a man after being in the RAF for so long. But he slurped, the noise going through me like a fork scratching on a plate.

His hair was grey at the temples. Thinning. And, hard to imagine, he was skinnier, the hollows in his cheeks outlining the skull underneath. He still did that queer thing with his nose, twisting it like a rabbit before ramming his white hankie up one nostril then the other. And the crumbs from his biscuit powdered his lips for far too long before he licked them off.

He stared for hours at the newspaper cuttings of Arthur's death. Reading them one by one. Running his finger along the words. I said nothing as I sat watching him. He pointed at the one with the dreadful picture of me. A mad woman desperate for someone to throttle. 'I was very upset. It was the most terrible thing ever happened,' I told him.

'Indeed,' he said.

I waited. He'll be wanting to ask me questions, I thought. Was there a funeral? Where was he buried? Did he say anything before he died? Was he happy, was he sad? But Bernard said nothing. Just carefully went through the clippings with that vein on the side of his head pulsing like he was chewing.

'He's buried up in Mansfield,' I told him.

He nodded.

He should have asked, 'Why the bloody hell Mansfield? Why not the Royal Borough of Kensington and Chelsea?' but he didn't. Didn't even ask what we were doing up at the Buxton farm.

'I managed to get a stone,' I said.

He nodded again.

And I thought, Time for more tea, Queenie.

I'd had the grandfather clock put in Arthur's old room. First thing you saw when you opened the door. Looked like a phantom in the dark. I hadn't been in the room for a long time. Just flitted round with a duster on a sunny day when I thought I ought. It was musty with damp. I went to open the window, but the sash had warped and wouldn't budge. Next thing I know, Bernard's behind me again. 'Let me help you with that,' he said. 'It's a bit of a knack.'

'I know,' I told him. He gave it three thumps then pulled it down. The air ran round the room, sharp as lemon. 'Thank you,' I said.

'Are you sure you'll be all right in here?' he asked.

'Oh, yes. Really. You take the other bed. I'll be fine.'

He went over to the grandfather clock next. Looked at his watch then back to the clock face. 'It hasn't been wound . . . not since,' I said, then wished I hadn't. Blow me, if he didn't open the case and start winding it up. Fussing with this and that. 'There's no need,' I said quickly. But it was too late. Tick-tock, tick-tock. Thought he was doing me a favour, I know he did.

'There,' he said, satisfied.

It was only polite to say thank you.

'Well, if you've got everything you need, Bernard, I'll be turning in now.'

'Yes, yes, of course,' he said, but he didn't move. Stood there studying the room in a sort of wonder – his mouth gaping – like he'd never been in there before.

'Goodnight, then,' I said. I went to the door to show him the way out. He came towards me and stopped still. A goodnight kiss, that's what he was wanting. A peck from a chicken's beak. But neither of us had the courage. Both said, 'Sleep well,' instead.

I locked the door after he'd gone. Turned the old key, rusty and stiff, in the lock. Gently, quietly tried the handle to make sure it had worked. When, ruddy hell, that blinking grandfather clock started to chime.

Early morning and he was out on the doorstep with Mr Todd. Their voices were muffled by distance – I couldn't make out what they were saying. But surprise and pleasure had Mr Todd's voice squeaking high as a girl's. And every few minutes they'd titter like the best gossips. It was a good while before they went quieter. Hushing down to a low mumbling that didn't want to be overheard. That cautious whispering prattled on for quite some time.

He'd moved a few things in the parlour. A china dog from the sideboard to the mantelpiece where it always used to be. An armchair shifted a few feet back in front of the fire. He was flushed coming in from outside. His shirtsleeves rolled up. The top button casually undone. He walked almost jauntily into the room, slapping his arms against the cold.

'Took me a while to find the teapot,' he told me. 'Not where it usually is.'

'No,' I said.

'Did you sleep well?'

'I did, thank you. You?'

He looked up – told the ceiling, 'It was very good to be back in my own bed.'

He'd made toast. Near as skipped to the kitchen to fetch it. He'd never done that before. The skipping, I mean. Brought it in on a silver rack. Triangles neatly laid in a row.

'Where did you get that toast rack from?'

'Oh, it was my mother's.'

'Where was it?'

'In the sideboard.' I didn't say it – 'No, it blinking wasn't' – but I wanted to.

At the table he pulled the chair out for me to sit down. Settled in after me, tucking a napkin under his chin like we were in the finest restaurant. Passed me the toast. I'd taken one mouthful when he asked, 'So, how many lodgers do we have?'

'We' – he said 'we'. I put the toast on the plate. Picked up my napkin to dab the corners of my mouth. Might as well play along, I thought. 'Let's see. There's Winston and Jean in the middle landings and Gilbert and his wife at the top.' There was a genteel silence so I filled it with, 'Gilbert's wife has only just arrived.' A frown formed on his forehead gradual as shifting sand. And I knew what the next question would be.

'Are they all coloured?'

'No, Jean's not. She's a nurse.'

'That's not what Mr Todd called her. '

'I dare say.'

He slapped his palm on the table, quite startled me, and said, 'A prostitute and coloureds. What were you thinking of, Queenie?'

I didn't want to shout, not again. 'Listen to me, Bernard. I had to get lodgers. I had no idea where you were. There was no one going to look after me. I had to bring people in.'

'I don't doubt that, Queenie, but did they have to be coloured? Couldn't you have got decent lodgers for the house? Respectable people?'

'They pay the rent. And on time. Gilbert was in the RAF during the war.' He wasn't impressed.

'I'm sorry to tell you, Bernard, but this house is no palace. It got really run down during the war. I couldn't fix it up, and I had no one to turn to. They were willing to pay good money to stay in those dingy rooms. I had little choice. I mean, where were you? You haven't told me that yet!'

He started chewing again before softly saying, 'Well, they'll have to go now I'm back.' My toast was like sandpaper. I didn't have the saliva to swallow the parched bread. 'Mr Todd is moving, you know,' Bernard went on.

'Is he?' I said. It wasn't a surprise to me and would be no loss either.

'He and his sister have found a little house in Orpington.' I didn't doubt it. I tried more butter on the toast but it still wouldn't go down. 'Says the street has gone to the dogs. What with all these coloureds swamping the place. Hardly like our own country any more.' He poured the tea – handed me a cup, which rattled in the saucer.

'Blames me for that, I expect,' I said.

The shaking cup was momentarily silent. 'I've been doing some thinking,' he went on. 'We should move out. Get rid of all these coolies . . . the lodgers, I mean. Let them find somewhere more suitable for their type anyway. Sell the place. Move somewhere more select. Kent, maybe. I've heard just outside Ashford's nice.' He was quite jaunty again. Bold even, bouncing on his chair a little. When suddenly he said the strangest thing: 'Thought I might start a rabbit farm.'

I hadn't heard him right, I was sure of it. 'A what?'

'A rabbit farm. We'd only need two rabbits to start. A male and a female.'

'What are you talking about?'

'Rabbits. You know what they breed like?'

'Have you gone mad, Bernard?'

'Like rabbits.' And I swear he chuckled.

'What?'

'It's a joke. Don't you see? They breed like rabbits, rabbits.'

'What are you going on about?'

'Breeding rabbits on a farm. We can start it together. I'll do all the business side. You look after the stock. It will be something new, I know. A lot of work, I don't doubt that. But everything will soon be back to how it was. Just like it used to be. We can start again with rabbits.'

Every single silly word he uttered sucked the air from the room as sure as if he'd siphoned it. He didn't leave so much as a puff for me to breathe. I gulped – grabbing at my throat.

'Are you all right?' he said.

The toast was going down the wrong way but it wasn't that. No, I was sure I was being smothered.

Forty-eight

Bernard

Funny dream. Odd.

I'm in bed with Queenie at home. She's lying next to me. Sleeping. Peaceful. Tucked up warm. Suddenly I hear a plane. One plane. Single engine. A drone. Sounds a bit like a bluebottle (a very big but slow bluebottle). I watch the course of the plane above my head. Follow the sound. Pass my eyes over the ceiling of our bedroom. Across the crack that looks like the bow in the Thames. Past the bit where a chunk of plaster fell off when we had a very close one. Over the ceiling rose with the bare bulb, which starts swaying from the vibration. Somehow I know it is a Jap plane. A Japanese fighter pilot flying over Earls Court. Probably a Zero. It could never have happened, I know, but this was a dream.

The noise of the kite suddenly stops. And I'm aware he's coming for me. The bedroom door starts opening slowly. But I can't move. Paralysed. Even my eyeballs are stuck – fixed on watching the door moving inch by inch. Then he's there. The Jap. I see his head first, then the whole of him framed in the open door. And he's just like they were in the cartoons. Little. Big glasses. Squinting eyes, buck teeth, ears like two jug handles. He's wearing a grey peaked cap – they all used to. This one looks comical but I know there's nothing funny about a Jap. Fishy thing is, he's smiling at me. Friendly.

I want to shoot him. Stick one in him. Jump him. Smash his face into the ground. But he's still smiling and I start to think, Oh, well, maybe he's not so bad. Until I see his sword flash. Light cracking off it in a spark. I knew we were in danger. But suddenly Queenie sits up in bed, turns to the door, looks the Jap straight in the eye and says, 'Hello.' Just like that. Hello. Like she's talking to a neighbour. Hello. As if she'd known him all her life. 'Hello. Come in.' And that was when I woke up.

Forty-nine

Gilbert

'Winston,' I say, 'that you?'

'Oh, yes, yes – Winston. Let me in, man.'

Even through the wood of the door I knew the man vex. Cha, I come tired out from work dreaming on rest. But every Jamaican boy (and even those from the small islands) had come to learn the wisdom, all for one and one for all, in this Mother Country. Hortense was huddle up on the floor over a pan on the wretched gas ring. Her young back should not have been folded like a crone's – it should have been standing haughty and straight at a good cooker. But, come, like watching a right-hand person use their left, when she was cooking, she make every movement a torture to behold.

It look like Winston standing before me at the door. But to make sure I ask, 'You Winston?'

'Yes, man, Winston,' he say smiling.

So I invite him in. One second is all and my suspicion is arouse. I introduce Hortense and him just say, 'Yeah, man,' before carrying on with a blast of words that nearly knock me from my feet.

'The man gon' throw me out, Gilbert. That fool-fool ras clot say I must go. And by morning or him will call on the police. Police, I say – why him need the law on me? I am abiding as I must. He call me darkie and coon, so

I tell him him must show respect. Him say him want respect. His house him shout on me until me ear burn with it.'

'Wow!' I tell him. 'Calm yourself, man. Who you talking of?'

'The landlady husband who cannot find him way home.' He sat himself hard on the chair, throwing off the ferocious look Hortense sent him for disgracing up her ear with bad language.

'Winston?' I ask again.

'Yeah, yeah, Winston,' he say, and I know it is Kenneth.

'You Kenneth, man.'

'No, Winston, look.' He show me the back of his hand as if something there that will prove it.

'What you doing in Winston's room? Noreen throw you out again?'

'No cloud up me story, man. Him gon' throw me out.'

'Is Winston he is throwing out,' I tell him. 'You should be already gone.'

'You wan' hear me story or not? I been working, Gilbert. Keeping warehouse and stores.'

My mind could not believe what me ear was hearing. Was there some Englishman so fool-fool that he look upon Kenneth's tricky eye and slippery finger, then make the conclusion that this man will make a responsible storeman? Too many things in England surprise me but this news — I fall down hard on a chair with my mouth agape. 'Wait. You tell me someone employ you to look after their stock?'

'And, let me tell you, man, me do a good job. Counting and keeping and nobody is takin' away. The boss a-smilin'. No one mess with me. But today is payday. Me rub me hands. I have all sort of work that hard-come-by money must do. I get it in a little brown bag. Man, this envelope so light it could float off if me hand not on it. Hardly any money in there. It them that rob me and not the other way round. So I go to the office to call on them. "Where me money? Most of me money gone," I tell them. Gilbert, you have any rum because me nerves have been tried today, man?'

Hortense start banging together every pot she find in the room. This man was troubling her. But Kenneth just look to the noise and say, 'You lucky you have someone to cook you up something nice there.'

'Yes,' one half me heart say, and Hortense grant me a look that shrink me skin. 'Kenneth, come, nah – I am tired. You have a point for me there, man?'

'I am Winston.'

'No, you are not.'

'Okay. You are right there, man. But Noreen throw me out and a brother is a brother. Now where was I? Oh, yes. You know what they tell me when they look on the skinny packet they give me? Tax. I say t'ief. Him say tax. Gilbert, the day is still light and a white man rob me. What you think?'

'I think, Kenneth, you pay some tax.'

'What? No, man, they take me money. They tell me one thing I will get, they give me another. They t'ink me a fool can take me money when me eye is still wide. "Silly West Indian raw from the boat," they say, "he will not know when him being robbed." '

'Man, you tellin' me you never pay tax before? Kenneth, everyone pay tax.'

'Everyone? White man too?'

'Everyone. Is tax. The government take it.'

'What for?'

'For running the country.'

'No,' he say. 'They t'ieve me. I tell you them rob me. But, man, you know what?' He beckoned me to whisper but has to shout over the clatter Hortense is making. 'Me still have the keys . . .'

'No, man – I don't wan' to hear this!' I tell him. I stand up to show him the door.

'Wait, man, hush. I not tell you about the fool man downstairs yet. You must listen up – you next.'

I sat back in my seat to rest my chin on my hand.

'Come, no look so weary, me tellin' you this for reason, man. You mus' know what mood is on me as I come through the door of this house. I had just been robbed! I walk through the door and bump into this man. This Queenie's husband or so him say. I am vex. Maybe I say sorry for knocking him a little. Maybe not. Maybe I tell the man to watch where he is walking. I do not know for I am too concern to remember every little thing I do. Next thing the man is breaking down my door knocking on it so fierce.

"You have to leave," he tell me. "Why?" I say. "The house on fire?" He tell me not to be funny with him. I tell him to go away so I can rest. He hold on to the door and say he need the room. I am polite, Gilbert, I swear on my mummy's grave. I ask him what he need the room for in such a hurry that he must throw me out. His mouth open a little but nothing come through. I tell him goodnight. And, man, him start to glow red. I never see a human face go that colour. You ever see that, Gilbert, a white man go red? It one strange sight. Suddenly him start screaming he is selling the house. "Now," I ask him, "you selling the house this minute?" "Tomorrow," he shout, he want me out tomorrow. This man was so hot I tell him to calm down for his own sake. But he tell me he will not. I do him a favour when I shut the door on him face. One more minute and him would go pop. But him start bangin' on it again. Shoutin' through that he will not stand for nonsense. So I open the door and tell him that he must go somewhere else to fornicate. Although, Gilbert, because there is a lady present I am not using the actual word I say. This skinny man start puffing up himself. Him have two fists made. I would kill the man with one blow if I were to punch him. I do him a favour – I push him away. But, man, him so skinny him fall over. I swear I just touch him and him fall down. But I am not a rough man – I make sure he was all right. I stand over him. Wog, darkie, coon – all them words him start use in telling me he want me out. The bad language bring Jean to her door. And for one minute him look on her instead. She look one sight. Eyes rimmed with black and dripping like fingers down her cheek, hair straight up like fright and standing in her underclothes half naked. She start laugh on this puny man sprawled all over the floor. Him get himself up but this time quiet. All is over now, me t'ink. I go back in the room and shut the door.'

Kenneth, finishing his story, look on me for some response. Oh, boy. I lift me head and think to make a joke when I ask him, 'Is that all?'

My heart take up residence in me boots when he tell me, 'Well, I may have told him that his wife seem to like the company of black men. Maybe. I cannot remember. Plenty things said in the heat of the situation.'

I know trouble. When it come through the door, it place a hand round a delicate part and squeeze. Man, I had to uncross me leg to release this tension. 'Why you do that, Kenneth?'

'Is what I do?'

There was something I recognised on the face of Bernard Bligh. I glimpsed it on that first encounter for only one second, two. But I know it like a foe. Come, I saw it reflected from every mirror on my dear Jamaican island. Staring back on me from my own face. Residing in the white of the eye, the turn of the mouth, the thrust of the chin. A bewildered soul. Too much seen to go back. Too much changed to know which way is forward. I knew with this beleaguered man's return the days of living quiet in this house had come to an end.

'What you wan' me do?' I ask Kenneth.

'Well, I been doing plenty t'inking on the situation, Gilbert. And I come to this conclusion. We get a few of the boys and give him a good licking. Show him him mus' not mess with Jamaican boys.'

'Kenneth, I no lick a man for no reason.'

'What you chattin', man? Him call me wog and darkie. Him need lesson in manners. And you next, boy. Mark me word. And you have lovely wife who is cooking up something fine for you. You have obligation.'

'No rough stuff. Let me speak with Queenie,' I tell him.

'Cha, you no 'fraid of some skinny white man?'

'I sort out everything with Queenie. Come, you go now, man. Me dinner ready.'

Kenneth grin sugar and spice on Hortense. 'What you cooking there, miss?' he say. 'Smellin' good.' She scowl one bitter lemon back on him. But he carry on without regard. 'You a lucky man. What you getting, rice and peas, a little curry goat? Me don' know if me 'ave food for tonight.'

'Where is Winston?' I ask. 'Him know yet you get him thrown out of his room?'

'Me goin' sort this out. A few of the boys . . .'

'No, Kenneth! No trouble. I tell you already I will speak with Queenie. You don't even live here, man. You forget Queenie throw you out months ago?'

He breathe in loud, smelling the aroma every West Indian boy had come to love in this country – free food. 'Smell so good. You have a little left for me?'

Hortense sent him a look that would have made a sensitive man disappear in a puff of smoke. However, Kenneth take this as a good sign. He lift himself from the chair to stand over Hortense. But it only took a little while of staring over her shoulder on the cooking food before he quickly say, 'Now me come t'ink, I jus' remember I arrange to meet a few of the boys.' He was out the door and slamming it after him so fast you would think Hortense was chasing him to taste something off her spoon.

Not long before I know why. Hortense hand me one pile of mess on a plate. Not one thing did I recognise to start nyam. I nearly follow after Kenneth calling for him to wait. But Hortense was looking on me ready to berate me for ungratefulness. So I examine the food and tell her, 'Lovely.'

'He is uncouth, that man. How you let him in the room?' she say.

I think there was rice but I don't think it was boiled. It was crunching on my teeth as I say, 'He tell me him Winston.'

'I doubt this Winston is any better?' she say.

'You have not met Winston.'

'If the brother is anything to go by, I do not desire to.'

'Kenneth is not so bad.'

'How you say that? The man is rough and uncouth. You hear his language?'

'Him vex.'

'He is the sort of ruffian make me ashamed to come from the same island.'

'Cha, he is not so bad. Him just trying to get on in England.'

'Huh,' she say.

Something so chewy in the food I wonder if it is gum. We both chomping silent like cows in a field. Come, it was a pretty silence so why I say, 'But there is no need to fret?'

'About what?' she say.

'About what Kenneth has just tell us.'

'The man is a buffoon.'

'Maybe. But no worry yourself about being thrown from this place.'

Her fork stop half-way to her mouth. The little smile that formed on her lip gradually turned to a nasty smirk. 'I paid him no mind,' she tell me.

'Good,' I say but she had not finished yet.

'You forget,' she begin, 'that I will soon have employment in a good school as a teacher. Do not fret on my account. The man downstairs would do me a great service if he were to throw me from this run-down place. A room such as this is not befitting for a teacher such as I.'

The fork finally make it to her mouth. And I stare hard on this insufferable creature as she gaze to the ceiling chewing dainty on the nasty food.

Fifty

Hortense

Gilbert Joseph looked wide-eyed on me to exclaim, 'Wait, is that your wedding dress you have on there?'

So I tell him, 'At last I have an occasion that warrants such a fine dress.'

The silly carefree countenance slipped from his face with such force it bump on to the floor. He make me feel sorry for the words. His bottom lip protruding with their harshness. His eye displaying sorrow. I thought to apologise for that quick tongue. But then he start cussing – sucking on his teeth, and cha, cha, cha on me like a ruffian. So I paid him no mind.

Ah, even the sun was shining. Only a weak light but enough to raise my spirits higher than this stupid man's worry. My two letters of recommendation each contained words that would open up the doors of any school to me. Despite the slow start at the school for scoundrels in Half Way Tree, my headmaster had seen fit to call my teaching skills proficient. Looking for the meaning of the word in the English dictionary, I was honoured to see he thought me expert. Miss Morgan, the formidable principal at my college, declared me highly capable. And a highly capable expert I felt. This was the day I was going to present myself for a position as a teacher at the offices of the education authority and no pained-face, fool-fool man was going to imperil my elation.

Gilbert's explanation for how I might travel to this place called Islington took him more than an hour. The man insisted I take a note, then proceeded to deliver his instruction in one babble of turn-left-turn-right-no-wait-go-straight-on. The only lull in this breathless litany occurred when he asked, 'You write this down?' I am not a writing machine. Was it little wonder that when the man finally finish the only note I had written on the paper was the word 'bus'?

'This the only thing you write?' he said.

'You speak too fast,' I told him.

It was with one long agitated breath that he blew the words into my face, 'Come. I will go with you.'

Anyone hearing Gilbert Joseph speak would know without hesitation that this man was not English. No matter that he is dressed in his best suit, his hair greased, his fingernails clean, he talked (and walked) in a rough Jamaican way. Whereas I, since arriving in this country, had determined to speak in an English manner. It was of no use to imitate the way of speaking of those about me, for too many people I encountered spoke as a Cockney would. All fine diction lost in a low-class slurring garble. No. To speak English properly as the high-class, I resolved to listen to the language at its finest. Every day my wireless was tuned to the most exemplary English in the known world. The BBC. The Light Programme – *Woman's Hour, Mrs Dale's Diary, Music While You Work*, and of course the news. I listened. I repeated. And I listened once more. To prove practice makes perfect, on two occasions a shopkeeper had brought me the item requested without repetition from me. With thanks to that impeccable English evidenced on my wireless, I was understood easily.

But Gilbert was still sucking on his teeth. Every two bells the man said 'cha' and could not, no matter how I tried, stop himself exclaiming, 'Nah, man,' with every utterance. I worried that the refined and educated people at the education authority might look aghast at me if Gilbert Joseph were anywhere near. But I have to confess: 'Hortense, "bus" is not enough instruction to see you delivered safely.' So I agreed. 'Okay,' I told him. 'You may accompany me.'

It was a fine establishment. Brick-brown and ageing with all the dignity of learning. The building stately imposed itself on the rundown street with as imperial a demeanour as Miss Morgan in front of we girls. With trepidation my heart beat like fluttering wings. Gilbert walking in front of me placed his hand on the shining brass of the door.

'You can leave me now,' I told him.

'What, you no wan' me come in?' The man look on me in that same pained manner.

'No, thank you, I will be fine.'

'I wait here for you, then.'

'There is no need for you to darken up the place. I can find my way now.'

'What is there to find? I get you here.' He was trying my patience. So I told him politely that perchance the education authority would want to show me the school at which I would be working. It might take some time and I did not want to disrupt his day further. The man look on me for a long while. Then, quietly, he said, 'Hortense, this is not the way England work.' I then informed him that a teacher such as I was not someone to be treated in the same way as a person in a low-class job. He just shake his head on me and say, 'You won't listen to me, will you? I wait for you.' There was no persuasion could dislodge this man from the step. I could see his shape sucking on a cigarette through the glass of the door as I approached a gentleman at a desk. He made no attempt to keep himself hidden. Catching my eye while I waited for the gentleman to finish what he was reading, Gilbert raised his thumb to me grinning like a buffoon. This wretched man was lowering my tone.

I was heartened when the gentleman at the desk understood my request with only one asking. Straight away he answered me. Unfortunately he began his directions to the correct office in the same manner as Gilbert. Left-right-left-right-up-down-and-around. Not one pause for consideration. When he had finished he returned to perusing his newspaper. I was left with little choice but to ask, 'Excuse me, could you perchance repeat the instruction?'

The gentleman tutted then rolled his eye before yelling loud as a street caller, 'Seymour.' One gangly boy appeared. I had to avert my eye from him, for this young man's face was so angry with raw pimples and pustules he looked to have been wrestling a cat.

'Take her up to Inquiries,' the gentleman at the desk commanded.

'Thank you for your help,' I said, but he had already returned to his reading and I had to run to keep up with this red meat-face boy.

Three women sitting neatly at desks perused me as I came through the door. In a puppet dance all three quickly glanced to each other then returned to staring on me.

'Good day,' I said.

Two dropped their heads returning to their business as if I had not spoken, leaving just an older woman to ask, 'Yes, do you want something?' This woman smiled on me – her countenance gleaming with so much joy that I could do nothing but return the welcome. Her beaming smile was so wide I had trouble stretching my own lips to match the delight. She bathed me in this greeting for several moments before breath sufficient enough for a reply returned to me.

'I am a teacher,' I said, intending to carry on with some further explanation. But I was startled to find myself timorous in this woman's friendly presence. My voice faltered into a tiny squeak. I took a moment to cough into my hand. Having composed myself I began again. 'I am a teacher and I understand this is the place at which I should present myself for a position in that particular profession.' Through this woman's warm smile I detected a little confusion. Too well bred to say 'What?' she looked a quizzical eye on me, which shouted the word just as audibly. I repeated myself clearly but before I had completed the statement the woman asked of me sweetly, 'Did you say you are a teacher?'

'I am,' I said. My own smile was causing me some pain behind my ears but still I endeavoured to respond correctly to her generosity. I handed her the two letters of recommendation which I had taken from my bag in anticipation of their requirement. She politely held out her slim hand, took them, then indicated for me to sit. However, instead of studying the letters she merely held them in her hand without even glancing at their contents.

'What are these?' she asked with a little laugh ruffling up the words.

374

'These are my letters of recommendation. One you will see is from the headmaster at—'

Interrupting me, her lips relaxed for just a moment before taking up a smile once more, 'Where are you from?' she asked. The letters were still held in mid-air where I had placed them.

'I am from Jamaica,' I told her.

She was silent, we both grinning on each other in a genteel way. I thought to bring her attention back to the letters. 'One of the letters I have given you is from my last post. Written by the headmaster himself. You will see that—'

But once more she interrupted me: 'Where?'

I wondered if it would be impolite to tell this beguiling woman to read the letter in her hand so all her questions might be answered. I concluded it would. 'At Half Way Tree Parish School,' I told her.

'Where's that?'

'In Kingston, Jamaica.'

She leaned back on her chair and instead of opening the letters she began playing with them – flicking the paper against her fingers. 'And where did you train to be a teacher?' she asked me.

Her comely smile belied the rudeness of her tone. And I could not help but note that all gladness had left her eye and remained only at her mouth. 'I trained at the teacher-training college in Constant Spring, under the tutelage of Miss Morgan.'

'Is that in Jamaica?'

'Yes.'

It was relief that tipped her head to one side while she let out a long breath. I eased myself believing everything was now cleared between us. Until, leaning all her ample charm forward, she told me, 'Well, I'm afraid you can't teach here,' and passed the unopened letters back to me.

I was sure there had been some misunderstanding, although I was not clear as to where it had occurred. Perhaps I had not made myself as understood as I could. 'If you would read the letters,' I said, 'one will tell you about the three years of training as a teacher I received in Jamaica while the other letter is concerned with the position I held as a teacher at—'

She did not let me finish. 'The letters don't matter,' she told me. 'You can't teach in this country. You're not qualified to teach here in England.'

'But . . .' was the only sound that came from me.

'It doesn't matter that you were a teacher in Jamaica,' she went on, 'you will not be allowed to teach here.' She shook the letters at me. 'Take these back. They're of no use.' When I did not take them from her hand she rattled them harder at me. 'Take them,' she said, so loud she almost shouted. Her smile was stale as a gargoyle. My hand shook as it reached out for the letters.

And all I could utter was 'But—'

'Miss, I'm afraid there really is no point your sitting there arguing with me.' And she giggled. The untimely chortle made my mouth gape. 'It's not up to me. It's the decision of the education authority. I can do nothing to change that. And, I'm afraid, neither can you. Now, I don't mean to hurry you but I have an awful lot to do. So thank you for coming.'

Every organ I possessed was screaming on this woman, 'What are you saying to me?'

She went back about her business. Her face now in its normal repose looked as severe as that of the principal at my college. She picked up a piece of paper, wrote something at the top. She looked to another piece of paper then stopped, aware that I was still there.

'How long is the training in England?' I asked her.

'Goodbye,' she said, pointing a finger at the door.

'Must I go back to a college?'

'Really, miss, I have just explained everything to you. You do speak English? Have you not understood me? It's quite simple. There is no point you asking me anything else. Now, please, I have a lot to do. Thank you.'

And she smiled on me – again! What fancy feigning. I could not stand up. My legs were too weak under me. I sat for a little to redeem my composure. At last finding strength to pull myself up, I told this woman, 'I will come back again when I am qualified to teach in this country.'

'Yes,' she said, 'you do that. Goodbye.'

As I stood she rolled her eyes with the other women in the room. But I paid them no mind. I fixed my hat straight on my head and adjusted my gloves. 'Thank you and good day,' I called to them all, as I opened the door to leave. Each woman returned that pantomime greeting as if I had meant it. I opened the door and walked through. Suddenly everything was dark. I was staring on a ladder, a mop and a broom. I put out my hand and touched shelves stacked with bundles of paper. For one moment I wondered how I would find my way out through this confusion. Only when my foot kicked against a bucket did I realise I had walked into a cupboard. I had stepped in with all the confidence I could grasp, while the women watched me.

All three were giggling when I emerged from the dark of the closet. One behind a hand, another with a sheet of paper lifted up so I might not see. The older woman was, of course, smiling but pity encircled the look. 'It's that door,' she said, pointing her spiky finger at the other wooden opening. I thanked her, bade them all good day once more and passed through the correct exit, untroubled by the sound of their rising laughter.

Fifty-one

Gilbert

It was in bewilderment that Hortense walked from the place. Clutching her bag, her head held high. Four strident steps she took before she stop to look about her. Dismayed, she stand, fingers trembling at her mouth. She change direction for two steps. Then stop once more. She look up the street one way, then down the street the other. A paper drop from her hand on to the ground. She stoop to pick it up. Then bump against a big man who call at her, 'Oi, watch where you're going.' And the paper slip from her again. She chase it. Struggling with the clasp from her handbag she stuff the paper in before she start anew. Four paces this way then two paces the other.

I call out to her, she see me. All at once this woman finally know which way she is going. Anywhere that is away from me. Tripping along the road I try to keep a steady course beside her.

'How you get on?' I asked. She dodged round me to walk on. 'They tell you you have a job?' She feigned a deaf ear. And, man, she is walking faster than any Jamaican ever walk except when they run. I have to call after her, 'Hortense,' for I was out of puff. 'What they say to you?' Still this woman has no word for me. Cha. I am following on behind her like a lame dog. 'Wait, nah,' I called. She quicken her pace. So, as Auntie Corinne taught me when chasing a chicken round the yard, I make a jump to grab this woman. Two hands I use to seize her then swing her round to face me. 'Wait,' I said. Stiff as a rod of iron, her neck twisted misshapen to turn her eye from me. 'So what they say?' I asked. Suddenly she look on me, her nose go up in the air and, man, I am ready to duck. Aah, I knew that look.

'Why you ask me all these question? What business is it of yours?'

What little wind was left in me she cause to expel. Come, this was a good question. Why was I asking anything of this wretched shrew? I was ready to walk away. Plenty boys would by now be chasing the next pair of pretty legs that passed their eye, not wasting their time listening on a lashing tongue. So why I bother to say, 'You are my wife,' only for her to look on me like this was one pained regret?

'Leave me alone. I can look after myself. I was doing it for many years before you came along . . .'

So what was it? A quickening breath? A too-defiant shrugging shoulder? The gentle pout of her lip? Who can say? But something beg me stay. 'Hortense, no more cuss me. Tell me what 'appen.'

She purse her lip tight. Cha, I could do nothing but shake her. Not hard, for I am not a brute. But I rattle on her bone. It was the teardrop that splash on my lip, warm with salt, that cause me stop. She was crying. Steady as a rainpipe, the crystal water ran from her eye. She start contorting again to hide her face from me. A woman passing by begin staring on us. But it was not concern for Hortense's welfare, she was just ready to walk a wide circle around we two.

'What happen?' I asked her.

'Nothing,' she said.

So I tell her, 'Nothing is a smile, Hortense. You no cry over nothing.'

And the woman scream, 'Nothing,' at me again.

Man, let her burn. Come, this was probably the first time the woman's cheek ever felt a tear. She was insufferable! I walked away. Two paces. Then a hesitant third before I turned to look back on her. She was snivelling and trying with all her will not to wipe her nose on her good white glove.

I thought to smile when I hear it: Hortense reeling wounded after a sharp slap from the Mother Country's hand. Man, I was ready to tell her, 'Pride comes before a fall.' To leap around her rubbing me hands while singing, 'Now you see . . . I tell you so . . . you listening now.'

But her breath rose in desperate gasps as she mumbling repeated over, 'They say I can't teach.'

Come, no pitiful cry from a child awoken rude from a dream could have melted a hard heart any surer.

I guided her to a seat in a little square, she followed me obedient. So did a little scruffy boy whose wide eye perused us all the way. Softly delivered in my ear, Hortense informed me that she was required to train all over again to teach English children. And I remembered the last time I saw Charlie Denton. My old RAF chum grinning on me because he was happy he said, oh, he was tickled pink that he had become a teacher of history. Now, let me tell you, this man once argue silly with me that Wellington had won the battle of Trafalgar Square. And yet there was he, one year's training, and they say he can stand before a classroom of wriggling boys to teach them his nonsense. Hortense should have yelled in righteous pain not whimper in my ear. And still the goofy boy was staring on us. 'Shoo,' I told him. He poked out his tongue and wiggled his big ear at me, then ran away. But other eyes soon took his place. An old man was so beguiled by Hortense that, gaping on us, he leaned his stick into a drain and nearly trip over. A curly-haired woman crossed her eyes giddy with the effort of gawping. A fat man pointed, while another with a dog tutted and shook his head. Come, let me tell you, I wanted to tempt these busybodies closer. Beckon them to step forward and take a better look. For then I might catch my hand around one of their scrawny white necks and squeeze. No one will watch us weep in this country.

'What you all see?' I shouted on them. 'Go on, shoo.'

Hortense's hat had slipped forlorn on her head, just a little, but enough to show this haughty Jamaican woman looking comical. I straightened it for her. She composed herself, dabbing her eye with the tip of her white-fingered glove. I got out my handkerchief so she might wipe her face. However, this item was not as clean as it might have been. For several days I had been meaning to wash it but . . . Hortense held it high between her finger and thumb to pass it back to me. As she took out her own handkerchief from her bag, I saw the pretty white cloth had Sunday embroidered on it. 'You have the wrong day there,' I told her. Then, oh, boy, she blew her nose into that poor cloth with the force of a hurricane, before telling me quietly, 'I walk into a cupboard.'

'Why you do that?' I asked her.

'I thought it was the door to leave by.'

'Oh dear,' I said.

'But it was a cupboard and the women all laugh on me.'

My mind conjured the scene but instead of laughing hearty on the joke of this proud woman's humiliation, my heart snapped in two. 'And tell me,' I said, 'what was this cupboard like?'

Her expression flashed 'What is this fool man saying?' but she answered, 'There was a bucket and perhaps a mop.'

'Ah. Now, that was a broom cupboard. I have walked into many broom cupboards.' Reddened and moistened with tears, her eyes gazed upon me. And I believe this was the first time they looked on me without scorn. Two breaths I skipped before I could carry on. 'It true! I walk into broom cupboard, stationery cupboard . . .'

'This one had paper in also.'

'Interesting cupboard,' I told her. 'You say it have broom and paper.' And then it happen.

She smiled.

I felt sure Hortense had teeth that sharpened to a point like a row of nails. But they did not. They were small, dainty-white with a little gap in the front two. Come, could it be true that I had never before seen her smile? I thought carefully of what I should say next – for I feared a rogue word might chase away that astonishing vision. 'How long you say you stay in this cupboard?' I asked. And, oh, boy, that smile take on a voice – she giggle.

'Enough time for me to know that I am not dead but I am merely in a cupboard.'

'Long time, then.'

She laughed and I swear the sky, louring above our heads, opened on a sharp beam of sunlight. 'Enough time for them to think me a fool.'

'Ah, well, that is not so long, then.' Man, I had gone too far. No sooner were those rascal words said than I wanted to scoop them back up and stuff them in me big mouth. Like an apparition all trace of mirth vanished.

'Are you teasing me, Gilbert Joseph?' she said. I was ready to throw myself to the ground and have her walk across me. But the cloud passed. Playful, she hit my arm.

'What you do when you come from the cupboard?' I carefully carried on.

'I left the room.'

'You say anything to the women who were laughing on you?'

'What was there to say?'

'You must tell them that was an interesting cupboard.'

'You are fool.'

'It is what I would have said.'

'That is because you are a fool. No. I should have told them that their cupboard was a disgrace.'

'Yes. Good.'

'Because it was. It needed to be tidied. I bang me foot on a bucket.'

'Wait. Cha! You tell me you hurt your foot because these people cannot keep their cupboards in a tidy manner? You should tell them that you are used to clean cupboards where you come from.'

'But I am.'

'Oh, I don't doubt you there, Miss Mucky Foot.'

Her face was so pretty wearing merry, I wanted to kiss it. But no, no, no, no. Don't get carried away, man. One thaw is not the summer. 'Tell you what,' I said, for I had an idea that might prolong this glad weather, 'you wan' see the King?'

While Hortense looked out from the top of the bus at the city around her, I gazed at her. So roused was she at every site the bus passed even her well-bred composure could not keep her voice from squealing: 'Look, this is Piccadilly Circus. I have seen it in books. The statue is called Eros.' Gleeful, her head spun with the effort of seeing. And everything her glad eye rested upon she pointed out to me. 'Gilbert, can you see? That is the Houses of

Parliament and the big clock is called Big Ben.' Although I had seen all these sights many times before, I too spun my head to feign elation. So pleased was she with her view from the top of the bus, she held her hands as if on a steering-wheel, saying, 'You can pretend you are the driver of the bus from here.' However, excitement for that particular experience I could not affect. The driver of a bus — oh, God! — with my luck, one day I probably would be.

A cheeky pigeon in Trafalgar Square deposited his business on the sleeve of her coat. 'You have your handkerchief?' she asked me.

'Excuse me, Miss,' I said, 'but what happen to your Sunday cloth?'

'But mine is a good handkerchief and yours is filthy rag,' she told me. She have me there. Wiping off the muck she shrieked as two more birds landed on her head. 'Get them off me — I don't like them.' She ran a small circle flapping her hands to scare the birds from her head.

'So now you need my help?'

'Gilbert, please.'

I brushed them from her. 'What you think of Nelson?'

'He has too many birds,' she said.

Reverent as the devout before an altar, she gasped, astonished at Buckingham Palace. 'It is magnificent,' she said. A small girl carrying a doll touched Hortense's arm then ran away. No sooner was she gone than a small boy followed. Feeling his touch, Hortense looked around. 'Yes?' she asked the little boy.

He stared up into her face with that same expression she had used for the royal palace. 'You're black,' he told her before running off. Hortense, all at once aware of people around her, straightened her hat and pulled at her gloves.

'You like the palace?' I asked her.

Stiff and composed she replied, 'I have seen it in books.'

'People always stare on us, Hortense,' I told her.

'And I pay them no mind,' she snapped back to me.

'Good, because you know what? The King has the same problem.' But her nose had risen into the air and I feared I was losing her once more. I put my elbow out to her. 'Come let us stroll like the King and Queen down the Mall.' But she sucked on her teeth and turned her eye from me.

I bought her a cup of tea and a cake at a café. 'Why you waste your money on cake?' she asked me. 'It will spoil your appetite for the food I will make.'

Oh, I do hope so, was my thought. Of course I did not utter those words for this woman's mood was once more bleak as the dark cold fog I viewed through the window of the café. Who knows how long we sat there in silence eating on our cake, sipping on our tea? Not me, for three boys came greeting me with a cheery nod, looking on Hortense with a wink of: 'Okay there, man – you have a pretty coloured lady.'

'You know these men?' Hortense asked.

'They are from home,' I told her.

'And you know them all?'

'I know they are from home.'

'But you don't know them?'

'No, but I know they are from home.' I did not tell her that some days I was so pleased to see a black face I felt to run and hug the familiar stranger. She took off a silly white glove to wipe some crumbs from her lip and I sensed a little thaw. I am not a gambling man but I was a desperate one. 'So, how you like London?' I asked.

'I dreamed of coming to London,' she said. Her eye was not on me but focused on the stirring tea in her cup.

'Well, there you see, not many people have a dream come true.'

And hear this – with no warning she start to cry again. Damn – I was losing me touch. Tears were dropping into her tea. Out came the Sunday handkerchief. A shaking hand dabbing once more at her eye. I thought to apologise but feared that do-do might fall from my careless mouth. It was a timid hand I stretched across the table to place over hers. I waited for her to slap it away. But she did not.

'What am I to do now?' she said softly. 'I thought I would come here and teach.'

'Don't worry,' I told her. 'I can look after you.'

As I suspected, the do-do fell. She pulled her hand so rough from under mine, it slap on the table. Cha, nah, man, this woman had me no longer crafty. 'I am your husband...' I started. I said it too firm, I know I did. Looking on her pouting mouth I quickly changed, 'Well, come, let me see. What else can you do?'

She shrugged.

'Can you sew?'

'Of course,' she told me.

'Is that "of course" like you can cook? Or is that "of course" because you can actually sew?'

'I can sew. I have been sewing since I was a girl.'

'Good,' I said. 'Then I know where you might find some work.'

'Sewing?' She shout this, all tears outraged away. 'But I am a teacher.'

'And a teacher you will be even when you are sewing.'

She sucked on her teeth in a most unladylike manner. So I told her, 'Hortense, your mummy never tell you, "Needs must when the devil drives"? Look at me, for too long I have been driving lorries but one day...' I hesitated.

'What?' she asked

'One day I will study the law.' Man, those words sounded so foolish. Let out into the cold air of a London night that hopeless dream soared so far from reach I heard the angels laughing. It was my turn to look away. For I was a big-talk buffoon. Suddenly her hand, delicate and tender, gently place itself over mine. I dared not look to see if her touch was real. My doubt might melt it. A minute it rested there before she said, 'I can cook.'

'No, you can't.'

'My teacher, Miss Plumtree said my cake was the best outside the tea-shops of southern England.'

'Your teacher taste it?'

'Of course.'

'And still she say it better than one she eat in a tea-shop.'

'Yes.'

'She tell you where this tea-shop is, because we must be sure not to go there?'

'Are you teasing me, Gilbert Joseph?' Just as she said that another boy came to our table. He was old and cold. Two scarves were round his head with a brown hat squashed down on the top.

'Cold today, eh?' He smiled, with the few teeth he had left.

'Yes, man,' I said.

He did not smell so good, his brown skin dusted grey with dirt. It was a struggle for him to tip his hat to Hortense as it was pushed down so far. But finally it came off. 'Cold day today, Miss,' he said to her.

She glanced at him, from his scarf-wrapped head, past his baggy stained trousers, to his dirty shoes. She looked swiftly around her and, in the wink of an eye, she came back to this man. And she answered him, 'I have found that this is a very cold country.'

The man tipped his hat again. 'Ah, very cold, Miss,' he muttered, as he moved on, 'very cold.'

Fifty-two

Bernard

Felt like a thief. Silly, I know. A man can't burgle his own home. But the turn of the key in the lock. Unfamiliar objects in the room. Odd smell. Somehow made it all feel clandestine. I knew they'd be out. I'd seen them leave in the morning. Dressed up to the nines. Hardly aware of how queer they appeared. Would have been hard, I know, but they made no attempt to blend. His suit smart but baggy as a tramp. She completely overdressed — white gloves on a weekday. Still, I knocked a few times — just in case. Who knows how many more could be in there? Just a precaution. Not fear. Volatile creatures. No need to arouse them more than necessary.

There was a huge trunk blocking most of the doorway. Hardly room to turn. I banged a shin trying to navigate between bed and chair. A curious smell of gas. I wondered if they knew how to use it properly. Can't be too careful. Checked the tap but it was firmly off. The unpleasant odour clung like dirt. Tatty cloth sprawled over the bed. Armchair limp and wounded — riddled with holes. Dead flowers in a jam-jar. The place was a disgrace.

Ma used to use this room. Sewing, mending, reading and suchlike. Always when I lost her, me a little boy, I would climb the stairs. If the door was closed I knew she was there. I'd tap three times, softly.

'What are good little boys?' she'd say.

'Seen and not heard,' I'd tell her. Only then she'd tell me to come in. Beckon me to sit beside her chair. And I'd watch her fingers in the dim firelight nimbly darning socks on a mushroom. Or embroidering something splendid. Any other footsteps heard on the stairs she'd stop. Listen. Her lips silently counting the flights taken. A door shutting and she'd say (not to me, but out loud) a name. That would be the lodger who'd just arrived home or just gone out. Pa rarely came up here. At least, he never got all the way to join us while Ma was alive. She'd know his footsteps, you see. Be up and out, curious to know what he wanted before he'd come too far. Pa was born in this room. His father and a couple of the great-aunts before him. A woman's room, Ma called it. Not only because of the births. It was the view from the window. She could spy on the whole street without anyone realising, she said. It was the top of her world.

In Brighton (and out east), I often thought fondly of the creaking wooden stairs, the cavernous empty rooms, the stuck sashes of this venerable old house. Sometimes thought of it more than Queenie, I admit. But, funny thing, it was Ma I felt I'd let down, not Pa. The house was going to ruin. Of course, the war didn't help. Lucky, some would say, to survive still with bricks and mortar to call your own. But I was a poor steward none the less. Couldn't see anything out of the windows now. The curtains grubby and ripped. These coloured people don't have the same standards. I'd seen it out east. Not used to our ways. When in Rome . . . Lost on these immigrants. They knew no better, like children, Mr Todd believed. But I was having none of it. He'd never been out east. Never seen how cunning these colonial types could be. Children? Poppycock. Had to put him straight. I was more experienced, you see. The recipe for a quiet life is each to their own. The war was fought so people might live amongst their own kind. Quite simple. Everyone had a place. England for the English and the West Indies for these coloured people. Look at India. The British knew fair play. Leave India to the Indians. That's what we did. (No matter what a hash they make of it.) Everyone was trying to get home after the war to be with kith and kin. Except these blasted coloured colonials. I've nothing against them in their place. But their place isn't here. Mr Todd thought they would only survive one British winter. I hoped he was right. These brown gadabouts were nothing but trouble.

Didn't hear their footsteps on the stairs. Hearing not as keen since India. (Bullets and blasts saw to that.) I would have stood my ground anyway. No harm done. They looked a pitiful sight as they walked in. A pair of sodden minstrels once the gaiety's past. Decked in seaside colours the pair of them. Their clothes far too flimsy for our climate. Drooping and sagging with the damp. These people belonged in hot climes. It would be a kindness to return them to the backward place they came from.

We all looked at each other for a good while – pondering what next. A loss for words on both sides before the darkie fellow asked me what I was doing in the room.

'Looking around,' I told him.

Cheeky blighter tells me that this room – at the top of my house – does in fact belong to him.

'I beg to differ,' I said.

He looked puzzled by that. Gazed at me as if I was the foreigner.

'This is my house.' I said it carefully so the idiot might follow. But it made no difference.

According to this darkie I could not just come into *his* room. Somehow I needed *his* permission. I think not.

'I can go anywhere I please in my own house,' I told him. That started him off.

Rent, he shouted. Said he paid plenty of rent.

'I'm not interested in what you pay,' I said. 'This is my house.'

The conversation was over as far as I was concerned. He, of course, had other ideas. Had the nerve to ask me how I got into the room.

'None of your business,' I told him. But I showed him the keys anyway. Left him in no doubt as to who had the upper hand. My house, and I've a key to every room. But it seemed to be of little importance to this black chappie. Still told me to get out. Raised his voice. Unnecessary, of course. But I'd learned a sharp lesson already from these people – tutored by his foul-mouthed friend downstairs: there was no reasoning with them. Didn't want any more rough stuff. But I fought a war to protect home and hearth. Not about to be invaded by stealth.

'This is my house and I'll go into whichever room I please,' I informed him.

It was his privacy he started ranting about next. Said he paid rent therefore he deserved — yes, deserved — privacy.

Cheeky blighter had me lost for words. 'You deserve . . . you deserve!' What he deserved was to be thrown on to the street. Him and all the other ungrateful swine. He came towards me then. Eyes bulging like a savage's. 'I'll have the police on you if there is any trouble,' I had to tell him firmly. Put his palms up to me. Submissive. Telling me that he didn't want any vexation. Said he was only interested to find out what I wanted. But I'd seen all their tricks out in India. Straightened myself up — I was taller than him, you see. Told him, 'You're going to have to leave.'

Four times he asked me why. Standing so close I was having to breathe his air. Nothing for it. Notified him in the end, 'I'm selling the house.' And, funny thing, he announced to me that Queenie had never told him this. As if she would. Queenie, he called her. 'This is my house, not my wife's,' I said, 'Not for her to tell you anything.' Seemed I had hit a nerve. He really started ranting then. It was Queenie he paid the rent to. It was Queenie who let him stay here. It was Queenie he answered to.

'I'd thank you to call her Mrs Bligh,' I said to the cheeky blighter.

He took no notice. Was off again. Wanting to know if Queenie (said it to annoy) also required him to go. I soon shut him up.

'I'm Queenie's . . . Mrs Bligh's husband. It is my house and I wish you to leave.' I thought that was clear enough but the dimwit asked the same question again. 'Oh, good God, man,' I said. 'Do you understand English? You took advantage of her good nature. But now I'm back we intend to live respectably again. It's what I fought a war for.'

I thought he was calming down. He took a deep breath. Looked to his feet. Bit his ample lip. Mentioned, almost quietly, that he, too, had fought in the war. I didn't doubt it. I'd seen colony troops up in Blackpool. Brought over for clerical duties and suchlike. Useful, of course, but hardly fighting men. Apparently all he now required was the chance of a decent life. 'I dare say,' I told him. Barely needed to point around the pitiful room but I did. 'But look at this place – it's a disgrace.'

The woman started muttering then. Couldn't understand a word. Just caught something about trying to make the room nice. Nice? I nearly laughed. Those cosy times up here with Ma. A chair in front of a roaring fire. A pot of tea, a muffin each. That was nice. To look at it now made my blood boil.

'Well, my dear,' I said, 'you could try harder.' I didn't see it coming, it happened too fast. He pushed me hard on the shoulder. Shouting at me, this bloody darkie, to get out. Nothing for it. Pushed him right back. That bit taller, you see. Sent him reeling. Tried to stay calm. 'No, it's you that must get out,' I informed him. Hotheaded blighters, these dark immigrants. Once they're woken they're hard to get back in the bottle. He came back at me. Told me the place was falling down. 'Rubbish,' I said. Even Hitler only left it a little shabby. Nothing like the slum these people were hell-bent on. His audacity then astounded. Implied he was a friend of my wife. 'How dare you?' I said. 'A friend? With the likes of you?' Excitable, these darkies. Worse than the coolies. He started jumping up and down in some blinking war-dance saying something about bloodclots. He was going to bust my head, he said. I should watch my mouth or he would make me into mash. I should be careful what I said next. Shocking behaviour. I was pleased to see Queenie rush through the door, I admit.

'What's going on?' she yelled. She was puffing like a bulldog. 'What's all the noise?'

'I was just telling these – these people they have to leave.'

Wouldn't even let her catch her breath before he was at her. Demanding to know what was happening. Pleading to a woman. No shame.

'I'll thank you to address your questions to me,' I told him firmly.

'Shut up,' Queenie shouted. At me! Took the wind from me, I admit. 'Let me talk to them,' she said. Shouldn't have to hear that from your wife. 'Now what's going on up here?' Especially in front of coloureds.

'These people have to leave. I won't have wogs in my house.'

He poked his finger at me then. Told me he'd already warned me to watch my mouth. 'I'll say what I like—' I told him.

But Queenie started to shout. Wants me to be quiet, she said. Put a sock in it. Belt up. Calm down. Good God, where were her loyalties? Taking a darkie's side over her own husband. He saw it, of course. Jeered at me to listen to my wife. 'Gilbert, you can shut up too,' she told him. And not before time.

'Yes. Get out,' I said.

Off he went again. As if I had not made the situation absolutely clear. Ranting once more. His room and it's me who should get out. Pushed me. The blighter. Both women threw themselves between us. But I managed to get an arm out. Gave him a shove. I shouted then, 'Is this woman your wife or just showing you a good time?' Caught him better than any punch. All kinds of foul coolie abuse started spitting from him. Darkie woman tried to hold him back. Almost amusing. Except suddenly Queenie gripped her stomach. She was in pain. Face pale and blushing like raspberry ripple. Mouth wide as a cave. She howled fierce as a wild thing. All froze like some ludicrous tableau.

'Jesus Christ,' she was whimpering. Bent double with an 'Oh, God!' Grabbed out. Caught a handful of the darkie woman.

Concern made me find my voice: 'What is it, Queenie?'

She was panting, tongue fleshy as steak. Darkie woman tried lowering her on to a chair. She wouldn't sit, though. Her fist was clenching handfuls of the woman's coat. Blackie puts out his hand to steady her. 'Oh, no, you don't,' I told him. Pushed them both out the way (roughly, I admit). 'Come on, let's get you home.' Managed to take her weight but she was surprisingly heavy. Almost dropped her. He jumped forward, of course, ready to catch. Barely disguised, the lust in his eye. Fingers splayed, he laid both hands on her. 'Get your filthy hands off my wife,' I shouted.

She was hysterical, screaming, 'Get off me!'

Quite.

But it was me she batted away. Force sent me tripping over the trunk. This was absurd.

'Hortense, you help me,' Queenie said.

'Don't be ludicrous,' I told her.

Dimwitted darkie girl just pointed at herself. Totally baffled. 'Me?'

'You need a doctor, Queenie,' I said.

I went to help her again but she howled before even my fingertip touched.

'Hortense. Come on. Help me downstairs. Please.'

I had to push the black again. Lunging forward, he was, to get another feel. He made a fist. Nothing for it – I made two back. Beckoned him on. That bit taller, you see.

'Stop it,' Queenie shouted. Straightening up, the darkie woman took her arm. Brown coward dropped his guard. I made a final move to assist Queenie. But she was having none of it. Calm she was. Pleading, 'Bernard, please, just get away from me.' Then both women staggered from the room like battle casualties.

Fifty-three

Hortense

It was not enough to turn the key in the lock. Mrs Bligh commanded I take a chair to stand on so I might slide along the bolt.

'Your husband will be locked from his home,' I informed her.

But my protestations only caused her to say, 'Good.'

In truth my concern was not with locking him out but incarcerating myself with this writhing woman. I was fearful, for pain was twisting her face ugly. I pleaded to her, 'We must call a doctor. Please let me call your husband to bring the doctor.'

But she was insistent – only if I followed her instruction could her pain be eased.

'Can you help me to the bedroom?'

'Mrs Bligh, please, let me get some assistance.'

'Oh, for God's sake – just do as I say, Hortense.'

Two arms she wrapped round my neck in a mighty embrace. I struggled to stay on both feet as I walked her into the required room. She landed hard on the bed. Only briefly did relief spread on her face before she cried out again. I thought to join her – howl up the house until we both were delivered from this misery.

'Mrs Bligh, I am worried for you, please.'

In response she gave a faint smile. If she had not, I might have slipped to my knees to beg for her to release me. But she took my hand, enclosed all my fingers and said, 'I know what's wrong with me.' She then squeezed them all together as if trying to extract their juice. This time it was not only she who yelled with pain. Releasing my crippled hand she struggled along the bed like a beast. Not only panting but on her hands and knees. She began unbuttoning her cardigan. Shrugging it off with difficulty. Her blouse she almost ripped from her chest, losing several buttons. She wriggled as I helped her pull off her skirt. Her pink slip was wrenched tight across her. She drew it up to her chest, the strain on the seams popping blisters of white flesh through several little openings. I thought to avert my eye for this woman would soon be naked. But to my surprise I saw that, far from revealing her exposed skin, she was bound around the middle with a length of bandage. As she unlocked the knot on the bandage I feared for the injury it would expose. For had her husband not shown himself to be a violent man? The oozing gash from the flick of a knife. The pus-y indents of a vicious bite.

'Please let me get the doctor. Your wound may need new dressing.' Although not of a delicate disposition, still I worried I might faint. But she paid me no mind. With care she unravelled this cloth. I turned my eye so it might just peek. But there was no cut, no blood, no gash. Like bread dough rising in a tin, as she unwound, her stomach steadily swelled in front of me.

'Mrs Bligh, are you with child?'

Once the bandage was fully discarded it was plain as a drink of water. Her bulbous belly puffed, relieved that it was now freed from its bind. She lay back on the bed commanding me with a pointing finger to fetch the cushions and pillows to prop her up. As she did, another contraction was upon her. And this belly bucked and rolled as the child inside fought for release. 'Oh, God, I think it's coming!'

How had she kept such an ample secret wrapped so tightly to her?

'Please let me get the doctor, Mrs Bligh. You must go to the hospital.'

'No, there's no time. I've been having these pains since yesterday. They're worse now. I know it's coming.' Once again the pain was scorching her face crimson. It was not in my experience, giving birth. I had watched chickens, of course, laying their eggs, but none of them had ever required my assistance. I held on to her hand patting it gently, my mind fretting on what else should be done while willing my eye to keep back its fearful tears.

Her pain subsiding, she spoke through a panting breath, 'Don't worry, I know what to do.' She struggled with a little giggle, 'It'll be like *Gone With the Wind*. You know the scene . . .' before a contraction blurred the words into screeching. I knew the scene very well and I did not care for the comparison. What doubt was there that she was the prosperous white woman? So, come, did she think me that fool slave girl? Dancing in panic at the foot of her bed? Cha! I am an educated woman. I knew that this birth would happen. 'Cross your legs and see to your knitting, Mrs Bligh,' I could tell her, but that baby would soon drop from her. All I would have to do is catch. *Gone With the Wind!* I closed my mouth from its gaping determined to show this impertinent woman what it means to be raised in Jamaica in reach of the foremost hands of a Miss Jewel. I took off my coat and hat. And one after the other put a roll on my sleeve. 'Come, Hortense,' I said, 'better go boil some water.'

Her husband was yelling the words, 'Queenie, open this door – what's going on? I demand to know,' and the accompanying banging became so regular its beats no longer startled me but became the rhythm I worked by. Placing the kettle on the stove, collecting towels and sheets from a drawer, soaking a cooling cloth and carrying through a bowl of fresh water were all performed to this man's bluster.

'It's just a women's matter, Mr Bligh. Soon come. No worry,' I told him through the wood every time I passed the opening. No man is required at a birth but any fool could see why Mr Bligh would be considered an intruder. This ignorant man was not even wise to what was ailing his wife. And even the stupidest pupil at Half Way Tree Parish School – yes, even the wretched Percival Brown, using his fingers to count – would be able to tell that Mrs Bligh's come-lately husband was not the father of the soon-come child.

Mrs Bligh called for me with a yell so urgent the booming, bottomless tones seemed to come from the devil himself. In comparison, Mr Bligh's protestation squeaked puny as a mouse.

'What are you doing?' she asked.

I was ready to tell her that while all that was required of her was to lie back and expel the child I had been asked to perform as maid, midwife and doctor all in the body of one woman. But she raised her hand, calling me to her timidly – all she needed was I. I placed the damp towel on her head. She held it there – her mouth open in a soundless howl. The room was malodorous, stale and airless. But the useless window would not budge.

'Leave it. Just tell me what's happening. Is it coming? I can feel it coming.' She pointed an insistent finger to the region of her being she wished me to concentrate upon. Up until this time I had contrived to avoid gazing on Mrs Bligh's private parts. Unschooled in the process of birth, I was none the less aware that eventually it would be this area where my attention was most needed. I prised her fingers from once more crushing my consoling hand and I offered her the grip of the bedpost instead. I thought the metal of the bed would buckle as she yelled her loudest. It was with politeness and – it would be wrong to say otherwise – reluctance, that I asked her, 'Please could you open your legs a little wider, Mrs Bligh?'

'Call me blinking Queenie, for Christ's sake,' she shouted, just before she started to cry.

'Okay,' I told her, 'I will call you Queenie, Mrs Bligh. There is no need for tears.'

'I'm crying 'cause it bloody hurts!' she screamed.

I was learning that Englishwomen can behave in a peculiar fashion. And this one was conspiring to be the oddest one I had ever met. Suddenly she was smiling again, 'Oh, what's happening, Hortense? Tell me,' and seeming to all the world like she was pleased to be having this baby.

So I looked. What a thing was this! A wondrous sight perhaps – for there was the round head complete with curly dark hair matted in blood pushing out from within her. A new life for this world. But it was quite the ugliest sight I had ever beheld. Only a few days before this pretty white woman was going about her business – collecting her shopping, hanging washing on a line, passing the time of day with neighbours – now, prostrated by nature, she was simply the vessel for the Lord to do His work. This woman's private parts had lost all notion of being of the human kind. Surely they could not stretch wide enough to let the creature pass. Cha, all this straining, squeezing and screaming. I would not presume to tell the Lord His business but, come, the laying of an egg by a hen was, without doubt, the more civilised method of creation. Every tissue in my body was tingling with repulsion. But for the sake of this woman's well-being, not even an actor on a stage could have held a gaze of rapt wonder more steadily.

'The baby is on its way,' I told her. 'The head is there.'

'It's crowning,' she said. 'Can you see it?' The noise she then created brought to mind the relieving of constipation. I was wearing my good white wedding dress. What consternation befell me as I realised I would have no chance to cover myself. For this baby, like an erupting pustule, was squeezing further and further out. Soon its eyes were blinking into the dim light. I tenderly held my fingers to its warm, slippery head.

'You must push, Mrs Bligh,' I said.

And with one venomous yell of 'Queenie, call me bloody Queenie,' the head of the baby popped full out.

'I have the head,' I told her. For there it was, cradled in my hand, in this obscene resting place. Crumpled as discarded paper. Dark hair, nose with two nostrils and lips that waved in a perfect bow. Suddenly that fresh mouth sprang open to deliver forth a mighty shrill scream.

I lifted my head to tell her, 'One more push, Mrs Bligh.'

This baby's head then began to twist round – turning without aid from me. No further injunction was necessary before, in one slippery rush, I found myself holding the whole baby.

'It's here,' I said. 'I have it. I have it here.' But she had fallen back upon her pillows. 'It is born, Mrs Bligh – it is here.'

I lifted the baby carefully so she might see. She held out her arms. The slimy purple pink of a robust earthworm, with skin smeared in blood and wrinkled as the day it would die, and yet still Mrs Bligh's eyes alighted on this grumpy-faced child and saw it as someone she could love. This was truly the miracle to behold. Leaning forward she enclosed this baby in two grateful hands. 'Oh, my God, oh, my God.' And luckily my dress had remained clean.

'We must keep it warm,' I told her. A throbbing cord of bright silver blue still tied mother to child. I brought a towel to clean and wrap it, but this wretched cord hindered all our movements.

'We have to cut it,' Mrs Bligh said. 'Get the scissors – they're on the dressing-table.'

I had thought my work done but here was she once more commanding me to fetch. I washed the implement in the bowl of boiled water. Drying it carefully I handed the scissors to her.

'No, you'll have to do it, Hortense.'

As soon as my mouth protested, 'Me?' reluctantly I realised it was only I who could perform this distasteful task.

I placed the cord within the open blades. Was I averting my eye or closing them? I do not remember for all at once Mrs Bligh was shouting. 'No, wait.' String, Mrs Bligh informed me, I needed to make two ties in the cord – one near the baby, one near her – and cut in between. She was insistent on this fancywork, observing me tying the knots as strict as a teacher at school. 'Good. Now you can cut it,' she finally granted. The scissors cut through the gristle with an ease that startled me. At last, she took the baby into her arms, embracing it against her chest. Then like a fussy shopkeeper with his wares she began to inspect. Two arms she lifted to delicately count every finger. Ten toes she looked for. A gentle wind she blew at each nostril. She wiped an eye. Then, rummaging careful in the middle of its two legs, she said, 'It's a boy. He's a lovely, perfect boy.'

I had no time for this reverie for the room was cold, the mother gone fool-fool and the baby naked. Every blanket had slipped to the floor in all the confusion. Bending to retrieve them at the foot of the bed, I found myself awkward by the feet of Mrs Bligh. When, all at once, Mrs Bligh's private part let forth a burp then spat out on to the lap of my best white wedding dress a bloody-soaked lump of her insides. Looking like a piece of best liver it burst on to me as if I was some bullseye in a game. My anguished cry had Mrs Bligh straining to look between her knees at the commotion.

'Oh, good. That's the afterbirth. Don't worry, it's perfectly natural,' she told me.

Soaking pink with the bloody splattered tissue, my poor dress wept. I picked up this slippery excretion and dumped it in the bowl of boiled water (with no doubt in my mind that this Englishwoman would probably wash her vegetables in this same bowl tomorrow). Mrs Bligh tutted at the sight of my spoiled dress, then said, 'Come and look at him, Hortense.' She was crying again. 'He's a lovely little boy.'

And I said to myself, Hortense, come, this is a gift from the Lord – life. What price is a little disgust on your best dress? I decided to pay it no mind.

She had wiped all the blood and yellow muck from the baby's face and wrapped him tight in the messy towel. She pulled the cloth down, away from his chin, so I might get a good view. I looked at the baby. Then my eye went straight to Mrs Bligh, who was cooing with words incomprehensible to the fully grown. I looked back to the baby to make sure what my eye had seen was true. Once more to Mrs Bligh, I perused her face for signs that what I could see she saw also. But her only response was a loving smile as she tenderly wiped at the dark hair on his head. Was it possible this woman had not noticed?

'Your baby is black,' I said to her. For, no longer that slimy purple pink, his skin had darkened to be browner than my own. 'Mrs Bligh, you know your baby is a black child.' Dreamily she tell me to call her Queenie. 'Mrs Bligh, can you hear me? You have a coloured child.' The skin of this baby appeared so dark resting against the pale ghostly white of its mother that, for a moment, I wondered if this blonde woman had swapped her baby for another while I was otherwise engaged. How else would this happen? 'Mrs Bligh, can you see your baby is not white?' But she paid me no mind, beginning her counting again – ten fingers, ten toes, she tells me. Yes – and every one of them black!

This woman had ceased to make sense, when just then I heard the voice of Gilbert Joseph at the door. 'Hortense, what 'appening in there?' Was it the Almighty intervening to point a finger? As these words were spoken, Mr Bligh blustered on, letting Gilbert know that he should remove himself from the door, in what, after all, was his house. Outside together and still scuffling. I looked to Mrs Bligh with her baby, serene as a Madonna on the messy bed. And it felt like a vicious cruelty to have to ask her, 'Shall I let them in now?'

Fifty-four

Gilbert

Now, come – let me think where to start. I must begin with Hortense. Bloody as a murderer, she walked out of the door of Mrs Bligh's basement flat. The whole front of her good white dress was red. Her hands, delicately holding her coat and hat, were, however, covered in the congealing scarlet stains of a hapless butcher.

'You can see your wife now, Mr Bligh,' was all the explanation that was forthcoming from her lips.

As she moved past me to ascend the stairs to return to our room, her nose lifted so far in the air it was a wonder her neck did not break. Now this was the story that my mind conjured. Queenie had in some way insulted my fiercely proud wife. Her hat a little old-fashioned? Her English not so good? Who knows? But a slight none the less for which Hortense took grave offence. In retaliation Hortense had – with a knife, perhaps, or a hatchet – killed her. Not until I was standing behind Mr Bligh, trying not to make too much noise to vex him with my presence, looking on a bed that contained Queenie and a newborn very brown-skinned baby, did things enlighten sufficient for my senseless brain to finally realise that, oh, boy, no, this was bigger trouble than that!

Never had I heard such a noisy quiet. We three – no, we four – caught in a scene that defied sensible comment. Queenie fondled her pickney that was plainly still wet behind the ears. The blameless baby wiggled, unaware of the accursed situation it had squeezed itself out into. Her husband, staring on them straight-backed as if on parade, wiped a hand back and forth across his head in the exact spot where his cuckold's horn would rise. While I frowned. For I knew Queenie had put on a bit of weight but what an astonishment to find it was the type you could dress in a bonnet. Some word was needed to break this frozen clinch. So it was I who said, 'Shall we still get a doctor?' The fool husband then turned his gaze to me. So bewildered was his countenance, it was almost comical. But this situation's funny side was obviously not what was troubling him at that moment. His eye locked on mine. And in that steady stare lurked true pain. My tongue had just begun with urgency to click to the roof of my mouth to utter the words, 'No, man, this is nothing to do with me,' when he lunged at me.

Two hands grabbed scruffy fistfuls of my jacket. I was being lifted from the ground. My feet tripped trying to get some foothold as he rushed me from the bedroom out into the parlour. I lost a shoe. Cha, I was shrieking like a girl. Not fright but surprise. First time I noticed this man was taller than me. Skinny? This man swelled before me, pumped up fierce with rage. No force I had could quell him. He slapped my back hard against a wall. Every muscle and tooth in his face was put to the service of showing his fury. One inch from me his breath blasted from him, speechless. Fearsome as the wrath of Samson, I was puny before it. I raised my hand only to shield my face as he shook me like a dog with a doll. I tell him fast, 'It nothing to do with me, man. It not my baby.' He started cuss language I never realise white men knew. 'Not me, man. Not me.' He swung me round, this puny man. But I got a little footing on the ground, enough for me to push him. But, like rolling a solid rock, he stood firm before me, while his fist came up to mash my nose. Blood spurted so wild from it, him looked as shocked as me. 'What you do, man?' I yelled. The only pain I felt was the craving to get this man far from me. Fearful of getting bloody, he took a fateful step back. I hit him in the head. Stumbling, flailing, he tripped on a chair and was spilt on to the floor. 'Good,' I shouted at him. 'You hurt, man? Good.'

Cha, blood running wet down my chin and I wiped my nose on the sleeve of my one good suit. It soaked up the indelible liquid like sponge. I went to go. Leave these white folks to their problems. Looking at the front of my stained, ripped and ruined suit, I knew I had problems too. Plenty.

But he had not finished yet. He sprang up to jump on my back. This man was tenacious as a vine. I swung this way and that to dislodge him. His hand was clawing nails in my face. So I whacked him with my elbow hard in the stomach. He deflated fast as a pricked balloon, but not buzzing off round the room: he slipped almost gracefully from me on to the floor again – his knees curling him up tight. At last, I'd killed him! He stayed that way. Breathing heavy as a crying child, wrapped up rigid on the floor. Come, I had not hit him that hard. 'You all right, man?' I asked, after a little while. I got no reply except his anguished breath. So I told him once more, 'Cha, nah, man, I sorry for you. But this business is nothing to do with me.'

Softly I hear him mumble. 'It's everything to do with you. You and your kind.'

And hear this, soft-hearted man that I am, I go to help him up. For suddenly pity for him flowed over me like a wave. No man – no matter how fool-fool a white ras clot – should have to look on his wife suckling a baby that is not his. 'Let me help you up, man?' I said. But he thrust my hand away. Then, slowly lifting his head, he glared upon my face with unmistakable hate. The man attack me, pour blood from my nose, accuse me of all sorts of things I had never got the chance to do with his wife. Come, let me tell you, all at once I was pleased this dogheart English bastard had too-too much to bear.

Cha, I hobbled up the stairs to the room – one bare foot, one clothed – rather than stay another second looking for the item. Let them keep the wretched shoe, for I wanted no more of Queenie and her fool-fool husband's confusion. I was fed up. Perhaps Elwood was right. Of course he was. About what? I could not remember. But he was warm in Jamaica and I was here, bloody and barefoot. Come, that must make my cousin the cleverer of us two. When I got to the door of the room I found it was locked.

'Hortense,' I called. 'Come, let me in, nah?' How long did I wait before I realised she would not? Shivering and hopping on my shoed foot I called again, 'Hortense.' I worried she might be asleep for there was no sound from inside. I rattled at the lock. 'You in there? Come, I am freezing out here. Hurry.' Suddenly the door opened and there was she dressed neatly in her hat, coat and white gloves. Before I had a chance to enter the room she had told me, 'I will call for my trunk when I am settled in.'

'Settled in where?' I asked her. But she gave no reply except to throw her nose once more into the air before brushing me aside to pass. 'Wait, nah,' I called.

I intended to follow her but my bare foot stood on an open nail. The sharp metal entering my foot put me in mind of a fork sticking a pickled onion. I had to cry out. Hopping up and down on the landing I could just hear Hortense calling back to me. 'You disgust me, Gilbert Joseph.'

Come, I finally get it. She had weighed up the evidence and reached the same conclusion as the fool husband. The brown baby in Queenie's arms must be the child she had for me. Cha! Am I the only black man in this world? Why everyone look to me? I have been back in England for only seven months. Why no one think to use their fingers to count out that before they accuse?

'Hortense, let me explain,' I called to her. Man, as soon as I said that I wanted to stuff the words back in my big mouth. It did not sound good. I had nothing to explain. Only men that have guilt have something to explain. 'It not my pickney, Hortense. I only been seven months here with . . .' I was saying before the wretched nail pricked me again and I lost most of the words to another pain-filled yell. 'Wait,' I shouted.

As she reached the landing by Jean's room, Jean appeared at her door. It was late – she was dressed for work. Powdered and painted as an ugly doll. She looked on Hortense, who said a polite, 'Good evening,' to her, as she passed by. Then Jean turned her gaze to me, perused me curious, then threw her head back and laughed. I heard the front door shut. Where could Hortense go? She knew nobody but, worse, she knew nothing.

How long it take me to find another shoe? The only one that show itself to me is for the wrong foot. I hurried down the stairs after Hortense on two left feet. I could not see her on the street. The blasted cold misted my breath so the way ahead was hazy. Left or right? Cha, I followed my shoes – if she had gone the other way I was ready to blame them. Up towards the square I hobbled like a cripple. A man walking his dog came towards me. Only when I saw his look of terror did I realise what a fright he was beholding. A man with black skin, covered in red blood, walking ungainly in two left feet. Man, I swear, the little dog, looking on me, jumped in his owner's arms. I thought to say, 'Good evening,' but was sure this man would scream once he realised I was indeed real. Who could blame him? I was a sore sight in this green and pleasant land. If I did not find Hortense soon and return once more inside someone would surely call a constable. Come, I looked like a suspect. What crime? Oh, any will do.

Then I saw her. Unmistakable even from afar. Her haughty gait swinging her white gloves like two fireflies in the dark. But she was lost. She stopped by a corner on the edge of the pavement looking to all the world like this cold dark spot was precisely the place she had left Jamaica to be. But, just like this afternoon, she looked to the left then to the right. Which way held the most promise?

This woman had no plan. No place to go. No mummy, no brother, no friend, no cousin round the corner who would hold up their arms to take her in. This was London, not a stroll in the evening air of Constant Spring. But come, let us face it, to be far from me this woman would walk off a cliff.

I thought to call to her but my voice carried on the evening air might cause her to run. I walked slowly towards her, hiding in the street-lamp shadows. Just then I saw the headlights of a car. It pulled to a stop by Hortense. I watched as the passenger door swung open. Hortense, ever polite to strangers and more innocent than that pickney newborn, leaned down to talk to the driver of the vehicle. For a few moments she was doubled, her head to one side attentive, listening. I quickened my pace and cursed the odd shoe for slowing me. Suddenly she straightened. She leaped back from the car saying, 'No!'

Her next step bumped her into me. She screeched until I said, 'It's me.' And for the first time she looked on my face with the pleasure of seeing kin.

She clung to me – her head burrowing into my neck like a chastened child. Just in time I slapped the roof of the car. Grabbed the door that the driver was rushing to close and yelled at him: 'Fuck off, man. This woman is not your whore.'

Fifty-five

Queenie

There are some words that once spoken will split the world in two. There would be the life before you breathed them and then the altered life after they'd been said. They take a long time to find, words like that. They make you hesitate. Choose with care. Hold on to them unspoken for as long as you can just so your world will stay intact. But from whichever side you looked at it I owed Bernard an explanation.

I'd waited so long for him to come back. I'd resigned myself to it – taking up where we'd left off. I wasn't the only one to make the wrong bed and I was ready to lie down in it. (I'd only used my half of it for years so no bad habit would have me hog it when he got home.) For so long I just twiddled my thumbs. I went to find a job. But a married woman working when there were deserving men who could do any job better? Go home, they told me, twiddle your thumbs the other way, missus. I'd never felt loneliness like it. (Well, maybe, just after Auntie Dorothy died.) Waking every morning, I'd get two seconds of blessed forgetfulness when I could have been anyone, before the boring leaden yearning settled about me again.

It was after dark, there was a knock at the door and I'd called to Arthur to get it. He'd been dead three years. But whenever there was a knock at night I called his name. It was daft, I know. I called it, then shouted, 'Oh, don't worry

I'll get it, Arthur.' It made me feel safer. I only opened the door a crack. But even with one eye and a dim light I knew him straight away. The way he stood was casual as a cowboy. A coat slung over one shoulder, hooked on a finger. As I pulled the door wider he turned full to face me. 'Sergeant Michael Roberts,' I said. But he was out of uniform, dressed sharp in a dark double-breasted suit with a hat cocked jaunty on his head.

'No, just plain ol' Michael Roberts now,' he replied.

Of course I invited him in. Thought nothing of it, although he stepped in sheepishly, checking around him as if someone might jump out shouting, 'Boo.' He hadn't died, as I'd sometimes wondered. No, nothing like it – he filled the parlour, every inch of it, with life.

'You are alone?' he said.

'Yes.'

'Only I thought I hear you call out – your father-in-law?'

'No.' I turned my face away from him in case a tell-tale blush called me liar.

'Your husband?'

'No.'

Slowly his playful picture-house grin lit his face up like limelight. And she was gone. That Mrs Bligh. That thumb-twiddling old drudge who'd not long finished her washing-up. Her hands still hard from scouring soap. That grouch who'd not used makeup or scent for weeks. She took off her tatty apron and scarpered. For this woman – the one he looked at like a delicious dish to be savoured – she was handsome. She was breathtaking. The most desirable thing he'd ever seen. So exquisite he stared without a blink lest all at once she vanish.

He'd been flying a Lancaster in a raid over Germany. Got shot down over France. Plane was a blaze of fire. They scrambled to get out. Parachuting down he got split up from the rest of his crew. Kip, the pilot, went down with the aircraft. They never found either. (Franny's sister collapsed when she was told.) Ginger got out. Michael saw him floating down to earth like a tiny cigarette match against the dark. The silk wings of his parachute were on fire. Never saw anything of him again. Michael was lucky. He even had a soft landing. Sprained ankle, that was all. Spent the next few days pulling turnips out of the ground and eating them raw. He was found eventually by a farmer. The funny thing was, it was his black skin saved him. They looked on him more as an oddity than a threat, other locals coming round to rub the colour. They hid him, then handed him to the Americans who passed him to the British in the end. And he got home. Well, back to England. Never flew again.

He'd been anxious about the raid because he'd mislaid his good-luck charm. He didn't like to fly without it. He told me all his crew had them – a piece of ribbon from a sweetheart's hair, a tooth from an old pet dog. Kip evidently always had a tin of corned beef with him. And Michael's, as I thought, was that little leather wallet. The one with the photograph of the old coloured gentleman and his seated wife. And that little girl.

I was excited to tell him I'd found it, that I'd kept it for him. His lip trembled as he took this picture wallet from me. Like a little child ready to sob. But he wasn't caught by tears. He just held it reverent as a Bible. Opening it with such caution as if the contents might flutter up and fly away. I breathed with relief as he stared a look of wistful longing at each of the pictures in turn. Because the truth of it was, I'd nearly thrown it out several times. The tatty thing only got a reprieve because it got shoved down the back of a drawer and was left there. I had thought about telling him that I'd gone to the station to find him with it. To give it back to him before his train left. And about the bomb blast that held me back. But mine seemed such a silly feeble story beside his heroic tales of derring-do I didn't bother.

'Are they pictures of your family?' I asked.

He didn't answer me for a good while. Just sitting there drinking in every shadow and crease of the photographs. I didn't ask again because I knew he'd heard me. It was softly spoken and out of the blue when he said, 'I lost them all in a hurricane.' If I'd have asked any more questions, I'm sure he would have wept.

But then he surprisingly bucked up – made me quite jump. Looking up at me his roving eyes started nibbling me all over. He placed his large hand on top of mine. 'Tell me, you ever felt the force of a hurricane?' One by one he slipped his fingers between mine, forcing them apart while gently increasing his squeeze.

'No,' I said.

He put his lips against my ear his tongue lightly licking the lobe. 'Would you like to?' He bit me.

And I said, 'In Herefordshire, Hertfordshire and Hampshire hurricanes hardly ever happen.'

Three days and three nights he stayed with me. We kept inside, living like mice. I would scuttle around trying to make us something to eat – avoiding windows and their inquisitive light. Then I'd bring it back to him on a plate. Bread and jam mostly. We'd eat it in bed like newly-weds. Feeding it to each other, before licking the sticky corners from each other's mouth and wriggling about to get rid of the crumbs.

But I knew it wouldn't last (and not only because the jam had run out). He was on his way to Canada. Toronto. He'd trained there and talked of it, throwing his arms wide to demonstrate the open skies, the endless vistas of this wondrous vast place. No small island that, only needing a few fingers and a cupped palm to describe it. He didn't want to go back to Jamaica where he came from. Each time I asked why, he smothered the answer with kissing. Until he finally snapped at me, 'Why are you so concerned? Mind your business, nah?' And sulked – crossing his arms, closing his eyes. I had to tickle his toes with my hair just to see him smile again.

I dreamed of him begging me to go with him to Canada (not just me, all the Queenies did). We knew my answer – I would have gone. Locked up the house, waved the neighbours goodbye and started a new life. But he never asked. And neither did I. He left on a Monday morning at nine o'clock. I watched him walk away, hoping for a whiff of hesitation – an over-the-shoulder glance that expelled a sigh. But with his coat casually thrown over his shoulder, his hat cocky, his gait was as purposeful as a fleeing thief.

I didn't kid myself that Michael loved me, that I was his best girl or anything soppy like that. He had nowhere to go in London while he waited for his ship to sail. I was a piece of luck – no more, no less. A lonely pretty almost-widow to spend his last nights with. But I didn't bloody care. I knew

I was pregnant. If that miserable doctor I'd seen before the war was right, then I had to be. They might not strictly have been conjugal relations but, by God, I blinking enjoyed them.

I was so sick, though, my precious rations floating in the toilet every morning and every night. I wanted rid of the baby at first. I bound myself in an old roll of bandage I found in a drawer. Holding my breath to squeeze in the unwelcome swelling. I wrapped it tight as a mummy, round and round, until bending to put my shoes on took most of a morning. I even had to encase my breasts, once they resembled two barrage balloons. I wanted it kept from nosy-parkers – Mr Todd and his horrible sister. Nudging, pointing, whispering. 'What a how d'you do? Poor Bernard, what did that blessed man do to deserve her? The darkies are bad enough but now an illegitimate child. Whatever next in that house of ill-repute?' I wasn't ashamed, I just didn't want prying eyes making it sordid.

I'd hump things round the house – a chest-of-drawers from one side of a room to the other, a wardrobe that simply had to be taken up two flights of stairs. The heavier the better. And in between I'd jump the stairs – three at a time to the top and two at a time to the bottom. Every bath I ran was so hot I feared I'd blister. But none of it worked. I cursed those bloody old wives – could they get nothing right? Then one night as I was lowering myself into the bath for another scalding, I felt a tiny kick. A little bounce inside me. A tiny foot protesting that our bath was too hot. A little elbow nudging to ask me what I was doing. I turned the cold tap on in panic. Lowering myself down in cool water I swear I heard it sigh. I felt queasy thinking that the little mite was probably scared of me. Who else alive was there who could protect it? I was so sorry and I told it so over and over.

I was lucky – I never got too big. Never lumbered around like some I saw, gasping for breath leaning on a lamp-post or rubbing at an aching back. At night in bed I'd unwind the binding – let the little mite breathe – my belly puffing up like a fat man's. And I'd talk to it, tell it my plans. Perhaps we'd go to Canada on the money I'd saved from the rents. I could make up a tale of its hero father slaughtered in the war. What was to stop us? The war had been an enormous bomb blast. Everything thrown up, tumbling, turning and scattering high into the air. Now it was over; the whole lot was coming back down to land. But it was all settling in different places. A mother with a lone child – a little unusual we might be, but not wicked.

However, Bernard crashing back to earth soon put an end to that fancy.

There are some words once spoken split the world in two. Before you say them and after.

He listened to me right through. Never saying a word. Never interrupting or wanting a clarification. Never tutted, shook his head. Never once exclaimed 'Oh, Queenie, how could you?' He sat across from me at the table smoking a cigarette, gently tapping off the ash. But his eyes never lifted to look at mine, not even a glance. When I'd finished – when there was no more worth saying – he scraped his chair back across the lino, stood up and left the room. And for the first time I was thankful that Bernard Bligh could be relied upon to have absolutely nothing to say.

Fifty-six

Gilbert

I come to dread a knock on the door. Is this the way a man supposed to live in England? If it is not the jackass from downstairs come to shake me from this room or try bloody my nose again, then who?

Kenneth. Standing before me rubbing his hands, telling me keen, oh, he has a little business proposition for me. I folded my arms then blocked the door so his eager eye would not pull the rest of him inside. 'You listening, man?' he say.

'Oh, yes, I listening, Kenneth.'

'No, man, me not Kenneth, me Winston.'

I placed me tongue in me cheek while I carried on listening to the stupidness this man have for me this time. His story start with him telling me he had come into a little bit of money. How he come by this? Some of the boys from his district back home start a pardner. He have a little saving so he join them. His turn soon come round for the hand. Now with this and some money his grandma give him from selling her land to a big-time movie star, he find he have enough to buy a house. Here, in London. Finsbury Park was the precise location, which he inform me, with a finger pointing helpful like a compass, was in north London. He carry on to tell me the place need fixing up a bit, which was the reason he could purchase it at a preferential rate.

413

'You have a point for me there, man?' I ask. I was weary waiting for the moment when I might shut the door with a no-thank-you. But something was puzzling me. Slowly it come to me what. The man standing before me was actually speaking sense. I stopped him. 'Wait,' I say, 'you Kenneth?'

'No, man, me Winston. Come, you no tell the difference yet?' And he showed me the back of his hand for proof. I look upon nothing there.

'Why you show me this? What am I to look for here?' I ask him.

'Kenneth hand no have these two freckles on the back. See? One here, one there.' He placed his hand up under my nose pointing to the blemish that none but his mummy could ever see.

Carry on, I tell him. Only one sure way to find out – if he ask me for money he was Kenneth, if he did not he was indeed Winston.

'I wan' you come fix up the place, Gilbert. You can come live there with your new wife. Other room we board to people from home. Not English-woman rent. Honest rent you can collect up. And then you see the place is kept nice.'

'Why you need me? Why you no do this yourself?'

'Me a businessman, Gilbert. Me have me eye on another little place. Me do the same there. But me can't be everywhere.'

Could I at last see the beam in his twinkling eye? 'So you wan' me pay you money?'

'Gilbert, you help me fix up the place – weekend, evening. But me no pay you nothin'. You look after the place. Still me no pay you nothin'. But you give me small rent. We can agree on this?' His gaze was firm on me. Not once did him look shamefaced to the shine on his shoe or the dirt in his nails. 'Cha, why you no trust me, man?' he ask.

'So where is your brother?'

'Come, you no hear? Kenneth gone live in the Midlands.'

'Why?'

'A boy in London chase him for money he owe.'

'You no worried this boy will find you instead?'

'No. I am the boy chasing him. But, Gilbert, tell me what you think, man. What you say to me proposition?'

414

'Why me?'

He sucked on his teeth. 'I trust you. All the boys I meet since we come, it is only you I trust. You look out for me. You find me this room.'

'You don't wan' me give you money?'

'Cha, nah, man, me no wan' your money! Is a little work and a little business. But if you no wan'. . .' He began to walk away.

But I caught his sleeve and cried, 'Oh, Winston! Where you been, man?' And I hug him up right there at the door, as he primp himself.

'Cha, mind me suit, man. Just been pressed,' he say.

No longer welcome in Queenie's house, Winston was my cavalry. He rode in at my hour of need. (Hour! I was not the only boy to find his time of need was spanning more than just an hour in this Mother Country.) Keen to see the place Winston had for me, I took a little detour in my post office van. (Come, everyone know we silly darkie postmen were always getting lost.) It was a fine house, I could tell as soon as I turned the key and pushed open the door. What a size! Four floors of solid substantial rooms. Ceilings so high my voice echoed in them. The garden stretched far enough for the end to be caught in mist. The flat at the bottom of the house had two bedrooms, a kitchen already with a sink and stove and a bathroom of its own. The sitting room had windows so tall they reached from floor to ceiling. Man, after that one room in Earls Court, I saw before me a palace. But still my heart started pumping from in my boots. Why? How would I persuade Hortense that this house was somewhere she could live? She would certainly look upon it with disappointment. Quizzing me over and over with the words, 'Just this?' Frowning on me, convinced that God had placed me on this earth with no other purpose than to drag her down into an English gutter. Come, she had only just been persuaded that I was not the offending father of Queenie's baby. Winston was not a liar – in need of a bit of fixing up, he said. And, oh, boy! In need of a bit of fixing up it was. Surely she will only see that those windows that spanned from ceiling to floor had old-fashioned shutters dangling crooked and broken on rusty hinges. That each of the solid rooms was gloomy as a bad dream. Peeling dark brown paint, bare floorboards strewn with the rubbish of old newspaper and holes in the plaster so deep the wooden slats of the house construction were revealed. She would definitely notice the nasty smell in the kitchen. Damp from the ground or from a stray cat's backside – would she be able to tell? Of course she would see the dead pigeon fallen in one of the bedrooms. But only after she had observed that every piece of glass in the windows was cracked. 'Is this the way the English live?' she would say to me. The mournful lament sighed on each and everything she would see. And dirt? Just waving her white gloves in the air would see them turn black.

But Hortense was impatient to inspect the place in Finsbury Park. She was eager at the thought of leaving behind our one room in Earls Court. Keen to see the back of Mrs Queenie Bligh and all the confusion that resided there. And that gas-ring – she longed to wave goodbye to that blasted gas-ring. So keen was she, her mind on a higher life, that I was forced to nag ceaseless that she must remember that the place needed fixing up. Dressed in her coat, her green hat upon her head and white gloves, I led her into the first room. Nervous as a man presenting his sweetheart to his fearsome mummy – hear this – I had bought a bunch of flowers. The afternoon before I had placed the winter blooms in a jar on the mantelpiece. I had swept up the scattered newspapers into a pile. Man, I had even buried the pigeon. My feeble mind thought this silly bit of dressing might avert Hortense's scorn. But now, instead of cheering the place homely, those flowers looked as woebegone as the room. Heedfully, she perused the mantelpiece, the floor, the ceiling and the derelict wooden shutters. At the window she looked out quizzical upon the scene. She rubbed her gloved finger on the pane of glass. Examined it but said nothing as she brushed away the dirt. But, man, I was ready for her. Let her tell me the place is too run-down. Let her ask me why I bring her to this cheerless house. For all the answers were on my lips. Rehearsed and ready to go. There had just been a war. And, yes, this was the way the English live – and many live worse. What! She think she a princess to turn up her nose at such a fine house? She was lucky, I would shout, lucky to have any place to live at all.

My eyes followed her as she paced about the room in a silent shock. When she had finished her harsh inspection, she turned her gaze on me. Her chin was high, her nose was in the air as her lips slowly parted and her breath sighed. 'Just this?'

There, she had said it as I knew she would. The same discouraged tone as when she first stepped into the room I worked so hard to find in Earls Court. Just this? Soon she would lament, her eyes downcast, 'Is this the way the English live?' as she saw before her the gutter I was determined to drag her into. It was one deep breath I took to calm myself.

'How you mean?' I said. Cha, this irritating woman began tapping her knuckle on the wall listening to the sound with a sharp ear.

'I mean,' she said, 'is it just this?'

'Just what exactly?' I asked. She looked on me puzzled, or was it the sound from the wall causing her concern?

'Just this?' She threw out her arms wide. Come, this was an enormous room she needed to throw them wide. It was cold but my forehead trickled with sweat. 'Just this?' she said again. I was ready. I was vex. Then she slowly asked me, 'Just this one room we are to have or are there any other rooms?'

'How you mean?' I said.

'Gilbert, what is wrong with you? This is a simple question. This is a good room but is it the only room we are to have?'

'Wait, you like the room?'

'Yes, it is a good room.'

'It is very run-down,' I said.

'We can fix it up.'

'But look,' I told her, 'you no see the paint peeling from the walls? And those windows? Every one is cracked.'

'These things can be fix up.'

'It will be a lot of work.'

'Gilbert, come, you no scared of a little hard work. I can help you.' She spun round in the room. 'With a little paint and some carpet.' She moved to the corner leaning over to spread out her arms and say 'And a table and chair here,' before rushing to the fireplace with the suggestion, 'and two armchairs here in front of an open English fire. You will see – we will make it nice.'

All words froze on my tongue. For before me I suddenly saw quite the most wonderful woman. Proud, haughty – come, let us face it, even insufferable. But still, all I wanted to do was kiss her. Press her to me, right there in the middle of this ramshackle room. Feel her breath, then her lips soft against mine.

'But what I need to know, Gilbert,' she was asking, 'is, is it just this one room or are there any more?'

This beautiful woman commanded nothing but the best. Never again would I think to oblige her to settle for just this. Pretty in her hat and white gloves I would make this life around her good enough to fit that fine apparel. Lift her up so high until that one room in Earls Court became as distant a memory as if glimpsed in a dream. It was with love that I smiled at her. 'Oh, no, Miss Mucky Foot,' I said. 'There are many, many more rooms than just this one. Come, if you take my hand I will show you them all.'

I had got used to folding myself up on to the armchair to go to bed. My limbs had become collapsible. There was no winged creature that could tuck and bend itself away as neatly as I. I might have been crumpled as a moth from its cocoon every morning, but with the light, blood soon pumped through me to make me a man again. And under my big blanket I was snug as a bug. Like every night before, I turned out the light and wished Hortense pleasant dreams. But on this night, when all was dark and quiet, I heard her softly spoken voice say, 'Gilbert.'

Cha! What was it now? I thought. The mice, the tap dripping, the smell of gas? 'I tired, Hortense – let it wait till morning, nah?'

'Gilbert.'

I made the noises of sleep with the hint of a feigned snore.

'Gilbert, you wan' come into this bed?'

I did not answer. Why? Come, I believed that I had gone to sleep and was now dreaming those words. I was convinced if I were to speak she would awake and chastise me for disturbing her with my talk.

'Gilbert,' she say again, louder this time.

It was with great trepidation that I timid say, 'Yes, Hortense?'

418

'You no hear me, nah?' she ask. And I knew I was awake. Come, never before had every part of me been so alert.

'I not sure,' I say.

'What you think I say?'

'I not sure.'

'I say, do you want to sleep in the bed with me? Plenty room.'

She moved the covers. I felt the breeze from them as she opened up the bed to me. I moved on the chair – not to get up, mark you, but to make a noise to see if she toying with me. Would she tell me she changed her mind? Or laugh to say it was a joke – a good joke that made her laugh, ha ha? I stuck out a leg ready to catch it back if my dignity required it. But she say, 'You coming because I am getting cold?'

Now, there was not a man in the world would refuse. And if there was, let me tell you, he was not a Jamaican. I flew from that chair. Not once did my feet meet with the cold floor before they were squeezing down between the two sheets. The rest of my grateful body soon followed, settling itself down into the warmest place on this earth. At that moment if the Caribbean sun had been shining on me, while naked girls fanned me with banana leaves, it could not have felt any more pleasant. For all around me I was caressed by the smell of Hortense. Her soap, her perfume, cha, even her not so sweet sweat. But that startling headiness was not going to make a fool of me. I kept myself turned from her, lying rigid as a stick. Scared if any part of me, rude or innocent, were to touch her she would start to scream. She closed the blanket over me, efficient as a mother. And I felt her foot press lightly against my leg. I moved my leg away. But soon the little cold foot followed.

'You comfortable?' she ask. There was no sensible breath left in me to speak. If I were to open my mouth she would hear me panting like a dog. She brought her face up close to the back of my neck. With her breath fluttering over my ear light as a kiss, she say, 'Tell me, Gilbert, will there be a bell at the door of our new house? And will the bell go ding-a-ling, ding-a-ling?' While her foot – the mucky one – began gently to stroke up and down my leg.

Fifty-seven

Bernard

Queenie kept him in a drawer. Odd way to start a life. The bottom drawer. Largest one of a chest that belonged to Ma (she'd kept laundered linen in it). She'd secreted away baby clothes. I saw her struggling with a chair to fetch them from a suitcase on top of the wardrobe. Everything knitted. Funny thing, I recognised the wool. Watched her knitting it up several times before the war. It had been a cardigan and a jumper before it was booties and a bonnet. She'd even hoarded nappies in preparation. Pulled a pile of them from a trunk under the bed. The big pins had been on the sideboard for all to view. Never crossed my mind to regard them as a clue.

I idled away in Pa's room. Pleased for the comfort those familiar four walls could bring. Everything about this dreadful homecoming was awry. Nothing of the life that played before me was recognisable. I felt I'd stumbled into someone else's existence by mistake and was now busy trying to find my part. But how long can a man gape at his own circumstance? Senselessly bat his eyes against the glare from the unusual? Silly thing I know, but I envied Pa. Shock just sent him under. Rendered him speechless and useless. I longed to wake up unable to struggle through, with no choice but to surrender to it. Sit in a chair dribbling with Queenie feeding me, cleaning up the mess. But unfortunately this shell-shock – my shock – was proving to be quite bearable.

I moved around only when I thought she was at rest. Nocturnal, almost. Silly, I know, but I feared the chance meeting. Crossing in the kitchen, passing in the parlour. Not the dismay of seeing her suckling an impostor child. Or the fear that rage would overcome me. Or pity have me weep inappropriately. It was her expectation. Glimpsed in an inquisitive look, a backward glance. She wanted me to replace silence with words. But the truth of it was I was numb. I longed for something to stir me once more to opinion. Anger, hurt, disapproval. It was pitiful. I was blank as a sheet of white paper. No idea what to feel.

Heard him starting to shift as I was on my way to bed. Small whimpers that even I knew heralded a howl. (He cried every night and most of the day.) Opened the door a touch. Queenie was asleep. Deep enough for a muttered snore. She needed it. Just given birth, the doctor told her to rest. He came to look her over. Check the baby was all present and correct. Ordered sleep and double rations. I showed him out. He took me to one side as he left to enquire after the whereabouts of her husband. 'Before you,' I told him. That stunned him into staring at me as if I were a freak. A long moment. Then he wittered something he thought comforting about the war. I nodded. Why not? The war. It had been over for three years. But, yes, maybe the threads of that fraying cloth were still in a tangle.

I stepped into the room on tiptoe. No need to wake her. Just to check nothing untoward was happening. The drawer was on two chairs near the bed. I looked in. His mouth was moving cautiously into a downward grimace. Something was making him sad. And there it was for all to see on his face. No artifice, just glum. Downturned U of his mouth clear as a cartoonist's sketch. I thought my presence might quiet him. But the whimpering was getting louder. Queenie stirred. I was ready to run. His lips, puckering, were about to yell. I put my hand down. Held it gently to his stomach. (Saw a woman do it once to her child.) His belly was as warm as a hot-water bottle. I rubbed it a little, and his expression changed. Not so sad now. His mouth relaxed. No need to cry. He opened his eyes, searching for me to come into view. His dark skin fresh as a polished shoe. Flat nose. Nostrils, tiny pips. Lips elegant, as if recently drawn. Little fists tightly clenched swinging in front of his mouth. Feet kicking under the blanket. Happy to have me there. His tongue tasting his lips. Gave him my little finger to hold. He grabbed it tight. Tiny black fingers wrapping around. Sound grip. Then quite a pull to get it to his open mouth. Was soon sucking on my finger. Clamping his gums around, soggy, wet. And warm. He sucked like it was nectar. Quite content. Actually, he was a dear little thing.

He was fighting sleep. His eyes closing only to open with a start. Trying to find me again. His suck easing on my finger, I took it away. Back came that guileless grimace – those stuttered whimpers. 'All right,' I told him. My voice seemed to calm him. Eyes focused on the noise. 'There, there,' I whispered. I thought of a song. Ma used to sing one. Lost in some nostalgia but she must have sung it to me. My voice cracking, off-key. No singer. But even so his eyes closed almost as soon as I began. 'Lullaby and goodnight, may sweet slumbers be with you.' Couldn't remember all the words. La-la-la'd where I had to. But his eyes closed. Two lines under a furrowed brow. The vacuum of his suck gone, I took my finger away. Covered him over again. Job done. I turned to leave.

Queenie was sitting up in bed, staring at me, her mouth agape with astonishment. The little chap stirred again. I leaned down to him, breathing baby-talk. There, there, sleepy-time. Utter nonsense. But no doubt my voice was soothing. Silly thing, but with Queenie listening I suddenly said, 'I was in prison, you know.'

Her voice unmodulated seemed to shout: 'What? When?'

I hushed her with a finger to my lip. Didn't want him wide awake. His eyes were fluttering closed again. Soft murmur of a fledgling snore coming from him. He looked so like Queenie. Her son, no doubt – despite his skin. Spoke the words softly to him. Bare facts. No need of embellishment. But the sorry tale none the less of why I couldn't come home. The missing gun. The court-martial. His clenched fists gradually relaxed as sleep overcame him.

'Why didn't you tell me before now? Write or something? Anything?' she asked.

Had to shush her once more. Too loud. And I hadn't finished. His eyes fluttered open again. 'Oh, no, he's awake,' I whispered, before telling the honest truth of my stay in Brighton. In the quiet I could hear her every breath. Each one laden with queries too puzzling to ask. And I could feel her shock. Its brightness laid my face bare.

'Bernard, you should have told me this before.'

'No, I couldn't,' I said.

'Why ever not?'

I let the question hang. That much, I knew, should have been obvious beyond words. The little chap started stirring. Soon kicking against his covers again. Hands back against his open mouth. And I said, 'I'm so dreadfully sorry.' There was just enough light coming from the hall to catch her face in its beam. She never looked prettier. Plump and rosy from mothering. I always knew it: she was far too good for me.

'You should have told me all this before, Bernard. You should have said before.'

'It's all over. All done.' The little chap's mouth was open wanting something to eat. I gave him back my finger. But he wasn't having any of it. Must have heard his mother's voice. Mouth started turning down. A yell any minute. 'I think my finger won't do any more,' I said. She went to get out of the bed. But I beckoned her stay. Leaned down, bundled the little chap into my arms. Picked him out of the drawer. Remarkably stout. Queenie was ready. Her arms open. Anxious.

'I'm sorry I haven't been a better husband to you,' I said. And I passed her someone else's son. She took him. Snuffling her face into his. 'I'll leave you,' I told her.

And as I walked from the room she called out, 'Thank you, Bernard.'

Fifty-eight

Queenie

They were leaving. Gilbert had told Bernard. In a commotion, of course, on the stairs. A near fight that had Gilbert yelling for Bernard to stick his house where the sun don't shine. 'The top lodgers have found somewhere else to live,' was how soberly Bernard relayed the information to me.

'I know,' I told him. 'I heard, and so did the rest of the street.'

Pleased he was, though. Bernard wanted me and him to move to the suburbs. A nice house, semi-detached with a rose garden out the front and a small lawn at the back. 'Manageable' was the word he used. Not like this house with its memories, its prospect haunting his every thought. He was wanting a new start. Didn't they all, those fighting men? I mean, they'd won. They deserved something out of it, surely. What else was the victory for? Bernard was never half so interesting as when he was at his war. He thought I'd find his story – of the prison and all that happened to him out east – shocking. But no. I just wanted to laugh. Shout loud and congratulate him on failing to be dull for once in his life. I know two wrongs will never make a right but at least now we could stand up straight in each other's company. Even if it was caught in the clinch of two skeletons in a cupboard. Oh, Bernard Bligh, who'd have thought? But when he said it, about the new start, he wasn't looking at the baby, he had his back turned to him and he spoke it in a whisper.

Giggling together they were, Hortense and Gilbert, as they walked up the front steps to the door. I'd been listening out for them for hours, wanting to catch them before they started up the stairs. I was in the hallway before they'd shut the front door behind them. They were both startled by me at first but then their smiles faded, leaving their eyes saying, 'Oh, bother, she's caught us again.' My presence did that to them now. There was a time when Gilbert would smile on seeing my face — a cheeky grin that always left me feeling special. But not any more. Our eyes had not spoken since I don't know when.

'Would you like a cup of tea?' I asked. You'd have thought that I'd just bade them come watch me dance naked, they were that stunned. They looked at one another like I was playing some sort of trick. They no longer trusted me. Why not? What the blinking heck had changed all that? They were silent, neither of them wanting to answer in case the other got angry because of a wrong reply.

'Just for a minute,' I had to say. (I could have said, 'I won't bite.' I should have said, 'Weren't we friends once?') 'Just for a cup of tea and I've got cake. I know you're moving, I just thought it would be nice.' And I meant it when I added, 'For old times' sake.'

Gilbert's shoulders relaxed when he realised, no, it wasn't a booby-trap just a cup of tea. 'Okay,' he said, but Hortense could barely hide her scowl.

Bernard took one look at them and said, 'What's all this?' I'd wanted him to be out. Hoped he would be, gone on an errand or to see Mr Todd. Anywhere but there — sitting at the table reading the paper.

Gilbert started puffing himself up, 'Your wife invite us in,' he said.

Bernard was poised, searching for a cutting quip. The two of them like stags about to lock horns again.

'Oh, stop it, please, you two. Bernard, I've invited them in for a cup of tea.' And his look said, Why, in heaven's name, would a woman like me want to do that?

'I don't want them leaving without saying thank you,' I told him.

Bernard tittered doubtfully before going back to his paper. He was a bloody thundercloud sitting in the corner. This wasn't how I wanted it. He was making it awkward.

'We can go, Queenie,' Gilbert said.

'No, sit, sit.'

Both of them perched so tentatively on the settee, the cushions would hardly have known they were there. They were ready to run. I couldn't leave them alone in the room with Bernard and that mute anger. They'd have scarpered or a fight would have broken out. And, oh, God, I didn't want that.

'Bernard, could you make a pot of tea, please? And bring us all a slice of cake,' I said. The poor man was too shocked to protest. His mouth open, eyes blinking, dumbfounded, he was left with no good reason why he could not. When he left the room – scraping his chair back, folding his paper with a flourish – it was a blessed relief, like the sun coming out.

I was surprised to find myself tongue-tied, staring across the room at them. Desperate to say something right. 'I haven't thanked you,' I began, 'for, you know . . . helping me.' I'd said it to Hortense: her face was as stiff as an aristocrat's. She lifted her hand waving it at me a little. It was either saying, 'No, really, it was nothing', or 'Please, don't bloody remind me, missus' – it was that hard to tell. There was silence after that before I asked, 'Where are you moving to?'

'Finsbury Park,' Gilbert said.

'Is it nice?'

'It need a bit of fixing up.'

'Has it got furniture?'

'Not yet, but . . .'

'Gilbert, why not take the furniture from the room upstairs? If you like. We'll not be needing it.'

'No, thank you – it is kind but we will be all right, Queenie.'

'No, take it, Gilbert. Honest, take it.'

'I could not take your husband's furniture,' he said very deliberate and slow.

'Look, give us a quid for the lot. Then I'll have sold it to you.'

Gilbert shifted on his seat. Wouldn't even glance in the direction of my eye. I'd said the wrong thing, but what? I'd never seen him look so awkward. I wanted to shout out, 'Let's just start again – let's just do that scene again.' But it was too late. Gilbert and I used to laugh together, what changed all that? The perspiration under my arms was seeping up like a wellspring. 'Well, you decide, but you're welcome to it if it would come in handy.'

There was a silence again when I heard the baby stirring. My ears were keen as a bat's when it came to him. Couldn't hear the wireless from the other room but if he so much as sniffed I knew about it. Felt it in my skin as if we were still attached. 'Would you like to see the baby?' I asked them. 'Only you haven't since he was born. He's a bit less of a fright now. In fact, he's beautiful. I'll go and get him.' I jumped up. I'd no intention of either of them telling me not to bother. But I caught them glancing to each other discreetly with a look of 'How, in God's name, can we get away now?'

The little mite was rubbing the sleep from his eyes. He gave a wide gummy yawn before his face started crinkling up ready to yell. Then he saw me watching him and began kicking his legs. I took out the shawl – the one Mother had used to christen me in our bleak local church. I'd kept it wrapped in muslin in a drawer. It had sat in there so long it was hard to rid it of the smell of mothballs. I'd washed it five times. It looked so white now – clean and fresh against his brown skin.

'Here he is,' I said, as I handed him, this lacy bundle, over to Hortense. I didn't give her a chance to tell me she was nervous to hold him. She was flustered, messing around with her gloves, straightening up her coat. She took him, though. But, God, she was awkward with him! Held him out like he was a bolt of cloth she was taking for measuring. 'Let me help you,' I said. I had to grab him again in case she dropped him – she looked that unsure. 'Just bend your arms and cradle him on them,' I told her. She was so cack-handed I could hardly watch. I was short with her when I said, 'Have you never held a baby before?'

'Of course,' she told me.

I'd affronted her, which wasn't hard, but it did the trick. She shifted, moving him into the fold of her arms until he was resting snug as a baby should with a woman.

'He's a lovely boy,' I told them both. 'Good as gold. No bother at all.'

Her face, looking down at him, still carried the pinched lips of someone annoyed. But it soon began to soften. He could do that to anyone. His adorable heart-shaped face, glinting eyes and perfect bow mouth couldn't be looked at for long without even the coldest soul warming. She leaned her head a little closer to his and said softly, 'Hello.' It was a start. She looked up to me to hand him back.

'Oh, no,' I said. 'He likes you. Listen, can you hear the noise he's making? It means he's happy.' In truth I was worried he was about to cry. 'You hold on to him for a bit,' I said, before realising Gilbert couldn't see him. 'Show him to Gilbert. Gilbert, come over here.' He lifted himself from his seat to look into the shawl. I patted away some of the fabric so he could get a better look. Hortense obliged me by moving the baby round a little.

'You have name for him?' Gilbert asked.

'Michael,' I said.

Hortense flinched. She looked up at me so quickly she startled the baby. He began to whimper. 'Oh, careful,' I said. Her wide eyes were still on me. 'You all right?' I asked her.

'Oh, yes.' She comforted him nicely back down. She rocked him a little. His whimpering just faded. She made sure he was comfortable again before she said to me, 'Michael was the name of someone dear to me.'

'You have a brother call Michael?' Gilbert asked her.

'Yes, my brother. He was killed in the war, you see.'

'Oh, I'm sorry for your brother,' I said. 'But it's a lovely name. I like it very much.'

'Yes. It is a favourite name of mine,' she said.

'Wait, you tell me Gilbert not your favourite name?' Gilbert said to her. Then returned her weak smile with a little wink.

She looked down at the little mite again repeating, 'Michael,' softly, twice like she was christening him with it. I wanted to hug her, thank her for caring what he was called. But I couldn't. I just looked around me like an idiot and wittered something daft about the tea.

Michael started whimpering again. She was ready to hand him back to me. What must she have thought of me springing away from her sprightly as a flea? They both looked perplexed. 'The tea – I must just help Bernard with the tea.' And I was gone. Although I didn't go into the kitchen, I went behind the door and watched her through the crack. She was doing all the right things with him. Swinging him gently in her arms on her lap, while Gilbert, looking down at him, carefully gave him his finger to chew. He said something close into her ear. Whispered it so I couldn't make it out. She pouted her lips at Michael saying something in baby, then smiled. Gilbert did the same. They looked so right with him.

'What on earth are you doing?' Bernard asked. He'd caught me spying on them, craning my neck at the crack of the open door.

'Let me help you with the tray,' I said. He wouldn't let it go and we entered the room still tussling over it. Bernard plonked the tray on the table with such a thud the milk spilled from the jug. He went back to his paper without bothering to wipe it up. Grumpy blighter. I poured the tea, asking about sugar and milk. Two sugars for Hortense. Three for Gilbert, which made Bernard tut behind the news. I handed Gilbert his tea. But Hortense had Michael so she couldn't take hers. I was holding her tea out to her not knowing how I could get it to her mouth. I knew she'd want to hand Michael back to me. She started shifting all awkward in the chair. There was no time left — I had to say it then.

'Will you take him?' I asked her.

She was puzzled by what I'd said. 'I thought,' she began, 'that you might hold the baby so I could drink my tea.'

'Will you take him?' I said again.

'But I already have him, Mrs Bligh.'

'No. You don't understand, listen.' I was still holding the blinking cup of tea, the cup rattling on the saucer as my hand shook. I put it on the table and carried on, 'Will you and Gilbert take him with you when you leave?'

'Leave where?' Gilbert said.

'The house. When you move. Will you take him with you?'

I'd never seen frowns so deep. Both of them staring at me, trying to find some meaning or joke on my face. I knelt down on one knee. Took both of Gilbert's hands in mine. He pulled them back but I grabbed them again. 'Gilbert,' I said. I squeezed his hands. 'Will you take him with you? Look after him for me. Will you take him and look after him?'

There was a moment of stillness in the room before it fizzled like a live squib, once they realised what I meant. Both at once, questioning, 'What you saying? . . . What you mean? . . . What you want?'

I pleaded to Hortense, turned to her. I was on both my knees now. 'Take him and bring him up as if he was your son. Would you, would you, please?'

'Mrs Bligh . . .' was all she could get out.

'Hortense, please. I trust you and Gilbert. I know you. You're good people.' I was begging, I know I was, but I didn't care. She was trying to hand him back to me. I pushed him towards her again. Shoved the little mite back into her arms.

That was when I heard Bernard. 'Queenie, what in God's name are you doing?' He was on his feet standing over me.

'I want them to take him, Bernard.'

'He's your child. What are you saying?'

'Listen, Bernard. He needs a home. A good home.'

'He's got a home.'

What the hell was the stupid man talking about? I just wanted him to shut up. Shut his bloody mouth. What was this to do with him? 'Don't speak, Bernard. Do you hear me? Just don't speak,' I yelled at him.

'What are you thinking?' He was red as a berry, pure anger looking down at me. But I needed to persuade Hortense and Gilbert and he was just getting in the blinking way. He grabbed me. Pulled me up from the floor. And Michael started crying. And Gilbert was on his feet telling Bernard to leave me or else.

I faced Bernard. Took a breath. 'I need someone to look after him.'

'You're his mother.'

'I know, but I can't look after him. Bernard, we can't look after him. Don't you see?' I pulled away from him. Gilbert sat and I got back on my knees. Michael was still whining but Hortense was softly shushing him.

And I heard Bernard ask, 'Why ever not?'

It was so desperately spoken that we all stared at him. So earnestly asked that it should have been funny. Had he really no idea why we, two white people, could not bring up a coloured child? I was winded. I never expected that – Bernard questioning what was so obvious.

'We can't look after him,' was all I could think to say.

'Why not?' Bernard asked.

I thought my argument would be with Gilbert or Hortense. I couldn't believe what I was hearing. 'Because I don't know how to comb his hair, Bernard,' I said.

'But that's ridiculous. We'll work something out.'

'Bernard, what are you saying?'

'We'll bring him up.'

'Oh, yeah? And what will we tell him when he asks? That we left him too long in the sun one day and he went black?'

'There's been a war, all sorts of things happened. Adopted, that's what we'll say. An orphan. Quite simple.'

Bernard had no right to be so sensible. So just. So caring. Words. He'd found them but he had no business to try to use them now to persuade. Make me think I could be wrong. Because I wasn't — I knew I wasn't. Crikey, I've never even seen a humming-bird! Not even in a book. Who'll tell Michael what one is like?

'He's coloured, Bernard.' I was crying. Drinking fat salty tears. 'And . . . and he's not your son.' That shut him up. Flung him back in his seat with the blow. 'You might think you can do it now,' I told him, 'while he's a little baby saying nothing. But what about when he grows up? A big, strapping coloured lad. And people snigger at you in the street and ask you all sorts of awkward questions. Are you going to fight for him? All those neighbours . . . those proper decent neighbours out in the suburbs, are you going to tell them to mind their own business? Are you going to punch other dads 'cause their kids called him names? Are you going to be proud of him? Glad that he's your son?'

'Adopted, that's what we can say,' he said, so softly. This was blinking daft.

'Bernard. One day he'll do something naughty and you'll look at him and think, The little black bastard, because you'll be angry. And he'll see it in your eyes. You'll be angry with him not only for that. But because the neighbours never invited you round. Because they whispered about you as you went by. Because they never thought you were as good as them. Because they thought you and your family were odd. And all because you had a coloured child.' He

431

was going to say something else. Opened his mouth but nothing came out. 'It would kill you, Bernard,' I said. 'Have you thought about all that? Because I have. I've done nothing but think about it. And you know what? I haven't got the guts for it. I thought I would. I should have but I haven't got the spine. Not for that fight. I admit it, I can't face it, and I'm his blessed mother.'

At last I could turn back to Gilbert and Hortense. 'I'd have to give him away, you see,' I told them. 'To an orphanage.' I took Gilbert's hand again. This time he let me. 'And they don't want them, you know – the coloured ones.' I needed to stop crying – I had to explain carefully. I gulped on the tears. 'In the newspaper they said they were going to send all the half-caste babies that had been born since the war – sons, daughters of coloured GIs mostly – they were going to send them to live in America.' I giggled, but God knows why. 'Gilbert, can you imagine? You remember, don't you? The Americans. They'd want Michael to go up to the back of the picture house.'

Bernard turned himself away from us. And I knew why. It was the sight of me on my knees in front of these darkies. He sighed, or at least it sounded like it.

'If I gave him to an orphanage,' I carried on, 'I'd never know about him. Never. And he wouldn't know how much I loved him. And how all I wanted was to be a good mother to him.' They were just staring at me. I must have looked – no, I was – pathetic. 'You might let me know how he was getting on. You might write to me and tell me. I know it's a lot to ask.'

Gilbert's troubled eyes were asking all sorts of questions.

'I can give you money, if that's the problem,' I said.

'No,' Gilbert snapped. 'Don't sell your baby, Queenie.'

'No, no, you're right. I just want him to be with people who'll understand. Can't you see? His own kind. But I'll do it any way you want to. Any way. But you have to say you'll take him.' Michael started to cry. I pressed both my hands together. 'You know I'm begging. But it's not for my sake. Honest to God, it's not for me. I know you could give him a better life than I ever could. Don't do it for me – please, do it for him. That's what I'm on my knees for – my darling little baby's life.'

Fifty-nine

Hortense

I never dreamed England would be like this. Come, in what crazed reverie would a white Englishwoman be kneeling before me yearning for me to take her black child? There was no dream I could conceive so fanciful. Yet there was Mrs Bligh kneeling before Gilbert and I, her pretty blue eyes dissolving beneath a wash of tears, while glaring on we two Jamaicans, waiting anxious to see if we would lift our thumb or drop it. Could we take her newly-born son and call him our own? Not even Celia Langley, with her nose in the air and her head in a cloud, would have imagined something so preposterous of this Mother Country.

Gilbert insisted Mrs Bligh came from her knees. He lifted her, still snivelling, from the floor, supporting her with a careful arm round her waist. And he placed her down on the settee beside me. It was not the time to talk of such things but the baby's backside was damp under my hand. I paid it no mind. Gilbert tried to squeeze himself down on the chair between Mrs Bligh and myself but there was no room. So it was then he that took up the kneeling position.

'Queenie,' he said, with as gentle a voice as a woman might have, 'how can you think to give up your baby?' Those tender-spoken words caused Mrs Bligh to sob with such ferocity that the sleeping baby was once more aroused.

433

But Gilbert's look carried such concern that I forgave him. 'How you believe that we would be better for your child than its mother? We are strangers to him.' But questions were useless, for this woman's anguish had rid her of the power to speak. Still he waited patient for her sobs to subside. When they did not, he wriggled himself once more between us on the settee so he might place a comforting arm round her shoulders. Returning the consolation, Mrs Bligh lifted her hand and placed it on Gilbert's arm. With the vigour of a blast, that delicate touch was enough to see Mr Bligh on his feet and exploding, 'Get your filthy black hands off my wife!'

Gilbert was soon squaring up to this tall man. The two of them standing facing each other. 'What is your problem, man?' Gilbert said.

'My problem is you, with your hands on my wife.'

'You sure that it is my black hands on your wife that is worrying you, man?'

'How dare you, you savage?'

It was at this point that Mrs Bligh, tired of all this rough stuff, fled from the room. Leaving me alone to comfort the crying baby.

'Now look what you've done.' Mr Bligh pointed a finger almost inside Gilbert's nostril. Gilbert batted it away. While I stared down into the chasm of this baby's mouth, where the little pink knobble at the back of his throat was wiggling with the wind of his howl.

'Please mind the baby,' I said, with the thought to calm the situation. But little notice was being taken of I or the child. Join the sweet little baby and howl, I thought, for the situation was taking another bad turn.

Gilbert pulled himself up until, I swear, he was almost the same height as Mr Bligh. 'Listen, man, your wife just ask us to take her baby and all that is worrying you is that a black man might think to comfort her.'

'I don't want to hear any more from you. Just shut your mouth!'

'Well, you gonna. You gonna hear plenty more from me.'

Mr Bligh stepped back one stride, not in fear of Gilbert but only so he might better show his disdain by perusing him up and down. 'Why, in God's name, would Queenie think to entrust the baby's upbringing to people like you? That poor little half-caste child would be better off begging in a gutter!' he said.

434

Gilbert sucked on his teeth to return this man's scorn. 'You know what your trouble is, man?' he said. 'Your white skin. You think it makes you better than me. You think it give you the right to lord it over a black man. But you know what it make you? You wan' know what your white skin make you, man? It make you white. That is all, man. White. No better, no worse than me – just white.' Mr Bligh moved his eye to gaze on the ceiling. 'Listen to me, man, we both just finish fighting a war – a bloody war – for the better world we wan' see. And on the same side – you and me. We both look on other men to see enemy. You and me, fighting for empire, fighting for peace. But still, after all that we suffer together, you wan' tell me I am worthless and you are not. Am I to be the servant and you are the master for all time? No. Stop this, man. Stop it now. We can work together, Mr Bligh. You no see? We must. Or else you just gonna fight me till the end?'

Gilbert had hushed the room. It was not only Mr Bligh whose mouth gaped in wonder. Even the baby had fallen silent. For at that moment as Gilbert stood, his chest panting with the passion from his words, I realised that Gilbert Joseph, my husband, was a man of class, a man of character, a man of intelligence. Noble in a way that would some day make him a legend. 'Gilbert Joseph,' everyone would shout. 'Have you heard about Gilbert Joseph?'

And Mr Bligh, blinking straight in Gilbert's eye once more, said softly, 'I'm sorry.' Of course, I thought, of course. Who would not be chastened by those fine words from my smart, handsome and noble husband? But this Englishman just carried on, 'I'm sorry . . . but I just can't understand a single word that you're saying.'

Gilbert's august expression slipped from his face to shatter into tiny pieces upon the floor. He leaned down to me and took the baby from my arms. Straightening himself he handed the bundled baby to Mr Bligh. He then took my hand in his and guided me silently from the room.

Gilbert mounted the stairs in a furious anger. The first two flights he took three stairs at a time, his feet banging loud as a giant's foot. I decided not to keep pace with him, for still those stairs rose like an empty bookcase in front of me. But by the third flight, whether through exhaustion or concern for me, he slowed. In the quiet of the gloomy hallway Mrs Bligh's voice could be clearly heard shouting a tormented, 'No'. By the fourth flight Gilbert had stopped. The baby was crying. The sound encircling me appeared to grow louder as I climbed to where Gilbert stood. Both his hands were pressed firmly over his ears. As I approached him he suddenly struck out and punched the wall. Then, hopping with the pain from the ill-advised wall mashing he wailed, 'Damn them, damn them.' He sat down hard on the stair. I rested beside him and took his throbbing hand in mine.

'Your mother never tell you that a wall is hard?' I said.

For the briefest moment he looked on my face before hanging his head back to his boots. 'Hortense,' he said. 'What can we do, what can we do? I can't just walk away. Leave that little coloured baby alone in this country, full of people like Mr Bligh. Him and all his kind. What sort of life would that little man have? Damn them.'

I squeezed his hand to be kind but had to stop when he said, 'ouch'. This man was still a buffoon. Nevertheless I began. 'You wan' hear what I know of my mummy? A flapping skirt, bare black feet skipping over stones, the smell of boiling milk and a gentle song that whispered, "Me sprigade," until my eyes could do nothing but close. That is all I remember of her. As a little child I was given away too – brought up by my cousins because I was born with a golden skin.' He placed his hand over mine and lifted his chin to kiss my cheek.

'And this Michael?' he asked.

'Oh, Michael Roberts, he was my cousin's son, we grew together.'

'You loved him?'

'Of course.'

Jean opened the door of her room. Just enough so her nose could poke through, smell the darkies on the stairs and shut it again to laugh.

'They took me from my mummy because, with my golden skin, everyone agreed that I would have a golden future.'

'Well, then, a golden future you must have, Miss Mucky Foot.'

'I intend to, Gilbert Joseph. That is exactly what I intend.' The baby's crying was enfolding us again. 'You wan' us take the child, Gilbert?' I asked.

It was not hesitation that caused him to pause – it was his breath once more

436

filling his lungs. 'Oh, Hortense, perhaps you are right – I am a fool. And you wan' know why? Come, I truly believe there is nothing else that we can do.'

Gathering the baby's things into a drawer, Mrs Bligh kissed each of the garments as she folded them away. Then she hugged her baby to her until the embrace caused him to whimper, before handing him carefully to me. Michael Joseph would know his mother not from the smell of boiling milk, a whispered song or bare black feet but from the remembered taste of salt tears. Those tears that on that day dripped, one at a time, from her eye, over his lips and on to his tongue.

They made such a fuss with my trunk. 'You mind if we just throw the damn thing out of the window?' Gilbert asked me. He had managed to carry it up all the stairs those weeks ago but now it was too hard to get it down. I opened my mouth to cuss him when he said, 'What, you still don't know what is a joke?'

'Oh, yes,' I told him, 'a joke is something that is funny.'

It was Winston who called for Gilbert to try lifting it again. 'What you have in there, anyway?' Gilbert wanted to know.

'I have everything I will need, Gilbert Joseph, everything I will need.'

Oh, how they groaned and strained, banging my good trunk against the frame of the door, crashing it on the floor of the landing, and thumping it on each stair. The baby was shaken from his bed with the commotion. The drawer that was his crib bouncing around the room with each and every thud. I picked him from where he lay and hushed him with whispered words. Drowsy, he looked on my face with languid eyes before a smile briefly stretched his lips. One day this boy will want to look on a bird's nest and I will have to lift him to show. He will torment spiders and dress up a cat. 'Me sprigadee,' I said, and I kissed his forehead.

As I was about to place him back down my hand rested upon something hard around his backside. Thinking his nappy needed straightening I tried to smooth it. But it would not. Laying him down I found, stitched into his garment, a knitted pouch. To release the item I was required to search for scissors so I might cut the ties. The baby was as good as Mrs Bligh promised he would be. He fell back into his sleep as I fumbled with the pouch. Opening it I found a bundle of money tied with soft pink wool and secured with a dainty bow. Three hundred pounds in dirty notes. Never before had so much money caressed my fingertips. But then at the bottom of this bundle was a photograph. It was of Mrs Bligh taken, I was sure, in a happier time. Head and shoulders, her eyes angled to the viewer, gazing out with a gentle smile. I had never thought to enquire about the father of Mrs Bligh's child. Who was he? Some fool-fool Jamaican with an eye for the shapely leg on a pretty white woman. Where was he? As far from her as he could run? I thought to call Gilbert to show him this bounty. But this man's pride would surely insist that the items were returned to her. And I had something else in my mind for them. Come, I would put them to good use when they were required. Placing them in my bag I determined to keep a secret of both the money and the photograph.

I held the baby awkward as I finally closed the door on that wretched little room. No compunction caused me to look back with longing. No sorrow had me sigh on the loss of the gas-ring, the cracked sink, or the peeling plaster. At the door to Mrs Bligh's home I stopped. I tapped gently three times. There was no reply. I tapped again, this time calling her name. Still no one came. But with only a flimsy piece of wood between us I could feel her on the other side. The distress in a halting breath. A timorous hand resting unsure on the doorknob. She was there – I knew. 'Goodbye, Queenie,' I called, but still she did not come.

Gilbert nearly knocked me from my feet as he rushed towards me. His shirt outside his trousers and buttoned up badly, panting like a dog. 'I have the trunk in the van,' he said. 'Come, hurry, nah.' He took the baby from me. I adjusted my hat in case it sagged in the damp air and left me looking comical. A curtain at the window moved – just a little but enough for me to know it was not the breeze. But I paid it no mind as I pulled my back up and straightened my coat against the cold.

Never in the field
of human conflict has
so much been owed by
so many to so few

Winston Churchill

Acknowledgements

I would like to thank the following people, publications and organisations for their help and assistance with this book – they were all invaluable: Pip Mayblin, Amy Levy, George Mutton, Ray Bousfield, Jim Munday, John Collier, Philip Crawley, Leone Ross, Michael Munday, David Reading, Danny Collier, Heinz Menke, Stephen Amiel, and Katie Amiel.

Robert Collins, *The Long and the Short and the Tall: An Ordinary Airman's War*.
Squadron Leader 'Bush' Cotton, *Hurricanes Over Burma*.
Sam King, *Climbing Up the Rough Side of the Mountain*.
Donald R. Knight and Alan D. Sabey, *The Lion Roars at Wembley*.
What did you do in the War, Mum? An Age Exchange publication.
Robert N. Murray (Nottingham West Indian Combined Ex-services Association), *Lest We Forget – The Experience of World War II West Indian Ex-service Personnel*.
E. Martin Noble, *Jamaica Airman*.
Mike Phillips and Trevor Phillips, *Windrush: The Irresistible Rise of Multi-racial Britain*.
Ray Sansome, *The Bamboo Workshops*.
Graham Smith, *When Jim Crow met John Bull*.

The Burma Star Association; Kensington Central Library, Local Studies; Royal Air Force Museum, Hendon; Mass Observation Archive, University of Sussex; Post Office Heritage Archive; Colindale Newspaper Library; Prospero's Books; Hansib Publications Ltd; and the Internet for, oh, so many little things.

I would also like to thank the Authors Foundation for their generous financial assistance, my agent David Grossman, and Albyn Hall and Bill Mayblin for their indefatigable support and guidance throughout the writing of this book.